# PRAISE FOR *AT THE ISLAND'S EDGE*

"C. I. Jerez's enchanting novel *At the Island's Edge* is a captivating and poignant debut about a young mother's struggle to heal from the scars of war following her deployment to Iraq as a US Army medic. Jerez's deeply moving prose dives into the realities of war for women in combat, the complexities of serving while balancing motherhood, and the sacrifices made. This heartwarming novel captures the beauty of Puerto Rico's culture and leaves us wanting more!"

—Robert Dugoni, author of *Suspense Magazine*'s 2018 Book of the Year, *The Extraordinary Life of Sam Hell*

"C. I. Jerez's *At the Island's Edge* is an astonishing debut—an eloquent, moving, and heartfelt story about a young mother's efforts to claw herself back from the precipice for the sake of her young son, even as she is convinced that she is beyond redemption. Jerez's compelling prose and deep insights into Puerto Rican culture elevate this thoughtful and thought-provoking novel. I loved this book!"

—Karen Dionne, author of the #1 international bestseller *The Marsh King's Daughter* and *The Wicked Sister*

"Rich with culture, vivid characters, and elegant prose, *At the Island's Edge* is a knockout debut by an author who is sure to leave a bright literary mark on this world. I was swept away."

—Boo Walker, bestselling author of *An Echo in Time*

"C. I. Jerez's debut novel is a fresh and immersive delight. Somber and heartfelt, *At the Island's Edge* offers a flawed but substantive protagonist plagued by the psychological trauma of war as she returns home to face her family's failed expectations. It is also a love letter to the island of Puerto Rico and its people, a richly woven tapestry, filled with wonderfully palpable details. From beginning to end, I was utterly transported."

—Barbara Davis, bestselling author of *The Echo of Old Books*

# AT THE ISLAND'S EDGE

# AT THE ISLAND'S EDGE

*A Novel*

C. I. JEREZ

LAKE UNION
PUBLISHING

This is a work of fiction. Names, characters, organizations, places, events, and incidents are either products of the author's imagination or are used fictitiously. Otherwise, any resemblance to actual persons, living or dead, is purely coincidental.



Published by Lake Union Publishing, Seattle

www.apub.com



ISBN-13: 9781662523427 (paperback)
ISBN-13: 9781662523410 (digital)

Cover design by Shasti O'Leary Soudant
Cover image: © Nelson Vega / Alamy; © 24BY36 / Alamy;
© Olga Nosach / Shutterstock

Printed in the United States of America

At the Island's Edge *is my love letter to the island of Puerto Rico and the amazing people who call it home, especially the teams I worked with in Dorado, Arecibo, and Aguadilla. Thank you for sharing your island magic.*

*To the brave members of our armed forces and their sacrifices in the name of duty: Thank you for your service to our great nation. I am forever honored and humbled to have been a part of the team.*

Mother is the name for God in the lips and hearts of little children.

—*William Makepeace Thackeray*

# 2009—Operation Iraqi Freedom

I hate the taste of desert earth and fuel exhaust.

The wind from the helicopter above us lifts the papers attached to my clipboard. After completing my walk-around, I scrawl a messy signature at the bottom of the page, finalizing the inspection of our Humvee. I pull at my sweaty uniform, already damp from another sweltering morning as we wait to leave the wire. Truth is, I'm exhausted, battle weary, and ready to end my second tour across the pond.

I knew what I was getting into returning to Iraq, but the situation with my son back home is worsening, making the normal pressures of war even heavier. I'd just graduated from high school the year I turned on the television and watched the towers fall on 9/11. I burned with protest, wanting to take a stand and fight back. We've occupied Iraq for six years now, and after last week's losses, I'm beginning to wonder if I made the wrong choice.

I look out at the soldiers ahead, loading their packs and checking their own vehicles. They have families, too. Kids, just like me. Do they wonder if they're missing out on what really matters—at home? I do.

Except right now I can't think like that. Anything can happen during a convoy. If someone gets injured, I'll need to operate at my best. Which means it's time to tuck away my doubts and the images of the explosion during last week's "routine" convoy. Worst case: life and death hinge on my ability to do my job.

*Stay alert, stay alive.*

I cap my pen, slide it into the pen pocket on my sleeve, and strap into the passenger seat. Reaching down, I tap my medical bag for assurance, transitioning for what still lies ahead.

I tally the vehicles, one behind another, seven in total. Mine is second to last—the designated ambulance. The unit chaplain sits alone in the back seat. His graying temples indicate he's probably been at this awhile.

The executive officer's voice breaks through the static on the radio. "Convoy in position. All soldiers prepare for departure."

I have an extra stethoscope tucked into one of my pant pockets and a roll of wound-packing gauze in the other. The last mission served as a painful lesson in all the things that could go wrong when you're not readily prepared. I once ran out of nasopharyngeal airways for the number of wounded soldiers who needed them, the same mission where I reached for rusted scissors that didn't allow for a clean and efficient gauze cut. I won't let anything like that happen again.

Wiping the sweat from my brow, I close my eyes for a moment before glancing down at my watch. It's only five thirty in the morning, but time is irrelevant here—it's always hot. The Iraqi dry heat has turned the cab into an oven, and I'm baking to a golden perfection underneath my armored plates. Sergeant Fuentes, our driver, swings open his door and moves into position. He reaches down to the console between us and reviews the order detailing our mission.

"Hope you two hit the latrines, because we aren't stopping for potty breaks," he says with way too much cheer. "And remember, there's a no-return policy on this cab. All sales are final once we hit the road." He smiles when he turns to me. "Buckle up, buttercup."

I give him a half-hearted smile in return. I can't imagine it's easy to keep a sense of humor under the circumstances. I certainly don't. But that's because I'm wondering whether my little boy will ever truly understand why I had to deploy, not once but twice. I don't know much about my driver, but I know he doesn't have kids. I've already asked.

Fuentes just arrived from a sister unit south of us. Rumor is he had contact with the enemy but survived and insisted on staying in country to finish his tour. He's still getting his bearings—shifting in his seat, pressing buttons, running the wipers.

The radio below the dashboard crackles to life, filling the truck with static.

"All clear," the commander calls out.

I release a deep sigh of relief. "Finally." I look over at Fuentes. "I hope the rumors about your good luck are true. On our last mission, two soldiers didn't make it back alive."

"Don't you worry, Sergeant," Fuentes chides. "Only the good die young. Isn't that right, sir?"

The chaplain looks over and smiles softly. "Oh, I don't know about that. I think we all have a date, and when the time's up, it's up. Nothing anyone can do about it."

I shake my head. "Sir, respectfully, I don't agree. A lot of people die because they aren't paying attention or refuse to take proper precautions. Not me. I'll make damn sure I get back home. My son, Teó, is counting on it."

"Gotta lotta fight in ya, Sergeant," he says, revealing his thick Irish brogue. "Good for ya. For us, too, I suppose."

I do have a lot of fight. It comes from mornings like today, when I wake up angry. Last night I used the remaining ten minutes on my prepaid phone card to call home, only to hear Teó's getting worse. It's been nine months since his diagnosis of Tourette's syndrome, and because I had to deploy only a month after we found out, I still don't fully understand what we're up against.

The military pediatrician assured us his condition could be easily managed in my absence. He signed off on my deployment paperwork, stating Teó would likely grow out of this around his eighteenth birthday, like nine more years weren't a big deal. Nothing more than an adjustment, he said. Nothing to worry about.

The doctor was wrong. He never considered the bullies in the schoolyard, or the impact they and his absent mother would have on worsening his symptoms.

Tía Kika, one of my father's two sisters and the only family I have in the continental US, left her life and her city—twice—and relocated to North Carolina to take care of Teó for me. Not wanting to worry me yesterday, she kept it light, but I could still hear what she wasn't saying: *His health is declining. He needs more medical care. He needs his mother.*

And I need the Army to provide that medical care.

My foot taps impatiently as each truck, front to back, confirms its readiness over the speaker. At our turn Sergeant Fuentes leans closer to the radio. "Vehicle six, ambulance, confirmed. I'm here with our medic, Sergeant Lina LaSalle, and the chaplain, Captain Michael McGinnis. Vehicle six, out."

I like how he says my name. If I had to guess, I think Sergeant Fuentes is either Puerto Rican or Cuban. I'll have to ask him once we get on the road.

I pull down my sunglasses and watch the tires up ahead rotate.

*Here we go. One more convoy, Teó, then Mamá is coming home to take proper care of you.*

Fuentes doesn't look nervous. It's as good a time as any to ask. "I heard an accent. Where are you from?"

He glances over at me and smiles. "Puerto Rico." The two words are full of pride.

I return his smile. "Me too. Except I left twelve years ago. My parents sent me to live with my aunt so I could go to high school in Florida and pursue the American dream. I never went back."

He frowns. His eyes shift over to the road.

I bet he thinks I'm a traitor for leaving the island and not returning. What does he know?

I force myself to focus, knowing my duties to the US government force my little boy to once again wonder if I'll make it back alive. Today it's up to me to do exactly that.

It's been nearly two hours, halfway there, and nothing but standard radio traffic. The engine's hum is still the only sound on the quiet stretch of road. So far, so good.

My head nods with the hypnotic lull of sleep threatening to take over. The increasing heat makes fighting the drowsiness damn near impossible.

Breaking the hum, the truck swerves to the left, avoiding a large pothole. My helmet collides with the armored door, jostling me awake.

I look up to see beyond the vehicle in front of us. Buildings are scattered up ahead. The sun's fiery rays are blinding, despite the standard-issue Oakleys.

Sergeant Fuentes radios in an update. "Vehicle six is green. We are all good."

"Are we?" My newly racing pulse heightens my senses. The Army has trained our bodies to shift in one instant from relaxed and sleeping on a convoy to battle ready.

Something doesn't feel right. I can sense the danger like a storm cloud moving in fat with rain.

Fuentes leans his head down toward his shoulder playfully. "Relax. It was just a pothole. Sounds to me like you need a distraction. Tell me, Sergeant, why do they call you 'Stone Cold'? Is the rumor true? Do you get ice cold when you're in action?"

I keep my eyes straight ahead, watching the empty horizon, straining to see what no one else can.

"Come on," he presses. "What did you do to get that nickname?"

He's flirting. He's definitely Puerto Rican. "Let me guess. You talked to the infantry guys, right?"

His smirk answers for him.

"And what did they tell you, Fuentes? Why did *they* say they call me 'Stone Cold'?"

"Listen, in my defense, I wasn't asking about you," he says with a laugh. "When I told 'em I was driving the ambulance, they warned me to watch out for the sexy medic. They said your pretty brown eyes could melt hearts but that I shouldn't be fooled because you were stone-cold ice."

"I've been demoted. I was a stone-cold healer before. Do you want to hear the real story?"

"For sure." He chuckles, but his focus remains straight ahead.

"So last week they cried and I didn't when the unit's rescue mutt, Sparky, died. I tried to help him, but it was too late. One of the infantry guys said I was stone cold. I guess the name stuck."

He considers my account. "So why didn't you cry? No feelings, LaSalle?"

My chin rises. "I have feelings, Fuentes. I just don't act on them when I've got a job to do. I tuck them away, exactly how my father taught me. I think it makes me a damn good medic."

None of these guys need to know how I returned to my CHU that night and cried for the dog or whispered a prayer for his journey over the rainbow bridge. They don't get that, while it's all right for them to cry in public, the standards are different for me. Crying in front of them would only push the narrative that I am weak, emotional, and a lesser soldier than they are. I need them to trust me with their lives. So I tuck it away until later, when I'm alone.

Fuentes turns and winks at me. "And you got great hands. I bet that makes you a damn good medic, too."

I ignore him but find myself staring down at my long, slender fingers.

"Fuentes, don't you have some pretty girl back home waiting for you?"

My question grounds him. He reaches up and wipes the sweat from his brow, smiling wistfully. "Yeah, actually, I do. She's pretty special, for sure. I think she might be the one."

I purse my lips. "I bet she has great hands, too."

"Ah, come on, LaSalle. I'm messing around," he teases. "Can't blame a guy for noticing how pretty you are. But I'm harmless, I promise. Besides, I bet you get hit on all the time. I'm surprised your family in Puerto Rico didn't push you to compete in the beauty pageants. You know how competitive we are when it comes to fighting for the Miss Universe title."

His compliment makes me blush. "My mother did. At first. But I was a lost cause—too much of a tomboy. No surprise I ended up in combat boots and camouflage."

Fuentes isn't wrong about getting hit on. Guys here do flirt, maybe because I'm one of only four women in the unit. Some of them watch me, even whistle when I brush my long hair back into a bun. I have kept myself in good shape. My job demands it, and the guys notice, but it's not for them; it's for me. I need power and strength to execute a fireman carry on a wounded soldier.

The rhythm of the convoy changes. The engine's hum shifts, accelerating and decelerating, buzzing alongside the clanging of the truck's metal frame. We slow to a jostle along the graveled desert road. Clouds of gray dust splay across the windshield under darkening skies.

Sergeant Fuentes and I lock eyes, realizing at the same time that it's not dust—it's ash from the smoke ahead.

We are entering into danger. I feel it. The darkness means an explosion.

I sit up straighter, immediately picturing my son. *I'm coming home to you, papito.*

That's it. That's all I can allow.

I force my mind to go blank. If I want to stay alive and do my job, I must be focused.

The convoy slows even more. The truck ahead is closing in, forcing us to crawl to a complete stop. The darkened air against a blaring sun makes visibility noticeably difficult.

The radio crackles again. "Possible IED, one hundred meters ahead. Stop to deploy the robot."

The robot sits in the large truck behind us. It can detect an explosive device and provide visuals to soldiers in harm's way. This is not good.

I look up, channeling my grandmother, Mama Lina. I was only seven when she died. Ever since, I've prayed to the woman who loved me best.

*Please protect us.*

My head whips from left to right. I'm scanning the perimeter, forcing my breath to quiet so that I can hear anyone call for a medic. *Stay alert, stay alive.*

Sergeant Fuentes calls into the radio. "Vehicle six, requesting further instruction."

It's too late to turn back and change course. I've done this enough to know the commander will insist we press through.

The village outside Fuentes's window is awakening. The danger from the explosion heightens the tension in the air. I can tell by the tightening in his jaw that he feels it, too.

I look through his window to see a commotion of movement from the village. My heart pounds, but I take a deep breath, bringing it back into a steady pace—my training taking effect. Open doors from the stacks of rectangular clay buildings slam shut. Five or six groups of Iraqi men huddle together less than fifteen meters from where we've stopped. They sprinkle the landscape on street corners and storefront entrances, watching suspiciously as our convoy comes to a complete stop.

My watch reads 7:50 a.m.—too early for them to be out gathering. Something is up.

The cab crackles to life again as the commander's voice breaks through. "Vehicle Six, make sure the medic is on standby. We have a visual. Possible IED."

Now my toes and fingertips tingle as my body releases adrenaline to keep me alive. "Ay, bendito," I whisper. This can't be happening. Not now. I picture Teó in distress on the other side of the world. This is fear taking over. I can't let that happen, not when I'm so close to going home.

I reach down and lift my medical bag onto my lap and scan my area of operation. I need to lean into my training to regain control. If I don't, I'm the one stacking the odds in the wrong direction. I can't do that. I take a deep inhale, the familiarity of my tools grounding me back into muscle memory. *Don't be nervous, Lina, be ready. Stone cold.*

The radio crackles desperately. The convoy commander is now shouting. "All personnel dismount and set up a perimeter. We need to take a defensive position."

Dismount? My head whips over to Sergeant Fuentes. "Is he for real? We are stopped, wide open. Those guys out there are watching us. This is not good, Fuentes. We are sitting ducks."

"LaSalle, move," he says, his words curt. "He gave a command." Fuentes leans over the seat. "Sir, you too."

The chaplain, silent until now, reaches for the door, transitioning into action. We all know the drills. There's no ignoring the reality of our situation. This is a war zone, and our convoy is in danger.

I pull open my door, ignoring the pressure in my chest from fear's grasp. After grabbing my stuff, I shuffle to the front tire on the passenger side of the truck, knuckles stretched tight from the death grip on my medical bag. I can't see the village from this side, but my job is to listen and be ready when and if someone shouts for a medic.

The two-man team in the vehicle ahead move their truck forward before coming to a full stop and widening the gap between us. The truck's lights shut off as the driver and the lieutenant beside him dismount.

Angry yells carried by desert winds echo in the distance, growing wilder. I can faintly hear the shouts from our unit commanding the villagers to get back and the angry Arabic responses. From what I gather, no one is really listening on either side.

An eerie calm comes over me as I begin to assess. I want to run back to the safety of my Humvee until we get the "all clear" and I can return home, where I'm needed most, but my system knows instinctually what to do. I lean in.

Scanning my right flank, I identify movement behind a crumbling stone wall approximately fifteen meters away, on the opposite side of the village. It's the only activity on this side of the convoy. My side. The hostility from the villagers grows on our left.

A puff of dirt floats up from the ground in the shuffling of loose rocks. I strain to focus, but the noise surrounding us distracts me. The lieutenant up ahead runs toward the beginning of the convoy, essentially leaving me wide open.

I shake my head. *There goes the LT trying to play the hero.*

My eyes move back, following the chalky cloud of dust to the dirt-smudged face of a young man still lacking the confidence of a seasoned adult. He struts a few steps forward with intention, but the look in his eyes is so similar to my son's when he's unsteady and afraid.

My heart pounds with familiarity. I'm on the other side of the world, and yet the stubbled skin of a beard not yet grown in and those large almond eyes, blinking with regret, remind me so much of how Teó will look during his transition to manhood.

With quivering steps, he moves around the stone edge, stopping to assess us. He looks right at me. My instincts are to run out and push him back where he will be safer, but I know that's impossible. Moving from my position would endanger my unit. I strain to catch his gaze, ignoring the reality of what is right in front of me, and silently urge him to return behind the wall.

The rustling behind him draws my attention. There's movement. Someone else is behind that same wall—yelling. An older man. He pushes the trembling volunteer forward.

The man's face juts out. He's still shouting in a tone that sounds like a command. I strain to listen. He hollers again in Arabic: "Ezhab!" *Go.* The man is urging, directing his protégé farther out into the open and into view.

The young man looks over toward the commands being shouted at him, then turns back to face me. His eyes are wide with terror. He shakes his head. "La," he says. *No.*

"Go," the bearded man shouts.

I watch as he stumbles forward. My gaze narrows, and I pray that somehow his course will change at the last minute. It's obvious he's scared.

He looks back in my direction, raising his hands slowly and clasping them behind his head.

My eyes trail down, confirming what I already knew in my gut to be true. His soccer jersey rises, revealing the olive-green edges of a belt wrapped around his waist. A glint of foil exposes shiny duct-taped bricks tucked into the belt's pockets.

The pounding against my ears intensifies, while I helplessly search the row of trucks and endless miles of sky and sand, wondering whether anyone else has noticed this threat. But the convoy is spread out now, and the only other person on my side is the unarmed chaplain facing the rear.

Darting back to look at the bearded older man, I see that his other hand holds something much more dangerous. A cell phone.

A detonator.

My stomach drops with a horrific realization. We are all going to die. Teó will be left alone in this world, not only by a father who abandoned him before he was born but by a mother who broke her promise and never returned home. A second passes where I can't tell the difference between my son and hers . . . whoever this boy's mother may be.

*No. He can't take me from my son. I won't let him.*

My heart hurts at how much this young man looks like Teó. He still retains soft, rounded cheeks and familiar messy, dark curls. How can such innocence be the enemy? In many ways he's still just a child with a world of possibilities ahead of him.

My eyes shoot over to the bearded man. I want *him* to be my target, but he is even farther back. No way I can get an accurate shot with a pistol at this distance.

I peer across the front of the truck, shouting, "Sergeant Fuentes, there's a threat. One hundred meters at my three o'clock. He is wearing an explosive device."

My sentence is capped with an explosion from the village in the opposite direction of where I stand. The ground shakes below us as the skies darken further. I try to hold my breath and calm my pounding heart.

Fuentes peers from around the other side of the front bumper. "What, LaSalle? Can't hear you."

I open my mouth to shout again, but Fuentes is still hollering commands in my direction.

"Stay low. Snipers . . . Get ready to help."

The voices around me are growing louder. A series of directions streams through the radio in the vehicle. Even with my door open, I can't make it out clearly, but there's something about the robot being deployed to the IED. I look back, but the team behind us is not coming across my side.

The young man takes a step forward.

He is crying. I can still easily see the little boy within the changing body of a man. Gray streams of dirt, sweat, and tears slide down his cheeks.

*Please,* I beg, *please stop. Let me help you.* I want nothing more than to rip that damn belt from his body.

Almost as if he can hear my thoughts, he hesitates.

*Come on, kid. Don't take another step. You don't have to do this.*

I can see it in his face. He doesn't want to do this. Neither do I.

The man behind the wall shouts again. The resolve is too strong; the young man's features shift, conjuring determination. He isn't going to stop. I reach down to touch the 9-millimeter on my hip. If he won't stop, then neither can I.

"Sergeant Fuentes!" I shout again, but there's no response.

"No hay otra," I whisper tragically. If I don't do something right now, my son will be left an orphan.

I won't let that happen.

"I'm moving, LaSalle," Sergeant Fuentes finally says in the distance, but two shots—enemy fire from the village—punctuate the end of his sentence.

The chaplain and I drop to the ground.

In the distance, I hear someone shout, "Take cover! We need to get back!"

Another round of fire fills the air. "I'm hit. LaSalle, help."

Sergeant Fuentes lands with a thud in front of our vehicle. I smell the iron rust of blood before I see it. But from my position on the gravel, I have a direct view beneath the cab. Our eyes meet. The light behind his expression is fading.

*Oh God. No, please.*

I rise to render aid, but from my periphery, I see the young man push through his hesitancy and begin advancing toward us.

"Sir, Sergeant Fuentes is down. Help him," I scream at the chaplain, pointing to the front of our cab.

The chaplain looks up and sees the young man slowly approaching and the obvious bulk at his waist. His eyes fill with the horrid realization I discovered only moments ago.

"Jesus, Mary, and Joseph," he shouts, rising to his feet, crouching low. He runs past me to Sergeant Fuentes and grabs Fuentes's rifle.

He doesn't have the training to use it. I do. "Give me his weapon," I yell.

The chaplain slides it over to me.

Bullets firing from both sides fill the skies.

I grab Fuentes's rifle and lie on my stomach, elbows firmly planted in the dirt. I peer through the scope and settle on my sight picture.

The target has stopped moving. His hands are on his knees, his chest palpitating as he leans forward. The heavy explosives weigh his body down, giving me precious seconds to take proper aim.

I point the muzzle slightly above his head, ensuring an accurate shot, and focus inward, holding my breath.

*Now, Lina. Do it.*

I force the transition. He is not someone's son; this is a target, a black silhouette on a white sheet of paper. An enemy combatant. A weapon.

I pull back my trigger finger, numb, and brace against the blast of my rifle.

My nose fills with the peppered scent of metal and sulfur as his skinny body falls to the ground.

A few seconds pass, then another rifle shot rings out. This time it comes from the vehicle up ahead. The team finally saw the bearded boogeyman behind the wall. He falls in a crumpled heap at the wall's edge. The detonator tumbles to the ground beside him.

My head drops to my chest. It's not over yet. The belt could still detonate.

I close my eyes and wait, picturing my sweet baby boy's big blue eyes and wide, silly grin. If I'm about to die, I want to be thinking of my tesoro, my little treasure, when it happens.

A quiet breeze passes along the back of my neck. Still holding my breath, I wait, but mercifully, the young man's belt does not detonate.

I exhale, my lungs pounding.

The sulfur of gunpowder combines with the scent of Sergeant Fuentes's rusty blood, trailing beside me like a river in search of an ocean.

The rifle tumbles from my hands to the ground. My chest aches with the pressure of what I've just done. I swallow it deep and hold it down. I cannot break. Not yet.

"You saved us," the chaplain says, kneeling above me.

I don't believe him. The team ahead of us took out the real threat—the man with the detonator. What if I had just waited another couple of seconds?

"Look at me, Lina," he says, using my first name.

I raise my head but don't turn to face him. My focus is out on the horizon. *Murderer.* The word repeats itself over and over in my head.

I imagine a mother somewhere in the distance, mourning the loss of her son and all the dreams she held for his life. Over and over I see her son's body crumpling to the ground.

I had to do it.

I had to stay alive for my son. I had no choice. I swallow and repeat the words in my head.

*I had to do it.*

My heart pounds at the realization—again—somewhere out there a mother has just lost her son. Now she will be forced to bury him and sever the living connection between them. And it is all my fault. *Murderer.*

When I finally look over at the chaplain, his fingers move deftly down his face and across his chest as he crosses himself. "You did the right thing," he offers gently.

I know in my head I had no other choice . . . did I? No. Teó needs me. I had to do it.

In his darkest moments, my father used to quote a famous Puerto Rican expression: Tanto nadar para morir en la orilla. *I've swum so far, only to drown on the coastline.*

# CHAPTER ONE

"Mamá, did you know the ocean makes up seventy-one percent of the earth? And if you add the lakes, rivers, and streams, it makes up seventy-five percent!"

Teó blinks in rapid succession, then sniffs twice.

"Mamá? Did you hear what I said? Seventy-five percent! That's three-quarters of the whole wide world—made up of water."

"Teó, were you watching *Bill Nye, the Science Guy* reruns on YouTube again?" My son's high IQ and love of science are endearing, but we need to pack. "The movers are coming soon. Have you finished boxing everything up?"

He looks up at me guiltily, a slight grin at the corner of his lips. His large sapphire eyes blink nervously He has my papi's Spanish blue eyes.

Attempting to gauge my mood and determine whether he can get away with being funny is what Teó does when he wants to sidestep a lecture. He could also avoid uttering another word, given my bad mood, and get back on task.

Predictably, he takes a chance.

"I plead the Fifth Amendment," he says, raising his right palm in the air and covering his heart with his left.

I want to reprimand him, to shout "Get to work!" My chest fills with an angry retort, but a brief flash of apprehension in Teó's eyes, fear at my loss of control, stops me in my tracks. When the hell has my son ever been afraid of me? I swallow the knot in my throat and fake a smile. Teó deserves better. I have to be better.

"You're not in court, Teó. You're in my house." I try to meet him halfway with a joke. "And in the confines of this jurisdiction, you're not protected by any US constitutional rights but must instead follow orders, soldier. Understood?"

He looks up at me. "Huh?"

I give up. That was all the joy I could muster. "Teó, please finish packing the boxes in your room before the movers get here."

"Okay, Mamá," he says, relieved, probably because I didn't lose it this time. This loose temper of mine is new but frequent in the last two months since I returned from Iraq. I keep chalking it up to being tired, overwhelmed, and jet-lagged from the change in time zones. But does jet lag last two months?

Teó turns and runs back down the hall toward his room, singing, "Bill Nye, the science guy"—*sniff*—"Bill Nye, the science guy"—*sniff*—"Bill, Bill, Bill, Bill, Bill."

Stacks of books, mostly medical thrillers and Spanish classics, lie toppled on the ground in the corner of my bedroom. The silver framed photos of Teó over the last nine years and one of my parents and me when I was just a baby are taken down and stacked in a neat little pile beside the books. My most recent Army award, a Silver Star, from my actions on the battlefield, is still tucked in the green plastic sleeve and strewn on the floor. Most people would think I'd be nuts to treat such a prestigious award so callously. I don't care. Our kayaks and camping gear have somehow migrated from the storage closet to the front of my bedroom door. Each of the six dresser drawers is filled to the brim with clothes and options for four seasons.

I won't be needing the winter stuff anymore.

One thing that's evident amid my clutter is my solitude. There are no photos with gal pals, no love letters, no wilting bouquets from a lover. The agony of going through my pregnancy all alone at such a young age and brokenhearted traumatized me from entering into another relationship. My tía Kika stepped in to be the support system I needed, especially when I spent my senior year of high school pregnant. She helped me see everything I could accomplish on my own if I believed in myself. Then having a baby boy gave me an easy excuse to substitute a man's place in my life with my son's. With a full-time career in the Army, single motherhood, and online classes to earn my undergraduate degree in biology, I had little time for friendships. As a result, I built my entire life over the last nine years around my roles as a mother, a soldier, and an aspiring doctor. Today the isolation weighs heavy.

I look over at the uniforms lying on my bed.

You can always tell when a unit is reintegrating back to life stateside. My freshly pressed uniform pants and jackets look like they haven't seen a minute of field activity, still emanating the faint scent of laundry soap. My black, rounded beret is new and molded to lie meticulously across the center of my forehead in a near-perfect parallel to my eyebrows. The new deployment patch sits proudly on the upper portion of the right sleeve, just below the American flag.

The unit we deployed with to war brands us now whenever we wear the Army uniform. Except I won't be putting on that uniform any longer. Today begins my terminal leave, which means the Army will pay me for the thirty days of leave I've accrued, but I'm essentially on my own time, free as a bird. After those thirty days, my release papers will be finalized and I'll be back to civilian life—permanently.

Although, truth be told, I became a civilian in my own mind the moment I stepped off that bird and onto the tarmac in North Carolina. My tía Kika and Teó were there to receive me and bring me home, but rather than celebration, that night was filled with long silences, awkward half sentences, and uneaten food, despite my aunt's best efforts in the kitchen. My appetite was gone. Teó followed suit and ate very little from his plate. No one touched the tres leches cake. I never expected to be surrounded by family and feel lonelier than ever. Returning to my apartment, to my son, to the life I'd known before deploying, felt like the motions of a stranger, disjointed, lost. For the first time I understood the actual feeling of being on the outside looking in. I was returning to Sergeant Lina LaSalle's existence, her home, her child, her job, and yet my soul felt disjointed—even stuck back overseas.

Which didn't make any sense, given how badly I'd wanted to come home. After what I'd done, the young life I'd taken on that damn desert road, I knew I'd never go back to Iraq or to the military. I broke something inside me out there. I lost my sense of purpose and my ability to concentrate. Fortunately the timing worked out. Once we returned home, I was a few months from the end of my enlistment period. Before deploying, I'd planned to re-up, see if I'd qualify for a program to be temporarily released from active duty, though still under Army benefits, while attending medical school. But now Teó's worsening symptoms mean he needs specialized care. The only ways I can provide that are to either remain on active duty, which is not an option, or, as my tía Kika pointed out, return to Puerto Rico, where the government subsidies for health care, the available specialists, and my family's home and support could help me do right by my son. My tía even pushed me to consider applying to the local university medical school after settling in on the island. All my options felt impossible. I couldn't see myself remaining in uniform, but returning to Puerto Rico meant I was returning home a failure to an island and a family that had sent me away twelve years before.

Since leaving, I've never gone back; I've always found an excuse.

I look around at my bedroom filled with stacks of empty cardboard boxes. Piles of toys, shoes, and knickknacks that still need to be boxed up. There's so much to do.

It's easier to just trash everything or burn it all.

It's dramatic, but for the last two months, everything has made me want to cry, scream, or light fires. There isn't a why. It's just my new normal state of mind since we got back. My commander says it's to be expected. Especially for me. I got only the weekend off after returning from service abroad. In fairness, I could have requested leave, but I wanted to conserve as many days as possible and expedite my exit from the Army. So I reported to duty the following Monday morning, just like any other day, except that during PT, I fought the urge to scream at the top of my lungs throughout our four-mile run. That feeling still hasn't gone away.

I requested to work in the motor pool for my remaining two months in uniform, knowing I couldn't return to work at the clinic on post. No longer a healer, and branding myself a murderer, I felt it didn't make sense for me to try to return to an existence I no longer deserved.

Except I wasn't very good with vehicles and equipment, either. Worse, I kept losing my temper and ordering the young privates in the unit to drop into the front leaning rest position (a fancy term for a push-up); then I'd fight the tears I'd feel coming on at the erratic swings of my behavior. The motor pool soldiers complained. My first sergeant called me out on it. He told me to get my act together and stop acting like an erratic little girl. "According to the United States Army, you're a doggone war hero," he shouted from behind his desk. "Start acting like one."

I still have no idea what that means or where to begin.

I haven't told my parents the truth about my decision to leave the Army. If I tell them about Iraq, I'll have to relive it all and face my feelings about the notion of what everyone in uniform keeps telling me: I did the right thing. I was a hero out there. I was incredibly brave and selfless when my unit needed me most. *Selfless*—I hate that word; nothing about my actions out there that morning was selfless.

I pulled the sympathy card instead, highlighting Teó's condition and my desire to have my family's support. Tía Kika backed me up, defending my choice against my parents' begrudging concern that I was throwing away such a major opportunity and returning home.

My tía Lisandra, my father's oldest sister, has remained unusually silent, although I'm certain I already know her stance on things.

Her faith in me helped me cradle the dream to become a doctor and heal people, giving my transition to Florida greater purpose. I held on even tighter when I arrived at my tía Kika's one-bedroom apartment, because I needed a mission to help craft my identity. Then, a month before I graduated from high school, my cradled dream was replaced with a real one, one wrapped in a blue blanket—all eight pounds of my new baby boy, Matteo.

Alone with a new baby, everything changed. I'd managed to graduate, but I still had to find another way ahead, one that would allow me to provide for my son. Even with the odds stacked against me, I knew I could chart a new path to success, even if it was on a different road.

My tía Lisandra had a different perspective. When she found out about the baby, she didn't send a gift, a note of congratulations, or an alternative idea to the dream she'd helped plant. Instead, she sent a bouquet of dark-purple roses with one line typed on a blank white card. It read, "I held such high hopes."

She'd given up on me, at first, but when I told her about joining the Army, her faith in me reignited. It was my tía Lisandra who discovered the Army's medical school program and urged me to push through my undergraduate studies. This is why her silence doesn't surprise me. Returning to Puerto Rico will only reinforce what I've continued to show her time and time again: I don't have what it takes to go the distance. Well, she doesn't matter right now. Teó does.

I've already researched the name and contact information of a prominent neurologist and a psychiatrist in San Juan. They're safely tucked away in the pocket of my backpack. I'll have to figure out everything else about work, my future, and where we're going to live after I arrive. At least we can stay with my parents and grandparents until I get on my feet. Whatever that looks like.

"Mamá," Teó hollers, "I have a question."

Sighing, I stand up and walk down the small hallway to his bedroom. "What is it?" I ask, noticing the cover is missing from the top of the fish tank. "And where's the . . ." I stop, my question answered. The green plastic net is still in Teó's left hand. A brown-and-gold angelfish circling a water-filled ziplock bag is in his right.

My eyes squeeze shut while I push down the scream forming at the base of my throat. I want to grab the clutter in his room and throw it up against the wall. I take a deep breath and let it out before reopening my eyes. "Teó, what are you doing?"

*Sniff.* "Can I take Mr. Stripes on the airplane?"

I swallow. It's never been so hard to retain my composure. Why is it so hard now? "I'm sorry, son, but no. The fish won't survive the trip."

Teó stares up at me, his eyes watery saucers behind his glasses. His chin twitches up in my direction. This rare tic presents itself during high-stress situations. I am stressing him out.

I wonder what my parents will say when they see the tics.

Knowing Mami, she will offer a swipe of Vicks VapoRub on his feet, a cup of sopa de plátano, and a warm hibiscus tea with ginger and honey as a cure for his neurological ailments. For her, healing is all about nature, and our life's journey is all about fate. She uses her famous expression—*If only things went the way they were supposed to go*—anytime life doesn't go the way she expects. Papi, on the other hand, is the wild card. I'm unsure how he will process the reality that his grandson isn't in perfect physical condition.

I kneel, suddenly calmed. That's the thing about these mood swings: they come and they go, and I try not to feel victimized by their whims.

"It's okay, honey," I say, taking his face in my hands. "Puerto Rico is a tiny island in the middle of the ocean, surrounded by millions of fish. We can go snorkeling when we get there, and you will see some of the most beautiful fish God ever created."

"But what about *my* fish, Mamá?" Teó asks, holding up the ziplock bag. "Who will take care of them when we leave? Abuelo says little boys should have pet fish, remember? What if we can't find another little boy to care for them?"

Even at a distance, Papi makes an impact. He spent my entire childhood wishing I'd been a son—a makeup kid for the stillborn one he and Mami lost eleven months before I was born. Teó is his recompense. He has never met him in person, but Papi doesn't allow that to keep him from asserting his opinions during their weekly phone calls.

And now, by moving back, I'm diving right in the middle of the storm and Papi's two cents . . . on everything. The earlier calm disappears, and I feel my jaw tighten.

"Son, I promise we will make sure your fish have a safe new home before we leave tomorrow."

"You promise?" he asks. *Sniff.* He drops the net to the floor and removes his glasses. Using the back of his hand, he wipes the tears that didn't grow thick enough to spill over.

"I promise," I reiterate.

"Will Abuelo be sad I didn't bring my fish?"

I stop myself from rolling my eyes. "I'm sure he will understand. And I bet he will want to take you fishing and show you the huge marlins that live in the deepest parts of the ocean."

Teó's eyes light up with excitement. "Yeah, Mamá, you're right! That's what Abuelo said the last time we talked. He said when I got to Puerto Rico, we men would go fishing while the women were busy cooking and shopping." He wraps the arm holding the ziplock bag around my neck. "You're so smart, Mamá."

I swallow the retort about Papi's opinions. If I start complaining about him now, I don't think I'll make it on that plane tomorrow.

"Okay, so how about we return Mr. Stripes to the tank and finish packing. Tomorrow we can take him and the others to the pet store on our way to the airport. They will make sure all of them have a new home, okay?"

"Okay," Teó says. "I'm sure Abuelo will understand."

Sometimes I want to scream at my father's machista attitude and the ideas he puts in Teó's head. I want my son to be different. I don't want him to feel superior or entitled because he was born male, not female. I don't want him to sit at the head of the table and expect the women of his household to serve him and cater to his every mood—good and bad.

I return to my room to tape the last box of books. That's it for the small stuff. The movers can get the rest.

Satisfied, I head to the kitchen and open the cabinet along the back wall. My fingers pass over a bottle of brandy I bought almost a year ago for a sangria I made during a bachelorette brunch. I've never drunk brandy by itself before. I bought it because the sangria recipe called for one cup of the stuff, and now brandy is the only alcohol I have in the house, following my commander's recommendation not to stock any at home. She warned me it would be easy to overdo it on the days I felt sad or overwhelmed.

She was right—it is easy. But today I've been responsible and focused on packing.

Looking at my watch, I note I haven't had a drink in almost twenty-four hours.

I'd forgotten about this bottle, hadn't given it much notice . . . until yesterday, when I moved it from the back of the cabinet to the front, wanting a direct eye view. I could have thrown it away then. It was more than a year old, but . . . I couldn't . . . I didn't.

Today I told myself I would pour it out, making sure I didn't tempt myself unnecessarily while Teó and I were home alone.

Now I stare longingly at the bottle, trying to convince myself it won't be so bad to have one small drink.

I am an adult, for God's sake. I served my country. I've been to war. I've killed in war.

The thought stops me cold, ending any rational logic left in my mind, breaking my will.

I grab a small Styrofoam cup and the bottle of brandy, and twist off the sticky, crusted cap. I splash one ounce into the cup—only one ounce. I have willpower. I can drink responsibly.

The liquor burns my tongue like cinnamon candy. Heat flows down my esophagus and into my belly. I let out a whoosh of breath, feeling hot air flow from my lips up into my nose. My breath smells like smoked cedar. I will the contents to settle in my stomach and not return the same way they went in. Brandy tastes nasty.

"Damn, that was strong," I mutter.

*Sniff.* The first is followed by another. *Sniff.*

I turn, horrified by what Teó may have seen. Up until we got back from my tour, I had never had more than coquito at Christmas or a glass of champagne on my birthday. Now I keep a bottle of rum in the drawer of my desk at the motor pool for my end-of-day shot (or two or three), and I use my son's twice-a-week after-school science club meetings as an excuse to have a glass of wine (or two or three) while I wait. The on-post bar and grill is a short walk to his school; from there we can walk to unit housing, so no matter how much I drink, I never get behind the wheel.

I drink every day now. Not a lot, but it steadies my anxiety and helps push away the constant replay in my head of the boy's body crumpling to the ground. But I've never had a drink in front of Teó.

If he sees the shame in my eyes, he doesn't acknowledge it. He smiles, although it looks to be masking a nervous glare. He pushes the black horn-rimmed glasses higher on his nose.

"Mamá, my room is all packed up. Can Abuelo and I take a boat far out to sea when we get to Puerto Rico? Bill Nye says the most direct way to explore the water's ecosystem is to dive right in. He says there's more difference in pressure between the surface of the ocean and ten meters deep than between the surface of the earth and Mars."

He's talking, but I'm too embarrassed to pay any attention. Teó isn't supposed to see me treating my issues. He needs to know his mother is strong and sound and ready to focus all her energies on caring for him.

"Yeah, sure, son," I say, wanting desperately to be left alone again. "Whatever you want."

The warmth from the brandy covers me on the inside, like a down blanket on a snowy afternoon.

"Teó, you should do one final check to make sure everything is ready to go."

"Do I gotta?" he asks.

I glance over my shoulder at the brandy. "You do."

"Ooookkaayy." Teó rolls his eyes and turns sharply.

He glances back at me from over his shoulder. I flash another fake smile until I'm left standing alone. His footsteps fade down the hallway before I stare guiltily at the empty Styrofoam cup.

With trembling hands, I reach for the bottle and pour a little more.

# CHAPTER TWO

The flight attendant greets me with "You almost didn't make it," but my death stare forces her to paste on a plastic Colgate smile and wave us down the aisle. Clearly she hasn't traveled in a crowded airport with a curious nine-year-old who insists on stopping at every bookstore in search of something about the ocean or the solar system.

Finally worn out, Teó is fast asleep in the seat beside me. His head rests against my arm. The tablet on his lap plays a documentary on the life and death of Buddy Holly. Since Teó discovered the 1950s artist, he's become obsessed. He even insisted on matching eyeglasses, hence the new horn-rimmed frames.

I pause the video for him and allow my eyes to move around the tiny cocoon of my backdrop.

The tight confines of the plane heighten my senses. The overhead blower pushes out a cool breeze, burning my nostrils with whirling circulated air. Every vibration shudders through me as the plane banks left and right, working to remain steady at the onslaught of our descent. The engines buzz like a swarm of cicadas on a summer evening. Despite the overhead fan, beads of sweat accumulate on my forehead. I reach up to wipe them away, focusing on my breathing, keeping my respiration quiet, not wanting to draw any attention to my fear or wake Teó. It's better he sleeps through the landing so that I can stay focused on my own unraveling nerves. "Keep it together," I murmur, trying to shift my thoughts from the miles of endless ocean beneath us to a faraway place, where I am happy, free, peaceful . . . drunk.

Taking a deep breath, I work to stay calm. We're almost there.

I've never been afraid to fly before. The last time I was on a plane, I was crouched beside fifty soldiers in the tightly packed section of a C-130. At least now there's a reclinable seat and a window view. This time the plane is returning me to an entirely new home—my childhood home. Conflicting thoughts pound against my chest with every heartbeat. My parents said I can take things one day at a time, but that's an easy promise to make. The reality is I'll be staring into the reflection of Papi's unspoken expectations. Will he see nothing but a failure now that I've left the military? Especially now that I'm returning without a solid plan or an identity.

The pilot's voice crackles over the intercom. "Good afternoon, folks. I hope you've enjoyed a smooth flight so far. Variable winds from the north are coming in at seventeen knots, so we anticipate a bumpy landing. I've turned on the seat belt sign. I'm asking everyone to return to their seats to ensure a safe arrival."

I sense the tightness in his voice, not the cheerful banter he used at takeoff. The seat belt lights turn on as the captain instructs the crew to prepare for landing. I gently kiss the top of Teó's head, breathing in remnants of baby shampoo in his soft brown hair. My mind flashes to another image of a head full of dark curls, and my fingers wrap around the edges of the armrest. I squeeze tightly. *Please, God, let us land safely.* It isn't logical to worry about dying on a commercial flight. The odds are one in a million, but my new heightened alertness has me constantly worrying about dying and abandoning my son. I fought so hard to get back to Teó—I can't imagine the irony if we would die beside one another in a one-in-a-million encounter.

The flight attendant translates the pilot's message for the Spanish speakers. As a native, I can tell she left out the part about the wind speeds. I get it. Why alarm a plane full of Puerto Rican passengers who have a flair for the dramatic on a regular day? Let alone on a bumpy descent toward a runway less than a kilometer from the ocean.

Some passengers snicker at the young woman's poor translation. Others chatter nervously and whisper prayers. The older woman on Teó's right murmurs toward the ceiling, begging La Virgen to return her home safely. She laments boarding a plane to visit family in the States. I'm sure she is among many locals on board terrified by the flying experience. I wish I could ask her to pray for my soul, but then she might ask what I've done. Once I told her, we'd have to agree prayers would be pointless; my soul is damned.

As we descend below the clouds, the drop in altitude sends a jolt to my stomach. The cabin fills with a unified gasp. I squeeze the armrest a little tighter.

With just a few minutes remaining, I look around, needing a distraction. Why didn't I pack the travel bottles of rum? *Because I would have drunk them all and likely missed our plane, or lost my child at the airport while moping around with a strong buzz.*

Pulling up the visor, I sigh, grateful to see the island's northern edge enter into view. My breath catches as I watch white-crested waves advance, then crash against light-brown, sandy beaches. The aquamarine waters at the island's edge spill outward and blend with the deep royal blue of the open sea. Despite my racing heart, I find myself smiling at the familiar sight of the Bahía de San Juan, the semicircle of ocean leading to the island's busiest port.

The reality settles in my chest: I've stayed away twelve whole years. I wanted to reject her the same way she rejected me. Now I'm back, maybe even worse off. Pathetic.

My eyes trail north to the peninsula of Old San Juan. I picture one-lane cobblestone streets and brightly colored buildings filled with the scent of coconut beverages and the rich musk of pink beans and rice. The memory of it slices through me. *Dammit, Puerto Rico, here I am, back and on my knees, feeling like I've failed, like I never made it past the starting line.*

In the final stretch of our descent, the cabin grows increasingly quiet.

The approaching runway moves closer and closer as the familiar beachfront view of high-rises bordering the metro area welcomes us. This is San Juan, the capital I once loved. It's the city where I saw my first concert and succumbed to my first kiss. It's also where I boarded a plane, rejected and alone, confused by the excitement of what lay ahead of me and the pain of being sent away.

San Juan is where I first began dreaming of becoming a doctor. I remember the exact moment when the dream sprouted into a possibility, and it began with my tía Lisandra—her ambitions for my life and her stories of the greats. Together, these things helped me understand what she saw in me.

José Celso Barbosa, born in 1857 in Bayamón, Puerto Rico, became the first Puerto Rican to receive a medical degree in the United States. Initially he was denied admission to Columbia University because of his African heritage, but less than twenty years after the end of the Civil War, Barbosa attended the University of Michigan's medical school, graduated as valedictorian, and returned to Puerto Rico destined to become a legend. Barbosa was the earliest hero I ever remember choosing for myself. I was only eight years old when my tía told me about him, quoting Barbosa with pure flamboyance.

*Superiority is not proved by color, but by the brain, by education, by willpower, by moral courage.*

At her words I dared to dream. I held on, despite my sense of betrayal when my family sent me away. When I initially resisted, feeling alone and afraid, Tía Lisandra chastised me, insisting I not be simple-minded. She said moving to Florida was my first step to greatness, just like Barbosa's had been. I believed her then.

The rear tires touch down. The plane bumps forward, safe and sound, back on land. Wind whirs loudly outside the windows until the aircraft slows to a complete stop and taxis to the gate.

The interior lights flash on, and passengers erupt into loud applause. The people of the island always cheer at their safe arrival home.

I pause but then release the armrests to join them. It is tradition, after all.

Teó raises his head groggily and stares at me. "Mamá, why are you clapping?"

"Because, papi," I reply. "We didn't die."

Stepping into the airport leaves no doubt we are no longer in the continental United States. Salsa music blares from the speakers. The sun shines brightly through glass walls. The ambiance is joyful, designed to bring the beauty of the outside tropics in. I'm surprised at how overwhelming it all feels.

At least one familiar scent grounds me. Roasted coffee beans from the smaller café a few steps down from Starbucks permeate the air. I muse at the long line forming in front of the Seattle-based establishment.

Fools. Those people have no idea what they're missing.

I take Teó's hand, leading him to the local coffee shop. We are first in line.

"Dos cafés, uno claro y uno oscuro," I order. Two coffees, heavy on the milk for Teó and darker, lighter on the milk, for me.

"¿Azúcar?" the young man asks before actually adding the traditional two tablespoons of sugar.

"Sí, morena," I reply, hoping the once-beloved local brown sugar doesn't taste bitter against my agitation.

The handsome cashier smiles and winks, except it isn't his face I see. It's another's. Large, almond-shaped eyes flooded with fear and shame. He stares down at the register, but I see him looking at the foil wrapped around his waist, then looking back up at me, begging for me to help.

"¿Señora? ¿Estás bien?" When I don't answer he tries again. "Lady? You okay?"

I look down to see Teó squeezing my hand as he stares up at me. I've scared him—again. "Yes," I say. "Sí, I mean . . . yes . . ." I try to offer Teó a reassuring smile, but I bet it looks more like a grimace. "I'm okay."

"One moment," the cashier says, and within a few minutes, he hands us each a Styrofoam cup, not giving a second thought to a young boy drinking coffee. Here, that is normal.

We choose a round table with two seats in the corner of the small seating area. Teó seems nervous and excited to be traveling. It's his first time outside the continental US. I wonder how that will evolve when he really realizes we aren't going back.

I study the excitement on Teó's face, noticing the distinct contrast with the terror in the young man's eyes that fateful morning he approached our convoy.

*Stop it.*

I pull out the chair for Teó to sit, forcing myself to focus on the here and now.

Teó's big blue eyes—a bold contrast to his natural tan—look even larger behind the thick lenses of his glasses. He notices me staring at him and offers a smile with lips rosy from the steam rising from his cup. We sip the dark roast together, allowing a few seconds of silence.

*Sniff.* "Is Abuela coming to pick us up?" Teó asks anxiously. He's shifted from calling her *grandma* to calling her *abuela*. Tía Kika must have taught him that. I haven't done a very good job teaching him Spanish. Another way I rejected the island the way it rejected me, I guess.

"Nope. We are going to rent a car here at the airport. We get to use it for the whole week until we buy one. Your abuelos are at home, waiting for us." Having them wait at their house was my idea. I intentionally delayed the reunion, wanting to experience my first few moments back in unfamiliar territory alone with my son. I needed a little more time to steady myself, knowing I was returning to the vise of Papi's unmet expectations, no longer a soldier and returning instead a broken drifter.

I glance at my watch, my stomach grumbling loud enough for Teó to look up from his cup. It's the first time I've ached with hunger since returning from deployment.

"Let's get going, papito. There's got to be a feast waiting for us when we get to Abuela's house."

Teó licks his lips. "Does Abuela make beans and rice and chicken and potato salad and arroz con leche, like Titi Kika does?"

His favorite meal doesn't come from his mother; it comes from my stand-in. I know I should be grateful, but I'm jealous, and petty, and pissed off at how on edge I feel after eight waking hours without a drink. "I'm sure they have all those things and more."

He grabs my hand and pulls me up from the table. "Then let's go, Mamá. There's no time to waste. I'm a hungry man!" He rubs his belly with vigor. For the first time in two months, I snort, an almost laugh.

Hand in hand we walk across the street to the parking garage. After a brief transaction at the rental car station, Teó and I pull out of the airport.

I lower the windows and breathe in the thick tropical air, needing to feel my lungs expand.

Teó stares out the passenger window, his neck craned upward at the gloriously tall palm trees swaying in the breeze. We move past them like a parade. They stand on each side of the road, mocking my return.

I turn up the radio to block Teó from hearing the prayers under my breath.

The deepest parts of my soul cry out. "Papa Dios, I know I keep praying the same prayer, but please let this move be the solution to Teó's condition. Amen." The next part I pray silently, petitioning the heavens to end the ongoing nightmare where a young man is bent at the waist, begging me not to pull the trigger.

# CHAPTER THREE

I recognize the colmadito on the corner. Its doors and windows are boarded with plywood.

"Teó, do you see the orange building with the bright-red roof over there?"

He strains to look in the direction I'm pointing, so I slow down before the store is too far behind us. "Over there, papi, the boarded-up building on the corner with the palm trees painted on the walls."

"Yes, I see it!" he replies excitedly. "Did you paint those trees, Mamá?"

"No, those have been there since I was your age, but I did spend a lot of time there. It was our local grocery store. I would ride my bike a couple of times a week to get fresh fruits and vegetables, rice, coffee, Ajax for Abuela, or cigarettes for Abuelo."

Teó sticks out his tongue in disgust at the mention of cigarettes. "Did you know that smoking causes disease by damaging the alveoli?" he says. "Those are tiny air sacs in your lungs." *Sniff.* "They take your healthy pink organs and turn them into charred purple blobs, making your lungs look like eggplants."

I nod. "You're right, sweetheart. Abuelo doesn't smoke them anymore."

Life was so simple back then. Going to the colmado for groceries was my journey out into the world. I had no idea what existed beyond the banana and plantain trees of my neighborhood. I didn't yearn to see anything more, until Tía Lisandra began to plant the ideas, the dreams, in my head. She saw how I was drawn to ask questions, to diagnose, to read. She insisted my parents let her pay for private school, but Papi was too proud to let his older sister step in and *manage his responsibilities.* He had a better idea, and it involved sending me to the US with his younger sister, my tía Kika. Before I left Tía Lisandra told me that she'd planted the idea in Papi's head and pushed for it without him realizing. *Your papi is a simpleminded man. It wasn't hard to let him think it was his idea,* she'd said. *But trust me, this is what is best for you and your journey to greatness.* Meanwhile, in the last days before my move, Papi kept carrying on about two birds and one stone: he got to "top" Tía Lisandra's ideas about my education *and* spite her by implying that Tía Kika in the US could do even more for me than she could. I don't know what ignited the sibling rivalry between Papi and Tía Lisandra, but I do know that it had a profound effect on my life.

I sigh, wanting to stop the flood of emotions and drive away from the abandoned building and the imprints of my early childhood memories.

Following the last bend, I gasp, reaching the majestic flamboyán at the edge of my old street, the "flame tree" with its broad canopy of bright reddish-orange flowers. These trees are everywhere throughout the island, but I've never seen one with an umbrella of foliage as grand as this one. Its three-foot-wide trunk and hundreds of upward-arching branches serve as our neighborhood's primary landmark. Not that I needed one.

Twelve years away have made no difference. I knew exactly how to get home.

Reaching the corner, I bite down on the inside of my cheek while my fingers fidget atop the steering wheel. At the final right turn, my wavering thoughts calm at the sight of the dead-end block backed against the largest monte in the neighborhood. The dense thicket still covers it in a blanket of green, but the hill looks smaller than I remember. I was much smaller the last time I saw it.

The car rolls to a slow stop in front of my parents' salmon-colored, one-story home. The rooster's crow in the neighbor's yard brings me back to my grade school days, chasing the chickens down the street. *Cock-a-doodle-doo.* The red-breasted beast perches on the fence across the street. He crows again, reminding me who's in charge of these parts.

"Are you okay?" Teó asks. "You look like you're thinking really hard."

"I am, I think. The house looks a lot smaller than I remembered." Although it's much larger than the apartment I shared with my tía Kika, which closed in on us even more after Teó was born. When the Army offered Teó and me our first on-post housing, I'd thought I'd arrived. My childhood home isn't much different in size, but there will be so many more of us crammed into it.

Papi and Mami stand arm in arm in the doorway, waving. Neighbors on both sides of the street step out into their yards. The González family from across the street makes their way over with a new baby bundled in Señora González's arms. Mami mentioned the woman had a new granddaughter. Señor Aguila stands and waves from his porch as he washes down the concrete with a faded green water hose. Teó waves back at him from his seat.

When we step out of the car, the neighbors applaud our arrival in unison. I should be grateful, but my cheeks flame with humiliation. They are welcoming home the prodigal child; they don't realize what I've truly become. Murderer. Failure. Incapable.

Teó's voice breaks into my inner tirade. "Everyone's always clapping around here. First, the people on the airplane, now them. Why are they clapping?"

"Because." I shrug. "Puerto Ricans don't miss an opportunity to celebrate and clap for anything."

He smiles at my response and reaches up to hold my hand. "I like that. I bet they can teach you to be happy again, too."

I glance over at him sharply. What does he see when he looks at me?

Mami steps out into the front yard, wearing a simple flowered dress and worn leather sandals. Her hair is slicked tightly into a flawless black bun. She opens her arms wide at her sides.

"Bendición," I say, asking for her blessing and stepping into her embrace. It's all I can utter past the growing pressure in the center of my throat, thick with emotion.

"Que Dios te bendiga, mi hija," she replies. She kisses my cheek and wraps her arms around me, pulling me tightly against her small frame. I'm overcome by the same feeling I had when I returned from Iraq, like I'm someone on the outside looking in, like it isn't my body she's holding but someone else's, a lost little girl who can't find her way back home. I step away from her embrace, suddenly unable to breathe. "Gracias, Mami," I whisper. I can't muster anything more.

A celebratory cheer fills the street as the neighbors give us one final welcome before joining us in the front yard. They enter past the small wrought iron gate and greet us with a hug and a kiss on each cheek and wishes of good fortune. I don't know how to process all the touching, so I actively shut down something inside and move robotically, as though I'm not really here at all.

Mami shifts from me to Teó, her hand moving slowly down his cheek. "Mira sus ojitos," she whispers.

Teó's blue eyes represent a strong family trait that continues to present itself every other generation. Papi has them, and he often bragged about all the girls who wanted to date him in high school because of it.

I must be summoning him with my ire, because he exits the doorway and enters the yard, smiling at the entourage and loving every second of lavished attention.

"Bendi—" I begin but stop as he walks directly over to his grandson. Lifting Teó into the air, Papi grips him in a tight embrace and kisses his cheeks.

*Nice to see you, too, Papi.*

Teó looks terrified and disoriented, but Papi's eyes fill with joy, staring at the boy, who looks so much like he did at that age.

"Lina," he bellows, noticing me at last. His deep voice commands attention. "Bienvenida, hija," he says, welcoming me with arms spread wide. The curved muscles of daily work in the fields, harvesting plantains and fruit, are still prominent, making him look youthful.

He bends down to hug me, lifting me off my feet. My nerve endings crackle to life at his proximity. *I don't know you anymore,* I think. *Don't touch me.*

I'm immediately filled with shame; he's family.

Something in his eyes tells me he either sees or senses my rejection, but he pastes on a smile and brushes it off. "It's about time you showed up, girl. What took you so long to return to your senses? No matter, you're here now. Now my grandson can carry the LaSalle legacy here in Puerto Rico."

It's not what he says that strikes me (not entirely); it's how clearly he says it in English. He's been practicing. I've never known him to have any interest in the language before. I can't help but feel immediately suspicious. What is he up to?

"Come here, Teó," Papi says. "Let me get a good look at you."

He grabs him again, picks him up, and swings him in a circle. I hear the fear in Teó's squeal.

"Papi, he doesn't like that."

"Nonsense, all boys like to play rough. Especially a tough boy like Matteo."

Teó looks back over his shoulder at me, his glasses crooked, his eyes wide. I shake my head. "Please put him down. And he goes by Teó, Papi. You know that."

Papi rolls his eyes but obliges me. "It's good he is here now, Lina. The boy needs a father figure."

I swallow hard. I don't like my father's entitlement over my son, but we just got here, and this isn't the time to argue.

*It's only our first day,* I reason. I'm bound to be a little protective.

This isn't a visit, it's a permanent change of station, so I must be prepared for what that means. At least until I can get a job and a place of our own. I know Papi can be a force of a man, the kind who takes up the entire room and makes everyone else in it seem small.

Mami offers me her outstretched hand.

I take her peace offering, clasping her tiny worn fingers between my own. She channels her strength from her palm to my soul. I reluctantly accept, inhaling her and hoping her power will move through me.

Mirroring us, Teó reaches up, an offering of trust, then takes Papi's large, calloused hand in his own tiny one. Papi looks down at him with great pride. "Matteo, you and I are going to take a boat out far into the ocean and catch some of the biggest fish you've ever seen."

Teó's eyes widen with awe. "Really, Abuelo? Bill Nye says . . ."

They are too far ahead for me to hear my son's newest fun fact. Together, Mami and I follow them into the house, behind the concrete blocks of my childhood home, the last place I lived before I was sent away. I try not to think about that. Not now. I need to start over—beginning today.

# CHAPTER FOUR

Tropical flowers, dry cooking wine, and Fabuloso from freshly mopped floors greet us warmly. The familiarity is similar to the sun-kissed, leathered skin of Mami's bony arms when she wrapped them around me in the yard earlier. I know this life, but I don't trust it. I'm not a part of it any longer. Any of it.

My maternal grandfather sits on an old leather La-Z-Boy watching a baseball game on the television with the volume turned all the way down. He doesn't look at me, seemingly unaware of my arrival. Mami forewarned me that his mental state has declined to the point he is unaware of most things—except baseball. While rocking lightly back and forth, Abuelo's eyes light up as one of the players in a Puerto Rican jersey comes to bat.

Clanging pots chime in the kitchen when my grandmother peers out.

"Bendición, Abuela," I say in greeting while she wipes her hands on her apron. Her outstretched arms reach toward me, and she carries the slight hunchback of aging and a degenerated spine. My arms reciprocate to receive her. I bend down to allow for a kiss on my cheek. For the first time since I arrived on the island, I feel like I'm back in my own body.

When we embrace, the top of her head reaches the center of my chest. She shrank since I last saw her.

"Que Dios te bendiga, mi amor," she says.

The waft of delectable scents from the kitchen follows her into the living room, and my stomach growls. I am again surprised by my hunger. They say the island air has this effect. I guess it's true.

"Come, Lina. Look at what your abuela and I have prepared for your arrival," Mami says from the kitchen. I nearly announce how they "shouldn't have gone to so much trouble," but stop, remembering anything less than extravagant gratitude at the feast before me would generate unspoken offense.

"Wow, Mami," I force out, eyeing a kitchen filled with a variety of different colors and various-size pots. These have been handed down from at least one generation, possibly two. They rest on each of the four burners. "The food looks delicious. Thank you for going to so much trouble for us."

Mami blushes with pride. "It's no trouble."

I kiss her cheek, then look around for Teó, but Papi has already taken him away. They must be in the backyard, admiring the vegetable garden, the plantain and fruit trees, and his prize chicken coop.

By the size of the pots and the rich aromas filling the small space, I can already guess the traditional dishes inside each of them: arroz con gandules, ensalada de papa, pollo guisado, and boiled batata.

Three covered aluminum trays sit on the kitchen counter, one stacked atop another. I can easily guess the contents of each. On the top, a green salad with thick, crescent-shaped chunks of avocado, the large kind, fresh from the trees of the Caribbean. The second must be ensalada de coditos, with thick squares of ham, peas, and mayonnaise dressing. Lastly, for Teó, the bottom is dessert. I'm pretty sure it's rice pudding. Tía Kika would have given Mami a heads-up in preparation for our arrival.

"Lina, te ves muy flaca. Tienes que comer," Abuela says, admonishing me for how thin I've become.

"I know, you're right," I agree. No matter the excuse, there's no justifying weight loss. It is always better to look a little *fuller*, vibrant, and well fed in this house than thin. Here thin means misery. *Touché.*

Mami's eyes search me. I bet she's assessing how bad I've gotten. She doesn't know what happened overseas, but she sees the weight loss, coupled with my sudden departure from the military, despite my previous assurances I would use the Army's programs to go to medical school, serve twenty years, and retire by forty to open my own private practice. I'm sure

Tía Kika has offered her two cents on the matter. The woman she picked up on the tarmac wasn't the same as before. Everything else could be surmised.

"There's a gift from your tía Lisandra on the coffee table," Mami says. "She wanted to be here, but she is the president of the housing authority in her urbanización, and they're having their monthly meeting tonight. I promised to make sure I gave it to you."

Tía Lisandra, the oldest, became the family matriarch on Papi's side following Mama Lina's death three months after my grandfather's. Tía Kika, the youngest, says my abuela died of a broken heart after fifty years of marriage. She called it romántico. Papi remained mute on the matter. Tía Lisandra scoffed, infuriating everyone with her assessment that her mother's death was caused by a lifetime of foolish infatuation and servitude to a man who never respected her independence and individuality. It was a harsh stance, but following her own divorce, Tía Lisandra frequently referred to herself as a wise feminist. Mami said she was a man-hater.

I can't imagine what she decided to give me. For her, leaving the Army was a professional failure. She finally broke her silence and said as much via voicemail last night. To her I am quitting, giving up on my future, relinquishing my potential and any possibilities she ever dreamed I might achieve. I force back the angst at the memory of the dark-purple roses. I don't think I want to see another of my aunt's "gifts." Her presence here to receive Teó and me would have meant so much more.

The gift bag glares at me ominously. I walk past my abuelo with trepidation and reach for the glossy silver bag filled to the brim with bright-gold crepe paper. "Is this the one? For me?" I call out.

"Sí," Mami says, stepping out into the open space and casting a worried glance over at my grandmother. Abuela eyes the bag as though something is ticking inside. "Go ahead, Lina. Open it."

I reach in, my fingers running against a soft and light material. *That's weird.* I pull out a bright-red satin-and-lace nightgown with a small handwritten message on the gown's tag.

*Since you've chosen to trade in your uniform and your independence, here's a little something in your journey to finding a husband.*

My face warms, and I assume I match the material. For a split second I believed her gift might be a genuine token of affection. I know better. Her gifts are always a test. This one is a reminder of how she sees my worth now that I'm returning home and walking away from the bright future she envisioned for me. I think about her favorite reference—a simple mindset, a woman who grows up to be nothing more than a silly wife.

"Did you guys know about this?" I ask, looking up.

Abuela shakes her head in disappointment. "That woman always has a unique way of making a point. Don't worry, Lina. We all know you are going to achieve great things here in Puerto Rico. Your tía Kika tells me you want to go to medical school."

I shrug, the idea suddenly sounding far-fetched when spoken by someone else. Maybe Tía Lisandra is right—maybe being someone's silly wife is all I can hope for at this point.

Mami, ever the pacifist, says, "It's lovely, Lina. I'm sure she doesn't mean anything by it. Now let's eat."

She walks over to a small CD player in the dining room corner. Salsa music from the 1980s fills the room as she bellows Papi's nickname in the hallowed call for lunchtime. I shove the inappropriate gesture back to the bottom of the bag.

On cue the back door slams shut. Papi chuckles at Teó's triple sniffs as they make their way down the hall. He doesn't understand Tourette's syndrome. He believes the sniffs are an exaggeration—Teó trying to be funny. Papi's generation didn't pursue medical care for things like this. They chucked a medical condition off to a case of bad luck. If only it were luck, luck that could be reversed.

"Son, wash your hands for lunch," I instruct when they reach the living room. I point to the small, pink-tiled bathroom in the middle of the hallway.

I follow behind him when a door at the end of the hallway opens. A young woman steps out in little more than a sports bra and a tiny pair of shorts that could pass for underwear.

She looks young, maybe seventeen or eighteen. Dark streaks of yesterday's mascara pool under her eyes, and her disheveled jet-black hair is piled messily atop her head. I struggle to recognize who she is. One thing's for sure: she appears to have had one hell of a night. From the looks of things, she is barely waking up. I'm shocked. It's typically considered a mortal sin in my mother's house to be out of bed any later than seven thirty in the morning.

Who is this creature? And why is she allowed to break every conventional tradition my parents hold dear?

Teó and I stand frozen in the doorway of the small bathroom and gawk at her.

"Hola, prima," she says to me, her eyes still adjusting to the daylight streaming through the aluminum shutters on the windows.

"Prima?" I ask, working hard to place the woman addressing me as *cousin*.

She reaches out and wraps her arms around me in an embrace, kissing my cheek with teeth yet to be brushed. I bristle at the touch, wondering if all this hugging is ever going to get easier. I step back and look at her. Dolores? It has to be.

Tía Lisandra's sole child is the only one from our generation with light eyes. Except hers are gray, like storm clouds, not the bright-blue sapphires Papi and Teó proudly bear.

It has to be her. Dolores was six years old the last time I recall seeing or even hearing about her. Once I left the island, she vanished from my life. My aunt kept her tucked away from everyone, including me. Looking back now, I wonder whether Tía Lisandra wanted to remove as much life on the island from my new reality in Florida as possible. She probably thought it would be a good way to get me to move forward. Now, twelve years later, Dolores is a stunning, if sloppy, eighteen-year-old exotic bird.

"It's been so long." I press Teó's chin upward, closing his gaping mouth, and nudge him gently into the bathroom. "Wash your hands," I say a little more sternly.

"¡Qué bella! You are even more beautiful now, Lina," Dolores says.

I'm struck by the compliment, especially when I measure myself against the young woman. I am doing everything possible to keep my eyes on her face and not the private parts threatening to spill out from the tiny sleep attire.

"Dolores." Mami smiles. Somehow this openly hostile stance on the traditional LaSalle-Rivera household rules has no effect on her.

"Qué bueno que pudiste dormir. Ve y báñate, que vamos a almorzar."

*Seriously!* The girl comes out in the middle of the afternoon—in underwear, no less—and Mami is pleased she was able to sleep well and recommends she shower before lunch? What kind of spell does this freak of nature have on my parents?

Papi walks over and slaps Dolores playfully on the shoulder. "Come on, it's time to eat," he jokes.

I have entered the twilight zone.

She grins wickedly at everyone. "Okay, okay." She sashays toward the same bathroom Teó exited.

I walk over to the kitchen sink, dumbfounded by what I've witnessed. I wash my hands and grab the remaining plates and glasses to help Mami finish the place settings.

Papi takes his seat at the head of the table while my mother buzzes around him, placing his glassware and cutlery down. Little has changed. He is still the king preparing to dine with his paupers.

I swallow my disdain.

This is our culture. I know it, but I've never liked it, and I silently vow to teach my son to be better. Except how will I do that when I've dropped him right in the middle of it all? Well, we're here now, two eggs in the proverbial frying pan. How do I find a way to hold more influence on him than his new environment does? My stomach sinks, not only because of the gravity of my choice to come back here, but because, if I'm honest with myself, I'm not sure I'm up for being much of an influence on anyone. I'm barely hanging on.

Teó jumps into the chair beside Papi, already enthralled, which doesn't surprise me. My father is and always has been the star of the show. It bothers me how little space remains for Mami and all her grace, but you'd never know whether she minded it. She always appears perfectly content to operate in his shadow, seemingly grateful that of all the women on the island, he chose her. I think she's devoted to the notion that the remainder of her life will be an exercise of said gratitude.

That bothers me, too, but it seems frivolous when it doesn't bother her. In any case, I have more than enough to sort through without adding my mother's life choices to the mix.

Everyone except Abuelo sits down at the table. Abuela sets aside her own plate to eat with her husband separately, but she joins us with a bit of pan de agua, a local loaf of bread, and butter.

The rest of us are serving our plates from the feast of offerings strategically placed in the center of the large table when Papi's voice rings out. "So, Lina, now that you've come back home, what are your plans for work? With a degree in biology, I'm sure you can get a job at one of the local farmacéuticas. Maybe even in the quality department."

I stare down at my hands at the mention of going to work in Puerto Rico's most prominent industry, especially on the production line of a local pharmaceutical manufacturing facility. While I can't disagree with the logic, everything about returning to the island and relinquishing my dreams to practice medicine feels like failure.

"That's a possibility, Papi," I answer quietly, hoping he changes the subject. "Teó and I are going to get settled in this week before he begins school next Monday. I'll have a solid plan by then."

His eyebrows raise as though he isn't sure he believes me, but he remains uncharacteristically silent and pours some ice-cold Coca-Cola into his glass before passing the two-liter bottle to Teó.

"Only a little," I caution. "It has a lot of sugar."

"Nonsense," Papi replies. "He is a growing boy, and you just got here. We are celebrating. Relax, Lina."

I remain silent at his admonishment—this time. I know when to pick my battles. Today isn't one of them. I'm too edgy and too sober.

The food is served, Papi says grace, and we all dig in. Flavors of garlic, achiote, culantro, and fresh tomato sauce fill my senses with sentimentality. Tía Kika taught me how to cook, but there is something distinct about Mami's hand in the kitchen. The warm, starchy saltiness of her garlicky tostones reminds me of more innocent times.

I take a bite, and I'm a young girl again, playing trompo with our spindle tops or cheki morena, a game where you had to "shake it" in the center of the circle of singing children.

"Lina," Mami calls out, snapping me back to the present. "Why you no take Dolores a pasear?"

"To hang out," Papi corrects her gently.

"To hang out," she repeats, smiling at him.

I look over at Mami, confused. She's speaking English, too?

Dolores's voice bellows through the house as she holds a concert in the shower. My parents smile, endeared by the girl's exuberance.

"Is Dolores visiting you guys?" I ask.

"No, Lina," Papi answers. "She lives here now."

"She lives here? Why didn't you mention that when we talked about me moving back? Where will Teó and I sleep?"

"Lina, tranquila." Mami's voice drops. She stretches her arm across the table and places her hand on mine. "We added another room at the back of the hall. Papi built it last year. You and Teó will sleep there—"

"Yuck!" Teó interrupts. "I don't want to sleep in the same bed with my mom. I'm too big!"

Papi chuckles and ruffles his hair with his large hands. "Of course you are, Teó. That's why I put a sofa bed in the room for your mamá. You sleep in the big bed."

"Así mismo," Abuela agrees.

I roll my eyes at them both and take a forkful of rice and chicken, then a swig of the soda, wishing desperately it had two shots of rum to accompany it. Good thing there is always a supply of chinchorros, *roadside bars*.

Hanging out with Dolores may be exactly what I need.

I inhale the rest of my food as though I haven't eaten in weeks. I guess I really haven't, not much anyway. I am swiping up the last grain of rice from my plate when Dolores steps out into the hallway, wearing nothing but a small towel around her tiny figure. She kisses Teó on the top of his head, causing him to blush a bright shade of crimson. He battles a series of blinks, trying not to look directly at her. *Sniff.* "Mamá," he says nervously. *Sniff.*

"Teó, deep breath," I whisper, not wanting to draw any more attention to him. It will only make it worse. He looks up at me and inhales deeply until his nervous system quiets again.

Dolores backs away from the table, clearly disquieted by Teó's reaction to her.

"Buen provecho," she states politely, a local custom of wishing everyone a pleasant meal. "Lina, let's hang out, okay?"

I nod, forcing away my discomfort at the invader. At least she presents an immediate solution in my desperation for a drink. "Sure, sounds great." I punctuate my sentence with a tight-lipped smile, only halfway caring if she's buying it.

My mouth waters at the thought of an adult beverage. Invader or not, my cousin's presence is exactly what I need to help me relax and deal with the return to life on the island.

# CHAPTER FIVE

After lunch, Mami cleans the kitchen. I insist on helping her, but she shoos me away.

Teó and I wait in the living room as Dolores gets ready. I'm too on edge after a full day of sobriety to tackle unpacking. An afternoon rainstorm lasting all of ten minutes pelts the ground. I sit on the couch, feet raised, my arms wrapped around my legs as my body trembles, listening to the storm outside. I lower my head into my lap, trying to block out the sounds of the convoy, the small-arms fire, the shouts of the soldiers . . . the man—more boy—approaching our convoy on the battlefield.

"Mamá," Teó calls out nervously. "Are you sleeping?"

"No, just resting," I say amid a quivering breath. I look over to the window, using every ounce of energy to hold it together. Fat droplets of water fall in deep sheets from the sky, transitioning the outside dark and eliminating any trace of the sun. The raindrops rake against the aluminum shutters like bullets.

Finally, following the momentary pour, the gray cloud moves on, continuing its journey toward the ocean. The bright-blue hue returns to the sky as though the storm never happened.

I slowly stretch out my arms and legs. Teó is staring down at his hands. I'm overwrought with guilt and immediately think of the cool, cold sting of a rum on the rocks. *I have to get some air.* "Follow me," I tell Teó, opening the front door.

He looks up at me reluctantly. "Huh?"

I extend my hand. "Come on. Come with me." He obliges. "Now take a deep breath."

He looks up at me curiously, but he does it. "That's it. Breathe it in. Teó, you will never experience this scent anywhere else." The warm, wet air serves to calm my quivering insides.

"What scent, Mamá?"

"The scent of warm, wet soil and rain lingering in the air."

He pinches the bridge of his nose, contemplating what I've said. "You know, girls have a better sense of smell than boys. Scientists think the prefrontal region of girl brains is better. Others say it's nature's way of helping the mamas bond with their babies."

I put my arm around him. "How do you know all of these things, silly?"

He shrugs. "I don't know, I just like science. Maybe my father liked science. Do you know if he liked it?"

My muscles tense, including the ones I need to respond to him. My mouth won't move. My boy has been alive for nine years and has asked me about his dad only once, four years ago. It caught me off guard and I wasn't ready with a response, so I changed the subject and never came back to it. He never asked again.

Teó pushes away from me. "It's okay, Mamá. Never mind. Sorry I brought it up." *Sniff. Sniff.*

Staring at my child, I'm left speechless and unaware of how to take his hand and walk him through this land mine of our history. How do I broach the subject that his good-for-nothing father abandoned us after I told him I was pregnant? Or that I was just some summer fling while he was visiting the US, but he forgot about us both when he returned to Puerto Rico?

"I'm sorry, son." It's the best I can do.

He half hugs me, his little arm wrapping around my shoulders before he brings his head to tap lightly against mine.

Mami saves me from the further humiliation of having to explain how I wasn't special enough to keep his father's interest when she and

Dolores step out to join us. Dolores is dressed in a tiny black jumper with shorts that barely skim the tops of her long, fully tanned thighs. She's gorgeous. I look down at my T-shirt, baggy cargo pants, and flip-flops, suddenly feeling like a plain mush of missed potential. Perhaps that was her point.

Mami smiles sympathetically as she looks from Dolores over to me, thinking the same thing, I'm sure. She reaches out a hand to Teó. "Lina, the boys from the neighborhood are going to play baseball in the park. I'd like to take Teó. You go pasear con Dolores."

Unrelenting fear clenches my heart and squeezes. Trusting someone besides Tía Kika to care for my son is a significant leap forward. I'm not sure that today, our first day here, I'm ready for that.

But Mami steps forward, grabs Teó's hand, and simultaneously pushes Dolores in my direction.

Dolores looks bright and sunny, flashing a wide smile. What is she doing here anyway? What happened with Tía Lisandra that caused her to move out from my aunt's manicured gated community into our modest home?

Mami presses. "Go, Lina. Todo estará bien." *Everything will be fine.*

She's right. It's my mother. She will guard him with her life. I relent.

"Be careful with his glasses, Mami. He cannot see well without them."

My words fade with the wind at her off-handed wave as they exit the yard.

"Mami, por favor," I call out.

She looks back, smiles, and then continues hand in hand with my baby boy.

Dolores runs over to the passenger-side door. She flashes me her wicked grin, and I shake my head. Something about that smile gives me a sense of foreboding. I need to get to the bottom of what brought her here and apparently thriving in my parents' house.

Chiquitas Bar & Grill is a cliffside bar at the top of a three-story hotel. The outdoor space offers an open-air ambiance, giving an authentic tropical vibe for those on the island wanting to experience a slice of the trendy nightclub scene surrounded by the outside elements. It's directly accessible via an exterior stairwell. The stairs lead from the parking lot to the outdoor bar and grill, complete with a high-pitched, straw-covered ceiling and a pine bar extending the length of the entire side wall. The tables and dance floor all have 180-degree views of the Atlantic Ocean.

Chiquitas is the only commercial operation in Barrio Namestal, aside from the neighborhood colmado.

Of course there is music. There is always music. Sometimes it's a live band. Other times it's local voices, belting lyrics against the tropical rhythms of a karaoke machine.

The first time I ever came here, I was twelve, and Papi sent me to buy him cigarettes at the bar. The energy from the lights enthralled me. The music and the enticing aromas of charred churrasco and tostones made me anxious to return one day.

Now I'm here. I'm back and it feels cold and empty. I just want a drink.

Dolores seems ready for a good time. As we step out of the vehicle, I figure now's as good a time as any to ask.

"So how long have you been staying with Mami and Papi?" I work hard to mask the accusation in my words. Especially because I'm not sure what exactly I'm accusing her of.

"Almost a year," she says, her voice floating like a feather.

"They never mentioned you," I say coolly, wanting my words to hurt.

"They probably wanted to protect my privacy," she said.

"Privacy from what? We're family."

"The drama, Lina," Dolores says, the exasperation spilling as though this should all be obvious. "Your mami is a rare saint that doesn't like bochinche in the family."

I nod. She's right. Mami isn't one for gossip; she'd much rather pretend we all live in an uninterrupted state of bliss. I never picked up that trait from her. It's obvious Dolores doesn't want to get into the details behind her move into my old room. I think about the roses and the lingerie. Something tells me my aunt's impossible expectations might have something to do with it. I want to feel bad for Dolores, but she's also sleeping in my room, enjoying my family. They *love* her. I need a drink. Until I get one, I choose to let it go.

I lock the car as she saunters up the stairs. Six-inch, hot-pink heels adorn her feet, and no trace of last night's escapades lingers on her face. Her jet-black hair flows down her back like an iron curtain of Taíno heritage, Puerto Rico's native inhabitants. I must admit, I am in awe. I can't believe the sweet, shy little girl with the curious gaze has grown up to become such a confident powerhouse of a woman.

She looks down the stairs at me and smiles, waving me up. "Come on, prima. It's time to have some fun."

My mouth is parched from the self-induced prohibition of nearly twenty-four hours. My son is presumably safe, so I can embrace the sense of freedom and numb my nightmares.

When I reach the second story, Dolores is already gone.

The steps waver beneath my feet. The ground below rolls like waves through the ocean. I've never been afraid of heights, but this could be another one of those things I've never experienced before, not until my return from deployment.

With a racing heart, I stop short of the third-floor landing, flooded with nausea. I fear the plate of tostones, rice, and chicken may remake their appearance at the foot of Chiquitas's entrance. Dropping to my knees, I grip the railing. My hands tremble against the wrought iron that my mind believes is wiggling like a wet noodle beneath my fingers. It feels like the entire stairwell is going to fall apart. The parking lot spins, and I'm faced with the real possibility of fainting.

"Dolores," I call out, my head bowed. From this angle I have a direct view down three stories.

She can't hear me. She is too far ahead. My shout for help escapes my lips as nothing more than a gasp.

"In, Lina . . . breathe," I mutter. *One. Two. Three.* I pause, holding my breath and using the breathing techniques we were taught to keep our cool in war. I exhale. *One, two—*

A large hand—a man's hand—reaches around me. His thumb digs deep into the crevice of my underarm as his forearm secures itself around my waist.

"Whoa, there," he says, lifting me to my feet and onto the landing.

The quintillo of the güira and the tambora greet my return from panic to the present. The stranger pulls me closer and over to the wooden planks of the restaurant's entrance, where I no longer have a view directly below.

"Are you okay?" he asks. His voice sounds far away despite his closeness.

I'm surprised by the American accent.

The lean, thick muscles in his chest press against me as his arm cradles my back, pulling me closer. We are nearly nose to nose, facing one another, when he looks deep into my eyes. It isn't a romantic stare—more of a worried gaze, assessing whether I am lucid and able to stand on my own.

He smells of frituras, sweat, and cologne.

The cologne is familiar—American, not the spicy, potent fragrance of the locals. His scent and the mop of curly blond hair—spun gold—confuse me. His sea-green eyes look worried, probing the depths of my own dark ones. I feel safe, protected, and rooted in the present. Staring back, I'm uncomfortably aware of the close proximity of my body against his.

"Wepa, prima," my cousin calls out teasingly, already seated at a stool in front of the bar. She doesn't get it. She thinks I'm standing here, flirting, not recovering from a panic attack that could have tripped me backward three floors down and onto the gravel parking lot. Idiot girl.

I wonder whether I am referring to her or me.

My throat clears as I place my hand against the stranger's chest, pushing away from him and taking a few steps back in an overwhelming need to break the spell of his grasp.

He is unfazed by my gesture for space and continues to hold me close and stare. The gaze is full of questions. "Ma'am, are you all right?"

His southern drawl is an odd sound, known mainly to those around here from the movies. The accent is unique in any environment but feels entirely foreign against the merengue music in the background and the growing aroma of freshly caught fish, roasted pork, and fried plantains.

"I'm okay," I answer, still a bit flustered. "Thank you."

"No need to thank me." He bows slightly at the waist. "Elijah Montgomery, at your service, ma'am, but you can call me Eli. Most people do, 'cept my mama, of course. She prefers the original version."

His easy smile melts away my worriment. He is beautiful, but I am more fascinated by his features than attracted to them.

His bronze tan, indeed, a result of island living, brings out the row of perfectly straightened white teeth. He's a damn Ken doll. What's he doing here? This isn't a traditional spot for tourists like him. Chiquitas is for locals.

"Nice to meet you, Eli," I say curiously. "I'm Catalina, but everyone calls me Lina."

"Anyone ever call you Cat?" he asks.

Unable to help myself, I smile. "No, I can't say anyone has ever called me that. It would mean *gato* here."

"Gato," he repeats, tasting the sound of the accent. "Okay, Lina it is," he agrees. "Well, you already look a little better. The last thing I want is for you to hurt yourself in my bar." Giving me a final once-over, he says, "Looks like you could use a drink. What can I getcha?"

I'm desperate to say "Whatever's closest," but instead I say, "Your bar?" I'm confused by his accent and the obvious fact he is not Puerto Rican.

"Yes, ma'am." A mischievous smile spreads across his face.

Puerto Ricans expect tourists. We anticipate them from all over the world—Europeans, Canadians, and Americans alike—but usually roots are planted because of family or a legacy to the land. What's even more intriguing, given my years in North Carolina, is that he is a Southerner, and they, like us, tend to stay close to home. I've always known Southerners to have a great deal of pride in their origin southern state, each with a distinct brand, history, and culture.

Not only is this Southerner living here, but he's purchased a local bar in a barrio. Not a tourist trap but a neighborhood place, a secret treasure kept private among the locals.

I find that very odd.

Then, when I think he has completely surprised me, he motions me to the bar, using his left hand. Except it isn't his hand, not his original one.

Nearly gasping, I snap my lips closed. My eyes trail over Eli's left extremity, opposite the arm most recently wrapped around my waist.

There is no longer a human limb there. In its place is a secured, sinewy combination of titanium rods and steel brackets, leading down to a rounded joint where his wrist would typically be and extending into two black pincers that serve as the left hand.

He follows my gaze to the prosthetic arm but does not appear offended by the surprise in my eyes. He's likely become used to people staring at it—a missing arm from the elbow onward. It's impossible to camouflage.

My disability, debilitating as it threatens to be, maintains the advantage of concealment.

"It's a war wound," he says. "OIF."

*Operation Iraqi Freedom.*

Just the mention of Iraq brings the sound of the shot to my ears, the image of the body crumpling to the ground. Stuck in place, I stand there speechless, a bad habit when my emotions overwhelm me. I want to tell Eli I served, too. I understand more than he might realize. I want to assure him I'm not put off by his prosthetic, because I've carried limbs on the battlefield alongside the wounded. I want to tell him that while I couldn't possibly, in some ways, I could understand.

Instead, I remain silent.

He recognizes my discomfort, although I don't think he could ever guess its source.

"I tell you what," he says mercifully. "How about you let me spot the first round for you and the pretty lady over there? She's been waiting patiently, and I'm fixin' to get a death stare if I don't deliver you over soon."

I offer one of my infamous fake smiles, relieved by Eli's sense of humor and ability to let the topic go. Surprisingly, despite my race to get out of North Carolina and the Army, I like how his deep southern accent brings a little bit of the US back to Puerto Rico.

# CHAPTER SIX

Eli is wrong. Dolores's stare in his direction looks more like *interest*. She barely glances at me as we make our way over. Her gaze works its way up his tall physique, landing squarely on his golden face.

"Hey, Dolores," he says, kissing her cheek.

"I see you already met my prima, Lina."

"Your cousin?" Eli's question sounds ripe with possibilities. "I should have known beauty would run in your family."

The mischievous grin returns while he walks around the end of the bar and rejoins us on the other side. He doesn't just own the place, he's the bartender, too.

Dolores leans forward in his direction, offering a prominent view of cleavage while tossing her hair to one side.

To Eli's credit, his gaze remains on me. "Lina?"

My name on his lips interrupts my thoughts. His drawl adds a lyrical tone to it.

Dolores rolls her eyes at his lack of attention.

"Yes," I answer, parched with thirst. *I need a drink.*

"What can I getcha?" he asks.

I turn to Dolores. "Do you mind driving us back?"

She grins. "Go ahead, prima. I can drive."

I lean forward against the bar, more from anticipation than interest in showing off *my* cleavage under the tight white tank top. "I'll have a rum and Coke. Make that a double."

"Agua Perrier for me," Dolores says.

"One Perrier and a double shot, Cuba libre, coming right up." Eli spins on one heel and heads back to the end of the bar to grab a bottle of rum.

Given the gravity of what he's endured, I'm impressed by his affable nature. His prosthetic arm reminds me of the smell of benzene—a common scent postexplosion. It also gives a fresh new memory of the village, the shouting, the gunfire, the kid . . . I wonder how it happened for Eli, although I assume it must have been an IED. He did say he served in Operation Iraqi Freedom, enough for me to infer the obvious.

I can't believe I've flown thousands of miles to escape the realities of war only to come face-to-face with a distorted mirror. Another disabled veteran, a beautiful one, but permanently disfigured. We are the same in some ways, but he seems so light and carefree . . . maybe because he didn't have to kill on the battlefield. Eli probably never came face-to-face with someone on the cusp of a whole new chapter in their life, entering adulthood, and then ripped it away from them with one shot. I bet Eli never has to wonder why the hell he didn't wait just a few more seconds for the real threat to get taken out before choosing to kill.

That's me. I'm the murderer. But I can't even consider myself wounded. My scars are on the inside, eschar in the cracks of my inner identity. I didn't lose a limb or a loved one. I did my job and returned physically intact—a war hero, according to the US Army. Hell, they even managed to give me a Silver Star. Not that I was proud of that, even if I was one of only three women who'd received the honor since 9/11. My commander said as much, making it abundantly clear that I was to accept the medal gratefully as a tribute to all the other women who've served and not been recognized. Now here I am, crumbling from climbing up a set of stairs, while people like Eli, real heroes, have lost something they can never get back. These guys are the real casualties of war. Guys like Eli can't drink away their memory of what happened.

I'm lucky I can. When I need to forget, I know the recipe to get to numbness. I guess that makes me even worse.

My fingers drum on the shiny mahogany as he maneuvers behind the bar effortlessly. He looks like he can make our drinks without a trace of disadvantage. I wish I weren't the kind of girl who silently urged a disabled vet to hurry up at the bar, but I am, especially now. The corner of my lip twitches with anticipation as he scoops ice into a red plastic Dixie cup.

His pursed lips are whistling, although I can't hear the tune above the music playing through the speakers.

He looks happy. I don't think I'll ever feel like that again.

Okay, enough. This afternoon is supposed to be an escape from the darkness on the other side of the Atlantic.

Eli uses the pincers to hold down a fresh lime and his right hand to slice it in half, then in quarters.

"I hope you were originally right handed," I call out before considering the idiocy of my words.

Why the hell did I say that?

My cheeks warm with embarrassment. Dolores looks over at me, surprised.

Thankfully Eli appears unscathed.

"As a matter of fact—yes," he says, following it with a wink in my direction. "Lucky for me, I've always been right handed."

Overwhelmed into silence again, I press my lips shut, afraid of what other dumb stuff will fly out of my mouth.

"Eli, my cousin, Lina, was in the Army, too. She even went to Iraq. Two times."

Dolores is either attempting to change the subject or making an excuse for my awkwardness.

He looks up at me, surprised. "Really? You served in the Army? Why didn't you say so?"

I really wish she hadn't said that. My service, especially my deployments, is the last thing I want to talk about. In fact, all this talk about the military and seeing Eli has only made me edgy and irritable. *I need a drink.* "There isn't much to say."

My answer draws a sharp look from him, but he shakes it off and pours two shots of Bacardí into my cup, followed by a generous spray of soda.

"Well, thank you for your service," he says, sliding the cup over. I don't know how to respond to something like that coming from him. My service was supposed to be about healing; instead, it became about the exact opposite. I'm a fraud, what's to thank?

"You too," I mumble, relieved to see the rim of my glass adorned with the misty spray from the carbonation. *Bottoms up.*

Eli slides the tray of freshly cut lime over, followed by an icy-cold bottle of sparkling water for my cousin.

Dolores takes a sip of the water and slides off her barstool like a cat. "I'm going to go play some pool."

I toss her a pointed glare that says—*Don't waste your time leaving me alone with this guy.*

She points in the direction of the pool tables at three young, good-looking locals who have just cued up a new game.

Ahhh, I get it now.

Eli watches closely as the men settle on a round high-top. He processes them, mentally recording important details of each patron. It's a soldier thing. I was trained to do the same. Situational awareness. Life and death could be in the details. He knows it. Me too.

I mouth *cuidado* to Dolores as she saunters toward them, her hips swaying in excess with each step.

Eli reaches down and pops open an ice-cold bottle of Corona, then steals a wedge of lime back from my tray. He squeezes the juice into the beer bottle.

"Salud," he says, raising the bottle to toast.

The sound of the Spanish word combined with the thick accent of a Southerner makes me smile. An actual, genuine smile.

"Salud," I affirm, tapping my red plastic cup against the bottle. The moment feels like solidarity between a brother- and sister-in-arms. I don't want comfort in the familiarity, but it's there anyway.

Eli watches me. Awareness of the walls I'm erecting burns bright in his green eyes while he sips his beer. I would bet my life his assumption of what's making the bumps rise on my arms and legs is wrong.

"I should probably go check on them," he says, puckering his lips and using them to point toward the group of young men now actively gawking at Dolores.

I laugh at the gesture. Eli has already picked up the Puerto Rican mannerisms, using our mouths rather than our fingers to point.

"She seems to be handling herself just fine. I have a question for you. Do you usually tend bar even though you own the place?" I ask.

"Aw shucks no," he says, chuckling. "My bartender, Alvin, is at the hospital. His wife went into labor last night. And my daytime waitress, Anita, should be arriving any minute now. She tends to run on island time."

Eli seems nice. His employee is late, but he doesn't sound upset about it, although he does glance over at the entrance, almost willing her to walk in. He doesn't appear in a hurry to leave me sitting alone. As long as he's on the serving side of the bar, I'm perfectly content to have him keep me company. *Just keep the drinks flowing, cowboy.*

My Dixie cup is empty in three gulps, the earlier irritability sliding down my throat alongside the rum. I want another one.

Eli eyes me cautiously. "Would you like a bottle of water?" he asks.

Pricks of shame ping my stomach, but pounding despair in my chest hurts much worse.

"Sure," I reply, "but I'll have another Cuba libre, too. A double."

He nods at me, walking away a little slower this time. In only a few minutes, he returns with another Dixie cup and a twenty-ounce bottle of water. "You'll wanna stay hydrated," he assures me. "The island heat can getcha."

This time he leaves me at the bar alone, but not before giving me one more of his all-knowing glances, a gesture that's beginning to get under my skin. *Is he judging me?*

He heads over to the table with the three young men. Dolores is now seated between them. Her laughter fills the space with an ambiance of carefree, relaxed joy.

Now that I'm alone, I can finally relax. The tingle from the rum lifts my attitude. Right now, I'm free, liberated from any military responsibilities, from Teó's tics, from the pressure of pet fish and right and wrong. A few more shots of rum, and I'll be released completely.

I breathe in the salty ocean breezes and coconut oil streaming in from the beach below, blending with the restaurant's pungency of roasted cooking. The trumpets and timbales of the salsa music package it all together in perfect harmony. The serenity of these moments, where nothing is serious, and life is about simple pleasures, is why people call Puerto Rico the "Island of Enchantment"—*La Isla del Encanto*. Except I don't feel a part of it; instead, I feel lost.

I ignore the water Eli brought me and close my eyes, gulping my second drink. The alcohol warms my senses. The buzz enhances my reflections on everything around me. Three more gulps, then drink number two is nothing but ice.

The bottle of water begs me to open it, but I leave it untouched.

The drunk creeps in like lush velvet. Everything is far away—life, reality, animosity, death. It's another life happening to someone else, not me. I get to sit here, eyes closed, and forget, numb, indifferent. I inhale, filling my chest with the air I never seem to have enough of, and then exhale, doing my best to release the nonstop anxiety.

"Mira el gringo lisiado," a voice mocks from behind me. It's one of the hyenas from Dolores's new group, calling Eli a cripple. Their banter is followed by empty, obnoxious cackles. And as quickly as it was good—my moment sours.

How dare they call him that?

My eyes blink open, searching for Eli to see whether he notices.

The tall blond ad hoc bartender is making his way back to the bar—still smiling, still whistling, utterly unaware of the prejudice and barbaric comments these idiots are throwing in his direction. Dolores looks uncomfortable, watching my head whip back toward them. She knows I heard *exactly* what they said.

As Dolores stands to take her turn at the pool table, a young, bright-red-haired woman walks in. She has a Chiquitas logo embroidered on her polo shirt and a tiny black apron cinched at her waist. I can only assume she's Anita, the waitress Eli told me about earlier. She walks directly past me, shouting apologies for being late and carrying on about thunderstorms in the area.

Thunderstorms? The word shivers down my spine, coated in fear.

The skies on the other side of the half wall remain clear. The midafternoon sun shines brightly, scattering diamonds across the blue ocean landscape.

My stomach turns, and my hands tremble. I've experienced only one major storm since returning home from deployment. It wasn't good. Teó needed me to comfort him, but I rendered myself useless, crawling under my bed and crying in terror. He was in tears and needing comfort, and I hid from him, wanting to shield myself in the darkness and away from the explosions in the sky. I failed him when he needed me.

The more I've thought about that moment, the more I realize that if I'd been drinking, I'd have been brave, not irrational and ridiculous. I know the science behind alcohol's impact on the brain—I'd be a piss-poor premed student if I didn't—but regardless of the textbook's explanations, there's the real deal, in the moment, quieting my thoughts after a few shots and giving me the ability to handle a little rain without freaking out.

I know the unprovoked panic will alleviate when the storm passes; I just have to wait it out. Soldiers talk about this stuff all the time: random bouts of fear or rage. It passes. This irrational fear of storms will pass with time, too. Until it does, what's the big deal about having a few drinks to avoid the stress? Especially when I have a kid to care for.

I strain to hear any indication outside that the weather is about to turn, but my ears are met with rhythmic waves crashing against the rocks below. Their harmony reassures me—all is well.

The waitress must be making it up. She could be embellishing a weather condition to justify her late arrival.

Eli glances over, eyeing the unopened bottle of water.

I concede. He's unlikely to serve me another drink if I don't meet him halfway.

I reach over, uncap the bottle, and take a big swig of water. "Okay, okay. Yeah. There you go." I slap the plastic bottle back down on the bar.

"Can I fix you something to eat?" he asks cheerfully, although it sounds more like *sum'n jeet?* I giggle at his accent. The rum is kicking in.

"Not yet," I reply. "I came here from a large family lunch, but I will take one more of your famous Cuba libres."

My words slur slightly. Eli notices.

"How about you finish that water there and wait it out before having another one? The last two were doubles, after all."

"Are you policing me?" I ask. The trembling in my hands at the mention of thunder is a stark reminder my faculties are still too intact—I'm not drunk enough.

"I'm just sayin', you should be careful now. These drinks are meant to be savored. They'll creep up on ya."

"Shouldn't I be the judge of that?" I ask. "How about you just appreciate the hefty tab I'm running up and mind your business?"

Eli's eyes widen, and he raises his hands in retreat. "Whoa. Easy there."

I have a direct view of a smooth pink palm on one side and a shiny metal tube topped with a curved black pincer on the other.

My stomach drops at the reminder of war and real loss. "I'm sorry. That was rude."

He is about to respond when the heavens come alive. A loud crack of thunder whips above us, followed by two, possibly three, deep rumbles of a bass drumming in the sky. The bar's open design makes the celestial sound reach in as though we are out in the elements.

My ears pound with the thumping of my pulse as my instincts kick in, searching for a place to find safety.

"You all right?" Eli asks, but his voice sounds far away, in a different dimension. "Lina?" he calls out.

I lay my face on the bar and bring my knees up to my chest. The strengthening of the breeze whips along the back of my neck as my long ponytail flies up sideways. The edge of the bar digs deep against my shins. Wrapping my arms around my head, I create a cocoon of protection.

Memories of the chaplain crossing himself flash before me. Tears well against closed eyelids as another round of thunder claps its wings in a loud boom.

It's happening again. The sounds of war in the skies remind me that my worst nightmare was only a trigger finger pull away.

Dios mío. I brace for the pop of shots fired.

# CHAPTER SEVEN

"Hey, it's okay," Eli says, placing his palm on my shoulder. "The thunder stopped. I walked outside, but the clouds were already heading in a different direction."

I lift my head, blinking back tears, thankful the sun has resumed its post, warming the heavily oiled sunbathers below.

A tiny hand is rubbing the center of my back. Dolores. She looks at me curiously despite my recoil at the gentleness of her touch. She isn't familiar to me yet. I'm not ready.

"¿Estás bien?"

I nod. "Sí. I'm okay, thank you."

She is a curious one, my cousin. At times she seems borderline aloof. Other times absolutely tender. "Prima, the thunder . . ." I trail off, but she nods. She gets it.

"You want to go?"

I shake my head. "No, not yet." Adrenaline absorbed most of the alcohol in my system, leaving me uncomfortably sober and frustrated.

Eli reaches across the bar with the drink I ordered. "It's not a double, but you look like you could use this last one."

He emphasizes *last*.

"Thank you," I whisper, refusing to feel any kind of way about it.

"But I'm going to need you to finish that bottle of water."

"Okay, fair enough."

I tilt back the bottle and swallow it all without taking a breath. I was thirsty. I let out a light burp and raise my Dixie cup in victory. "Salud," I say under my breath.

"Salud," Dolores and Eli reply in unison as she pulls out the seat beside me.

"Can I offer you something to eat?" Eli asks, placing a menu in front of us. "A little food in your belly may be a good idea before this one over here," he says, pointing in my direction, "ends up three sheets to the wind."

I give him my best give-me-a-break face, and Dolores smiles politely, but she doesn't understand Eli's southern colloquialisms.

She points at a picture of a sampler platter of fried Puerto Rican appetizers. "This one."

"Good choice," he says before heading back behind the bar to the kitchen.

"How well do you know Eli?" I ask. She doesn't answer. "At least tell me what he's doing here, running a bar in the middle of the Atlantic?"

"No sé." She shrugs. "Christian, one of his soldiers, was from here. Se murió."

One of Eli's soldiers died? I wonder how that could have led him to Puerto Rico.

I want to ask Dolores how she knows that, but the topic seems to make her sad.

This whole afternoon needs a pick-me-up. No more talking about dead soldiers.

After a few minutes Eli approaches us with a beautifully laid-out platter of fried delicacies and another bottle of water for me.

"Buen provecho."

"Gracias." Dolores and I thank him in unison.

I gulp the last of my drink while Dolores hungrily dips a sorullo, a Puerto Rican corn fritter, into a small dish of mayo-ketchup. She licks her lips and fingers, and I feel the stares of the young men behind us, watching.

This time I sip my drink. Eli is right. These are meant to be savored. I only want to feel far, far away from my body.

My eyes search the bar as a few more people walk in. Dusk will soon take over the skies. I'm sure Teó is starting to wonder where I am. A part of me wants to stay, see the sunset, and watch the dance floor lights come on. I want to feel the energy of a Puerto Rican night take over as the music gets louder and the dancing grows closer. I want even more to bear witness as the inhibitions fade and people remember how life is meant to be experienced.

My daydream stops abruptly as Eli observes me. I bet he's gauging my inebriation. I open the bottle of water and take a big swig.

He looks satisfied. "Anita's going to take over behind the bar. Would you like to go for a walk with me?"

What I want is for him to pour me another drink. I'm *almost* drunk enough, and it's starting to get late.

"I can't," I finally sigh. "We have to get back."

"Of course," he says, stepping back from the bar. I may be imagining it, but I swear he glances down at his left arm. "I understand."

My heart sinks.

"I have a son. Teó. He's nine. He's waiting for me."

Eli's cheeks turn pink. "Oh my, forgive me. I didn't realize you were married—"

"I'm not," I cut him off. "It's only me . . . and Teó."

He looks down at the Cuba libre in front of me.

I bet he's judging my drinking.

The silence gets awkward, but I'm not interested in filling it. Eli seems like a know-it-all. I bet he regrets asking me to go on a walk now that he knows I'm a single mother and a drunk.

Whatever.

"Lina is staying at our house," Dolores interjects, oblivious to the awkwardness between us. She pushes the half-eaten platter in his direction. "You should come to visit."

My head swivels from Eli to Dolores and then back at him. How does he know where my parents live? I think back to their familiarity when we first walked in and how he greeted her. They must have dated at some point.

Eli seems to know what I'm thinking.

"No!" he says abruptly. "It's not like . . ." But he trails off, shaking his head. "Let me go get your bill."

Once Eli is out of earshot, I turn to Dolores. "Did you date him?"

She throws me her signature smile, reaches over to grab another sorullo, and takes a bite. "No, prima, not me," she says between chews.

Eli returns from the register with our tab but slips it into his back pocket. Ringing up our bill was just an excuse to get away from us.

"It's on the house," Eli says. "Dolores mentioned she had a cousin moving back to the island, so consider this a welcome-back reception and my pitch for your continued patronage. Although, next time, don't let Dolores eat alone; try the food. I'll make sure you leave here full as a tick."

Suddenly tired, I force a polite "Thank you, Eli. It was nice to meet you."

He gives me another broad smile with his full pink lips and bright-white teeth.

"Likewise, Lina." His cadence sounds like a song. "The pleasure is all mine."

I put my hand out to shake his, but he reaches forward, takes it, and brings my hand up to his mouth, kissing my knuckles gently.

I try to ignore the intimacy of his gesture, letting my hand fall limply at my side as I stumble off my seat. I glare at Dolores, but she simply raises an eyebrow before wrapping an arm around my shoulder and guiding me toward the exit.

# CHAPTER EIGHT

Teó sits alongside his great-grandfather. My abuelito gently sways back and forth in the rocking chair beside him. The rocking chair has been a staple of the concrete front porch my entire life. It's the same chair Papi sat in at night when I was a child. I would climb onto his lap, and he would tell me about the constellations in the sky. In those moments it didn't matter that I wasn't his son. I was his child. He wanted to share something special with me, and the heavens had always fascinated him. It's likely where Teó gets it from.

"Hola, Mamá!"

"Hola, mi amor," I reply, endeared by the Spanish. He's learning so quickly, even though I've never taught him. Teó is proving much more open to island life than I am. Go figure.

He holds up a Styrofoam cup as pink liquid sugar drips down his chin. The tradition is still alive. Mami took him to the local piragüero.

I whisper a salutation to my grandfather, but he continues swaying back and forth, mumbling, unaware I'm even there. I can't believe how much things have changed in the last twelve years, how quickly his mental capacities have deteriorated. My abuelo was always full of life, with a turn of phrase that never made any sense. Some of my favorites were "El camarón que se duerme se lo lleva la corriente"—*the shrimp that falls asleep is carried by the current*—or "El gato con guantes no caza ratones"—*a cat wearing gloves does not catch mice.* Thinking of the twinkle in his eye and the playfulness of his tone makes me smile, but immediately behind it—I hurt. I missed his last moments of lucidity. Why? Because I wasn't here, because, at Tía Lisandra's insistence, they sent me away. Now he probably has no idea who I am.

Another fake smile. "Is that what I think it is?" I ask, reaching down and kissing Teó's cheek, hoping he doesn't smell the rum.

"It's a snow cone, Mamá! But Abuela calls them piraguas. She picked this one out for me. She says it's parcha. I don't know what that is, but it's deeelicious!"

His tongue swipes across his chin.

"It's passion fruit. And we can find it all over the island."

Teó nods. "It's sour and sweet."

"I'm glad you like it. Where's Abuela?"

"She went to the colmado to get more plátanos for dinner, but she said if we needed anything, we could ask Nana."

*Nana.* The word rolls over in my head. My "abuela" has now become "Nana." She is now a bisabuela, a great-grandmother. The title of *abuela* has been passed down to her daughter—my mother—a significant rite of passage. Nana's new title feels perfect.

The rum wears off in time for dinner. Mami arrived from the corner store with a small bushel of plantains to complete the arroz con pollo. Music plays softly in the background. This time everyone serves themselves and scatters away with their plates in hand.

Dolores eats in front of the television (I'm in disbelief the tiny girl can still eat an entire plate of dinner after the sampler platter earlier). Mami eats standing at the counter in the kitchen. Papi isn't home yet, but his plate is prepared and covered with aluminum foil, ready once he arrives. My abuelos are the only ones actually sitting at the table.

My abuela spoon-feeds Abuelo, one bite at a time. He leans forward and cautiously opens his lips to the approaching spoon. She lovingly guides small bits of rice and beans into his frail mouth, smiling at him as she does it. He recognizes her and smiles back.

Their bond is powerful, an otherworldly connection, a snapshot of what marriage is supposed to be—two souls joined into one—unity.

It's difficult to see my abuelos like this, realizing I gave myself away too easily. It may have been a few sweet words and the kind of summer romance people write books about, but then I found out I was pregnant, and it was all over. I never heard from Teó's father again. On the flip side, that gift came back to me a million times over with the birth of my son. I will never have a single regret about that. Maybe it isn't the same, but I have experienced the most selfless form of love and trust between two people—a mother and her child. And for that, I'm deeply grateful.

I rise from the couch to check on Teó. Heading down the hallway, I hear his little voice echo from Dolores's room.

"Hypothesis," he says, slowly sounding out each syllable.

"Hypothesis," she repeats.

"Good job," he says. "Now try this one—standard deviation."

"Okay," Dolores says. "Stan . . . dar . . . devia . . . ción."

"That was a good try."

My face relaxes into a smile. I can't quite get a pulse on Dolores, but I may have judged her a little too harshly today. She's gorgeous and confident and bold. Combining traits like that, I automatically assumed she lacked substance. I bet people get her all wrong all the time. I did. Not Teó. He can sense a genuine heart.

I decide not to interrupt the English lesson. It allows me to grab a quick shower. After I amble to the end of the hallway, my thoughts drift back to all the new characters who have entered my tightly controlled world in the past twelve hours. Opening the door to the room where Teó and I will sleep, I see our luggage spread open across the bed. The sofa bed is pulled out, and fresh linens are wrapped tightly around the mattress. A small hibiscus flower lies gently on the pillow.

Small tokens of affection like these from my family remind me I am welcome.

My eyes well up with heavy tears as my hand passes over the cool, freshly pressed sheets. This is love.

When I step out of the bathroom after showering, Teó is already in his pajamas, waiting for me. His glasses rest on the nightstand beside him, his body tucked under the sheets. The blades of the air-conditioning unit rotate up and down as cool air flows through the room. Either Mami or Dolores must have turned it on for him. Despite the hum of the unit, we can still hear the coquis, our native tree frog, outside. Their song mimics the beat of the human heart.

I bend down to kiss Teó's forehead and drooping eyelids, heavy with sleep, while his chest rises and falls slowly with relaxation. My son has easily slipped into the island's enchantment. I'm a bit jealous. I wonder if that will ever happen for me, too.

"Did you have an amazing first day?"

His eyes are nearly closed, but his lips curl into a lazy smile. "The best day ever."

"I'm glad you feel that way." I smooth back his hair. "Soon we are going to register you for school."

"Do they teach science?" His voice drifts off toward sleep.

"Of course they do. When I perused the website, I saw pictures of a pretty impressive science lab."

"Will they teach me in Spanish?"

"Only during Spanish class. The rest of your classes will be in English. It is a special school to teach kids like you from the US who don't speak much Spanish."

"Will there be other kids from the US?"

"Oh yes. In fact, most of them. Local kids who attend school there will speak English just as well as you—maybe even better."

He rolls his eyes and sticks his tongue out at me.

"You're going to love it," I assure him. I kiss his forehead one more time. "Now get some rest. We have a little time before all that starts."

His eyes rapidly flutter before descending against his cheeks. In minutes he is fast asleep.

I haven't seen Papi since returning from Chiquitas. He must be out playing with his band. As the lead singer of a local salsa group, he often performs in local bars or restaurants, even after a full day in the fields. Mami usually goes to watch him play, but my arrival took precedence tonight.

I'm drifting off to sleep when I notice an approaching shadow hovers at the bedroom door. I shoot up from the sofa bed, my senses heightened, fingers tingling with adrenaline. My hand reaches across for my sidearm, except I'm not in uniform and the only thing at my side is the waistband of my underwear.

"¿Prima?"

Dolores.

She tiptoes into the room and sits on the edge of the bed, fully dressed in pink sequined shorts, a white tube top, and platform sandals, smelling like a bouquet of tropical flowers.

I whisper, not wanting to wake Teó. "You're going back out? Don't you have a job to go to in the morning?"

She shrugs, although it's more like a playful bounce of her shoulders as she cocks her head to the side. "No. No job. Just like you. I am in luto."

Just like me? What does she know about my grief? I raise one eyebrow. "In mourning? You don't look like someone who's grieving."

The playful expression fades, replaced by serious eyes. "What grieving looks like?"

The question hits me right between the eyes. I have misjudged my cousin. I shrug. "I guess it comes in many forms, doesn't it?"

She nods slowly. "Sí."

Dolores grabs my hand in hers, squeezing her fingers against mine. Her hand is ice cold.

I don't ask her what she knows about me. It's impossible for her to know anything. She must sense it. "I'm going to look for a job once I get Teó situated in school."

Her response is a smile full of sympathy. "Prima, a job is just a detail. I so happy." She pauses, then corrects herself. "I *am* so happy you and Teó are here."

My defenses melt. I had no idea Dolores was processing a loss of her own, and still she finds joy in my and Teó's arrival home.

I sit up and lean my head on her shoulder. "Thank you, cousin. Me too. So you're going out?"

"Yes. To listen to Papi sing. And do a little dancing." She rocks her shoulders, reminding me of Chiquita Banana. "You want to go? Tía can watch Teó."

I may only be twenty-seven, but right now my body feels decades older than my exotic cousin and her boundless energy. Of course, Papi, turning fifty-six this year, also labored in the fields all day and is now swaying on a stage, singing his heart out and entertaining a bar full of people.

"I'm too tired. Have a good time. I'll see Papi next time."

She squeezes my hand again. "Okay, prima. You rest. Tomorrow we go to the beach. Maybe we hang out with Eli again." She grins as her eyebrows dance up and down.

"Maybe . . . Prima, how does Eli know where we live? Were you . . . ?"

Dolores stares down at me. She is quiet for so long I assume there was something between them.

"I loved him," she finally says.

"You loved Eli?"

"No Eli. Christian, el que se murió."

I don't understand. Dolores says she loved Christian, the soldier who died. How are they all connected?

"You want to talk about it?"

She shakes her head at me. "No. Not tonight, Lina. Tonight is dancing. Tomorrow is another day."

Dolores stands up and shrugs off the heaviness of our talk as though we never broached the subject of death. She blows me a kiss, closing the door behind her, and I pretend to catch it.

When the door clicks shut, I lie back on the pillow, putting my hands under my head. Something tells me I've only begun to unfold the layers of stories piling up around me.

The song of the coquis relaxes my body toward a state of sleep. Eli's easy smile greets me in the dark recesses of my peace. I consider the untold story hiding behind his bright-jade eyes. His easy nature and sunny disposition are admirable, but I'm not sure I can trust his sincerity. How could someone be so at ease after a tragedy has permanently disfigured him? I consider it, but it makes no sense.

# CHAPTER NINE

The next day and the seven thereafter welcome me with the *cock-a-doodle-doo* of the neighborhood rooster outside our window. Every day, his screech reminds me of the drinks I had the night before.

"Damn gallo," I mutter, half-awake.

Except this morning my frustration is replaced with wonder when I rub the sleep from my eyes and spot the brilliant emerald-green and sapphire-blue feathers of the zumbadorcito perched outside the window. I reach for my phone to take a picture of the tiny hummingbird, but she flies away before I can pull up the camera app.

The Caribbean air has consistently soothed Teó into a deep sleep. It's the first time I'm the one waking before him in years. This morning his little face is pressed soundly against the pillow with pure peace, surprising given that his tics tend to occur during sleep and result in repeated disturbances. My fingers caress his cheeks softly, wiping a shimmer of sweat glistening across his forehead. He is sleeping so soundly I'm confident I won't wake him before I slip out.

Piling my long dark hair on top of my head into a messy bun, I enter the kitchen to see Mami and Abuela hard at work. I wonder if they will comment on my tiny shorts, given how my little cousin has set a new precedent, although I'm not sure they'll even notice. Morning activities make for a busy start to the day.

Nature fills the landscape outside with native music, but inside, the house hosts its own sound. The battery-operated satellite radio sits on the windowsill of the open kitchen window, playing soulful salsa music. The music is comforting, but Abuela's whispered prayers are truly the most beautiful sounds in the room. She repeats verse after verse while buttering a slice of pan sobao. The warm fragrance of bread and butter fills the tiny space that makes up the kitchen, dining, and living room.

"Lina," Mami says, "por poco se te pega la frisa."

The expression makes me smile. I haven't heard it in more than twelve years. Its literal meaning implies the blanket is nearly stuck to me, but here it means I've almost overslept—a mortal sin under this roof . . . unless, I've learned, you're Dolores.

I reach over and kiss her cheek. This time I don't feel the immediate bristle inside my chest. "I'm up, don't worry," I say. "And after drinking a cup of that café you're making, I'll be running out that door, ready to tackle the world."

A small pot brews on the miniature four-burner stove. Mami pours heaping spoon after heaping spoon of Yaucono grounds into the boiling water. Lowering the heat, she lovingly stirs them, allowing the mixture to foam before pouring it through the colador. Our colador is the traditional kind. It looks like a worn brown sock. The boiling coffee is transferred from the first pot through the old sock into an aluminum percolator before the heat is raised, bringing the coffee back to a boil. Mami's hands lift expertly, then lower, straining out the best flavors from the grounds.

I savor the last step as the aroma of roasted beans fills the room and she pours the fresh batch into two awaiting mugs.

The coffee couples with the warm sweetness of freshly baked bread. Mami sings softly under her breath, syncing with the tune of my grandmother's whispered prayers. In tandem, they move through the kitchen, dancing the tango, surrounded by bright-colored paint on the walls and even brighter art adorning them. It's the same morning routine in the same kitchen I remember as a child. Twelve years away and things are still the same here.

It's comforting to know I can tap right back into it, but stifling, too. Now that I'm here, will I be stuck, too? Wasn't that the whole point of leaving in the first place? So that I'd progress? Tía Lisandra insisted I do exactly that. Isn't that why she hasn't even bothered to come visit? Because, here I am, back again at the beginning and more wounded than ever. I miss my tía Kika. She would know just what to say to flip my negative outlook on its back. I make a mental note to call her once I get Teó situated in school. He'll be excited to tell her all about it.

I look around at the kitchen, noting for the first time in a week that even the appliances remain the same. I know how Mami thinks. What reason necessitates change? If one cauldron makes magic, why search for another? But what does that mean for me? And how can I be both comforted and appalled by it in the same breath?

Sensing my growing angst, Abuela spreads a pat of butter on her baked bread and peels off a small piece for me, before dipping the remainder directly into her café con leche. Popping it into her mouth, she closes her eyes, savoring the first bite, then indicates with a tilt of her head that I should do the same.

"Lina, this one is yours," Mami says, pushing the second mug in my direction. "You and Teó need to have a good breakfast. I have the avena ready. Today is a big day for him. He's finally going back to school."

"Sí, Mami," I say. "He is excited about the science lab . . . Where's Papi?"

"He is still sleeping. He got home late last night."

I turn to Abuela. "Is Abuelito sleeping, too?"

"Lina, you are full of questions this morning," she chides, placing a full plate of bread and butter in front of me. "Nena, eat something and get going. You don't want that boy to be late on his first day of school. The teachers will think he comes from a house full of savages."

I glance up at the white analog clock on the wall and exercise my backward-planning skills from the Army to assess how long it will take to finish my breakfast, get Teó ready and fed, and drive to his new school. There's plenty of time.

I raise the ceramic mug to my lips and take a sip of steaming coffee. I drink mine black. Warm liquid fills my chest with heat, while Mami pulls something from underneath the table. My breath catches at the large white, glossy bag decorated with a red satin bow and blue-and-white crepe paper exploding from the top, the colors of the Puerto Rican flag.

"Mami, what is this? You didn't have to get me a present."

"Don't worry, Lina." She smiles. "It's not for you. It's for Teó. But you open it."

I pull the crepe paper out of the bag to reveal a brand-new navy-blue polo shirt with a logo on the top-right corner. "Wow, Mami. How did you know?"

"There's more," she says, grinning.

I reach deeper and pull out a pair of khaki shorts, crisp white socks, shiny brown loafers, and a small bottle of cologne. Everything is in Teó's exact size.

They purchased his uniform for school.

Mami and Abuela anxiously await my response, but I'm momentarily distracted by Teó's sleepy expression in the hallway. His little hand is enmeshed in Dolores's, who, by the look of it, couldn't have slept more than a couple of hours. His eyes meet mine.

"Mamá? Are you okay?" Teó asks. "Why are you crying?"

"I'm happy, sweetheart," I say, blinking back tears of gratitude. "Come here. Let me hug you. Say thank you to Abuelita and Nana for your new uniform."

"Gracias, Abuelita. Gracias, Nana," he says before sprinting back toward our new bedroom. He forgot my hug.

I want to reiterate my gratitude, but Mami and Abuela are already moving around expediently. The sentimental moment has passed. Princess Dolores takes the cue and returns to her room to sleep. I know the routine—I'm to get moving. There's not a second to waste in the mornings, especially not when children need to get to school.

I finish my coffee with one final gulp, then rise from the table to get us both ready.

"Mamá, my school looks like it's in the jungle," Teó says as we turn onto the road that leads to the entrance.

"That means you can pretend to be Tarzan on your way to class."

He rolls his eyes at me, but a smile creeps across his lips as he considers my proposal. The idea has merit.

Teó's right, though—it does look like a jungle. It's part of how things are designed here: lush, green, and full of plant and animal life. If I didn't know better, you could convince me we were in the middle of the Amazon rainforest, except the rainforest wouldn't lead to these state-of-the-art facilities.

This campus is a branch of an elite Swiss boarding school. The waiting list can be up to a year long, but we were granted immediate enrollment when I explained I'd recently returned from Iraq. Less than 1 percent of Puerto Rico's children will ever get the chance to receive an education like this.

It doesn't mean I'm not conflicted. A part of me is ashamed I want my son in the classroom with rich white children who can afford to be here. The other part of me knows what the alternative entails, a public school system still in disarray. After saving every last penny I could and living on very little, I prepared a cushion for Teó's future. His education here is part of that.

"Are you sure I'm gonna fit in here, Mamá?"

I squeeze his shoulder. "I think you're going to fit right in, son."

"I hope so." I hear the nerves creeping into his voice. "I didn't fit right in before. In North Carolina, people always asked, 'What was I?' They would say, 'Boy, you a light skin.' And I would say, 'No, I'm Puerto Rican.' And then they would always say, 'Ooooh, so you're an immigrant.' Then I would say, 'Nuh-uh—I'm American, like you.' And they would say 'Nuh-uh' and call me Speedy Gonzales. They were so dumb. I tried to teach them, saying, 'Speedy Gonzales is Mexican, not Puerto Rican,' but then everyone said—'Same difference.'"

He sighs from the relayed effort. I do, too.

I know more about his experiences than he can imagine. Tía Kika's small town in Florida had plenty of Latinos, but most of them grew up in the US and spoke English fluently. I spoke it, too, but not like they did. It took me nearly all four years of high school before I caught up.

"It's not the same, Teó. People from Mexico and people from Puerto Rico are different. Our world is a much more interesting place because it's not the same difference. Some people here look like you and others don't. Puerto Ricans capture every color on the rainbow. Look at our own family. Abuelo has dark skin and light eyes like you, but Abuelita has light skin and dark eyes like me. Our bloodlines have been touched by every race God ever made. That's what makes us beautiful."

He blinks and stares at me, a bit baffled. I'd like to ruffle his head, but he's gone overboard with the gel this morning, and I'm afraid of what will happen if I touch it.

He gets a reassuring smile and a wink instead.

As we roll into the guard station, I lower the window and explain to the guard I am registering my son for his first day of school.

I know this is how things are here—everywhere deemed "safe" has gates and security guards—but the borderline military-level measures are still surprising. The guard asks for my driver's license, annotates the car's license plate on his clipboard, and takes our picture. After signing an entry document, we get a parking pass to put on the dashboard. Then the gates open, and the mobile arm rises. Ever the soldier, I notice the 9-millimeter on the guard's hip as he wishes us a good day and waves us through.

Memories of my deployment aren't welcome, nor do I want to associate them with Teó's new school, but the reminders feel like they're everywhere. Security. Procedures. Protection. Protocols. I can't escape them.

My heart races from an unknown threat. I turn the key and shut off the engine. *Deep inhale, Lina.*

"Mamá?"

Teó sounds far off in the distance, even though he is sitting beside me.

"Are you okay? Mom?"

He begins sniffing two, three, four times. It snaps my eyes open. *Mom.* He never calls me that. I've scared him.

"I'm okay, honey." I turn toward him, putting my hand on his. I fumble to undo my seat belt. "Take a deep breath," I say for us both, but he is doing the opposite—holding his. "Teó?"

He lets his breath out slowly as his face visibly relaxes. He looks . . . victorious.

"It worked," Teó says. "Dolores taught me last night before bed." He opens the car door valiantly, a newfound strategy on his lips.

I'm stunned. Dolores found a way to help him manage his tics. Meanwhile I'm right beside him having a freak-out and making them worse. What the hell is wrong with me?

"I'm glad it worked, honey." My voice is quiet.

As we exit the car, an older woman with a pristine blue skirt suit approaches us. She's holding hands with a little girl about Teó's age, whose hair is so pale it's nearly the color of wheat, contrasting a pair of bright-blue eyes. I hope her parents have slathered her with sunblock. The translucent skin must take a beating under the brutal tropical sun. I heard stories when I was growing up about northerners who traveled to our beaches and ended up in the emergency room with second-degree sunburns. Locals teasingly called them chicharrones.

"You must be Catalina," the older woman says before glancing at Teó. "And you must be Matteo." Placing her hand on the little girl's shoulder, she continues: "This is Sophia. She has lived here all her life and has attended our school since kindergarten. I brought her to be your buddy during the first week."

The woman turns back to me and extends her hand. "It's nice to meet you, Catalina. I'm Director Strata, the head of school operations and admissions."

I take her hand and shake it, feeling small and off balance. It doesn't matter how old you are, school administrators have a superpower that will always make you feel lower on the proverbial power spectrum. "Just Lina for me," I say, staring down at the ground, watching my tennis shoe drag across the concrete. "And he goes by Teó."

My hand falls protectively over Teó's shoulder, but he shakes it away. I pretend not to notice.

I squat down to offer Sophia a shake, but she holds out her skinny arms, gripping my shoulder, and kisses my cheek. "Mucho gusto," she says.

"Mucho gusto," I reply but don't go as far as returning her kiss. It's customary here, but she is a little girl, and Army formalities still flow through my veins.

Director Strata nods courteously as I rise.

"Why don't you two follow me, and I can give you a quick tour of our facilities? Then Sophia and Teó can head off to class while you and I finalize the remaining paperwork."

She walks to the awaiting golf cart at the end of the covered entrance. Like ducks in a row, we all follow obediently, but as we get closer, my steps slow, allowing the kids to move ahead. It's important Teó handles the introduction and the new environment well, and I want to give him some room for what I know is coming. I tend to get a sixth sense about these things. When he breaks into a fit of sniffs and rapid blinks, we all stop walking. I freeze—my worries confirmed.

My heart drops, reading his face. Teó is mortified this is happening in front of his new classmate. Tía Kika told me about how episodes like this led to the schoolyard fights Teó was having in North Carolina. The bullies couldn't wait to use his condition as an excuse to make him their target.

I want to rush to his side and reassure him it's no big deal. But doing that makes it a big deal.

Director Strata is starting up the golf cart, unaware of what's transpiring a few feet behind her.

Powerless, I look on as Teó closes his eyes and holds his breath. He exhales slowly again, apparently the way my cousin taught him, and slowly regains control of his tics.

*Thank you, Dolores.*

I release my breath and the fisted hands at my sides.

Unfazed, Sophia grabs Teó and interlocks his fingers with hers, pulling him toward the golf cart. "Come on," she says. "We can sit facing the back and ride all the way there backward."

My insides fill with affection for this child. She didn't say anything about the tics. What a mature response for such a young girl. Her parents must be doing a great job teaching her empathy and understanding. Teó was so worried about fitting in and making new friends that a kid like Sophia is a godsend. Teó follows beside her, and I think he feels the same way.

We all take our seats in the golf cart. Sophia looks over her shoulder at me as she buckles her seat belt. She extends a wink and a girlish smile. I translate the gesture as a partnership—together we will look out for Teó's best interests.

For the first time since arriving at the campus, I relax and prepare for the grand tour. The director points forward to a large building and starts her exposition on the history of the campus.

Sophia leans over and whispers to Teó, "You might as well have some fun now, kid. In there you're on your own. Once everyone sees you're a gringo from America, they're going to make fun of you."

I look over at Teó, wondering whether he's thinking what I'm thinking. This is exactly what we were trying to get away from. New place, same struggle.

Teó shrugs, putting on a brave face for his new friend, but I can see the worry behind those big blue eyes. I turn back, hoping he'll release that breath he's holding before he turns blue in the face.

# CHAPTER TEN

I don't want to relinquish my baby antelope to a den of third-grade lions ready to pounce. The alphas in the pride always smell new blood. Those are the predators who stalk their prey before attacking. They isolate and surround the new kid to secure the kill. I know their kind because they don't grow out of it. I experienced them in basic training, too.

My glare aims at the obnoxious little sucker in the front row with a cocky snarl. Teó sees me and gives a desperate plea to *please stop* under his breath, followed by a squeeze of my hand.

I stop and offer a half-hearted smile, relenting in my duties. "You got this, big guy," I whisper near his ear under the guise that I need to tie my shoe. "I'll see you later at Abuela's."

I continue my tour of the school grounds, then follow Director Strata to her office. Her desk welcomes me with a mountain of paperwork piled high. With a handful of signatures, I will be signing away a sizable chunk of my savings for the remainder of the school year. This expedites my need to find work. I think back to the conversation Papi and I had at the lunch table on my first day back. Working at a local pharmaceutical is looking more and more like my best option. I sigh.

Teó is worth this, and it is an impressive school. He is lucky they allowed him to skip the waiting list and enroll so late into the fall semester.

My next stop is the VA Medical Center in San Juan. I'm not sure I'm ready for what will greet me there. My feet slog through imaginary quicksand on my way to the car. I want to come up with a reason not to go, but my mind draws a blank. I click my tongue against the back of my teeth and slide into the driver's seat. I have to go.

The digital clock on the dash comes to life, indicating there's time to spare before my appointment—just long enough to stop at the chinchorro on the way there. It will be a brunch of champions. Nothing like cheap liquor and fried food to consider myself a local once again. Although, given the state of my nerves, I don't think I can hold down any food.

A little liquid courage is the only way to make it past those doors and survive the questions the therapist will bring up. I'm confident in my abilities to hide that I've been drinking. If I could get out of the visit altogether, I would, but the only way I get approved for my rating and monthly disability payments for the rest of my life is to get these therapy sessions on the books. So I'll be a big girl, lie on the long white couch (at least that's how I imagine it), and tell the good doctor how being deployed has made me sad. That should be good enough.

It's not like I haven't been through this before—I have. The rear detachment unit screened all of us when we got back from deployment. Although, frankly, the focus was more on our physical status than our mental state. We spent more time getting screened for tuberculosis and other contagious infections than we did assessing our feelings and emotions. Our mental health screening lasted forty-five minutes, done by an inexperienced therapist. She read questions off a checklist, then handed us a couple of pamphlets and a business card. That was the extent of it. We spent the next eight hours inventorying our equipment and turning in our weapons. Then we got a case closed and were sent home with a pat on the back and a resounding *job well done.*

When I met with my separation-and-transitioning counselor before leaving North Carolina, he told me about the potential benefits to help soldiers battling mental stress available for Teó and me post-service. I'm not convinced I deserve them, that I should even be doing this therapy thing—but right now it isn't about me; it's about my son. There isn't anything I won't try to do to make his life better, and a monthly disability payment helps reduce the expenses of Teó's condition. The way I see it, all I have to do is sit through a few therapy sessions. Starting today.

I round the familiar bend and locate the bright-yellow chinchorro Papi always stopped at on our way to Old San Juan. An aluminum guardrail, two feet from the ground, and a small grassy knoll are the only things that keep cars from dropping over the edge of the rocky cliffs. I shudder to think about the driver taking the turn too fast and crashing into the Atlantic waves below. Not me. Not today.

It's one hell of a place to serve limitless orders of Puerto Rican rum, among other things, but it's how it's done here. The islanders form long, parked lines on both the right and left sides of the main road. The allure of loud music, fried fritters, strong booze, and cheap, cold beer is apparently worth the risk of walking up a poorly lit coastal highway, even one where vehicles routinely reach more than seventy miles per hour.

I'm here early enough to park alongside the kiosk in the grass. Safe and sound.

The bartender places a napkin in front of me. I shift atop the wobbly wooden barstool. "What can I get you?" he asks.

"Mojito de parcha—doble, por favor." The old man eyes me for a split second, then glances up at the clock, which has since struck 11:00 a.m. He turns around and silently prepares my drink.

"Ocho dólares," he says, sliding the tall cylindrical glass in my direction. The rum smells equally as strong as the passion fruit. I hand him a ten-dollar bill, indicating he can keep it in full. He nods, pulling back a smile. One thing I made sure to bring with me to the island was enough cash. Most small bars, including this one, are cash-only enterprises.

Giving me a straw was probably a bad idea. I finish the drink in three big sips. The roar in my ears grows louder, and I can't tell if it's the waves crashing below or my blood pressure rising. My eyes close on their own. I don't fight it. The sun warms my lids as the alcohol warms my stomach. I don't want to leave this place or this moment. Who am I kidding? I don't want to go to the VA.

"Uno más, por favor."

This time, he looks at me with a downturned lip and a heaviness in his eyes but simply repeats the price. "Ocho dólares," he says, making sure I don't assume there's a volume discount.

I nod and reach into my purse for another ten. After a few minutes he slides another equally strong, equally lovely, pink mojito in front of me.

Three more sips through the straw and I'm slurping a drained glass of ice and sugary mint leaves. I check my watch.

Forty-five minutes left to get to my appointment. I don't need to rush, which is good, considering there's a heaviness in my movements and a warmth in my respirations. The rum is working; the numbness is spreading. The idea of going to the VA now feels like it's happening to someone else. I am just a lonely observer, going along for the ride, watching as Sergeant LaSalle-Rivera dutifully does what she has to do.

I place the second ten-dollar bill under the glass.

"Gracias, amiguito," I tell the bartender, thanking him as though we are old friends. He smiles at me, except it never reaches his eyes and his lips lock in their corners.

"Cuídese," he says. *Take care.*

Okay, so I'm a little tipsy gripping the steering wheel firmly at ten and two o'clock. I focus on staying between the lines. It's only a few miles to the VA Medical Center in San Juan. And who cares? Haven't I earned the right to have a drink or two if the US government is going to force me to sit inside a stuffy office and relive the worst moments of my life?

I trained to be a medic, save lives, heal the injured. I was prepared to do that on either side of the fight if I had to. When the hell did I ever agree to take a life?

*When you raised your right hand and swore to defend the US Constitution.*

Okay, true enough. But when did our world change so severely that our enemy became so young? How can a boy who hasn't fully become a man be the enemy?

The answer comes in loud and clear: *When they strap an explosive device on their bodies and run in your direction.*

I'm not going to feel bad about drinking. No. I won't feel guilty about getting behind the wheel and possibly killing someone. I already did that.

I take the stairs up to the sixth floor because I'd rather not get into an elevator with the unpredictability of the local power grid. One gust of wind and I could end up stuck in that little box for hours. No, thank you.

I'm sweating when I reach Dr. Lourdes Robles Montoya's office. The sour scent from the alcohol escapes my armpits, filling my nose.

Walking into the waiting room, I sigh at the room full of people. How could I have forgotten? Seeing a physician here is nothing like the process in the US. Appointment times are generally placeholders, not actual scheduled times. Most people arrive as soon as the doctor's office opens and sign in upon arrival. They are seen by the order on the list, regardless of their appointment time. I'd completely forgotten about this.

I walk to the receptionist's desk and fill out my name on her clipboard. There are a couple of different doctors to choose from. I circle the therapist's name and take my seat, but surprisingly, I'm seated for only a minute or two before the young woman calls my name.

I stand up, startled.

"Yes?"

The room spins when I jump to my feet. The alcohol has a creeper effect. Or perhaps it's the fact that I haven't eaten anything today.

"La doctora will see you now," she says and points to the door at the back end of the waiting room.

I'm shocked by the punctuality. Things really have changed since I left.

"Okay, great," I say.

The back door opens, and everyone in the waiting room looks up. I walk over, doing my best to keep a straight line despite the wobble in my stride.

I force back a nervous giggle, imagining a cartoon version of my psychiatrist in a tweed suit with a pipe dangling from his lips, waving me into our first session. I really should have eaten something. But it's not the doctor at the entrance; it's a familiar face.

"Eli!" I say in a whoosh of breath.

His lips widen into that signature white smile, his green eyes glimmering with surprise. He is wearing a white button-down shirt, khaki shorts, and brown leather sandals. The white shirt offsets his golden tan. A handful of women, young and old, admire the tall, fit American with the golden curls.

"Now I'll be damned," he says, letting out a light whistle. "If it isn't Dolores's beautiful cousin. Hello, Lina." He tips his chin. A cowboy hat would have suited the gesture perfectly.

Given my T-shirt and tight blue jeans, such an admiring gaze leaves me feeling a bit inadequate. We both stand still, facing one another. Last week, at the bar, I was too preoccupied with my arrival on the island, my family, and getting a buzz to pay him much attention. But seeing him here—on neutral ground . . . it feels familiar. Maybe because he was in the Army, too. Except that doesn't explain the flutter in my belly at the admiration in his eyes. Attraction is unfamiliar territory.

My last relationship, not that I would call it that, was more of a fling. It ended right before my second deployment. Everything about that experience was practical: a nice, good-looking guy liked me, and I was curious about him. Once my curiosities were explored, I got bored. That's how it has always been since Teó entered my life and his father broke my trust in relationships. Teó is the man in my life; I'm happy this way. When it comes to intimacy, I tend to use them, then lose them. That's my pattern—rinse and repeat.

"Hi, Eli," I say, tucking a strand of dark hair behind my ear.

Taking Eli and all his sunshine in, I wonder if he, too, is seeing the shrink, but my question is answered when a nurse exits a back door and walks into the hallway behind him.

"Eli, remember to continue working on those repetitive drills. The PT only works if you keep running through the routines at home."

He looks back over his shoulder at her. "Yes, ma'am, will do."

A different, stern-looking older woman in a white coat exits another door farther down the hall behind him. She calls out, "Catalina LaSalle-Rivera?"

I shrug. "That would be me," I say quickly, wanting to slip away before Eli figures out why I'm here. I don't need anyone's judgment about therapy. This is all just protocol anyway.

I push past Eli, but he stops me, placing his hand on my arm.

"Mind if I wait for ya?"

Before I can answer, the lady doctor clears her throat behind us. "Catalina, that way," she says, pointing down the hall. "Last door on your left."

I pull back my arm, a sense of flight kicking in. I just want to get this over with and get out of here. I turn away from Eli and the waiting room now behind me and head in the direction the doctor pointed, leaving his question unanswered.

# CHAPTER ELEVEN

I'm not sure what to expect when I walk through the doors, but I'm a bit surprised by the warmth of the modern space, given the rigidity of the doctor's demeanor. Maybe it's the tightness of her smoothed-back bun, the perfectly manicured nails, or the immaculate, understated makeup, but this woman has a feminine style bordering military precision. It's familiar to me in its commitment to both island femininity and the Army's dress-right-dress standards.

Her office is separated into two rooms. The main door leads into a modern living space with a white leather couch (like the one I imagined earlier) opposite two sleek, rounded chairs surrounding a circular electric-blue coffee table. The accent pieces are done in bright tropical colors and the modern planters accentuate the space. On the walls a combination of landscapes from Old San Juan and waterfalls in El Yunque blend with modern abstract pieces that make me think of multicolored spaghetti. This modern, bright living space can be described as elegant with a tasteful style.

A set of glass-paned double doors along the back wall open into the doctor's private office. From this vantage point it looks like the decor in there is similar—tropical, modern, distant, but classy. Based on the artistic selection, something tells me her emotional walls are up, too; they're just painted a different color.

"Please have a seat, Catalina," she says, pointing toward her office.

"You can call me Lina," I say, taking a seat in front of her desk. The last trace effects of the earlier mojitos are all but gone. My hands are already beginning to shake. I'm nervous.

*I knew I should have had a third.*

Dr. Robles takes her seat. The desk has a large glass top, the kind you're almost scared to put anything on top of for fear of smudging or breaking something. Maybe that's the point.

"Lina, it's very nice to meet you. I'm glad you're here."

*Glad?* I'm not sure how to respond to that. So I don't. I sit still, mute, with no manners. Mami would be horrified.

"What I mean is," she says, "I've had the opportunity to review your file. You're a hero—a recipient of the Silver Star Medal. That's a significant achievement for anyone, but especially for you. And I don't mean because you're a woman, but you were born here. Correct? In San Juan?"

The weight of her praise suffocates me. It's been a few months, but I can still hear the first sergeant's voice ringing loudly in my mind: *Today, we honor one of only three female recipients of the Silver Star Medal since 9/11.*

I close my eyes, lean forward, and take a deep breath slowly, in through my nose. I hold it for three seconds, then let out a slow exhale.

The room is silent. Neither of us speaks. Finally, I break. "Yes, that's right—on both accounts. I am a recipient of the Silver Star, and I was born here, in San Juan."

"That's quite an honor—"

"But you're wrong about something. I'm no hero." Her eyebrows rise but drop just as quickly. She works to keep a neutral gaze, assessing.

"I was told about the award fifteen minutes before the ceremony. They wanted to make sure I couldn't back out. I tried anyway. But my commander . . . she was female . . ." I roll my eyes at the idiocy of my explanation. Of course *she* was female. Maybe the mojitos aren't completely out of my system after all.

I stop, but the therapist offers a soft "Go on."

I don't want to go on, but I can't help myself, remembering my commander's explanation word for word: *Refusing this award would be a huge setback for all of us, validation that combat awards don't belong to us because we refuse to accept them. How unjust would it be to the thousands of brave women who came before you or those who were never even given the proper recognition?*

"She said I needed to validate the women in combat that had never been properly recognized. She told me to do it for them."

"Did you agree?"

"The award's on my record, isn't it?"

"That isn't what I asked. You obviously accepted the award, but did you agree with her reasoning?"

"I guess so," I answer. "It made enough sense at the time that she got me to stand among the ranks, face her in proper military protocol, proffer my salute, and shake her hand for the cameras. But no, I didn't think I deserved an award. I still don't. I wasn't doing my job; I wasn't saving lives. In that moment I believed that if I didn't act, a pure desperate action, we were all going to die, and my son would be left all alone. I didn't have a choice. That's not a hero. A hero saves. A hero chooses."

"You make an interesting point," she says, surprising the hell out of me. Why does it sting that she agrees?

Suddenly annoyed, I ask, "Why do they call you *doctor*?"

There's a slight crane in her neck when she responds. "Excuse me?"

"Aren't you a psychologist? When I circled your name on the form in the lobby, it said *psychologist*. That means you can't prescribe me any medication, right? So why do they call you a doctor?"

She mimics my body language and leans back in her chair, and I'm relieved at the change in subject. "They call me *doctor* because I have a doctorate in psychology from Cornell University. And as a matter of fact, Puerto Rico is included along with a handful of US states and some entities, like the Department of Defense, that support a program called *prescribing psychologists*, of which I am licensed, board certified, and, yes, able to prescribe medications."

I love that her English accent is flawless. Every word is articulated perfectly—except when she says *Puerto Rico*; then the accent changes and it's spoken in Spanish. I think we all do that.

She points to a framed certificate on the wall, but my eyes stop at a smaller framed photograph on the glass table behind her. It's tucked behind a planter, small enough that most people probably don't notice it. But even after a couple of mojitos, I still can't help but process the details—it's my nature, and something tells me this one is important.

"You served in the military?"

Her eyes widen with surprise. "Why do you ask?"

"Your picture—that one, over there, behind you." I point. "It looks like you were in the desert. Is that an antenna beside you? That is you, right?"

She stares at me thoughtfully, pulling back the curtain for a second.

"Yes. US Army. Desert Storm—1991. I deployed as an E-4, a 31U—signal support systems specialist. I knew my way around radios and telephones pretty well back then."

"Did you see combat?"

The curtain swings closed.

"Lina, this session isn't about me. We are here to talk about you and your experiences while serving."

I don't want to talk about that any more than she wants to talk about *her* time in service. Maybe we can figure a way around this. Perhaps we can reach an agreement now that I know she's served. I can give her enough information to fill out the reports and get me the disability rating I need. Then Teó's school expenses will be taken care of without issue. This way she doesn't have to probe past more than I'm comfortable talking about. I mean, what's the point? Therapy is supposed to be about me, right? What I need?

Well, what I need is a monthly disability check for the rest of my life. I need to be able to afford a solid life here, and every dollar helps, even if I do go to work at a pill factory.

"Okay, Dr. Robles, what do you want to know?"

"Why don't we start with the basics?"

She opens a drawer and pulls out a leather binder filled with an empty notepad. Inside it is a black Montblanc pen. Either the woman has someone spoiling her with expensive gifts, or she is deliberately sending a message of success to the patients sitting across the desk from her. I'm not sure I appreciate the pretentiousness of it all, but it doesn't surprise me, either. Sometimes, on this island, it feels like we need to overcompensate and prove to the world that we matter . . . that we made it. We do this by ensuring what we wear and the tools we use display their pretentious brand names for the world to witness.

Isn't that what I'm doing by enrolling Teó in the fancy school?

I don't want to think about that. Instead, I picture my son in his lab coat as a grown man with a Montblanc tucked in his coat pocket. I smile.

"Something made you smile. Is it something I said?"

"It's my son."

"Right. Earlier you mentioned him. You have a son . . ." She leans back and brings the pen to her lips. She seems genuinely surprised I'm a mother. I think she knows about the convoy. About the young man. Most people would never come to expect that a young, single mother could bring themselves to kill. Something tells me my case just got interesting. She knew about my Silver Star, so it's not a stretch to think she knows the details behind how I got it. Although I'm not sure how she could; it wasn't in the award's citation or in any of the official records.

"Yes. He is nine years old. Teó."

"And his father?"

That question always leaves me breathless. I should be over it by now. I'm not. Leonardo was my first for so many things. First boyfriend. First intimate partner. First love. First broken heart. Only one time did he come in second, after Papi, to prove that my willingness to offer love wasn't enough. He left anyway. He wanted a summer fling in Florida before returning to Puerto Rico. I guess he got one, leaving me right before my senior year of high school and our unborn baby with barely more than an "I'm sorry." I swallow. "Not in the picture."

"Ever?"

"That's right."

She nods. Then writes something down.

My hands are shaking so badly I move them under my legs. I try to focus my thoughts on something else, calming the adrenaline coursing through my system, fueled by shame. The young man on the battlefield, Teó's father—these are all the areas of my life where I've failed, where my efforts failed . . . it's a Molotov cocktail of self-degradation and regret.

That day at the award ceremony pushes its way back into my memory. Again I hear my first sergeant. *Sergeant LaSalle-Rivera's bravery is in keeping with the finest traditions of military heroism and reflects distinct credit upon herself, the 207th Special Troops Battalion, the Fifty-First Brigade, and the US Army.*

Lies. Lies. Lies. Please let me get out of here.

"Lina? Did you hear me?"

I did not. The back of my neck is damp with sweat. "No, I'm sorry. Can you repeat the question?"

"I asked if you were eating and sleeping normally. Any major changes in your weight recently?"

"Oh." I smile at her, relieved for some easier questions. "Yes, I'm eating and sleeping fine," I lie. "I'm sure I'll be gaining a few pounds now that I'm staying at my mother's house here on the island. My grandmother will make sure of it." I wink at her, but her blank expression remains stoic.

She looks down and writes more notes.

"Lina, you don't look as though you're doing either one very well. I recommend some natural remedies first, perhaps a little melatonin for sleep. A good daily exercise regimen will also help tire out your system and increase your appetite. If that's not helping, we can consider an alternate course of treatment."

She stares down at my hands trapped on each side, underneath my thighs, then back up at my lips as I chew them nervously.

"It takes a special kind of woman to raise a child on her own, an even stronger one to do it and serve her country. You have a lot to be proud of, Lina. There's no shame in needing someone to talk to."

*Shame.* Hearing that word out loud makes my stomach turn. Now I feel nothing but contempt for this woman. She has no idea who I am, what I've done, or what I'm capable of doing.

"Are we done here?" Before she can answer, I stand up.

Dr. Robles closes the pretentious leather binder and caps the overpriced pen, then places it in the center of her book.

"I think that's enough for our first day," she says, slowly rising to join me. "But we need to prepare for deeper discussions. I do have some homework to take with you for our session next week."

Homework? Great. I was already planning to stop at the chinchorro one more time on my way back to the house.

Dr. Robles turns around and reaches into a cabinet above the desk behind her, giving me an opportunity to get a better look at the photograph. There are two other soldiers, one on each side of her. She looks so young. They are all smiling, arms draped around one another's shoulders. I began this session with contempt; now I feel a kinship. That's the thing about the uniform. It brings you all together to a similar place of unity—in our case, sisterhood.

She hands me a black leather-bound journal.

"I want you to write in this—every day. It can be a few lines or a few pages. It doesn't matter. Whatever is on your mind, whatever catches your eyes, whatever you are feeling. Write it down. Promise to do it every day for one week, until you return."

I'm waiting for the catch. The part where the good doctor says we must discuss what I wrote, or it has to have some central theme, or the word count must total three thousand words.

But that's it. Dr. Robles doesn't say anything else. She simply stares at me with her perfectly styled bun, meticulously applied makeup, and outstretched hand, waiting for me to take the damn journal.

"I can do that," I say, wanting to please. She may very well hold the possibility of a lifetime disability check. "Every day."

"Good, then I'll see you next week."

She walks over to the main door and holds it open for me.

"Thank you, Dr. Robles. I think this is all going to be very helpful."

My lips spread into a phony smile. I'm hoping for a sincere one in return, but I get nothing. Match point for the good doctor.

# CHAPTER TWELVE

After an emotionally grueling therapy session, my mouth waters at the idea of another fruity mojito and the numbness it brings. Technically, now that Teó is starting school, I need to start looking for a job, but the thought of the responsibility and the monotony of production work sends me spiraling. No, not a thing I need to tackle today. Today I can go get another drink, wait for my son to get home from school, and push off the job search until tomorrow.

As I step out into the sunny afternoon, my plans are thwarted when I see Eli waiting for me in the parking lot. I guess he isn't all that good at taking a hint. I tried to blow him off politely when I saw him earlier, but there he is, sitting cross-legged on a mound of grass between the two flagpoles—one for the US flag and one for the Puerto Rican flag. He's wearing a cover over the pincers to resemble the look of his hand. The reality of his disability tugs at my heart, making me think of my callousness that I hadn't even noticed it earlier.

The sleeve of the button-down shirt covers the hardware at the junction of his elbow.

He holds my gaze as I approach, slowly rising to his feet and once again flashing that brilliant smile with teeth that must have cost his parents a fortune in orthodontic bills. The hornet's nest behind my belly button comes alive. I swallow. Damn the hormones. I mean . . . it's been a while and I'm only human . . .

I catch a whiff of him. Eli smells like suntan lotion and lemons, annoying me even more. I want a reason to turn him away. "You're still here. Don't you have a car?"

"It's nice to see you too, darlin'," he says, leaning forward in a little bow.

An older woman walks past us and murmurs, "Ay, bendito."

*Ay, bendito*, indeed. I really don't need this right now. Saint Eli is better off driving away and forgetting he ever met me. I'm not a good person, and worse yet, I don't ever seem to measure up anyway. Besides, something tells me he's the relationship type. I'm not. That place is reserved strictly for my son. Pursuing anything here reeks of disaster. In the end, he and I will both only end up disappointed.

"You know by sitting outside people are inclined to think you're a homeless vet wanting donations. All you're missing is the cup."

He gives his leather sandals and loosely hung, buttoned-down shirt a once-over. "You've got a point," he says with a laugh. "I was gonna wait for you upstairs, but I saw that blue sky shining through the window, and I figured I needed to get me some fresh air. You'd have to come out here eventually, right?

"And yes, Lina, I do have a car. I was fixin' to drive out here from Chiquitas when Anita offered to drop me off on her way to the big shoppin' mall on the island. It was on her way."

Anita, the waitress at Chiquitas. I wonder if I've misread the situation between them. Maybe there is more to them than an employer-employee relationship, and I've been imagining his attraction to me this whole time. How embarrassing. I should have known.

My face must give away my thoughts because Eli says, "Anita and *her husband* have to buy gifts for a birthday party, and apparently, this mall is the largest shopping mall in the entire Caribbean."

I nod knowingly. "Yes, it is, and despite the continued complaints that the island's economy is suffering and there is no money, I have yet to drive past that place where the parking lot isn't completely full."

He shrugs. "Must be the tourists."

"Must be," I concur.

Eli glances at the watch on his right hand. "So what all you got planned for lunch?"

I shove my shaky hands into my pockets. *A drink, if you don't get in the way.* I shrug.

"Good," he says, "Would you like to have lunch with me? My treat. Although it'll mean you're driving. I hope that's all right."

The way he's worded the invitation, I don't really have an out without being outlandishly rude. Not that I'm not tempted, but I see the honest-to-goodness sincerity on his face and figure I can have a drink whether he's with me or not. His presence won't make a difference. I *do* have a couple of hours before Teó's school day ends, and I am starving.

I return his earlier bow with a surrender of my own, wanting nothing more than to sit somewhere local and drink something strong. "Okay, Elijah Montgomery," I say. "Since you insist, let's go eat. And because I'm driving, I get to choose where. Deal?"

"Deal." His smirk tells me he thinks he's won this round.

I choose Old San Juan because it's only a twenty-minute drive from the VA, and Eli says he has never been to one of the island's most richly historical areas.

"I know all about Old San Juan," he says. "I love studying history. I spent an entire semester in college researching the discovery of the New World. I've been meaning to come out here, but I haven't had any time. You may not know this, Lina, but I've been mighty busy running a swaggy business."

"It's true, Chiquitas is pretty swaggy," I say, remembering the buzz from the Cuba libres he prepared. "But Viejo San Juan is equally cool and much closer." *They also tend to have two-for-one drink deals.*

The bright-blue sky is nearly a mirror image of the cobalt waters beneath it. A light, gentle breeze of fresh ocean air kisses our cheeks and runs its fingers through our hair, inviting us to experience history. Despite my apprehension at coming back, I find that I'm proud of my island for showing off her best to her new foreign resident.

At Eli's insistence and his constant chatter about the city's history on the way over, we begin our tour of the area's most famous landmark: Castillo San Felipe del Morro, or, as most locals call it—El Morro, the island's citadel.

Upon arriving, Eli turns his head up in wonder. "Lina, this was a great idea."

I try to smile and not feel ashamed that all I can think about is savoring an icy whiskey and coconut water at the corner café, but it feels fake and forced.

Eli continues, oblivious. "I've wanted to come here since I first arrived in Puerto Rico. Did you know construction of the fort began under the order of King Philip II of Spain in 1539 and continued for over two hundred years?"

"I did," I tell him quietly, doing my best to be present. "It's the pride of Puerto Rico. This landmark reminds us that the island's fierce naval power once held firm against many of the world's superpowers."

Eli stops as we reach the beginning of El Morro's widened concrete entrance.

The green esplanade sprawls on each side of us. The lime and sandstone walls, built eighteen feet thick, rise one hundred and forty feet above the ground.

I tent my eyes with one hand and point over to our right with the other. "Do you see the lighthouse? It's the gray brick tower, capped in white?"

"Yes, ma'am. I reckon I do."

Moved a little by his enthusiasm, I give in. "It's the fourth of its kind and one of the oldest functioning lighthouses in the US. It's crowned by a crenelated parapet with an ornamental guardhouse at each corner." I'm surprised at how easily I repeat what I memorized in middle school.

I point to the dome-covered sentry box once used as a lookout to the perilous seas beyond. "That dome over there is called La Garita. It's now a cultural symbol for the island. This whole city is. My family and I used to come out here every year for the Fiestas de la Calle San Sebastián, an annual celebration in honor of Saint Sebastian, on the third Thursday in January." I note the nostalgia in my voice and realize—it's real. "The party down here lasts until Sunday, and not only is it a massive celebration, but it represents the official closing of the holiday season."

Eli's mesmerized by the horizon. I am pleased. I realize, then and there, what seeing the beauty of El Morro looks like through the eyes of someone else. It reminds me of the combination of both pride and rejection I feel from this land. I look up at the stone structure and try to see it with my own eyes. Despite the masculinity of her name, she is a mother of sorts. Being in her presence makes me feel a little stronger.

Eli tents his right hand up above his eyes. "I can't believe I waited so long to come here. What a sight."

"Yes, it is."

My attention shifts to the families clustered together on the manicured grass. Their picnic blankets are spread across the fort's vast open fields. Chiringas stream from the long strings gripped in the hands of chubby toddlers. They soar above us and fill the sky with an array of different colors and shapes.

We walk in silence for several minutes, and I force away the replay of my earlier session with Dr. Robles. The anxieties are still simmering inside me, but I don't want to fill the space between us with words. I don't think he does, either. He looks out at the fort ahead of us, and I glance at my watch, calculating the time before I'll be drinking again.

We walk in, and Eli looks around at the cavernous structure.

"Did you know this fort successfully held off attacks against the English—twice, including a force of up to thirteen thousand men in the late seventeen hundreds? El Morro's last active fight ended with the Treaty of Paris, where Spain ceded Puerto Rico, Cuba, Guam, and the Philippines to the United States."

"How do you know all of this?"

He turns to me and smiles. "How *don't you* know it? Ain't this your patria?"

I laugh at how he says *patria* because the *a* sounds like *apple* when the accent intends for it to sound like *autumn*.

"Yes, you're right, but it clearly isn't *yours*. So what exactly are you doing here, running a bar in a local neighborhood?"

He doesn't answer. Instead, he looks out at the open expanse of the Atlantic Ocean.

I'm beginning to lose my patience with all the tourist stuff. "Eli, why don't we follow the path called Paseo del Morro. We can catch it from over there." I point down at the dip in the ground. "And it'll take us to the edge of the coastline. You'll love the landscape on the trail that leads to the San Juan Gate." *And the local bars.* "From there it's a short walk to a great restaurant with craft beer and traditional food. It'll give you a good jartera."

Eli shrugs easily. "That idea sounds fine to me, although I'm not sure what a jartera is, but I'll try anything at least once."

I grin. "A jartera means a full stomach. It's when you eat so much that your stomach stretches. Follow me, and you can answer some of my questions on the way there."

"Yes, ma'am, I'm sure you'll keep 'em coming," he says as we trek down a set of stone steps.

On the way, I reach for his hand to balance myself before realizing I'm standing on his left. My arm snaps down, while I jump ahead one step and grab the guardrail instead. I curse under my breath, praying he didn't notice what I nearly did.

The awkwardness bloats between us as we finish the remaining steps in silence.

I summon the courage to turn around and face him. "I'm sorry. I'm such an idiot."

He cocks his head and grins at me, pretending. "Why?"

My mouth opens to answer, but then I stop, caught in the net of his admiring stare. It was the same way he looked at me back at the VA, like seeing something rare for the first time. *Don't,* I warn him silently. *I'm not good for you—for anyone. I'm damaged and cold and broken.* I look away, breaking the possibility of a moment between us, and smooth the hair out of my face. Eli's curls glisten like gold beneath the open sky. *Stop looking, Lina.* I shift to the need for a liquid escape instead.

"You're beautiful," Eli says softly. "I've never seen such soulful eyes in my entire life."

My chest pulses at his reverence. I notice a dusting of freckles across the bridge of his nose. They look like Teó's. My son's light freckles are one of my favorite features on his face. I haven't noticed Eli's before. But that thought, the study of his face, reminds me of another—a young man with soulful, terrified eyes and a moment that destroyed me forever, making me unable to ever feel whole again. My anger rises. This needs to stop. Now.

"You know, Eli," I say, harsher than I intend, "I get the feeling you have been avoiding all my questions."

"Oh hush," he says lightly, but I see the disappointment on his features despite the attempt to ignore my efforts to raise the temperature. "I'm an open book. Ask me anything you wanna know."

His approach calms my inner turmoil. "What made you decide to buy the bar?"

He looks at me thoughtfully. He isn't trying to be secretive. There seems to be a lot to unpack there. "It's a bit complicated."

"Okay, let's try another subject."

He looks away, relieved.

"You said that was a war wound." I point at his arm, surprising myself at my brazenness. "What branch did you serve in?"

He exhales gratefully. "An easy one. I was in the Army."

"And what did you do in the Army?"

"I was a seventy-two delta, an environmental science and engineering—"

"Officer," I say curtly, cutting him off. "I know what it is. I was a sixty-eight whiskey, a health care specialist. Everyone calls us combat medics. You keep calling me *ma'am*, but I was a sergeant—an enlisted soldier, Eli. I should actually be the one calling you *sir*. You're an officer."

Now he's blushing. "Not anymore, Lina. That was another life. I'm a civilian now. Like you." He begins walking again. "How 'bout just Eli and Lina? No Army stuff. We didn't work together, didn't know each other before now." He inadvertently glances at his missing limb as he says, "I can't be called back. That life is over. So there ain't no reason for any Army formalities to get stuck between us now, is there?"

He has a point, but everything about him reminds me of the life I left behind. Why am I here? What am I doing? I look out toward the gate.

"Okay, no Army stuff," I say, wanting to believe that's possible more than he even realizes. "So you worked as a seventy-two delta—a scientist. My son, Teó, will be thrilled."

The words escape my mouth before I can take them back. I can't believe I just told him he would meet Teó. Why did I say that? I realize Eli has me emotionally bouncing like a pinball midgame. This wasn't a good idea. I'm not in any place to be on a pretend date with anyone, even if he's the one pretending.

Finally reaching the gate gives me a momentary distraction as I stare at my shoe.

"This is the gate I mentioned," I mutter, letting my hair fall forward to hide my embarrassment. "We can walk through and head up toward Calle San Sebastián."

This spot puts us fifteen minutes from the bar.

"I haven't been there in twelve years, but the place is a classic. I'm pretty certain we will find it exactly as it was back then."

"Sounds great," he says, moving my hair from my face with a soft brush of his hand. "I could use a sandwich something awful after skippin' breakfast this morning."

"You and me both," I say, trying to sound nonchalant.

"So"—he puts his arm around my shoulder—"your son likes science?"

By the time we reach La Taberna, I've discovered Eli is a graduate of South Carolina's Citadel, a US senior military college in Charleston. He tells me about a dual program, where he earned an undergraduate degree in biochemistry before transitioning to earn a master's degree in public administration from Clemson. He is the oldest of two. His younger sister is back home, living the debutante life. As he put it, they were "two peas in a pod" but have grown apart since college, a result of life moving them in different directions.

After completing his education, he began his commitment to the Army. He signed up to do four years on active duty and deployed twice. I didn't ask for details about his deployments. He was kind enough to return the favor. He did share the generalities of his mission, which included projects like influenza prevention, burn pit mediation, and raising awareness of public health threats.

The hostess escorts us to a table tucked alongside an open window, allowing us access to both the tourists and the locals as they walk along the streets. The music is loud, and the conversation louder. The walls are decorated with chalkboards displaying the meals for the day and the new draft blends on tap. My mouth waters, but it isn't for the food.

I remind myself I'm responsible for driving Eli back, and I have less than two hours before Teó will be home. My faculties need to be intact to receive him, although deep down I wish they didn't. It's so tempting to numb my senses, lie down, and go to sleep—too drunk even to dream.

"Lina?"

I snap back, realizing Eli and the waitress are staring at me, awaiting a response. I have no idea what the question was, but I take a gamble.

"I'll take a pint of whatever you recommend from the bartender's favorites and a chicken cordon bleu with arroz mamposteao."

"And I'll have the same thing," Eli says.

"A su orden," the waitress replies, recording our order on a small notepad, then flitters away.

"Do you have any idea what I even ordered?"

Eli leans back in his chair. "You do realize chicken cordon bleu is French, right? Lots of hillbilly Americanos have had it, 'specially in the school cafeteria growing up."

I smirk, surprised by my instinct to defend the local cuisine. "I'm sure you'll find this one is much better. What about the rice?"

"I have been living here for three months, ya know. Your cousin, Dolores, was the first to insist we add it to the menu at Chiquitas. She had Christian's mother whip up a batch one night and brought it to the bar for me to try. It's been on the menu every Sunday since. Ms. Fuentes cooks up enough to handle a day's worth of orders, and I make sure she gets a percent of the earnings that day."

I'm surprised by the casual ease with which he has brought up Dolores and Christian. I think back to Dolores's words—Christian, el que se murió. *The one that died.*

It gives me a chance to dig into my curiosity. Eli studied at two elite premier schools with a scientific background in high demand. He lost someone important to him, and even worse, he lost his arm somehow. I keep wondering how all that led him here to run a bar. What is he running from? Who is he running from? I know there's a whole lot more to this story than the easygoing, smiley southern officer is letting on.

When I open my mouth to begin asking, the waitress returns with two frothy mugs of ice-cold beer and places them in front of us. A busser follows directly behind her and sets our plates down as well.

"Buen provecho," Eli says as he takes a heaping spoonful of the combined rice and beans.

"Gracias, igual," I reply and take a big gulp of the frothy pale ale.

The tangy hints of citrus leave a sweet aftertaste. I take another gulp before reaching for my silverware and cutting my chicken into small pieces. Eli's eyes are momentarily closed as he chews. Satiated. My turn. Bringing a piece of chicken to my lips, I feel the vibration in my pocket.

I put down my fork and pull out my phone to see Mami's number light up the screen.

"Please excuse me. It's my mother," I tell Eli, pushing back my seat and standing up to take the call privately.

A look of concern registers across his face, but he only nods.

"¿Mami? ¿Todo bien? You okay?" The music is so loud inside I'm nearly yelling. I walk outside, where it's a little quieter.

"No, Lina. The school has been trying to reach you. Come home. Teó got hurt."

I don't hear anything else. A piercing ring fills my ears as my heart smashes against my chest. I end the call and run toward my car. Eli will have to understand. The sound of a rifle shot pierces my memories as I watch the body fall to the ground.

Teó is hurt. I have to get to my son.

# CHAPTER THIRTEEN

The odometer reaches ninety-five miles per hour on the island's autopista as I curve around the bend, imagining my son on the battlefield, his body crumpling to the ground. *Teó got hurt.* I hung up before she could say another word. I've missed two calls from Mami since, but I don't need to hear anything else. I need to get to him. I need to save him. Honed in with a combat medic's deep focus, I glide the vehicle across four lanes of traffic in one smooth motion, switching from the far-left lane to the far right, then braking only inches from the rear bumper of a bright-yellow McLaren. I don't care. All I can think about is Teó—maimed, bleeding, calling out for his mother, wondering why I'm not there to hold his hand. I imagine another woman holding a rifle—she's shot my son and taken him from me forever.

I grip the steering wheel and maneuver around a rusted Daewoo hatchback. A Puerto Rican flag waves out the missing rear window. The old beater is blocking my exit. I jam my palm on the horn and swerve around the driver, cutting directly in front of him. Within a nanosecond of passing the off-ramp altogether, I somehow end up on the feeder road.

"Teó, I'm coming, papito. Hold on."

I keep every instinct, every one of my five senses, on racing this car to my parents' house. A medic's focus. Teó needs me.

My stomach sinks as the upcoming streetlight turns from yellow to red. Thankfully it's a one-sided intersection and there's no oncoming traffic. I press the gas pedal and run the red light.

At the turn in front of the abandoned colmado, my mind jolts back to a different time. I'm dropped into the action on the streets of Iraq. Instead of palm trees and flowers, it's miles and miles of dry desert sand. The weight of my body armor bears down on my shoulders as the pressure from the metal plate presses tightly against my chest. My tongue dries from the memory of sandpaper in the air while blinking back the imagined compression from the Oakleys strapped to my face.

I can't see. I can't breathe. The snaps of bullets sound off in my memories as soldiers yell different commands. *Get down, dammit. Hold your position. We need more ammo up here.*

My foot presses down on the gas, shooting the car ahead on the uneven road. My heart pounds in my ears. I wipe my sweaty palms against the wheel, leaving traces of sweat, and make a sharp turn onto my street. To the left, the large, veined trunk of the flamboyán and her brilliant orange flowers ground me. She brings me back to where I am.

I am not in a convoy—I am in Puerto Rico, racing to get to my son. He needs me to save him.

My right foot lets off the gas pedal and slams the brakes, bringing the car to a screeching halt at the edge of the fence. There's a strange car—a fancy one—parked in front of the house. Might it be someone from Teó's school?

Forgetting the keys in the ignition, I push open the door and run inside.

The living room door slams against the wall from the force of my entry. My heart beats like a racehorse as my neck whips around every corner of the small room. Abuelo is in the same spot as yesterday—rocking in front of the TV as another baseball game plays.

I look past him toward the dining room, surprised to see Mami sitting at the table beside Teó. He is coloring quietly, no worse for wear other than a bandaged index finger, holding a purple crayon. What surprises me even more is the woman sitting across from them—my tía Lisandra.

I ignore the squeeze of my heart, seeing her, my eyes darting back to my son. Mami said Teó was hurt. So why does he look perfectly content?

"Teó, gracias a Dios, you're okay!"

I rush to his side and wrap my arms around him, inhaling his every scent. His warmth and stickiness ground me, even as he squirms against my embrace. Thank God my little boy is here, alive and well.

My arms stretch back, but I keep his shoulders firmly within my grip, looking him over with the trained eye of a combat medic.

"What happened, papi? You got hurt?" As the words rush out, I'm gauging the size of his pupils, feeling his pulse, assessing him from feet to face.

"Lina," Mami begins, but I ignore her, looking directly at Teó.

"Tell me what happened."

He blinks rapidly, holding up his bandaged finger. Solemnly, he says, "Did you know that zoonotic diseases are caused by germs spread between animals and people?"

"Yes, Teó. I'm a certified EMT. I do know that. What happened?" My pulse quickens at the mention of disease and germs.

"Lina." Mami tries again, but I shoot her a glare, daring her to interrupt my son.

*Sniff.* "I wanted to prove to my new class that I knew a lot about science." *Sniff.*

Tía Lisandra grunts at Teó's sniffs from across the table. Free from my initial pull to her and the fact that I'm beyond "hangry," it takes every bit of effort I have to not say something nasty to her. Teó sniffs again and blinks. I place my palm along his face, gently stroking his cheek.

"So what happened when you wanted to show them what you knew about science?"

His chest swells with pride. "Well, when the teacher went to check if it was our turn for almuerzo—that means *lunch*, Mamá—I went to the back of the classroom and opened the iguana cage. I told the class there are four equal quadrants inside an iguana's mouth, and each quadrant has between twenty and thirty teeth." He looks down at his shoes, then back up at me guiltily. "I wanted to carry him out and show them the teeth. But then the iguana's tail started whipping back and forth, and his head began bobbing up and down." He mimics the gesture. I'm taking it all in.

"Well . . ." He holds up his bandaged finger. "You can imagine the rest." He shrugs.

I must look horrified, because Teó begins blinking and sniffing again. I pull him close and hug him. "I'm sorry, sweetheart. I'm so glad you are okay." My words are muffled by his soft curls. I let out a deep breath, surprised by my actions after Mami first called. There were moments when I couldn't decipher where I was.

"Teó," I say, placing my chin on his head. "Didn't you think an iguana with twenty to thirty teeth in each quadrant would likely bite you?"

He pulls back from my embrace and looks at me as though I've said something outright foolish. "Mamá, iguanas are herbivores. Why would I think that?"

I smile and kiss his forehead. "Even herbivores don't like to be bothered, sweetheart. You should never have opened the cage, especially without asking permission. You know better."

"I do, Mamá," Teó says quietly.

"Why would you do something like that behind the teacher's back? That's not like you."

The next thing he says comes out as a series of grumbles.

"I wanted to show everyone what I know about science so they won't think I'm dumb with the tics and stuff."

His revelation leaves me stunned, and I cradle his cheek, giving myself a second for composure.

I let out a small breath. "Teó, why don't you finish coloring this beautiful picture for Abuela, and then we can put it up on her refrigerator?"

He smiles. "Okay, Mamá."

When I finally look up, Tía Lisandra eyes me curiously. She's been watching my every move. Chanel No. 5 fills the room and brings back memories of extravagant shopping trips at Plaza on Saturday—just the two of us. She is adorned with chunky gold jewelry and heavy makeup accented by thick, dark-brown hair blown out in an ironing-board-straight style. The designer clothes look freshly dry-cleaned.

She is the picture-perfect vision of what her generation considers success. It reminds me of all the moments we spent talking about my future as a doctor and the status that would naturally come with my greatness. *Everyone will respect you when you walk into the room, Lina, because you won't just be someone simple. You will be Dr. LaSalle-Rivera, someone important, with the ability to save and transform lives. You have the gift.* Through her faith in me, I believed in myself. Seeing her now, remembering the nightgown she sent me the day I came back home, I realized I've failed us both.

It hurts to feel the distance between us, so I ignore her and turn to Mami. "Why didn't the school call me? How bad is it?"

"They did call you, but the phone went directly to voicemail."

I glance down at my phone—two voicemails. With my focus on getting another drink, I didn't notice.

"I was the emergency contact," Mami says, "but Papi has the car, and he was already in the fields. I couldn't reach him, so I called Tía Lisandra, and she was kind enough to help. We went and picked up Teó together."

Mami looks over at Tía, who continues to silently watch me come apart.

"A greeting would be nice, Lina, after what your tía did for you today."

She's right, but I know better than to get too close and wrinkle the starched outfit. However, to not get up would be disrespectful to an intolerable degree, especially in my mother's home. I walk around and give her an air-kiss on the cheek and apologize for not greeting her right away. She nods at me like a queen addressing one of her many subjects. The family resemblance between her and Papi is stronger than ever. For now, at least, we make peace.

I'm surprised Mami turned to Tía Lisandra for help. They have never really gotten along. I've always felt my aunt believed Mami wasn't "good enough" for Papi. As the oldest of three siblings, Tía Lisandra believes she is the final authority on everything. That's why Dolores's presence here is such an anomaly. Her mother is not one to give up or admit defeat, especially not in parenting.

I return to Teó's side.

"Did they ask about Teó's tetanus shot? He is entirely up to date."

"No, they didn't need to ask," Mami says. "They still had the records from his registration on the principal's desk. It was a little bite, Lina. They washed his hands with soap and said to apply an antibacterial ointment for the next few days. Thankfully the iguana is a baby, and the bite wasn't very deep."

Her words ring in my ears. I can't help it. Maybe it's because I'm so hungry or exhausted from the intensity of my emotions, but anger bubbles inside me like lava. My hands grip the edge of the table as I lean over in Mami's direction. With my teeth clenched together, I seethe. "Then why did you tell me he was hurt? Did you purposely want to scare me?"

Tía Lisandra remains unwaveringly still, watching me unravel.

Teó and Mami look up at me with fear-laden eyes. A monster is reflecting in their expressions when a voice from behind me calls out.

"Lina, watch how you speak to your mami. I will not tolerate any disrespect in this house."

Abuela stands under the arch of the hallway, catching me off guard. I never even saw her approach, but the sharpness of her tone sends a shudder down my spine. I am a little girl again, an obedient little girl, who knows better than to utter another word.

"Sí, señora."

"It's okay," Mami says, but Abuela holds her hand up as she walks in. The matter is settled.

"Hola, Lisandra," Abuela says in greeting as she passes by the table on the way to the kitchen. "It's so nice you have time in your busy schedule to stop by and see us."

"Doña," my aunt replies, acknowledging her with a title that recognizes respect . . . and age. I've always considered the term insulting, controversial at minimum. By the look of Abuela's raised eyebrow, she agrees.

"Well, now that we know the nene is okay," Tía Lisandra says, "does anyone want to tell me where *my* daughter is?"

We all exchange awkward looks. Abuela steps into the kitchen as though she didn't hear the question and returns with a plate of freshly baked empanadas.

"Who is her daughter?" Teó asks, making an awkward moment even worse.

But before any of us can respond, Tía Lisandra says pointedly, "Dolores is my daughter."

*Sniff.* "Oh, I thought Dolores didn't have a mom. Like I don't have a dad."

Every set of eyes turns to me, including Abuela's as she places the plate down on the table. An unwed mother. A harlot. I know that's what they're thinking. I want the floor to open up and swallow me whole. It doesn't matter that this is how it's always been; sitting here, face-to-face, the culpability of my poor choices is fresh, raw, and unacceptable. I am a desgraciada—a shameless woman.

I reach over and grab an empanada off the plate and bite down before anyone can force me to utter a single word. Thankfully my new hero saunters into the room and somehow manages to shift the attention.

"What are *you* doing here?" Dolores asks, appearing from the hallway and under the arch. She glowers at her mother accusingly.

*Boy, if Abuela thought my tone was disrespectful . . .*

Abuela turns around quietly and returns to the kitchen.

"Bueno, I came to help," Tía Lisandra answers. "Now, is that any way to greet your mother? Where are your manners?"

Dolores doesn't answer right away. Mami and I share a glance as we wait for her response. The small space feels unusually crowded.

Dolores stands fixed under the archway. She reminds me of an old Wild West movie. These two cowboys are about to duel. When Puerto Rican women face off, you don't want to be within one hundred feet of them, especially mothers and daughters.

I can't help it. I want to yell, *Take cover*! Instead, I reach over and grab another empanada. This time so does Mami.

Dolores and Tía Lisandra continue to stare at each other. Neither dares to look away first, but my tía shoots her shot. "So what are you doing here in the middle of the day? Do you not work? I've already told you the allowance I'm sending ends next month."

"Lo sé," Dolores responds tightly. "In case you've forgotten, I'm grieving." She glances over at Mami. "My titi understands, even if you don't."

"Grieving?" Tía Lisandra says, followed by a tsk. "Please don't tell me you're still carrying on over that man who went off to the Army and left you here like dirty laundry. Foolish girl with a simple mindset. After all the times I warned you to focus on your own future and not get wrapped up in some shiny new toy."

Tía's famous turn of phrase—*a simple mindset*—pierces me, the unintended victim . . . I think. I brace for Dolores's response, but she holds steady, her posture a symbol of stoicism. She's tough. I'm overcome with pride.

With silence spreading like fog, I want to say something, anything, to break the space and tension between them, but with a mouthful of food and a mind that's gone blank, I remain quiet and chew. My cell phone rings mercifully.

It's a South Carolina area code. *Oh God, Eli.* I made such a fool of myself. I bet he thinks I'm nuts.

I swallow the last of the meaty pastry. "I'm sorry; I have to take this," I say, able to break the silence. "I abandoned someone in Viejo San Juan earlier. I need to make sure they're okay."

Tía Lisandra releases a sigh. "I need to get going, too," she says, rising from her seat. "I'm glad I was able to help you, Lina. I hope that was a *man* you were with today. Maybe you can put my little gift to good use. I mean, come on, joining the Army, coming back alone . . . some may wonder where your *interests* lie nowadays. It would be good for you to meet a nice man here. Especially now that you have so little happening in your life. Maybe try and put a little makeup on. Professional or not, women should never lose their femininity."

My stomach burns with humiliation. I did not get wrapped up in a relationship and instead focused on my own future, just as she taught me, but that wasn't good enough. Now she's implying I'm failing in another way entirely. So freakin' typical . . .

"I think I'll be fine, Tía. Gracias," I say, exercising restraint because she did help pick up Teó today.

"Suit yourself." She smirks before delivering a final blow. "I guess it's better than going around and looking like La Puerca de Juan Bobo." She shoots her daughter a pointed look, referencing a popular, over-accessorized pig cartoon.

My muscles tighten, preparing to see Dolores lunge. To my cousin's credit, she continues to hold still under the arch and waves her mother a mocking farewell.

Tía Lisandra ignores her and slides her Chanel purse over her shoulder.

"Gracias de nuevo," Mami says quietly as Tía proudly walks past us and out the front door.

"Ay, bendito," Abuela mumbles from the kitchen. Despite her best attempt to stay hidden, I know she's witnessed the whole thing.

# CHAPTER FOURTEEN

Dolores looks at me. Her makeup is flawless. I don't think she merited her mother's judgment. Her long hair falls to her waist in a cascade of full, jet-black waves. Her gray eyes are covered with thick coats of mascara and eyeliner, but the rest of her face is enhanced by light, neutral tones.

Teó smiles up at Dolores as she walks over and wraps her arms around him in a tight embrace. They're developing a close bond. Her presence calms Teó, reducing the tics.

"I'm coloring this picture for you, Dolores," he says.

"Gracias, primito."

As he squeezes his crayon and swirls diligently within the lines of the book, it's obvious he feels a kinship to his new cousin. Could this move back to Puerto Rico be what was right for him all along? Why am I the one feeling so lost when this is supposed to be home? How is it so seamless for Teó, who's never known this place before?

"Dolores, how come you live here with us and not at home with your mamá?" Teó asks.

I freeze, unsure if I should step in, except I've wondered the same thing myself. I wait, avoiding eye contact and allowing her the space to answer.

"Teó," she says, ruffling his hair. "My mamá isn't cool like yours. She wishes I was different—a boy like you. Here I get to be a girl with no apologies."

I turn to look directly at her. I know exactly what she means. I struggled with the same inadequacy in my relationship with my own father. I'm surprised how similar he and my tía Lisandra are. Tía Kika, their younger sister, is so different from them both. She is easygoing and accepting. I've never heard her have any expectations of anyone. She always said to me, *The only thing I have to do in this world is die, everything else is a nicety . . . or not.* When it came to my future or getting pregnant with Teó, her response was always the same—*What's meant to happen always does, Lina. Trust God's plan, however it unfolds.* It's uncanny how different she is from both her older brother and sister and their desires and expectations to raise a mighty son for their lineage.

I offer Dolores the slightest of nods as Teó looks up from his drawing. I know her story now, and it seems very similar to my own. I wonder whether she ever sees the parallels in Papi from her experiences with her mother.

"I don't think you should ever apologize for being a girl," Teó says. "I like you just the way you are."

"I like you, too, primito," she says, her voice light, but the shine in her eyes reveals the impact of his words.

"Lina, ¿vamos a janguear?" she asks me. "There's somewhere I'd like to take you tonight, someone I want you to meet."

Abuela turns to me. "We will take care of Teó. Your mother and I will bathe him and put him to bed. You go."

Dolores's face breaks out into a wide smile. "You heard Abuela, prima." She sways her hips from side to side. "Vámonos."

Everyone is staring at me, even Teó, who I'm sure has no idea what's happening.

"Okay, okay," I say. "But I need to make a phone call." I look down at the earlier missed call.

Eli answers on the first ring with a "Well, thank heavens you ain't bleedin' out in a ditch somewhere."

"I'm sorry for acting like a lunatic." I'm suddenly embarrassed at how erratically I behaved. I could have excused myself properly, insisted he find another way home instead of racing out of there like a woman assuming her son had been shot and killed.

"That's a good start," he says, his voice tense. "I was hoping you'd at least call, let me know you're okay."

"Yes, of course," I say equally tightly.

"So was it something I said?"

"It was my son. My mother called and told me Teó was hurt and I had to go home. I didn't think, I just sprinted into action. Casualty of the job, I guess." The word *casualty* sticks in the center of my forehead and pounds against my skull. "I had to get to him."

"Is he hurt?"

I probably should have led with that.

"No, he is fine. It was a minor accident—an iguana bite." Now that I know he wasn't seriously injured, I realize it's pretty funny. "He was showing off his knowledge about the inner quadrants of the iguana's mouth and decided to do a live demonstration."

Eli chuckles. "I see. Sounds like you really do have a future scientist on your hands. Although I'm sure his mama was madder than a wet hen when she realized it was a harmless scare."

"Yeah, something like that." I try to breathe away the lingering jitters, silently assuring myself that Teó is okay.

"I'm glad it wasn't anything more serious." The tone of his voice drops an octave. "I can already tell how much you live for that boy. Hell, you damn near abandoned me in the middle of nowhere."

I roll my eyes. "Not exactly the middle of nowhere. I'm sure you were able to find your way back to safety."

"I'm just sayin', I have a mind to pay you back somethin' serious, Sergeant."

I suck in air. "Oh, is that so! We're back to ranks, are we? I thought the Army stuff was in the past, *sir*!"

He laughs into the phone, and the sound warms me from the inside. I like it, but it bothers me all the same.

"Give me a do-over, Lina. Let me see you again."

"I can't. I promised to go with Dolores tonight."

He's quiet, but I can hear the disappointment in his breath. "How 'bout you bring Dolores to Chiquitas. I still need to cover the bar tonight, but it's Monday. I expect it'll be slow."

Honestly, I don't want to. Spending time with Eli earlier stirred up things I wasn't sure how to work out. It all felt like a little too much for one day.

Sensing my hesitancy, Eli relents. "If not tonight, can I see you again soon?"

If I plan to visit a bar, his is the closest to my parents' house. It would be illogical to say no. "Sure. Soon."

"Lina?" Eli's voice sounds almost frustrated. I can feel my defenses rise, prepared to fight back.

"Yeah?"

He lets out a sigh. "I can tell you got a lot going on, comin' home and all. I'm just looking forward to getting to know you better. I will talk to you soon."

The fight rushes out, leaving me hollow and sad. "Take care, Eli."

"Yes, ma'am, you too."

When I return inside, Teó is no longer at the table but standing atop an old wooden stool at the kitchen sink.

Abuela is on one side of him, and Mami's on the other, chopping potatoes.

"Teó, are you helping Nana and Abuela with dinner?"

"Sí, Mamá," he replies. "They said I could help wash the rice."

"Lina," Abuela says. "Todo está bien. Go on. We have work to do."

Mami looks up from the cutting board and turns her head to me. "Teó is going to be fine," she says and winks.

I shake my head, awestruck at the team I now have around to help me. Tía Kika repeatedly made the sacrifice to step into my home and take over when I couldn't be there during my initial basic training and two deployments, but out of respect for her normal life in Florida, I made sure not to keep her a day longer than necessary, which meant our time at home—the day-to-day stuff—has only been Teó and I. I've always missed my tía Kika when faced with the daily living of single motherhood. Teó, too. But after a few weeks, we've adjusted back to our normal routine and carried on as it always was—he and I, alone at home, doing our best as a tiny unit. I never felt that I had any choice but to carry the responsibilities of a single mother, parenting a child with challenges all by myself. The burdens of daily parenting were mine to bear and mine alone.

But not anymore. Not here.

# CHAPTER FIFTEEN

I turn the car around the bend of our street and head toward the main road. Left will take us toward the coastline. Right will take us to the autopista, which can lead anywhere.

At the intersection I ask, "Which way?"

"Turn right." Dolores leans closer, staring at me suspiciously. "You aren't very averiguada. Don't you want to know where we are going?"

"No, I'm not. And yes, I would like to know what you have planned."

"Turn right to get on the autopista and take the exit to Manatí. There's someone I need to visit. I go every Monday. I'm sure they are already waiting for me."

"Is this something dangerous?" I hate that I have to ask, but my cousin and I are still virtually strangers and the island's youth can easily slip into some seedy activities if they aren't guarded and intentional about avoiding it.

"No, of course not." She glances out the window. Her voice lowers. "It's Christian's mother. I go spend time with her. She is alone."

"Christian?"

"Sí, el soldado que se murió." *The soldier, the one that died.*

"Sí, lo sé. I remember you telling me about him. Eli's soldier."

She nods.

"You are helping take care of his mother?"

She nods again.

"Dolores, what happened to him? How did he die?"

Her eyes grow solemn. She whispers, "En Iraq . . . he was killed."

I want to apologize to her for her loss. But I can't speak. At the mention of Iraq, visions of the convoy and sounds of rifle fire come at me like bullets. It's taking every effort I have to focus on the white lines and keep my mind in this car, here with her.

At the exit, Dolores points deeper into the center of the island. The darkening skies make me nervous. I may have grown up here, but I've been gone for twelve years. I remember that the more central we go, the more rural it gets. That can mean many things. My concern, especially given that Dolores and I are alone, is that it could be dangerous.

The winding road leads to Ciales, a small pueblo known for its rich, gorgeous landscapes and cascading waterfalls. Except we won't be seeing any of those things tonight. There are no streetlights.

"Tell me about him," I say, wanting to avoid the sense that I'm back on a convoy among the heightened danger of an unknown area of operation. I need a distraction. "Tell me about Christian."

Dolores smiles. "Prima, he was so handsome and very proud to be in the Army. Before he left to go to Iraq, he was doing monthly drills at Fort Buchanan."

"So he was a reservist?"

"Yes, Army reserves," she says. "I met him in la superior. I was in twelfth grade. He was a teacher's aide but very young—only twenty-two. He offered English lessons even though he was very shy, but I was drawn to him, so I signed up. I told him about my issues with my mother, and he helped me with the transition to a new school when I moved in with your parents. Christian also worked nights at Chiquitas to pay for his sister's private school. Teacher's aides barely make minimum wage. After I graduated, we started going out. He told me the Army reserves helped him to have three incomes. It's what he needed to take care of his mother and his sister."

"He worked at Chiquitas before Eli bought the place?"

"Yes, he was trying to save money to buy it because the owner wanted to retire and move to the United States. But then his unit received . . ." She searches her mind for the word, then shrugs. "Ordenes to go to Iraq."

"Orders," I murmur. I want to change the subject. I realize a distraction isn't worth talking about someone dying in Iraq, but I also have a morbid curiosity about how Christian's life is bringing us up this jungled mountainside in the dark.

She points at a four-way intersection as we cross over a concrete bridge.

"Ahí. Turn left," she says, pointing at a small alley on our right.

I make a sharp turn to avoid missing it altogether. I would never have seen it on my own in the dark.

The alley leads to a desolate street. Two houses on each side of the road look dark and abandoned.

At the end of the one-lane road, Dolores points to a nearly dilapidated house raised high on four columns. It has a corrugated roof and old metal bars covering the windows. A dimly lit bulb is barely visible outside a side entrance. The door sits directly atop a set of wooden steps. *Wonderful.* It's another set of stairs where I get a clear, straight view to the ground below. Thankfully this one is only one story up.

"Over there," she says, directing me to a small patch of grass under one of the columns. "That's where you can park."

As the sun finalizes its descent, a lone rooster crows, announcing our arrival.

Then we are covered in darkness.

"Dolores, ¿eres tú?"

"Sí, Maria," she answers from the bottom of the stairwell. "Voy."

A white van is parked near the chain-link fence at the edge of the property. There's a decal stamped across the back doors with the universal symbol for medicine, the caduceus. It looks like a home health care vehicle, but it's too dark to tell for sure.

"Are you offering medical services?"

"No, of course not." Dolores laughs, then grabs my hand and leads me up the stairs. She lets herself in, as though she lives here, too.

"Bendición," she calls out. The room is unusually warm. There isn't an AC unit on the wall, only an oscillating fan running in the corner.

"Que Dios te bendiga, hija," a woman's voice replies from inside.

As we enter, a tiny, frail woman, who I can only presume to be Christian's mother, Maria, is seated on an old, worn-out La-Z-Boy. Her feet are propped up on the footrest, her arm outstretched with an IV attached at the crook. She is undergoing a type of infusion procedure. Cancer, I assume.

A nurse sits on a wooden dining chair directly beside her, jotting notes. The logo on her scrub top matches the one I saw on the van. This must be her home health aide. She doesn't bother to look up as we walk in.

Dolores walks over and kisses Maria and then the nurse in greeting. I prefer not to, but I know it's rude, so I follow suit and do the same.

"Maria, this is Lina, my cousin from the Army."

Maria looks sad when Dolores says *the Army*. She looks from me to a picture on the wall of her son wearing a graduation cap. I glance over, but I don't fully take it in, purposely trying to guard myself from the reality I've just entered.

The stark truth of it all hits me like a slap in the face. I have just walked into the home of a mother who lost her son on the battlefield in Iraq.

What am I doing here? Suddenly I feel like karma has delivered me to the feet of the mother whose son I murdered. Except that's impossible. That boy was a local—an enemy combatant. This isn't her. This isn't his mother. He spoke Arabic, not Spanish. My heart is racing as pinpricks of sweat form along the edge of my forehead and my palms grow cold and clammy. I shouldn't have come here. Why would Dolores do this? Why would she bring me to face the tragedy of a mother who lost her child in war?

*Because Dolores doesn't know what you've done. None of them know the truth about you.*

"I'm so sorry," I say to Maria, although I'm not entirely sure what I'm apologizing for. I think for all of it. I'm sorry that she is getting some type of chemo treatment in the middle of her living room. I'm sorry that serving in the Army means her son is now gone forever. Mostly I'm sorry because she is forced to share the same air with a murderer who also took someone's son away from them.

"¡Diantre!" she says breathlessly. "You don't have to apologize. It's cancer. It can happen to anyone. Please, sit down."

She points to the couch beside her. I take a seat, afraid my legs may give out.

"Dolores," she says, "you can get fresh squeezed jugo de guanábana in the refri—" She turns back to me. "My son was an English teacher, but sometimes I forget some of the words."

"I would love some juice, thank you," I answer, but I'm not thirsty; I'm babbling.

Her eyes widen, sensing my distress. Dolores is already up and moving around the kitchen with surprising familiarity.

"Nena," Maria says, calling me by an endearment meant for a young girl you know well. I think it's supposed to comfort me. I take a deep breath and try to settle the disrupted angry hive buzzing in my chest.

"This is Milly," she says. She smiles at the quiet nurse removing the blood pressure cuff from her arm.

"Mucho gusto," Milly says quietly. She isn't interested in visiting; instead, she remains focused on her task.

Maria looks apologetic at the nurse's standoffish behavior, which doesn't go unnoticed. Milly excuses herself to use the bathroom.

"She is here to do my treatment every Monday. Three weeks on, then two weeks off. It will continue this way for three months."

Dolores returns with two glasses of freshly squeezed juice. I wish more than anything I could reach into my pocket and pull out a flask of vodka to add the proper kick the juice needs. That I need.

Dolores sets the glasses down and disappears around the corner following an "I'll be right back." It leaves Maria and I momentarily alone. "I'm so sorry," I say again, feeling the pinprick of tears growing heavy behind my eyelids. I try to blink them away, but it may be too late. Why am I here?

Maria looks at me, confused. She must assume it's the treatment that has me so spooked. She points over to the empty chair directly beside her. "Come closer," she says. "Here next to me."

I concede because I don't know what else to do. I stand, contemplating a wild excuse to return back outside, but my legs are shaking so much, it's easier to drop onto the chair beside her. The medical equipment hums in my ear.

"It's okay," she says softly. "It doesn't hurt, and I'm blessed that Dolores can be here with me during my treatments. It's easier when you're not alone. I send my daughter to extra English lessons on Monday evenings, so she isn't here to witness this. Dolores is good company."

"I understand," I say. Then rethink my words, because how could I possibly understand?

"I have a son," I croak out, my racing thoughts and pounding heart releasing words I haven't fully thought through. I hope my revelation will make sense of what I'm trying to say. "I would want to protect him from this, too."

When the words are out of my mouth, I realize, like a complete fool, I've brought up the topic of a mother and her son.

I feel a tear spill down each cheek. I did this. This is what a grieving mother with no son looks like. Because of my actions, because I couldn't wait another few seconds, there's another woman on the other side of the world probably sitting alone in her living room, dying from her loss, too. Now I'm forced to sit here and stare at it, live in it, take in the suffering and the pain I caused someone else. No matter how far I run, it's here, surrounding me, strangling me with a pressured fist of grief.

I jump up from the seat and stare at the door. I need to get out of here.

Dolores returns to us with a book in her hand. She glances over at me, confused.

Maria stretches her ice-cold hand out and grabs hold of mine, preventing me from bolting out of the living room. "It's okay, nena. I know. I understand. The bond between a mother and son is like no other. You are his first love, and he is your deepest. I lost my son. I understand, it's okay."

My head shakes with denial. How could I have done this to another mother? "I'm—I'm so sorry."

I want to say more, but I choke past a sob that comes out strange and loud in the quiet room. I cover my mouth with my free hand, overwhelmed and humiliated.

"What is it, Lina?" Dolores asks at the same time the nurse returns from the bathroom and eyes me nervously.

"Are you all right?" Milly asks me coolly. The sharpness of her clinical tone grounds me from pure panic back into the reality of the hot, dim living room. She must see from the look on my face that I am back from my trip to crazy town because she heads into the kitchen without another word. I can nearly read the nurse's mind: *I don't get paid enough to deal with locas.*

What is wrong with me? What am I doing? I wipe my eyes with the back of my hands and press my trembling lips into a forced, embarrassed smile.

"Ven, nena. Sit," Maria says.

When I don't move, rooted in place with supreme humiliation, she repeats herself. "Come here, child."

I step closer and sit back down in the dining chair. Maria's clammy palm cradles mine. The cold, leathery skin reminds me of what dying feels like.

Dolores doesn't take her eyes off me until I retake my seat, then pulls up one of her own and opens a small spiral notebook with a plain typeface on the cover. "Okay, is everyone ready?" she asks; both she and Maria are looking at me. I offer a small nod, then open my mouth to apologize—again—but Dolores shakes her head. "Let's begin."

Maria leans back and closes her eyes as Dolores opens the notebook to the first page.

She reads a story about a young Puerto Rican boy, a jíbaro, who worked in the fields, and dreamed of moving to the US and fighting in World War I alongside his best friend from childhood. After twenty minutes she closes the book, just as the two boys prepare for basic training together. When she's done, I do not want it to end, but Milly has since returned with a fresh glass of water for her patient, informing us Maria's treatment is over.

"What a beautiful story," I say as we stand up to leave and give our goodbyes.

Milly helps the frail woman to her feet and escorts her to her bedroom.

As we reach the front door, I ask Dolores, "Why did you bring me here? You do this every week? Read to her while she has her treatments?"

I wonder whether someone is there to comfort the mother who lost her child in Iraq.

Dolores ignores the hostility of my initial question. "Of course. It's the least I can do for Christian." She turns and blows a kiss to the picture on the wall. I can't bring myself to look at the image again. "Besides," she says, "Nurse Milly doesn't have the personality to pull off storytelling."

I grimace. "No, she doesn't." I follow behind her. "Dolores, the story reminded me of *Don Quixote*. Who is the author?"

She looks at me sadly as we close the door behind us. "The best writer I've ever known—her son, Christian."

It's nearly pitch black out as the sounds of the jungle at night fill the air with hunger. I'm reminded how differently people here live than they do in the US. There aren't any streetlights here to light our way back to the main road, no expansive gas stations or Walmarts at the corner for midnight convenience. In these parts of Puerto Rico, the pueblo sleeps when the sun goes down, unless, of course, there's a chinchorro in the area.

Dolores slides into the passenger seat and pulls down the visor, using the mirror to freshen up her makeup. Her body emanates a combination of flowers and coconut. Everything about her screams young, vibrant, and feminine.

"Come on, you know you look beautiful. Where to next?" I ask, wondering how close the nearest bar is.

"You think I look beautiful because you don't realize how striking you are, prima. You have the body of a model and a face that can ignite the sun, if only you smiled more."

Before I can negate the compliment, her phone is already in her hand, thumbs scurrying across the screen. I reverse onto the dark, winding road and back toward the highway. "Who are you texting?"

"A couple of friends—my corrillo. They are going to meet us for a few drinks."

The smile creeps back on her lips, her sadness from our visit tucked away. Not me, but we are on the same page when it comes to a few drinks, especially after my meltdown in Maria's living room.

I reach over and squeeze Dolores's hand. I like being around her. "Point me in the right direction," I say, ready to get lost in a bottle of rum with my mysterious young cousin.

# CHAPTER SIXTEEN

The next morning I wake up to a pounding headache. Glancing over at my phone, I can see that I haven't woken up on time to get Teó ready for school. Not surprising, given that Dolores and I got home just before sunrise. She didn't drink last night, keeping a close eye on me instead. After arriving to see the earliest rays of dawn, we agreed Teó would have to stay home: I was in no condition to drive him to school, and she was too exhausted to get him there safely.

Papi's fist pounds on the door, followed by his deep baritone. "Lina, levántate," he shouts. "Why are you still in bed?" I look up from the sofa to see whether the incessant pounding has woken Teó, but the bed is empty.

I spring up, ignoring the heavy wave of nausea and the ache in my dehydrated joints, my heart pounding. *Where's Teó? It is morning, isn't it?*

The pounding continues, and I swing the door open. "What, Papi? Where's Teó?"

Papi glances down at me in disdain, and I can only imagine what he's thinking. I'm sure last night's makeup is still caked all over my face, although I can't imagine what I must look like now. I picture the quintessential sad little clown.

"Papi? Answer me." I ignore the disappointment I see swirling in his eyes.

"He's at school, Lina." His tone reiterates my failings. "I guess he got ready all by himself. That explains why he told us all to stay quiet and not wake you. Did you know your mami had to fix his shirt? He was wearing it inside out. I took him to school myself and arrived late at work."

Nothing he's saying is complicated, and yet I'm disoriented and confused. "What do you mean he's at school? What time is it?" *Didn't I just see the clock read 7:30 a.m.?* Did I fall back asleep?

"It's one thirty in the afternoon. Your mami and abuela are in San Juan today, renewing their driver's licenses, which you know is an all-day affair. She asked me to come in during lunch and check on you. Pero, diantre, Lina. I didn't expect to find you . . . like this. You need to get yourself together, nena. I know you are dealing with a lot of emotions, but you need to be strong and tuck them away. This isn't how a young woman should be behaving. Everyone has a wild night, but you're a mother now. This is unacceptable. You are—"

"I know," I huff. "*I* am unacceptable."

"Ay, bendito. Women." He shakes his head. "Listen, don't be so dramatic. I'm just saying. It's been almost two weeks. It's time for you to establish yourself and get back to work. We are here to help you, but . . ." He looks at me again from head to heels. I feel myself shrinking beneath his gaze, which only ignites the rage. "Get control of yourself and your feelings; otherwise they will control you."

"I'm sorry you had to take Teó this morning," I say beneath a seethe. "It won't happen again."

His features darken, his patience waning. "That is not what this is about. We love Matteo."

"No," I agree. "You're right. It's not about Teó, is it? It's about my inability to tuck away my feelings and so much more."

I step back and shut the door in his face before turning the lock, surprising myself at the lack of respect in my actions. But I can't deal with him right now. My head pounds, and I swallow back the bile in my throat. Closing my eyes, I wait for his fist to pound against the door in defiance at what I just did. I wonder what I will do when it comes.

It doesn't. Instead, his voice lowers, his mouth near the seal of the closed door. "Lina, please. Enough already. You're stronger than this. Pull yourself together."

He sighs when I don't respond.

The soles of his loafers slap against the tiled hall in resignation. I want to scream and hit something. I want him to give me the fight that I desperately need. Instead, he once again maintains the upper hand by leaving me to stand there, staring at the wall between us, alone in my misery.

# CHAPTER SEVENTEEN

Papi hasn't said more than a few words to me in the last week, not since he came home at lunch to check on me. I know better than to test his resolve, and I've intentionally stayed out of his way.

Taking heed of his frustration, I got on the ball and began to address my responsibilities. I scheduled Teó's first appointment with the local specialist, began the application for government health care, and finally scheduled my next appointment with Dr. Robles. I was supposed to have seen her this week, but I managed to come up with one excuse after another to push the date out a bit and avoid dealing with another grueling session. I even showed up at the local temp agency office to fill out an application for work in one of the local pharmaceuticals, knowing that, on the island, working in the most prominent industry would offer the best pay, stability, and benefits plan. The career counselor said I'd have no trouble, given my college degree and military service. I told her I couldn't wait to hear back.

She's called two or three times since. I haven't answered. I don't know what I'm waiting for. I need to get back to work. It's not like I don't want to. It's just that the idea of putting on a pair of booties and a hairnet in a sterilized environment while conducting quality checks at a factory feels like I've given up. I guess I have. I can't seem to summon the courage beyond surviving each day. Putting one foot in front of the other and finding a way to stabilize my situation for my son is taking every bit of energy I have left. This fog of despair and hopelessness threatens to suffocate me at times, but I press on with the need to survive and accept that things have changed. All the years I spent dreaming, following a path to becoming a physician, and now it's over. All of it is over.

It's taking me a little longer than I expected to make peace with that. Some nights, when it gets really quiet, I even find myself missing the military uniform. For seven years, the Army was my life, my safety net, my team. I was part of something bigger, something special. Now it's gone, too, and I'm lost and alone. The only thing getting me through the day is knowing the nights will come and I can finally find some peace.

For the last week I've waited for everyone to go to bed before sneaking onto the back porch and drinking a few glasses of rum on ice. I don't drink enough to make me sick or black out, just enough for the loneliness to fade and for the memories of that morning in the desert to get murky or disappear altogether. It's the only thing that has paved the way for me to rest my head on the pillow and fall asleep. I hide the bottle in a drawer and wash the glass each night after I'm done, eliminating all evidence. I can't afford to be out paying retail prices for drinks at a bar without a job, so I tell myself this is an act of responsibility. It also eliminates any risk of me driving under the influence. I am quiet and discreet, not bothering anyone with postwar theatrics or forcing anyone to bear witness to my pain. I drink, quietly and alone, and after that incident with Papi, I make sure to wake up on time and get Teó ready for school.

The monotony, though, of having nowhere to be, no sense of purpose, is beginning to make things worse. My family has resumed their normal routines, and Teó is thriving at his new school. I seem to be the only one lost in the shuffle of nothingness.

It makes me wonder about Eli and his postwar transition. He obviously found himself amid a real-war crisis, and now he seems pretty content with his life on the island. I'm curious how he found his way through the fog I'm stuck in. I haven't heard from him at all over the past week, and a part of me feels too embarrassed to make an appearance at Chiquitas. The last time we saw each other, I fled without warning from our lunch table and left him to find another ride home. He's probably thankful I haven't been by. I'm sure he's wondering how I ever even made it in the Army. It's better for everyone if I stay away from Chiquitas altogether, although today the idea of the open bar, the ocean breezes, and some good local music does pull a string of nostalgia somewhere deep inside.

While Mami is preparing the table for dinner, Dolores, almost in an act of sorcery, offers me an easy out. "Lina, you look too sad. I know moving back to Puerto Rico was a big change for you, but I think you need to keep remembering why it's so special here. You're home, prima. Come, tonight we go to Chiquitas."

Mami and Abuela look over at me worriedly, as though leaving the house at night will automatically result in another disaster. Their assumption bothers me, and now, not only am I anxious to get out of this house and breathe, but I feel like I need to prove to them and to myself that I'm not a complete and utter failure. I am a good mother, and I can manage to go out for a couple of hours and still return home to care for my child.

"I think you're right, prima. Let's do it." I look over at Mami. "Is that okay? I won't be home late, and I'll leave Teó ready for bed."

Mami nods softly. "Of course. Go. Teó will be fine."

I put on a formfitting, rose-colored maxi dress and platform sandals. It's the only dress I own in a wardrobe of sneakers, jeans, long shorts, T-shirts, and tank tops. Being a boy mom and a soldier didn't render many opportunities to wear anything beyond comfort or function. It does feel good to change tonight, to feel a bit more . . . feminine.

I slip on a pair of tiny silver hoops in my ears and prepare to brush my hair into the signature Army bun, but then stop and let it flow through my fingers, brushing it long and loose down my back. It's been a long time since I've worn it down instead of knotting it up tight and militant. I pull out the only tube of lipstick I own, a bold red. It's usually reserved for formal events, but tonight I want to feel like I'm not a muted ghost roaming the halls in search of my soul. I spread the color, a fire-engine velvet, across my full lips, then rub them together for evenness. Perfect.

The reflection in the mirror tells a story. The worry in my eyes is still there, the furrow between my brows beginning to feel like a permanent fixture. I hold my eyes closed for a moment, willing myself to open them and see the reflection of a young Puerto Rican woman with a glimmer of hope. Tonight I am Lina. Not a mother, not a soldier, not a murderer.

"Are you ready?" Dolores asks, popping her head into the bedroom.

She startles me, and I look away from the mirror, embarrassed.

"Yes, let's go," I say and grab my keys.

Teó's belly laugh rings out from the backyard. I open the screen door and look out to see him playing with the hens in the large pen Papi built. They run for their lives, with him close behind. My heart warms to see them wise up and counterattack. They stop running away and turn to face him, jumping up and flying a few feet in his direction. This time he runs away from them, laughing—no trace of his tics.

I feel Mami's eyes on me. She is sitting on a white plastic chair on the back porch. Our eyes meet, and she glances over at Teó while sipping a late-afternoon espresso. This isn't me exactly leaving him ready for bed.

Seeming to read my mind, she says, "He will be fine. Your father should be home soon, and you know he will enjoy having one-on-one time with Teó. Go on. Enjoy."

"Sí, Mami. Okay." I kiss her farewell, wishing for a way to heed her advice and enjoy life again, although, for me, that doesn't seem possible anymore.

The Chiquitas parking lot leads directly to the dreaded exterior stairwell. Dolores is chattering away as we approach, but I can't hear her beyond the ringing in my ears. Reaching the stairs, I grip the handrail and try to ignore the slats of open space between each step that make the whole thing appear unsteady. My foot grazes the first step cautiously. Thankfully it's so dark below I can't see the ground beneath me. My gaze aims up rather than down, focusing on the promised land beyond the metal gate and onto the third-floor landing.

With resounding determination and a held breath, I'm able to quickly climb three stories of stairs without nearly fainting.

The sound system is playing bachata, a soft, melodic rhythm originating in the Dominican Republic. It's one of my favorite styles of Caribbean music.

Colorful circles of light swarm around the dance floor, but rather than join the festive environment, I once again feel like I'm watching it all happen as a spectator on the outside. Dolores and I walk over to the bar, her hips swaying to the rhythm.

"I love to dance bachata!" she says. "Prima, you want to dance?"

The question hits center mass. I'm not ready. I need a drink.

Dolores senses my hesitation. "Come on, Lina. It's time to loosen up . . . un poquito . . ."

My eyes search for him down the length of the bar, but there's no Eli to save me with a distraction.

Before I can say anything, a young guy not much older than Dolores comes from behind her and grabs her hand. He spins her around to face him, moving his lower body in perfect synchronization with the song. Dolores listens for the beat, then follows suit. Not one word is exchanged. The man sways in one direction, and Dolores follows his lead. He spins her gently as her chest and hips sashay in perfect rotation. Her new partner watches, admiring her movement.

Completing her rotation, she faces him once more and nods. Yes. Invitation accepted.

He leads her to the center of the dance floor, and I admire the easiness between them as they continue the conversation between their swaying bodies. I bet outsiders would think they've known each other for years. I know better by the lack of recognition on her face. They just met. Their bodies flow at the same pace, in the same direction, without exchanging a word.

When the song is over, he takes a little bow, and Dolores leans over to give him a light kiss on the cheek, thanking him for the dance.

She returns to the bar, and we both grab a seat on the wooden stools. A few tiny beads of sweat glisten on her forehead, eyes shining. My little cousin looks invigorated. Watching her reminds me of who I was in my childhood and life, before the move to Florida. I used to love to dance.

"You're back already?" a voice says from behind us. "What would you like to drink?"

Anita's bright-red lipstick spreads across a beautiful smile. The shade is nearly an exact match to the curls on her head and the dusting of auburn freckles covering her face. Her features indicate an Irish or Scottish descent, but her body and sass are all Puerto Rican. It's true what I once said to Teó: our people come in all sizes and colors.

"I'll have a whiskey con coco," I answer, my mouth already watering at the idea of the buzz and the taste of the coconut water and whiskey blend.

"Mojito de parcha," Dolores says.

Before I can object to both her age and her ability to drive us home, Anita is gone to fill our orders. "Don't worry, Lina," Dolores says, reading my mind. "I will eat heavy before we leave and do plenty of dancing. I'll be okay to drive. If not, cogemos pon."

I don't like the suggestion that we will "get a ride" if she isn't okay to drive. Who does she think will give us a ride home? I'm not okay with a stranger driving us home, especially knowing Teó is inside fast asleep.

"I don't think so," I start, but Dolores cuts me off with the wave of her hand.

"Don't worry so much. Everything is good."

A rebuttal dies on my lips as Anita comes back with our drinks. That was fast. I let it go . . . for now. The pull of the alcohol is much stronger than settling the issue with Dolores.

"It's on the house. Boss's orders," Anita says.

Eli.

I try to be subtle, scanning the room in search of him again, forcing myself not to openly ask Anita where Eli is. The effort is futile. Anita points up to a camera in the corner of the ceiling.

"He's in the back, cuadrando los recibos." *Reconciling the receipts.*

"Oh, whatever." I shrug, but Anita smirks.

"I just think maybe you want to say sorry to my boss, because you abandoned him in Viejo San Juan last time."

I grow hot underneath my dress despite the thin material.

"I didn't mean to—"

"Good thing me and my husband could go pick him up. We were close by at Plaza."

"Yes, it was good you were close by," I say curtly, then take a large gulp of the icy-cold drink.

Anita's loyalty isn't misplaced. In fact, I respect her for it. Eli has bonded with her, which on this island tends to mean for life.

"What happened?" Dolores asks, listening to the bits unfold between Anita and me.

"It's a long story."

Anita is eyeing me suspiciously. She isn't sure what to make of me yet. I'm okay with that. I would feel the same way in her shoes. Truthfully, she has no idea the extent of what I'm capable of. Neither did I, until it was too late.

"Well, I'll be damned. You finally came by to see me."

The sound of the tenor coated in the southern drawl initiates a storm buzzing deep inside all my secret places.

"I figured I owed *you* one after leaving you stranded," I say coolly before taking another large gulp from the red plastic Dixie cup. I'm disappointed when ice clinks against my teeth.

I turn to Anita and hold up my empty cup. "Can I get another?"

Her smile is forced.

"Claro que sí," she says.

I commend the effort. I'm not her favorite.

As Anita walks away, Dolores's earlier dance partner returns. He extends his hand to her as a new song plays.

"I'll be right back," Dolores says to Eli and me over her shoulder, offering us a little privacy.

The new patrons must be tourists. The heavily tropical-patterned shirts; bright red, sunburned noses; and their obnoxiously loud entrance give them away.

I turn to Eli. "It looks like you're about to get very busy."

"Yeah, I suppose," he muses, glancing over at them. "Thankfully Alvin sent over his two teenage cousins to help cover while he is at home taking care of the new baby—a baby girl."

On cue an unusually tall teenager appears from around the kitchen. He's wearing a Chiquitas polo and escorts the newcomers to a table, handing them each a menu.

"Is that one of the cousins? He looks nervous."

Eli smiles. "Yes, ma'am. A good kid, catches on quickly. Anita will keep them in line." He turns his attention toward me and leans closer from across the bar. It's subtle—very subtle.

The reduction in space makes me want to run my fingers through the golden curls across his forehead and move them over to one side. They're nearly touching his thick, dark eyebrows. Those curls rebel against the high-and-tight hairstyle of an Army officer. I like that he's adapted to the island's relaxed beach vibe.

I take a moment to study his face. His nose is long and straight, posing little distraction from any of his other features. His bright-green eyes have tiny flecks of brown in the center. The specks are so small I didn't notice them until now, now that I'm only inches from his face. His lips are wide but plump and rosy. I can only assume he is a good kisser. God can't gift a man with lips that full and expect they'll go to waste. His silky-smooth face is freshly shaven. I can smell the aftershave—lemons. It's one military tradition he keeps.

Still feeling like I'm on the outside looking in, I bring my elbow up onto the bar and extend my hand toward him. I want to touch his face and press my cheek against his. It's an otherworldly action, a desperate act to get lost in . . . I don't know . . . something. I just want to stop thinking, hurting, remembering . . . My lips move closer to his, testing their ability to take me away and make me forget. I imagine them settling into the curve of his, feeling every press in the softness of a kiss. It's been so long. Will this work? His energy, the offer of an escape, draws me in.

My hand moves closer to his body, daring him.

He glances over and sees me subtly reaching. He leans in, obliging me. I tilt my head ever so slightly and move a little closer, my heart rate quickening with the anticipation of our lips touching.

"Mm-hmm . . . eh, con permiso." The voice is only inches from our faces.

*No, she didn't.*

And just like that, the moment is broken, and I'm smacked back into my current reality, no free pass to get away. I pull back with a loud exhale and lean back into my chair.

"Your whiskey con coco," Anita says, sliding the drink in front of me. I think she means it to be a barrier between us.

Eli's expression burns with frustration, but she saunters off, a perfunctory smile on her face.

He looks back at me. "Where were we?" But it's too late. I've decided my new drink will do just fine to help me escape.

I raise the refreshed glass in a toast. "Cheers," I say, ignoring the question. The moment has passed. I'm not entirely sure what came over me, but now I feel a bit awkward. Anita's strategy worked. All I want to focus on now is enjoying my drink. I think she knew that would be the case.

"Salud," he says, resigning the moment and taking the hint.

He turns and grabs a beer from the cooler behind him, and I notice he isn't wearing the hand prosthetic any longer. The circumference of the beer fits perfectly between the curve of the pincers. He pops the top from a Medalla, our locally brewed light lager, with his "good" hand.

Tipping the beer in my direction, he takes a large swig.

"Dolores took me to meet Christian's mother," I say, figuring this is as good a moment as any to bring it up.

His relaxed, carefree demeanor shifts. The moment reminds me of a toy I had as a child—a pair of red binoculars with a white disk in the center. By pressing down on the handle while peering through the eyeholes, the picture inside would change to the next image on the disk.

I've pressed the handle for Eli; his demeanor is different. Something has changed.

His lips squeeze together in a tight line. Darkness shades his eyes, transitioning them from bright green to olive. He is trying to hold a blank expression, unfazed, but I'm trained to recognize pain.

"Dolores reads to her on Mondays during her treatment," he says, confirming he knows what we were doing there.

"Have you been?" I ask carefully. "You know . . . during one of her treatments."

"I have not," he says, and takes another swig of his beer. My expression must relay my thoughts because he asks, "Does that surprise you?"

"I figured if you were close to her son . . ." My voice trails off.

"We were close. He was a soldier in my unit."

I wait for him to continue, but he doesn't.

"Lina, I need to do a quick check on things, make sure the young'uns aren't causin' a total ruckus back there. Don't go anywhere, okay? Promise?" He props his right elbow on the bar between us and extends his pinkie finger. "I mean it. I want a pinkie promise."

I swallow a mouthful of whiskey and coconut water and curve my pinkie against his. His hands are warm but—surprisingly for a guy who runs a bar—baby soft.

"I promise," I say, my insides tingling with the warmth of whiskey as the music transitions to reggae. "I'll be right here. And Eli? Maybe you can bring me back another one." I hold up the cup of ice.

He considers me again. "I can do that, and a bottle of water, too."

I nod grudgingly. "Sure."

As Eli walks away, Dolores's arms wrap around my waist from behind. I smell her before I see her. She's holding a bottle of water in her hand. Everywhere I look, people are smiling, happy, eating, talking. There's joy all over this place. Yet I'm alone, trying to calm the anger inside. Dolores's watered-down mojito is still half-full on the bar beside me. I consider whether I should come out and ask her if I can drink it. I shouldn't.

She is glistening with sweat.

"Lina, let's go dance! Come with me." She pulls my hand, wanting to lead me toward the dance floor, but I'm grateful at the pinkie promise that forces me to wait.

"I can't. I promised Eli I'd wait right here."

Eli walks to the far end of the restaurant, opposite us. He is checking on the seated patrons. Smiling faces look up at him and nod. Anita and one of the teenagers are working the other end. Everything appears to be moving along smoothly.

Still curious, I ask, "What's the story between Eli and Christian?"

Dolores huffs, annoyed I won't join her on the dance floor. She takes the seat beside me. Multiple sets of eyes from down the bar are aimed in our direction. We are both dressed for attention, but their stares make me unusually alert.

I reach for Dolores's mojito and finish it in one long drink. Her eyes widen, but she doesn't say a word.

"Christian told me about Eli in a letter," she begins. "He told me he met this rich gringo from South Carolina—a capitán. They played on the golf course in Mississippi when he was there to train. Whenever the unit gave them a day off, Christian liked to play golf, and somehow they began to play together."

*Eli is rich,* I repeat silently. I'm not surprised, considering he did buy a bar on a whim.

"Is that all?" I ask Dolores, watching Eli finish his rounds and walk back toward us. Time is running out, and I'm still missing a big piece of this puzzle.

"We can talk more later," Dolores says, seeing him, too. "But you should know Christian saved Eli's life."

"Howdy, ladies," Eli says cheerily.

All trace of his earlier seriousness is gone. I don't have the heart to bring him down again by mentioning anything more about Christian. Besides, both of my whiskeys and Dolores's mojito are taking effect, making me lightheaded and giddy.

Eli holds a water bottle in his hand, but not the whiskey and coco I ordered.

He uncaps the water and pushes it in my direction. "How 'bout we hydrate you. Then you let me take you for a little spin on the dance floor?"

"I don't dance," I say. "Not my thing."

"Oh, come on, everyone from 'round here dances. Besides, you need to burn some of that booze with some exercise." He eyes me carefully and points the water at me again. "At least, that is, if you plan to drink any more."

I grab the bottle and take a big swig. I already know how to play nice and drink the water if I want this bar to continue to serve me.

"You know how to dance merengue?" I say, relenting as a new song plays. The fast-paced beats fill the open air.

"Pretty lady, I can dance to anything until the cows come home. I'll just follow your lead."

"Okay, gringo," I say. "Let's see what you got."

I slide off the stool, dreading what's about to go down, knowing I haven't danced in nearly ten years.

Eli offers me his right hand. He sways his hips, shuffling his feet in rhythm with the fast-moving music. The trumpets and bongos keep us in sync with the song and each other. I'm baffled by the smooth motions of his body and the perfect alignment to the rhythm.

"Where did you—"

He twirls me around, then draws me close with his right hand while the other stays eerily still at his side.

"Anita," he says, winking.

Jealousy pricks my chest when I picture him with the beautiful red-haired waitress on this very dance floor.

Facing me, he breaks into a gorgeous white smile. It's contagious. I smile back, my hips in perfect rhythm to his.

When the song ends, he brings me close into a hug. His body is damp with sweat. I kiss his cheek, assuming we're done, when a new song, "La Quiero a Morir," by Sergio Vargas, a softer merengue, plays. Maybe we can keep dancing. I'm not sure I want to stop.

Eli senses my desire, because he twirls me again and resumes swaying to the music. I lean into him, soaking in the power of the rhythm, the longing of the words, and the dance at our feet. I've surprised myself with how much I've missed this. It makes sense—I grew up with music. Songs once helped me process my emotions and celebrate life's victories. My life's soundtrack is filled with salsa, merengue, mambo, and now even reggaeton, stamping memories in my heart forever.

I've also missed the feel of a man's body. There haven't been many relationships in my past. There was Leonardo—Teó's father—during the summer before my senior year in high school. Teó was born and the well ran dry for a couple of years, until I joined the military. I can't say I officially dated anyone when I was in the Army, but I did seize two different opportunities with a young, attractive soldier in a sister unit. He told me I was beautiful and deserved to be adored, insisting on showing me how much. For a couple of hours, on two late autumn afternoons, while Teó was in day care, I let him. It was nice. But it was over as soon as it had begun. I grew bored quickly, and I wasn't ready to introduce anyone to my son. The truth is, I didn't want to give my heart to anyone but Teó anyway.

I squeeze Eli's hand, ignoring the voice in my head that tells me to walk away. Eli is good, too good. I don't deserve someone like him, and I shouldn't lead him on when I know I don't have what it takes inside to connect. I won't have someone walk away and break my heart again. The power of Leonardo's rejection lingered for so long, I never want to feel so unwanted again.

We continue to dance, and I sing along to the chorus. I think about the words and what it would mean to Eli if he understood it. Would he think it's fate that we are dancing to a song about a woman who knows every wound, every war of life, and the pain of love?

When it ends, patrons seated at tables near the dance floor's edge clap for us. Maybe it's because for a split second the two of us looked happy. Or perhaps it's Eli's effort to dance and lead me despite being able to use only one arm. It doesn't matter. I blink back the tears from the corners of my eyes, flooded with conflicting emotions and sentimentality.

Eli hugs me again, but this time he holds it a second longer, pulling my body a slight pulse tighter against his. He leans down and kisses my cheek. I'm tempted to turn my face and return his kiss, but a sudden movement at the entrance catches my eye.

My feet are frozen. I cannot move. It's not possible. It's been ten years, but it's him. So much time, but he's barely changed, maybe a little more mature, but still the face I knew before. I'm struck dumb by the familiarity of his features.

"Hey there, you okay?" Eli asks, studying my face.

My eyes widen with terror, wanting this to be my mind playing tricks on me. I look back toward the door one last time.

Eli automatically pulls me closer—protectively. He follows my eyes to the front of the building, but he has no way of seeing what I see. For Eli, it's a young, beautiful couple waiting to be seated.

"Lina, you look like you've seen a ghost. What is it? Are you all right?"

I can't answer. I force my feet to move in the opposite direction, deliberately walking backward, away from the dance floor toward the rear wall.

It's too late. He sees me.

His stare burns into my skin, blinking back the realization that, yes, I'm here—in the flesh.

Taking purposeful steps, I move to the farthest end of the bar, searching for Dolores. I can't be here another minute. We need to leave. My eyes move from one side of the pine bar to the other, but Dolores is nowhere to be seen. I turn around to scan the room.

"Lina, I don't know what all is going on right now," Eli says worriedly as he runs up behind me. "But you look like you done lost it. Do you know the couple that just walked in?"

"You could say that," I mutter. I lean into the bar's edge, searching desperately for something to drink, but there's no one to ask. Eli's the closest available bartender, and he is on the wrong side of the bar.

"What d'ya mean?"

I figure after ditching him in San Juan and avoiding him all week, I've put him through enough surprises. I will just tell him. I bring my elbows up on the bar, placing my head in my hands. I hope he can hear me, because I'm only going to say it once.

"That couple at the door—the man who walked in—that's Leonardo, Teó's father."

# CHAPTER EIGHTEEN

Eli glances over at the couple as Anita approaches to seat them at their table. "I take it this isn't a good thing. I mean, his being here and all?"

I'm not sure I know how to answer that, so I ignore the question and inventory the different spirits standing like the queen's guard against the wall . . . vodka, gin, clear rum, dark rum, more dark rum. I lose myself in the imagery of the bottles. Puerto Rico is a tiny island, only thirty-nine miles from north to south. Knowing Leonardo most likely still lives here meant there was always a possibility we'd run into each other. I never expected it to be this soon.

"Lina, how about I get you outa here? We could go for a walk. There's a little path down to the water. It may be good to get some fresh night air."

Anita escorts Leonardo and his guest to a table on the opposite side of the dance floor. Small blessings. Leonardo's long, lean frame follows behind Anita, but his face is angled painfully back over his shoulder, presumably searching for me. I saw the recognition and shock on his face. I'm surprised his date hasn't noticed the odd behavior as he continues to scan the room. He isn't exactly trying to be subtle, even if the woman on his arm seems intent on staying blissfully ignorant. She's pretty, although I think it's more of a too-much-makeup-and-not-enough-clothes kind of pretty.

I let out a large sigh. "Maybe I should go over there and say something to him, get it over with."

"You think that's a good idea? It ain't my place to meddle, but lookin' atcha, you seem a little outa sorts. I don't know . . ."

Eli's right. What exactly would I say? Do I walk up to the table and strike up a conversation? *Hi, Leonardo, I know it's been a while, but no big deal. Our fantastic son is thriving without any effort or involvement from his father. Oh, and by the way—he has Tourette's syndrome. I found out a few months before I went to Iraq, picked up a rifle, and killed a kid, but no big deal. At least our son is doing great.*

"Of all the damn bars," I mutter.

Eli grins. "Yeah, well, I couldn't be happier that of all the damn bars in all the towns in all the world, you walked into mine."

"*Casablanca*? Really?" I force a small smile. I think it's sweet how he's trying to make light of a heavy situation. "You're right. A walk sounds like an excellent idea."

"That-a-girl. Now give me one minute to let the team know I'm heading out. I'll be right back. Don't go anywhere."

"No," I sputter, gripping the sleeve of his shirt. "You can't leave me here alone."

My panic catches him by surprise. "How 'bout you come with me?"

I like that idea much better. I nod and follow behind him, but we aren't fast enough to escape.

Leonardo heads toward us as we make our way to the kitchen. His date remains seated at the table, staring at her menu, oblivious to everything transpiring around her.

"Lina," Leonardo calls out.

He is too close for me to pretend I can't hear him.

"You want me to handle this?" Eli asks under his breath.

"No, it's fine," I say, relenting. "Go ahead. I'll be right there."

"You sure?"

The earnestness on Leonardo's face as he approaches us thaws my resolve. "Yes, I'm sure."

Hesitating, Eli turns around, looking squarely at me as Leonardo reaches us, speaking loud enough for him to hear. "I'll be right around the corner, Lina. If you need anything, just holler and I'll be here, right by your side."

Eli glares at Leonardo once more but then walks toward the kitchen, leaving us alone. Leonardo's eyes dart to Eli's prosthetic. A flash of empathy swipes across his eyes, but then it's gone, and the focus is back on me.

Leonardo's skin tone reminds me how Teó inheriting his father's coloring makes the blue in his eyes stand out so much more.

I crane my neck up to meet Leo eye to eye, reminded of his betrayal and abandonment. I ignore the living, breathing replica of my favorite person, not wanting to offer him an ounce of warmth, even if seeing him gives me glimpses of Teó all grown up. Leo's soft, dark-brown curls are an exact copy of his son's. The shape of their face is identical, and the tiny cleft in the center of his chin is a gift I'm thankful he passed on. Against the bright-blue eyes and horn-rimmed glasses, it gives Teó a warm-toned Clark Kent vibe. I can't believe this man, this stranger, standing in front of me with the warm brown eyes of a new puppy, is partially responsible for the most essential facet of my life. It's surreal and tragic all at the same time.

"I can't believe it's really you," Leonardo finally says, breaking the silence as Eli walks away.

"That makes two of us."

"What are you doing here? Do you live here now, or are you visiting your family?"

It feels like I'm being grilled, and I don't like it. "What does it matter?"

He's taken aback by my response. I don't blame him. The last time he and I saw each other, I was a timid high school girl, with little more than a few giggles and an "okay, sure, we can try that" kind of attitude. Not anymore. I've grown up. I trained to become a soldier. I've been raising a child—his child—for nine years, alone. I'm not the girl he remembers.

"I'm sorry, I'm getting this all wrong." He looks back to his table. The woman he left is no longer staring at a menu, but directly at us. There's some fruity concoction in front of her, but she isn't drinking it. I try to place her, but she's unfamiliar. I prefer that she and I never knew each other from before.

"That must be your wife," I say coldly. "Looks like you need to get back to your table."

"I do," he says, turning to look at her, but then glancing back at me. "I think we need to talk. Can you meet me tomorrow?"

How dare he think I might want to see him again. I don't. Nothing good can come of this.

While he waits for my response, I stare at the rosy lips twisting into a familiar sheepish smile. It's the same rosy grin and hope-filled eyes Teó wears when he confesses to some homemade science experiment gone wrong, hoping I'm not too upset.

Now that the three of us are all on the same island, there are probably some things we should discuss. It's better we set boundaries now. "Where and what time?" I ask, the relent in my voice palpable.

He glances back—at her—again. "How about here for lunch? Tomorrow, okay?"

"Tomorrow?" I glance over at his wife's increasingly irritated expression. "Seriously?"

"Yes, Lina. We need to talk. Don't you think?"

I really don't, but truth is, I guess I do. "Okay."

He smiles, relieved, then turns back to his table, relief immediately turning into nervousness. The scowl on her face is unmistakable.

"Good luck, Leonardo," I taunt.

"Please. Don't stand me up. I'll be here tomorrow at twelve o'clock."

"Okay, okay. I already said yes. Don't make me change my mind."

He grins again, and I see my son's face staring back at me. My heart stops, but before I can catch my breath, he's gone. His long, lean frame returns to the table, and I turn to leave.

It isn't until I round the bend, searching for Eli, that it hits me—Leonardo didn't once ask about Teó.

Before I make it into the kitchen, Eli is already pushing past the swinging door and heading toward me. He looks me over before grabbing my hand and leading me to a back exit.

Anita is watching us. She and Eli exchange a look of understanding before he walks me out to the back balcony. There are a few empty tables directly facing the ocean, opposite a wooden railing, but the space is empty. The dark skies make the sea look like a midnight abyss. Even this late at night, the waves roll, then crash, and topple onto the shore one after another. As Eli leads me down the length of the balcony, I feel unsettled by the darkness.

I've never been afraid of the dark before. Another new development, I guess.

After passing through a miniature swinging gate at the end of the walkway, we make our way down another wooden staircase. This one is at the back of the property. Its base touches the edges of the beach below. Going down the stairs feels easier than climbing up them. Go figure.

"Eli, what about Dolores?" I ask, realizing I forgot to tell her I was leaving. "She will get worried if she can't find me."

"No problem. Let me send her a text and let her know we are going for a walk. Anita will keep an eye on her."

He pulls his phone out of his back pocket and places it in the center of the pincers, tightening them around the device to hold it secure. It gives him the freedom to type using his right hand.

I think about all the regular, everyday tasks he's had to do in an entirely new way. It can't have been easy to learn how to live again in such an altered state, different from everyone else. Yet Eli is always jovial . . . always so relaxed. I envy his strength. Teó's strength, too, now that I think about it.

He's learned to do the same. I'm the weak one. I can't find my joy anywhere, except with my son. Even then, when I'm alone with him and I run my fingers through his curls, my mind flashes back to the image of a similar boy and a mother who will never kiss the top of her son's head again.

I press my nails into my palm, forcing myself to focus on the moment in front of me.

Eli returns his phone to his back pocket and extends his hand. I move closer and loop my fingers between his. After Leonardo's swiftly delivered heartbreak, I swore off hand-holding. The two guys I dated afterward were relegated strictly to the bedroom. To me, holding hands was intimate, vulnerable, deeper. I hold only Teó's hand, but there's something strangely natural and familiar about being with Eli . . . his presence is easy. It feels like we've known each other for longer than a few days.

We follow the sandy trail toward the water. "Lina, are you okay?"

Am I okay? No, I'm not, so I lie. "Yeah, sure. I'm okay."

"Things looked heavy between you and . . . uh . . . your . . . Teó's daddy."

"I hadn't seen him in almost ten years," I admit. "We met when he was vacationing in Florida for the summer. It was before my senior year of high school."

As we continue to walk, I wonder whether I should continue with this very personal story, but Eli's presence makes me feel safe. "Leonardo was my first. I found out I was pregnant very shortly after." I consider leaving it at that, but a flood of wistful memories, the more important ones, comes to mind. "My son, Matteo Salvador LaSalle-Rivera, was born on April 15, 2000, at 3:21 a.m. LaSalle is my father's last name, and Rivera is my mother's."

I delight in the little smile at the corner of his lips.

"I was only one month away from graduating high school when he was born."

Mami's voice from when I told her I'd gotten pregnant replays in my mind: *If only things went as they were supposed to go.*

Eli makes me feel open to talking about things I'd typically tuck down deep in a place where secrets are best kept. I've held them there for so long it's liberating to let one go free.

"I reached out to Leonardo's family in Florida when I realized I was pregnant. They gave me his email, but not before letting me know his girlfriend on the island was *also* expecting and due within the next couple of weeks. He never once mentioned having a girlfriend back home. So I sent him an email, figuring it would be the safest way to tell him privately. When he replied, he said he had no way of knowing with certainty that the child was his. We both knew that was a lie. He also said I was too young to be a mother and recommended I think through all my options."

Eli's interlocked fingers tighten against mine. The idea of terminating the pregnancy bothers him. I felt the same way.

"I replied to his email and told him abortion was not an option. And I told him I meant it. This was my baby and, for me, a gift from God." I pause and swallow deeply. "His email back said, 'I'm sorry, but I won't be a part of this.' That was it. Nothing else. I never heard from him again."

Eli lowers his head. "What a fool," he whispers.

The sand beneath our feet is wet now. We stop, allowing the edges of foamy water to glide up, closer to our feet. The heartbeat from the waves fills the air around us. I look out at the darkened water. *Preciosa te llaman las olas,* I think to myself. It's a famous expression about how the people of Puerto Rico feel about their island. *Even the waves call you precious.*

Eli turns and faces me, until our lips are only inches apart.

He leans down and slowly brings his face closer to mine. He is moving with slow intention, allowing me every opportunity to pull away and break the spell before it sweeps us both up. But I don't want to break away. I want nothing more than to breathe in his safety, his familiarity, his protection.

I tilt my chin up toward his.

After letting go of my hand, he wraps his arm around my waist and pulls me close, gently bringing his lips to mine. His kiss is sweet, like peppermint. It's gentle—an introduction. I don't want him to stop.

He breaks from me and follows with a light kiss on the cheek.

"You're trembling," he says softly, near my ear. "Are you cold?"

"No. I'm surprised." I can't think of a better word to describe the flood of feelings coursing through me.

"Pleasantly surprised?"

"Yes, something like that."

"Whew, good." He lets go of my waist and mockingly wipes his brow. "That's good to hear because I'm really enjoying spending time with you."

"You are?"

"Sit with me." He points over to a small mound of sand farther up ahead.

I follow him. The music from Chiquitas is fading farther into the background. I take a seat, enjoying the coolness of the sand beneath me.

I've revealed a lot, I realize. It's his turn.

"Dolores told me Christian used to work at Chiquitas. She said he was saving up money to buy the bar for himself."

Eli's body tenses. His hand closes into a fist and then slowly releases. "Yeah, Dolores ain't wrong."

"You're going to make me ask?" When he doesn't respond, I say, "Okay, I guess you are. What's the connection? Obviously you two knew each other. Christian was one of your soldiers. How did you end up here?" Then before I can stop myself, I finish with, "Living his dream."

Eli's head snaps up. I may have gone too far, but I'm tired and overwhelmed. I want to understand who he really is, especially because he's getting under my skin, and I'm in no position to take silly risks. I have a son to think about.

"He made me promise."

Eli says it so quietly I almost don't hear him.

"When we were trapped, waiting for the medevac . . . I think Christian knew he was dying. I didn't want to admit it then, but I knew it, too. The extent of his injuries . . ." He coughs loudly before continuing. "We'd been hit by an IED while I was getting soil samples. We were working on an analysis to implement a soil vapor extraction system that treats soil contaminated with halogenated volatile organic compounds."

I have no idea what he is talking about, but the mention of an IED automatically delivers the scene I've played in my head a thousand times. *Possible IED, one hundred meters ahead. Stop to deploy the robot.*

"Burn pit remediation," he explains, unaware of the inner torment swarming my thoughts.

His Adam's apple bobs with the depth of his swallow. I swallow, too, feeling the rapid drum of my heartbeat. I blink, trying to stop my own memories and pay attention to his.

"I never saw it, Lina. The IED. It was buried under a pile of rocks, camouflaged perfectly to the surrounding terrain. There was no way for me to easily spot it, but somehow Christian did. We should never have been out there alone, but that was my call. A bad one."

I can't help but think about another bad call. *All personnel dismount and set up a perimeter. We need to take a defensive position.*

Eli's fingers press against his closed lids, trying to block the images from his memory. I want to tell him he can stop, but I think stopping him now may do more harm than good. He'll sense my distress . . . it might lead him to ask about me.

*Sergeant Fuentes, there's a threat. One hundred meters at my three o'clock. He is wearing an explosive device.*

I take a deep breath as quietly as I can.

Eli doesn't notice me. He continues, lost in his own memories. "I specifically requested Christian," he says softly, "because I knew him and trusted him. We played golf together back in Mississippi while training for deployment. It was my own selfishness, handpicking him to join me, a decision that cost him his life. And if that wasn't bad enough, after the blast, he was the one who pulled *me* to safety. When he saw how bad I was bleeding, Christian tore off his T-shirt and applied a tourniquet above my elbow. His quick thinking prevented me from bleeding out."

His left elbow twitches at the memory.

"It was a miracle I survived, only losing my arm." He swallows again. "The impact of the blast shook us both up. The adrenaline kept him lucid enough to save my life. He even found a way to lead us back to our vehicle—damn near carried me there. I, at least, managed to radio for the medevac even though I was leanin' into shock. But something wasn't right with him, and we were running out of time." Eli pauses to catch his breath. "It wasn't but shortly after the blast Christian began to go in and out of consciousness."

Eli lowers his head toward his chest.

He feels responsible. *You have no idea how much I understand.*

My hand moves up to squeeze his shoulder. I want him to know that I am here.

"As we waited for the cavalry, I think we both realized something was seriously wrong. Christian knew the end was coming. He started telling me about his plans. He talked about Dolores and said he was crazy about her—was planning on proposing after he had enough money to buy Chiquitas. I kept telling him to hold on, not to give up. Still, he made me promise to find her and tell her if he didn't make it. Whatever happened, he wanted her to know how much he loved her. I promised him I would.

"When the chopper arrived, he lost consciousness and didn't wake up the rest of the trip back. I never saw him again."

*I know what that feels like.*

I think about Sergeant Fuentes and the young man whose body collapsed to the ground from the impact of my bullet.

When Eli doesn't say anything else, I return my head to his shoulder and wrap my arm around him, needing to take as much as I am giving. The moonlight reveals the moisture in his eyes as the memories take hold of our hearts.

"I'm sorry, Eli. I really am."

I don't think he hears me, because he continues to speak as though I haven't said a word.

"After my medical discharge, I made it my mission to fulfill my promise to him. It took me a couple of months after my surgeries and post-op care in Germany, but once I got back, I confirmed it—Christian had died in Iraq. I convinced our admin team leader to share his beneficiary information with me. That's how I got his mother's phone number and address. When I came down to finalize the purchase of Chiquitas, I found them both—Dolores and Maria, Christian's mother. I found them together at Maria's home during one of her treatments. I told them I was moving here to honor his legacy and fulfill a promise. And you know what his mother said?"

I shook my head.

"Maria said his death benefits provided her the resources she needed for chemotherapy. She said even in death, her son was a guardian angel taking care of her."

"She said that?"

He nodded. "Yup. Her perspective nearly knocked me on my ass. That's when it hit me—there was something exceptional about this little island. I started to do some research, and guess what I discovered."

He doesn't wait for me to answer.

"Time and time again, Puerto Ricans have been forced to look beyond their tragedy and find a silver lining. That's when I decided I wouldn't buy the place and have someone local run it. I would run it myself. There was something different about this island. I could feel the magic here, and I needed a little bit of that magic in my own life."

Pride warms in my chest. "I understand what you mean. Teó seems to have found it, too. As for me"—I shrug—"let's just say Puerto Rico and I still have a lot of things to work out."

I can tell he is relieved to be talking. I wonder how long he's bottled up that story.

"What about you, Lina? You were in the Army, too."

I don't think I like where this is going.

"Do you want to talk about what brought you here?"

I shake my head. "I can't. Not yet . . . maybe not ever."

"Isn't that what you're trying to do with Dr. Robles at the VA?"

His question catches me off guard. Then it hits me. Of course—he's seeing her, too. "Yes. We've only had one session. No breakthroughs yet, I'm afraid. I guess I'm just doing what must be done to qualify for my benefits." I'm unable to read the expression that passes on Eli's face. *Pity?* Time to shift the focus. "Are you a patient of hers?"

He offers a slight grin. "Yes, ma'am, I am."

I consider probing a bit more, but I've had enough revelations for one night. I get the impression he feels the same way, too.

"It's getting late. We should probably get back."

I move to stand, but he remains seated for a moment longer.

"Lina, I don't think meeting you was an accident. I think this could be something mighty special. Lord willin', you feel it, too."

I let my fingers ruffle his blond hair. "We have an expression like that, too."

"Pardon?"

"Lord willing," I explain. "In Spanish, we say 'si Dios lo permite.' It means 'if the Lord permits or wills it.'"

He rises and begins to walk back. I am following alongside him when suddenly he stops and places his hand on my cheek and kisses me again, this time a little softer, a little gentler.

"I like the way you sound in Spanish," he says. "You barely have any trace of an accent in English. I was beginning to wonder if you didn't speak it at all. It's very sexy."

I poke him lightly in the arm. "Come on, gringo. We need to get back. Dolores has to be wondering what's taking us so long."

He reaches for the phone in his back pocket. "Lemme text her and let her know we're on our way." As he swipes the phone back to life, his expression darkens. "That's odd. It ain't like her to be so quiet-like."

My instincts prickle. "What do you mean?"

"Well, she ain't replied to my earlier text. Normally she says 'okay' or something."

Eli's tone makes me uneasy. I'm reminded of earlier, when I spotted Leonardo—I searched the room and couldn't find her.

"Can you call her instead of texting?" I pull out my cell phone to see whether she's reached out to me. Nothing.

He holds the phone to his ear, and together we listen to three unanswered rings before the prerecorded message comes on, instructing Eli to leave a voicemail.

"Come on," he says, grabbing my hand. "Dolores is probably on the dance floor and doesn't know we are trying to reach her."

I follow, wanting desperately to believe he is right. Maybe she is dancing, but the growing ache in my stomach indicates something bad. The last few months have taught me that I'm only a beat away from a life-changing disaster.

As we reach the back stairs, my breath is coming in short bursts.

We jog up and push through the back door. As we round the bend into the main space, the darkened room looks just as we left it. Colorful circles rotate on the wooden dance floor. The room is surprisingly full, especially on a weeknight. I can't help myself and look over, noticing Leonardo and his wife are no longer at the table where they sat earlier.

I scan the room for Dolores, but there is no sign of her.

Eli's expression meets mine. "What the hell?" he says.

At the same time, I announce, "She's gone."

# CHAPTER NINETEEN

Anita approaches us, panicked. "What is it? What's wrong?" she asks.

"Have you seen Dolores?" Eli and I ask in unison.

"Yes, she left. She told me to tell you she was leaving."

"What do you mean, she left?" I ask. "Why would she leave me here? Where did she go?"

Anita stares at me with a mild case of annoyance. "Dolores said I should ask Eli to drive you home because she had to leave. That's all I know."

"Why isn't she answering my calls or texts?" Eli asks. "Did she leave with anyone?"

Anita's bright-red fingernails rise to her hip as she shakes her head. "She was alone. But it seemed like she was in a rush. All she said was something came up and she had to leave right away. Then she asked me to tell you to take her cousin home."

I bite my lip before thinking out loud. "I don't like this. Something isn't right. I need to get home and let my family know Dolores has gone off on her own."

"You think that's a good idea?" Eli asks. "You sure you want to worry everyone before you get a chance to call her and figure out what's going on?"

"Yes," I say, my irritation growing. "This isn't South Carolina. It's not safe for a young girl like her to be out alone at night." I realize everything indicates I should be logical here. Dolores is fine, but I can't trust things to be "fine" when someone just disappears. If there's something I learned in service, it's that letting your guard down gets people killed.

"Okay," Eli says, squeezing my hand in assurance. "How 'bout I call Dolores one more time. Then I can take you home?"

"Be my guest, but we need to leave now. If you can't leave the bar, I'll ask my father to pick me up."

"Eli, I've got everything covered here," Anita interrupts. "Alvin's little cousins are fast learners. They can handle the floor. I'll take the bar, and the kitchen is closed now. Go ahead and take her home."

Eli rests a hand on Anita's arm. "Thanks, Anita. I'll go grab my keys."

As he walks away, I call Dolores again. It rings three times as my dread grows, but the sound of her voice fills me with relief.

"Buenas," she says.

"¡Dolores! ¡Bendito, qué susto! ¿Dónde estás?" I say, chastising her for scaring me.

"Ay, nena, estoy en la casa," she answers.

I'm confused. She's home?

"What are you doing at home? Why didn't you wait for me?"

"Aren't you with Eli?" She sounds like she's teasing. "I made sure that Anita asked him to bring you home . . . alone."

Was that what this was all about? She wanted to leave me alone with Eli?

"I sent him off in a panic to go get his car keys. I was worried!"

She sighs into the phone. "Prima, Papi called me because Teó had a bad dream. He was crying. They tried calling you, but the phone went directly to voicemail. I think you should change carriers for something with better service on the island. Anyway, I didn't know how far you and Eli were, and I knew you were finally getting to know each other. You need a little romance, Lina. So I handled it. I rushed home to Teó like you would want."

I'm equally overcome with frustration that I've failed my son—again—and appreciation that Dolores rushed home to him. I'm not sure which emotion to give in to. "Can you put Teó on the phone?"

"He's already sleeping, prima. I told him his mami was dancing and happy, and then I told him the story of Rosamada until he fell asleep."

"You sent him to bed with a story of a woman who marries the devil and dies? Are you serious?"

"Don't worry." Dolores giggles. "He was asleep before I got to that part."

She isn't getting it. I am not accustomed to relying on others. If Teó needed me, I should have been there. I should never have left him alone. Anger and frustration bubble up at the corners of my eyes. "I didn't save him, Dolores. I should have been there to save him!"

There's silence on the other end of the call as Eli approaches me with keys in hand. He stares at me curiously, probably wondering whom I'm talking to and why I'm yelling into the phone.

"Lina, what are you talking about?" Dolores asks quietly. "Teó doesn't need saving. He is sleeping."

I am confused and overwhelmed, mixing things up in my own head.

"You're right, I'm sorry. I'm on my way home. Eli is here now."

"Está bien, prima. We see you soon," Dolores replies, confused. "Relax, nena."

I want to throttle her through the unreliable wireless connection, even though I know she is right. I do need to relax.

"That was Dolores," I tell Eli. His features soften.

"She's all right?"

"Yes, she is at home with my son. He woke up from a nightmare, and my parents couldn't reach me—again—so they called Dolores. She did exactly what I would have hoped—she rushed home to him." I offer a sheepish smile. "And I nearly bit her head off for it."

He wraps his arm around my shoulders as he leads me toward the exit. "It don't matter that Dolores rushed home to take care of him. You're his mom. I'm sure you wish you'da been there yourself."

"Thank you for understanding," I mutter.

"Of course. Now let's get you home to your little boy. It sounds like you both could use each other's company."

I take a deep breath and suck in the calm Eli brings me. He is exactly right.

# CHAPTER TWENTY

The next morning I'm awoken in the sweetest of ways.

"Mamá! You're back!" Teó hops onto the sofa bed and presses his little body against mine, nuzzling his nose against my cheek.

Without his glasses, he looks even younger and more innocent.

"I missed you last night. I wanted you to read me a story for bed, but you were gone, and I felt scared . . . I thought maybe you weren't coming back."

I wrap my arms around his tiny body and pull him even tighter against me.

"Teó, why would you think something like that? Of course I would come back. I always come back to you."

"I know, Mamá, but my best friend Melvin at my old school said that sometimes when parents go away to the Army, they don't come back. They die in the war, just like his dad."

I suck in a breath, shocked. Could this be what Teó worried about while I was deployed?

"Teó, I'm not in the Army anymore. I don't have to go to war. I went to dinner with Dolores."

"Then why did Cousin Dolores come back without you?"

My son always gets straight to the heart of the matter. I worried him. I know better. Tourette's makes him prone to slipping into a fight-or-flight response from worry, a result of his heightened senses. I have to be more careful.

"I was still . . . um . . . having dinner," I lie. The truth about running into his father is out of the question. Leonardo made it abundantly clear he didn't want anything to do with our child. I won't allow him a chance to reject Teó face-to-face.

"Dolores was already finished, so she rushed here to be with you."

"I think Dolores might love me, Mamá."

I rest my chin atop his head. "I think you may be right. Dolores is family, and that's what family does. They look out for each other, and they love one another."

"I think I might love her, too. But only if that's okay with you."

"Yes, papito. It's okay with me." I kiss the top of his head. "It's why we came here. I want you to have a houseful of people you love. Now it's time to get ready for school, and don't think for a second I've forgotten about that iguana attack last week. Promise me you'll stay out of that tank, okay?"

He looks up at me solemnly and raises one hand, covering his heart with the other. "I promise to tell the truth, the whole truth, and nothing but the truth."

It's the second time he is swearing into mock court. I laugh, wondering what exactly he's been watching on YouTube.

"I have no doubt you will always tell me the truth, Teó. But I want you to promise me you won't bother that iguana again or any other wild animals you might find outside."

"I won't, Mamá. I promise."

"Your glasses are on the nightstand." I point to the small table next to his bed as he gets up to brush his teeth in the adjoining bathroom.

"How about you, Mamá? Do you promise?" Teó asks above the sound of the faucet.

"Do I promise what?"

"To always tell the truth. Abuelo says I have to watch out because girls can be mentirosas. He said that means liars."

I swallow the retort on my lips, shaking away the ridiculous notion. How could Papi say something like that to a little boy?

Although I'm not really surprised by his chauvinistic opinions. He's always said women cannot be trusted, that he picked Mami, even though his family considered her plain, because she was the first honorable woman he'd ever met outside the women in his own family. I worried bringing his grandson under the same roof could prove controversial. My son represents another "man" in the house for Papi to bond with. Teó fills an ache to replace the boy he lost at birth.

I've never been enough, and Papi made sure I never forgot it. Growing up, I was subject to constant comparison. He would say, *Lina, boys always eat all the food on their plate,* or *If your brother was still here, I bet he would eat all the beans.* When I called him from Florida to tell him I was joining the Army, he said, *Lina, the Army would have been a good choice for your brother if he was with us, but for you—I think it's a mistake. The Army isn't the place for women. They're too emotional.*

That last comment made me race to the recruiting station. I couldn't sign up fast enough.

Papi's values are still very old-fashioned, including the idea all women are mentirosas. I had worried he might try to impose his beliefs on my son. It's our first month here, and he's already proved me right.

"Teó, I'm your mamá. I will always tell you the truth." I'm not sure he can hear me over the sound of the running water.

When the words escape my lips, I think about seeing Leonardo the night before. I may not be able to make good on my promise. I have no intention of telling Teó about seeing his father last night or my agreement to meet him at Chiquitas later in the day.

Maybe Papi is right, after all. Girls are mentirosas, but at least in my case it's only when absolutely necessary. At least that's what I tell myself.

I dress Teó in his uniform and walk him to the bus stop. I don't pack him lunch because the cafeteria at his school offers amazing meals.

I've already learned about Teó's partiality to frappés, acai bowls, and sweet, creamy oatmeal on the morning menu. I wouldn't be surprised if he fills out after a few weeks on the island. Except everything he consumes, he burns. Boys are lucky that way.

When I reach our yard, Papi is sitting on the front porch beside Abuelo. He looks like the quintessential mascot for the jíbaro—a local farmworker. He sits, sipping coffee, dressed in a cream-colored guayabera and khaki pants, wearing the token pava on his head. He gives the mug of steaming café con leche a good slurp. It must be Abuela's famous brew. Abuelo has a similar mug in his hand as he sits in the other rocking chair, staring off into the distance.

Abuelo is singing. I smile when I recognize the chorus of the famous 1970s hit "Boranda," by La Sonora Ponceña.

Even in mental obscurity, Abuelo holds music in his heart. We all do.

"Buenos días, Papi." I wonder what he is still doing at home.

"Good morning, Lina. Did you have a good time last night? I was surprised you didn't make it back with your cousin."

I blush, which irritates me.

"I didn't realize you were home last night, Papi. I thought you'd be with the band at one of the clubs."

"No, we don't play on Mondays." He presses his lips against the side of the cup a little longer than usual, irritated, I think, that I didn't remember.

"What about today? Are you off from work today, too?"

He raises his right eyebrow, surprised by my inquisition. He isn't used to being the one questioned, especially by me.

"That's right. I am off on Tuesdays from fieldwork. It's the only day I have off, except on Sundays, when I work a partial shift every other weekend." The left eyebrow joins the right one, arched high in consternation. His lips pucker with sarcasm. "Is there anything else I can answer for you?"

I hate that he still has a way of making me feel like a twelve-year-old in trouble. "No, señor."

I start to walk past him into the house when he reaches out and grabs my arm. "You didn't answer my question, Lina."

I pull from his grasp, proud of the surprise that registers across his face. "What question?"

He exhales loudly, thoroughly annoyed. "Why weren't you with Dolores when she came home last night? It's not safe for you to be alone in the streets. You know that."

And yet Dolores—my much younger cousin—seems to come and go as she pleases without a second thought around here. I don't get it. I've been on my own for more than nine years. I'm not here to be judged or monitored by my parents. They lost that right when they sent me away to complete high school in Florida.

"I wasn't alone," I say, my voice rising. "I met someone, and he brought me home."

"You met someone? What does that mean—you 'met someone'? You just got here."

"It means I made a friend, Papi—that's it. He was in the Army, too. He owns Chiquitas, and we were talking, and he offered to drive me home."

It's frustrating how much I'm revealing and justifying myself. I'm a grown woman. This isn't any of his business. It's not like I brought Eli inside their house without discussing it with him first.

"If this was your brother, Lina, it would be different. It's different with boys."

*Here we go.*

"You're a young woman. The island isn't safe for you to be making friends with strange men that run bars."

"Papi," I huff, "I'm a soldier, por Dios. I'm trained to defend myself." *I'm trained to kill.*

I swallow the growing lump, unable to say anything more about the Army. Not what I saw . . . or what I did. Papi would be forever ashamed.

"I know, Lina. You were in the Army, and I'm very proud of you for joining the service."

A mixture between a laugh and a snort escapes me. "Proud?"

He rolls his eyes. I made my point.

"Maybe I disagreed with you joining the Army, but you did it anyway, and you became a nurse. That's admirable. But it's not like you were out there on the front lines, in combat, Lina."

That's what he thinks.

Every muscle in my body tightens. My mouth dries up. I don't know what's left to say. Is it better this way? What would he think of me if he knew the truth?

"I didn't become a nurse, Papi. The Army trained me to be a combat medic. It's like an EMT—the ambulance team in combat."

"La misma cosa," he says proudly. It's not the same thing, but he hates to be corrected.

"The man I met, the one who owns the bar, his name is Eli, and he is from South Carolina. He was also in the Army and recently got out, too. So, yes, we have a lot in common. I think he's very kind."

Papi leans back in the rocking chair and takes another drink from the mug. He removes the pava from his head and holds it to his chest. The wild fibrous edges nearly cover him.

He looks directly at me. I can't tell what he's thinking, but something very unfamiliar is happening. He's giving in.

"I don't want you to get hurt, mi niña." His voice is resigned. "You're my only daughter. I've already lost a child. Your mother and I . . ."

When he doesn't finish, I give him grace and step in. "I am a parent now, Papi. I understand. I won't take chances, I promise."

"Lina," he says, his voice gentler, "we will always worry about our kids and do whatever it takes to protect them. I know you can understand that. Especially because you're a mother now. Matteo only has you. Being careful and protecting yourself is the most important priority. No matter what you have to do, the price is never too high to get home to him safely."

His words pierce like bullets. Thinking of bullets reminds me of the little body falling to the ground. I think of Teó and my desperation to live. That's it. That's what I felt in that moment. I had to do whatever it took to get home to my son. But at what cost?

*My soul.*

"Sí, Papi."

I wipe the single tear streaming down my cheek. I grab the pava and put it back on his head, then lean over and give him a kiss. The spiky stubble smells like my first day of kindergarten and Sunday mornings beside him at church. It's not often I agree with Papi or his views, especially when they're so skewed to male superiority, but this morning his bold words make me think. I can see how much he's already bonded with Teó. His words about parents and their children carry wisdom. Is he right? Am I justified? I find that too hard to accept still.

At least when it comes to doing right by Teó, Papi and I are certainly on the same side.

I pull the black leather-bound journal from the bottom drawer and take a seat on the sofa bed. The smell of Teó's cologne still lingers in the room. I grab the T-shirt he slept in, still hanging over the armrest, and breathe it in. His scent calms me. I settle down to write.

> *October 2009*
> *4th Journal Entry*
> *Today Papi said the price is never too high to do what needs to be done to get home to Teó safely. I know he meant to do whatever I needed to protect myself here on the island, but couldn't the same be said about my actions overseas? I had to get home to my son.*

*But why did I have to be the one to pull the trigger? The Army's mission is clear: enemy combatants posing a threat must be taken out. But it isn't supposed to be the medic, the healer.*

*And he wasn't just the enemy. He wasn't a black silhouette on a white sheet of paper. He was someone's son, a man who'd just transitioned beyond childhood, who believed the lies of the selfish and sick bastards he trusted. What else could he do but what he was told when pushed out into the open that morning?*

*I think the question that plagues me is—why me?*

*I am a mother. My identity is defined by the woman Teó sees when he opens his eyes in the morning. How will that change if he discovers what I've done? Will he be comforted knowing I made it home? I am a healer. My identity has been shaped and defined by my dreams to help people, to care for them and use my calling to make them well. I don't want to be a murderer. I know what I signed up for when I joined the Army, but I guess I didn't really believe I'd ever find myself behind the trigger. I committed to serve in a different way, to help, to heal. Will I ever experience peace again? The scales of justice continue to haunt me. Someone else's life was the price for my own.*

*Is it always one for one?*

*Will I ever come to understand or accept that, for one morning in the desert, it was?*

# CHAPTER TWENTY-ONE

Dr. Robles will be pleased to know I've begun to write in the journal she gave me. I'm not sure I feel much better, but there is something cathartic about writing down the questions that haunt my daily life. In my heart of hearts, I try to find comfort in the truth: I didn't sign up to kill anyone. I signed up to save lives.

The irony is suffocating.

I wish I could say my actions were noble. I want to justify myself by believing I was motivated to protect all the men and women in that convoy. Obviously they factored into my decision, but there was a greater driving force—I needed to stay alive and return home to my son.

I finish applying my makeup and spray a light perfume on my neck. Perspective is exactly what I'm going to need with Leonardo today.

I'm not sure what to expect. What could he possibly want to discuss after all this time? I need to make sure Leonardo understands—Teó is the most important person in my life. I will not allow anyone to hurt him. We came here to focus on his medical care and lean on my family for support. We are starting over, moving forward, and trying to embrace our new life here. Leonardo was never a part of that plan. When I told him I was pregnant, he made it abundantly clear he didn't want anything to do with a child. Has he changed his mind? If so, is it only because he saw me? We've done just fine without Leo in our lives.

I don't see why any of that should change. If Teó wants to meet his father when he's an adult, it'll be up to him, but for now I won't risk Leo wanting to meet his son out of curiosity and then rejecting him in person. I won't let him hurt my little boy.

I need to make sure he gets the message loud and clear.

When I arrive, Anita and a young waiter I haven't met before are the only ones at Chiquitas. The lavender-scented Fabuloso used to mop smells just like my parents' living room.

"Eli isn't here yet," Anita says as I walk through the front entrance.

"That's okay," I tell her. "I'm here to meet someone . . . someone else. Mind if I take one of those tables out on the back balcony?"

"Be my guest." She waves her hand toward the outside seating area facing the ocean.

I don't think she likes me very much.

"Are you planning to eat something? Or only drinking?" Anita asks with her hand on one hip. Her lips pop into a sarcastic half smile, enhanced by the side-eye.

Now I know she doesn't like me very much. Has Eli said something to her about my drinking? Was she watching me that closely?

"I'll take a Cuba libre." Who is she to cast any stones? "In fact, make it a double."

"A su orden." *As you wish.*

"And Anita?" I call out, forcing her to turn around.

"¿Sí?"

"Can you direct my . . ." I'm stuck. What do I call him? "My guest to the table in the back?"

"Claro," she says curtly.

I select one of the square wooden tables overlooking the ocean. A Puerto Rican flag hangs over the edge of the railing. It looks as though it has been left there to dry. I wonder how Eli feels, living on an island where the US flag, the one he swore to give his life for, is rarely seen.

Does he miss the US flag with its fifty stars?

I'm not sure I do. The US now intermingles so much with my experience in the Army. However, the red and white stripes and the lone star against the bright-blue triangle of the Puerto Rican flag don't pull me in, either. She rejected me when I was just fifteen. She sent me away to "improve" myself, as though I didn't belong here. I sigh. I'm a woman without a country.

Still, I sense a distant gratitude to sit out here under the bright-blue skies with waves singing their lullabies at my feet. This land is so far from where I've been, so different from the dusty, barren streets of the Middle East. Now I'm here, surrounded by the beauty of my homeland. I get why they call her the Island of Enchantment, even though I'm still waiting for her to hug me first.

Puerto Rico is not only unique because of the multitude of colors, sprawling beaches, and crystal-clear waters—it's the inhabitants' open and generous hearts. Our culture stems from deep within, combining the Taínos' love of the land, the unwavering spirit of African slaves, and the adventurous, iron will of the Spaniards into one bloodline. These three different cultures have merged DNA, history, and legacy to create an entirely new populace. And although they've blended in other parts of the Caribbean, like Cuba and the Dominican Republic, there is an amalgamation here that's all its own.

A breeze passes along the back of my neck, and I can almost hear the island's whisper: *Somos puertorriqueños.*

"Cuba libre, doble." Anita places the double shot of rum and Coke with a splash of lime in front of me. The heavy pour of rum overpowers the traditional chocolate color of the soda. It's much lighter.

"Gracias."

"There's a young man outside who arrived all by himself. He pulled up in a red convertible and is parking the car. Maybe your . . . guest."

I can tell she's expecting I'll say more. I don't.

"Maybe."

She purses her lips, making her red freckles stand out sharply against her creamy white skin. "Do you want to order something to eat?"

I really don't. Despite a light breakfast of coffee and toast, I'm not hungry, but having food on the table will be a good distraction for this conversation. If Leonardo says something that makes me want to scream, I can always fill my mouth with food.

"Tostones rellenos de camarón."

The small dish of cup-shaped fried plantain, filled with fresh grilled shrimp, is the perfect size to pop into your mouth when you don't want to say anything further.

Anita nods and walks away, leaving me alone on the balcony. My solace is short lived. I can literally feel his stare pointed at my table.

This is it. This is the point of no return. I am here. Leonardo is here. Whatever he needs to say needs to be said now. I want to clarify his intentions and make sure he isn't planning on popping up to see Teó, because I don't plan on ever seeing him again.

"Hola, Catalina." Leonardo walks over to the table and leans down to kiss my cheek.

His scent is the same. It takes me back to 1999. How can a man still smell exactly the same after ten years?

That scent releases a series of images in my mind. Leonardo is kissing me, pulling at my buttons. He's naked. I'm embarrassed, insecure, unsure, but he seems so . . . confident . . .

I remember the pregnancy test—the light-pink, blurry plus sign.

When I discovered I was pregnant, it took me two weeks to work up the courage to tell Tía Kika and Mami. Tía, in her usual practical sense, shrugged and said: *At least the baby will be born right before graduation. You're an adult and will have a high school diploma. No one can ever take that away from you.* Mami's response was starkly different, more along the lines of: *Ay, bendito, Catalina. This news changes everything.* Then she sighed and exhaled loudly while I braced myself for exactly what I knew was coming: *If only things went as they were supposed to go.*

I was alone when I found out I was pregnant. I walked in circles outside for hours, trying to decide what to do. Who would help me?

My savior turned out to be my son, born a little less than nine months later.

All this comes back with the brief inhale of Leo's body chemistry. My son. Our son. I remind myself of his abandonment—forcing Teó to live fatherless. I hate him for it, but a part of me is thankful because I didn't have to share our beautiful boy. Teó has been all mine. Now it's too late. I won't let him go. I won't share.

I reach over and take a long sip of the rum and Coke. The burn of alcohol and carbonation fills my throat, forcing me to swallow. The buzz is my security blanket. I need the buzz. I can't do this on my own. One thing I remember about Leonardo is how convincing he could be.

"Siéntate," I tell him, attempting to assert my authority. I point to the seat.

"Gracias," he says, his voice shaky, and for the first time I notice he looks nervous, too. "Hace mucho tiempo—" he begins, but I cut him off.

"Why don't we have this conversation in English?" I want him out of his comfort zone. I need the upper hand here, and I don't know how else to get it. "You do still remember how to speak English, right?"

It's harsher than I mean for it to sound. My defenses are in complete control, but I won't apologize. It has been ten years. Leonardo abandoned me. He abandoned Teó. I can't forget that—I won't.

"You are still angry," he says. "That's okay. You have every right."

I open my mouth to respond, but Anita comes back, interrupting me with two glasses of water.

"¿Algo para tomar?" she asks, requesting his drink order.

"Una Medalla," he replies, ordering a beer.

She looks at me pointedly. "¿Otra?"

She watches me finish the remnants of the one in front of me.

"Sí, por favor," I say, refusing to be ashamed. Given the circumstances, this is one time I'm entitled.

She generously graces me with another sarcastic expression before spinning on her heel and heading back toward the bar.

Leonardo places the silverware perpendicular to his glassware and moves my water glass to rest directly across from his in perfect alignment.

"Why did you ask me to meet you here?" My question sounds like the first shot fired.

His expression tightens. "I am ashamed so much time has passed and we never . . . you know . . . connected, especially after . . ." He clears his throat. "The pregnancy."

I raise my eyebrow in disdain. "You mean after I gave birth to our son."

This time his eyebrows rise in shock. He swallows deeply. The bump in his throat ripples like a wave. "What? What are you talking about? I have a son?"

I'm confused by his question. I never thought he would doubt Teó's paternity. When Teó was born, he had a headful of dark-brown curly hair and a large birthmark smeared like a swipe of dirt across the right side of his chest. The birthmarks are lovingly referred to as a mancha de plátano—a plantain stain. Leonardo has the same one.

"Of course you have a son. The birthmark on his chest—it's exactly like yours. I told you via email I was going to have the baby. Don't you remember? Your response was pretty short, but surely you don't forget something like that."

He shakes his head, completely at a loss. "Lina, I have no idea what you're talking about. I never saw an email."

Now I'm shaking my head, too. I'd laugh at how silly we must look if this weren't so serious. None of this makes sense. "Leo, I received a response from you!" I say, my voice rising. "It was your email address, replying to my message. It said, 'I'm sorry, but I won't be a part of this.' And that was it."

His expression darkens, unwilling to believe me. He stares in my direction, searching across the memories, his mind somewhere else.

I am telling him the truth. How can he not remember?

Then I see it. He knows. He remembers, and I am relieved the innocent act is over.

"Ziomara," he says.

"What? Who is that?"

He lowers his head, ashamed. "Lina, I wasn't completely free when I went to Florida that summer. I had somebody back here—a girlfriend. When I left, we agreed to take a break, but she was already pregnant." He takes a large drink of water. "I should have told you."

"I already know about her, Leo." I lean back and cross my arms over my chest. "Your uncle in Florida told me about her." Puerto Rico is like a small town. There are no secrets. "But what does she have to do with you abandoning our son?"

"She must have accessed my email. It was her. It has to be. She was the one who responded to you—not me. She must have deleted your email, because I never saw it. I never saw your response after I told you to . . . um . . ." He clears his throat again. This conversation is making him uncomfortable. "To . . . well, you know . . . consider your options. I assumed you didn't go through with the pregnancy. Especially because I never heard from you again."

I gulp the last of my drink and sit back thoughtfully. Leonardo never knew about Teó. His next revelation nearly knocks me out of my chair.

"And your family never said anything about you having a baby."

"My family?" Now he isn't making any sense at all. "What do you mean? What are you talking about?"

"My . . . uh . . . wife"—he nearly whispers the last word—"Ziomara. She has a little sister, Gina. Gina is the same age as your cousin Dolores. One day, almost two years after I returned from Florida, Dolores was at Ziomara's house with Gina. She mentioned her cousin Lina in Florida, living with her tía. She said her cousin was joining the US Army. I knew it might be a coincidence, but when I asked her tía's name, she said Kika. That's when I knew Dolores was talking about you. I asked what you were up to and why you were joining the Army, but something about me must have scared her, because she wouldn't say another word."

My lips purse with concentration as he recounts what happened next.

"I needed to know, Lina. I needed to find out if you had the baby, so I followed Dolores after school one day. Gina told me where I could find her. I'm sure I scared her, because she wouldn't say anything about you. Dolores told me to speak to your parents directly. Then she gave me their address."

He pauses to take another drink of water.

Anita returns at the same time with his beer, my second Cuba libre, and the tray with the appetizer I ordered earlier.

Leonardo looks relieved and takes a large gulp from the icy-cold bottle. Anita looks ready to take our lunch order, but seeing the expression on our faces, she walks away quietly to give us privacy.

The unraveling of everything I believed to be true is giving me an out-of-body experience. I hear Leo and I see him, but I don't feel like it's really me sitting across the table, taking it all in.

"I can't believe I have a son," he says. "What is his name?"

"Finish the story," I say. "What happened after Dolores gave you the address?"

"I'm sorry," he says, "of course. Armed with an address, I went to speak with your parents, but didn't tell Ziomara I was going. They were quite surprised when I showed up one evening. I introduced myself as your friend from Florida. When your father didn't make the connection, there was no other choice. Risking my safety, I told him I was the one who got you pregnant in the summer of 1999 and wanted to know if you had the baby. I thought he might kill me right there and then while I stood at his front door. It had been two years, but your papi was obviously still furious about the whole thing. I told them I knew you were joining the Army, and if you had the baby, I had every right to know about my child—"

"But I don't understand," I interrupt. "Didn't they tell you about your son?"

He takes another drink from his beer, and this time he looks upset. If what he is saying is true, I don't blame him.

"They told me you never had the baby. They didn't go into details about what happened. I assumed you decided to . . . you know . . ."

I nod. I know. I'm disgusted that he naturally would assume this, because not only had his girlfriend—or, uh, wife—intervened, but it was sounding like my family had, too.

Leo wads up the napkin, hugging the beer in his fist, and squeezes it until his fingers turn white. When he speaks again, he doesn't look at me. He looks far off into the distance, obviously reliving every last detail of that moment. "They said you put me and the whole experience behind you, and I needed to move on and stay far away from you and them."

I'm at a loss. I don't know what to say. One look at Leonardo and it is obvious he is Teó's father. The similarities in their features are striking. The one big difference is Teó's blue eyes, and we all knew those came from my side. I'm still shaken by how similar Teó and Leo look. Sitting across from a practical stranger who looks so much like the boy I love is odd. My son and everything about him connects us, whether I like it or not. My parents must have seen it, too. They had enough pictures of Teó to easily see the similarities. Why did they lie to Leo? Were they trying to protect me? Protect Teó?

"So my father told you I didn't have the baby? Was he alone when you arrived at his house?"

His face looks curious as he thinks back, but the memory unveils itself slowly. He takes another drink of his beer. "No, Lina. It wasn't your father who said it. In fact, he seemed confused by what I was being told. I didn't think much of it then, but remembering it now, I don't think he planned to lie to me."

"So who told you? Who said I never had the baby?"

He leans back and looks up toward the sky, equally as perplexed as I am. "It was your tía Lisandra."

# CHAPTER TWENTY-TWO

I pop the plantain cup, filled to the brim with shrimp, into my mouth. I may have miscalculated the actual size, because my entire mouth fills with food. I quickly discover I can't possibly chew it all with my lips closed. This is awkward. I take a sip of ice water, hoping it will help me get it down, but it's no use.

My cheeks puff out like a chipmunk's as alarm streams from my eyes like some lunatic while Leonardo stares at me, trying not to look too concerned, but it isn't working. I don't think he knows what else to say. If he attempts to say anything even remotely requiring a response, I'm in no condition to offer one.

He reaches down, picks up a plantain cup of his own, and takes a small bite.

I'm being guided on table manners.

I force down the first swallow and consider what he said. *My tía Lisandra.* I can't believe she lied to him. Why would she do that? How could she not tell me? Why didn't anyone else say anything? I could sense the layers of secrets among my family, but I never thought those secrets would have anything to do with me.

It's pretty naive now that I think about it.

These lies directly impacted my son's life, which only pisses me off more.

The indignation fuels me to swallow the rest of my food, and albeit embarrassed, at least I am free to speak again.

Leo looks up at me. "What is his name?"

The raw sincerity in his voice breaks me. For him, this is the same moment Teó was swaddled and placed in my arms. This is his moment to cherish the truth that he is a father.

I hadn't thought of any names for a boy. I was sure I was having a little girl and chose Natalia, which means "gift from God." We put a lot of thought into names here. My son's name needed to have meaning.

After giving birth, I lay in my hospital bed, holding my new baby. The staff could sense my increasing distress, staring at his round, red, nameless face. Thankfully, Tía Kika came to the rescue. She knew I saw this child as a gift from God and wanted the baby's name to reflect the sentiment.

"Matteo," she told everyone in a voice that left no doubt. "Matteo Salvador. It means *gift of God*, and *Salvador* means *savior* because this boy will save his mother in ways she does not yet know."

The sound of his name was perfect as it exited her lips. The matter settled.

"Matteo Salvador," I say now. My chest swells with pride.

"Gift of God."

I'm taken aback that he knows the meaning.

"It's a good name."

"I call him Teó." My voice sounds wistful.

"Teó," he repeats, tasting the name for himself. "Tell me about him."

As I open my mouth to speak, Anita's head pops out of the back entrance. Leo's beer is still half-full. I reach down and raise my water glass and shake my head. No more drinking, not through this conversation. She nods back at me and disappears.

"He is perfect," I begin. "I know all mothers say that about their children, but Teó is special. His IQ is much higher than the average person, and he loves science. I think he is Bill Nye's number one fan."

"Who?" Leonardo looks confused. Bill Nye may not be as famous here as he is in the States.

"He had a TV show in the nineties for kids about science. Teó watches the reruns on YouTube all the time." My voice is filled with joy. "He's also obsessed with Buddy Holly."

Again, Leonardo looks confused.

"You know Buddy Holly," I tease. "The guy with the glasses and the tuxedo from the 1950s. The artist who plays the guitar. Come on, 'Peggy Sue, Peggy Sue.'" I sing the last part with the same rhythm as the song.

He remembers. "¡O, sí! Buddy Holly . . ."

"Teó has matching eyeglasses. You know, the thick, black, horn-rimmed glasses. He loves them."

"So he needs glasses? I never needed glasses," Leo muses.

"He also has the same birthmark as you across his chest. Teó's is on the right side," I say protectively.

"Lina, I didn't mean—"

"It's fine," I cut him off. "I would understand if you had doubts."

"No." He shakes his head. "I don't have any doubts."

He is tapping his finger in a type of rhythmic beat. He follows my gaze to his hand and stops but reorganizes the plate and cutlery in front of him.

I've done enough research to recognize potential symptoms, especially in adulthood. Teó's birthmark may not be the only thing he got from his father. This obvious possibility, one I've never considered before, spreads inside me. All this time . . . How could I have never taken this link into account?

I have to tell him.

"There is something else," I say. I'm unsure how to talk about this in a way that he understands—I am not ashamed of my son, and neither of us needs to feel pity for him.

I take another drink of water and lean forward, needing to be a little closer. I need Leonardo to listen without judgment.

"Teó has a condition that makes life a little harder for him than for other children to focus and learn. It's what makes him remarkable and resilient."

Leo remains quiet, allowing me to continue.

"He's been diagnosed with Tourette's syndrome."

"I don't understand," he says, shaking his head. "What is that? Is he okay?"

Leonardo sounds like a father. My eyes well with tears of lost opportunities. For the first time in nine years, I am sharing the hardship of my son's diagnosis with the only other person who can even begin to understand how I feel, how I felt when I discovered Teó had a condition that would affect his ability to live a normal life.

I nod.

"Our son is okay. He is more than okay. He is perfect . . . but he has these tics. He can't help them, and it's not good for him to try and force them to stop. He blinks repeatedly, and he sniffs like this." I mimic one of Teó's sniffs. "Sometimes, when he's under a lot of stress, his chin juts up like this." I illustrate the movement. "Children with this condition often struggle with attention deficit, but not Teó. He is a straight-A student. He loves school, especially math and science. The doctors say he will likely grow out of his tics when he becomes an adult. Still, as he grows up, his condition could evolve into behavioral conditions like obsessive-compulsive disorder. He is already showing potential symptoms, like being very particular about how I organize things and insisting on eating his food in a particular pattern. I explained this all to the directora at his school. So she knows they need to try and accommodate him as best they can."

I'm rambling, but I'm stopped by the tear that slides down Leo's cheek. I reach my hand across the table and place it on top of his.

"It's okay, Leo. He is okay."

He shakes his head. "No, Lina. You don't understand. This is my fault. He got this condition from me."

His words stop me. My hand stays frozen on his.

"What do you mean?" I ask quietly, certain I already know the answer.

"I—I," he begins, tapping his foot frantically on the ground. "I had the same problems as a child. The blinking . . . and my neck . . . parecía torcido de un lado al otro."

He moves his neck from one side to the other, showing me the uncontrolled head jerking he suffered as a child.

"My son . . . ," he says, dropping his head against his chest. Another tear spills onto our joined hands.

I can't move. I want to stand up and comfort Leonardo, but the weight of his revelation is pounding through me. By the time he and I met, he would have likely begun to outgrow the tics. I lean back to look at him and then remember the blinking. *Oh my God.* I had forgotten. When Leo and I first met, he was still blinking—like Teó. I swallow hard. How did I not remember this?

But I know the answer to that.

All this time I needed to believe it was me. Teó's condition needed to be my fault.

He was diagnosed right before I left on deployment. I knew the condition could be hereditary—the scientific journals are clear about this—but I refused to believe it.

Teó inherited the gene from his father.

Realization rolls over me. I stand and walk over to Leonardo. He stands, too, and we embrace.

His arms wrap around my back as my arms grip around his waist. He holds me tightly while I rest my head on his chest. He brings his head down to rest on mine. There is only sorrow between us, a mixture of abandonment, lies, and our child's condition.

What began with two young kids away from home—away from their island, giving in to their impulses—evolved into a little boy's life. And that little boy changed my entire world for the better. Through tragedy arose a gift.

I hug Leonardo, thanking him for the precious gift of my son but also grieving for the challenges Teó must still overcome. I hug him apologetically for believing the worst of him for the last nine years. I'm surprised at how easily I assumed he abandoned me and his son, and I'm filled with indignation at his wife's selfishness. I try to swallow the rage pounding in my chest, wondering what is going through his mind and whether he is angry, too.

When we finally release our embrace, he takes hold of my hands and stares at them, intertwined with his.

His chin rises. There's more.

"Lina, I have a daughter. Her name is Fiona. Her mother, my wife, Ziomara, was already pregnant when I spent that summer in Florida. We were not together at the time, but she was pregnant with my child. I'm not proud of what I did. Fui infiel." *I was unfaithful.* "I've carried that shame for a long time. It's a big part of why I rushed to get married when I returned. Not that I regret it," he says quickly.

I'm not sure I believe him.

"All this time, I believed you ended the pregnancy. I had a feeling it was a boy. I've lived the last ten years believing my son was gone, and I deserved every bit of the loss in my heart afterward. It was God's punishment for not being faithful to Ziomara. But now I know he is alive! And he is here on the island."

He lets go of my hands and grips my waist, lifting me off my feet and spinning me around. "God has not punished me. He has blessed me. ¡Qué bendición!"

As he puts me down, I know what is coming next.

"When can I meet my son, Lina?"

There it is.

Truth is, I haven't decided he can. I don't know if I'm ready for that. I don't know if Teó is prepared. I need a minute. I need to think through this and weigh out the options to make sure I choose what's best for Teó. But before I can answer, he grips my face, pleading directly into my eyes.

"Please, Lina."

I have started to respond when the sound of someone behind us catches us both off guard. Leonardo drops his hands from my face. We both look over toward the entrance.

"Howdy," Eli says, waving awkwardly. "I was fixin' to head to my office when Anita mentioned you were back here. She probably shoulda mentioned you weren't alone, so . . . yeah . . . I'll just be on my way. You two lemme know if you need anything at all."

"Eli, wait," I say, stepping away from Leonardo and reaching for my purse, but when I turn back, Eli is already gone.

# CHAPTER TWENTY-THREE

"Lina, we need to discuss this," Leonardo says, grabbing my arm when I attempt to follow Eli.

"I need some time," I tell him. "Let me think about this. I need to do what's best for Teó."

"He has family, Lina. He has a sister. A father. Don't do this."

I turn around and face him square on. "I'm not doing anything, Leo. But don't push me. I'm asking you for a little bit of time."

"You've had nine years with him," he says quietly.

He opens the gate to the anger I'd been holding back. "¿En serio?" Why is he pushing so hard and so soon? He isn't considering Teó in this at all, only what *he* wants.

"I'm sorry." He realizes he is losing. "I know I'm pushing. It's that . . . he . . . he is family. Family is everything."

"Yes, I agree. And right now, *I* am his family. He doesn't know anything about you."

That one stings.

"I'm sorry," I say, regretting my harshness. "Look, this is a lot. A little time isn't asking much. I will call you. We can talk about how and *when* you can meet Teó."

I hand him my cell phone, and he punches in his phone number.

"Thank you." He gives me another hug. "Please don't wait too long. I need to meet my son."

"I know. I will call you soon."

When we walk back into Chiquitas's main dining area, I glance back toward the kitchen. I need to clear things up with Eli before I leave.

"Take care, Leo." My voice carries a promise. He hears it.

"Cuídate."

I thrust my chin toward the front entrance, and Leo takes the hint. He looks so nervous, glancing back at me as he walks out. I think he fears I may take Teó and run as soon as he leaves my side. Part of me wishes to do exactly that, keep my son all to myself. But I can't. I won't.

My family lied to him, to both of us. Why would they do that? How could they think keeping a man from his child was the right thing? All this time they lied to me, to Teó. I'm furious for me, remembering the heaviness of the betrayal, the knife of Leo's rejection once again plunged into my heart. My family could have rectified it all . . . just by being honest. What the hell? I seethe at the confrontation that awaits them, but before I go, I need to make things right with Eli. I know how it must have looked. I'm sure he recognized Leonardo from last night.

The place is still empty. It doesn't look like much of a lunch crowd until I notice what time it is. That crowd has already dispersed.

I make my way to the kitchen door, knocking lightly to be polite, even though I know I'm going in no matter what. Anita is washing dishes at a large stainless-steel sink, and it looks like she is about to usher me right back through the door, but then thinks better of it. She gestures with a nod toward the back of the room.

Two men dicing vegetables stare at me strangely as I pass them and walk to the wooden door in the center of the back wall.

This time I don't knock. I don't have time. Teó will finish school soon, and I want to confront my parents before he gets home. My aunt lied, but my parents were there. They could have made this right. They didn't. Instead, they held her lies and remained silent. What about my grandparents? Abuelo is the only one with an excuse, but Abuela kept this secret, too. She doesn't even like Tía Lisandra. Doesn't anyone in this family care about honesty?

I let out a huff as I walk through the door.

Eli sits at a small desk, a series of spreadsheets open on his computer. He types deftly with one hand. His left arm remains eerily still at his side. I should be used to this already, but I'm not. Anytime he's tackling daily life as though he isn't missing half his arm, I want to hug him and cry simultaneously.

"Hi, Eli," I say softly. "Listen, what you saw back there, it's not what you probably thought it was."

He spins around in his seat, genuinely surprised, but the smirk on his face relays his amusement.

"I have a mind to give you an application, Catalina, waltzing in here all full of fire. This area is restricted to employees only."

He winks at me, but I know better. I'm learning Eli uses humor as a defense mechanism. He hides all the tougher feelings, his discomfort, fears, among other things, behind that beautiful smile.

*Not today, Eli.*

"Please. You're going to pretend you didn't care at all about what you think you saw. Don't give me that, embustero."

"Lina, I'm not exactly sure what you called me, but it sounded sexy as hell."

"Is that so?" I bring my hand up to my hip. "Because I called you a liar."

"Well, bless your heart," he says, bringing his hand to his chest. "I don't know what all you're worked up about. Who you have lunch with is none of my business, even if it is inside my restaurant."

"Okay, have it your way." I really don't have time for silly games. I grab the doorknob, prepared to let myself out. "Well then, I'd best be going, Elijah." I say this last part in a sarcastic southern drawl.

A flash of insult pricks the edges of Eli's eyes, and I immediately regret it. I went too far.

"I'm sorry. I'm being a jerk. Today I found out some things I believed to be true were not, and now I have got to get home and figure out why my family has been lying to me for the last seven-plus years."

His expression softens as he rises from the chair. "Shucks, Lina, I'm the one being a jerk. I was enjoying getting a rise outa ya, but I took it too far. I have a bad habit of doin' that. No harm, okay? Still friends?"

He put out his hand as though we are to shake on it.

I take Eli's outstretched hand in mine and squeeze it, relieved the misunderstanding is over. "Yes, still friends, but I really need to go."

"I understand," he replies. "Now listen, Alvin is coming back this weekend. He can keep an eye on things while I take a night off. How about you let me surprise you with dinner next week?"

My first inclination is to reject his offer. After everything I've recently learned, my circumstances are beginning to stress me out. It's not a good time for me to start dating. I shake my head. "I don't think—"

"Come on, no pressure. How about this? Let me take you and your son somewhere I think he will love. It's a public place, and there will be lots of other people there. I'll make sure you two have a great time. Scout's honor." He holds up three fingers.

"You were a Boy Scout, too?" I roll my eyes.

"Eagle Scout," he says proudly.

"Of course you were."

It's thoughtful to include Teó. I can do that. At least I think I can. "Okay, next week, the following Saturday. What time?"

"I can pick you both up at four."

"Let's meet here."

"Deal, at four. And Lina?"

"¿Sí?"

"Go easy on the family. I'm sure if they lied, they had their reasons. Hear 'em out before you go all . . . you know . . . Puerto Rican on 'em."

I smile, reaching for the door. "I'll try, Eli. But no promises."

"Fair enough," he says. "I'll see ya soon."

This time when I arrive home, my grandparents are together on the front porch. Abuelo is in his usual spot, sitting quietly in the rocking chair. Abuela is sweeping the patio floor beside him. He glances in her direction, and I see a moment of lucidity as I march up the pathway. He looks over at me, then returns to stare straight ahead, gone again.

I wonder whether he ever feels trapped in a mind intent on dragging him into senility—a mind full of secrets we know nothing about. The older generations are not known to spill their stories or the secrets held within them, especially when it comes to the happenings of the family.

Now I'm faced with the reality of how deep the secrets they keep really are. Seven years ago, Leonardo showed up at this doorstep. He deserved to know the truth. Tía Lisandra thought otherwise, and my family apparently agreed. She interjected herself intimately, without hesitation, into my personal situation, setting off a ripple effect of consequences for me and my son, and no one did a damn thing to stop it. My hands tremble at the adrenaline coursing through them, ignited by the deepest kind of betrayal. I can feel my skin warm from the rise of the pressure inside me, pumping blood from a broken heart. I trusted them.

"Bendición," I say out of habit, not because I really want anyone's blessing. Mami steps out to greet me at the door.

"Que Dios te bendiga," Abuela answers, eyeing me suspiciously. She senses the hostility I've armed myself with on the way here.

"Mami," I say breathlessly, zoning in on her. She drops her arms from an intended embrace. "Tenemos que hablar." *We need to talk.*

Language is irrelevant. That expression never precludes anything positive.

Abuela looks from her daughter to me, leaning the broom against the wall. The bristles are made from a large cluster of heavily overgrown weeds. They are wrapped to the wooden handle with twine. She follows my eyes over to it but shrugs as though there is nothing out of the ordinary about using a cluster of thick weeds to sweep the concrete floor. Still pretending to ignore my ire, she pulls the garden hose coiled in the corner and turns on the spigot to wash the dust from the concrete floor. Abuelo automatically lifts his feet into the air.

Mami reaches out her hand. "Let's go inside."

I follow her into the small living room.

"What's wrong?" she asks, turning to face me.

I don't answer, trying one last time to justify their decisions in my freight train of thoughts. It's impossible.

She tries again. "¿Qué te pasa?"

I don't answer.

Mami moves closer as Abuela enters the room, wiping her wet hands on her apron. The door closes behind her, but she stops, assessing us from the entrance.

"What is it, Lina?" Abuela asks, innocently observing the standoff.

This only angers me more. My hands continue to shake with indignation but also with fear. I've never confronted any of them about anything like this before.

I begin with Mami. "How could you do it? You all lied to me. Tía Lisandra stood in this house and lied to Leonardo, and everyone protected her." I'm shouting the last few words. "¿Por qué? Why did she lie to him?"

Mami's eyes widen with awareness. She rushes forward and tries to put her arms around me. "Lina, you don't understand."

I pull away forcefully, ignoring her gasp. I need to know the truth. I need to understand.

"Lina, cálmate," Abuela says, the warning sizzling in her tone.

"I will not calm down," I say, an equal warning in mine. I turn back. "Tell me, right now. Why?"

Mami's chin rises indignantly, but I see the tremble. I open my mouth to speak again, but she raises her hand to stop me.

"Tía Lisandra did it to protect you. Papi agreed. It was not our place to go against him." Her voice rises. "That boy disrespected you.

He began something with you despite knowing he had a partner here in Puerto Rico. He is shameless, abandoning you without a second thought. He's lucky Papi didn't kill him. Your tía's actions gave Papi an alternative. By lying to him about the pregnancy, she spared him your father's wrath. And if we had the chance to do it again, we would do the same thing. Your tía was right. You needed a clean break to pursue your future."

There is truth in her words. But the response to Leonardo's actions was wrong. My family let him think I never had a child. What about Teó? Did anyone stop to think about the impact on my son? The one who believes he doesn't even have a dad? Leonardo seemed genuinely distraught at the years lost between them. He is desperate to meet Teó. This was a decision taken from me—made *for* me. My family didn't trust me enough to believe I would do what was best. That is unacceptable.

"You all had no right!"

"Lina, please," Mami pleads. "Calm down."

She turns to Abuela. "Mami, please give us a moment to speak privately."

"No," I shout. "There's nothing to discuss. Tía Lisandra had no right, and you all just allowed it to happen." I raise my finger and point at the tiny woman at the front door. "Abuela, don't you understand? You all made a life-altering decision without even discussing it with me. And then kept it a secret."

They both look confused. The flood of English words pours out too fast for them to understand everything I'm saying. I can't help it; after so many years in the US, my rage exits in English—my new default, distancing me from these two women even more.

But Abuela doesn't need to understand the literal translation of each word. She understands enough. She shouts back in Spanish, "For you, Lina. You still don't understand? You were going to the military. You were rising above your circumstances. That's what was most important. We made sure you moved forward, and no one, I mean no one, would hold you back. We did it for you."

I shake my head at her justification. "Qué barbaridad," I say, my expression of despondency exiting in my native tongue. Funny how *that* emotion still materializes itself in Spanish.

Maybe a part of me was hoping there was a better reason, something they knew about Leonardo that made it detrimental for him to know about his son. But there was no such thing. They did what they thought was best. They made a life-altering decision for me because they believed it was the best option. I didn't need to be consulted or even made aware. They knew best, Teó and I be damned. The realization settles into my stomach like spoiled food.

What if they hadn't intervened? Would it have changed things?

The timing of Leo's visit to my parents' house seems to have coincided with my leaving for the Army. Had I known, it might have changed something. Maybe I wouldn't have left for basic training. Maybe I wouldn't have been on the convoy that morning.

My family made a choice about my life, believing they were doing what was best, but what did it really cost me? What has it cost Teó?

"No tenían ningún derecho." *You had no right.*

Abuela crosses to where I'm standing in three steps and raises her hand, poised to slap me. I brace myself, but Mami jumps between us both before she can.

"Mami, no," she yells at Abuela. "Por favor."

Anger and indignation fire brightly in our eyes as we face off, a mirror image—grandmother and granddaughter—one and the same. For the first time I see my grandmother's individuality. She is molded by the ferocity of her convictions, the fighting spirit I recognize deeply within my own soul. I don't like where it has led her, or that she's justified her convictions by intervening in my life and keeping this secret. I don't know how I will get past it . . . but I'd be lying if I said I didn't understand it.

# CHAPTER TWENTY-FOUR

Papi's voice booms from the entryway. "¿Qué está pasando aquí?"

Abuela brings her assailing hand down and smooths down the front of her light cotton dress, swiping back the slicked gray hair from the crown of her forehead to the bun at the nape of her neck. In the flash of a second, she is the epitome of control.

"Nothing," she says, a master of deflection.

He walks in and watches her apprehensively, then looks over at Mami, who is already ushering me out the door.

I open my mouth to hurl another round of accusations at Papi, but Mami grabs my arm. I can't remember a single moment in my life when she's ever put a hand on me. The gesture leaves me speechless and limp. Obligingly, I allow her to pull me through the front door.

"We are to go pick up Teó on the bus," she tells him.

"We *are going* to pick up Teó from the school bus," he corrects.

She waves her hand at him offhandedly, then says, "Sí, sí," and closes the door behind us.

We walk to the car in silence, keeping it until we pass the colmado. I idle across from the bus stop. Anxious parents are parked along the street as they await their children's arrival. I pull in behind a black Maserati but leave the car running. The air-conditioning—a must.

No more silence.

"Mami, how could you all lie to me? To Teó? All this time? Why didn't you ever tell me about Leonardo?"

She doesn't look at me. Her lips move, but no sound escapes. She looks down at her wringing hands, trying to speak, but remaining speechless. I've seen her like this only once—the night before I went to live with Tía Kika in Florida. Papi had insisted it was for the best, that my whole future depended on me leaving and jumping on the opportunities in the US. I still don't know if Mami fully agreed. She was the only one who actually looked pained about sending me away. Then, like now, her mouth moved, her features twitched, but she remained silent and obliging, allowing Papi to make the decisions for us all, even when it meant giving her daughter away four years too soon.

"Mami," I urge.

"Lo siento," she says, her voice barely above a whisper. I'm sorry. "Your tía had her reasons. Papi and Abuela both convinced me she did the right thing," she says in Spanish. "You aren't the only warrior in the family, Lina. Your blood, your strength—it all comes directly from her."

She turns away from me, but there's more. I know there is more.

"What does that mean, Mami? What aren't you telling me?"

She bites her lower lip and wipes the tears spilling from her eyes.

"Lina, Abuela wanted to join the Army when she was young. Her family did not support this idea, even though she dreamed of traveling the world as a nurse in the military. She wanted to help the people recovering after the Second World War. She went to meet the recruiter by herself, in secret, and signed the papers."

"She wanted to join the Army?" I never knew this.

"Yes, she was only a few days from leaving when she found out she was pregnant with me. She was not married. The Army would not accept her in her condition. They told her to go home and take care of her baby. She had no other choice. She gave up her dream."

I'm speechless.

Mami reaches across the console for my hand and rubs my palm with her thumb.

"When Abuelo discovered the pregnancy, he knew he must do the right thing and married Abuela immediately. They never told anyone she was pregnant before they married. It would have disgraced her. I never knew about any of this until she finally told me on the night before my quinceañera. Fifteen years later and the pain of your abuela's sacrifice was still pounding through her. That night she said I was becoming a woman, and it was time to tell me the truth. She urged me to protect myself, to watch out for the boys, and not fall in love. Follow your dreams," Mami says wistfully. "I didn't know how to tell her my dream was to become a mother and raise a family here in my home. I was a disappointment."

Mami raises her hand to my cheek, caressing it gently. "I am living my dream, but she still doesn't understand why I didn't want to do more, like she did."

I grab her hand and bring it down, away from my face. I'm not ready to forgive. Neither of us says a word. I can't believe no one ever told me about Abuela's military dreams. Instead, they allowed Papi to make me feel like an outcast about pursuing something meant for men. Abuela could have been my strongest ally, and yet she admired my service in secret. Why?

My family's tendency toward secrets continues to reiterate how different my approach will be with Teó. I won't lie to him. Although the thought reminds me of Leo, and I realize that I need to tell Teó about his father sooner rather than later.

Mami must sense the distance in my demeanor and the frustration bubbling inside me, because she lets out a sigh before continuing.

"When Leonardo came to the house, we all saw the risks, especially your abuela. She and Tía Lisandra don't have much in common, but they both believe strongly that women rarely get the chance to go off and become something besides a wife and mother. They both recognized your potential and didn't want a man's affections to drag you back home. For your abuela, this was indemnity. She didn't get to follow her dream, but now she was watching her beloved granddaughter do what she couldn't. They believed Leonardo could stop you from moving forward. He could convince you to come back here and prevent you from achieving everything you worked so hard for. Your father couldn't allow that to happen. When your tía spoke to Leonardo, and your father agreed, I knew I had to be quiet, Lina. Especially when I saw your abuela agreed with the decision, too. It was my fault she never realized her own dreams. I could not watch her or anyone else lose this opportunity for fulfillment through you. For Abuela, your success, your story, was her second chance. Not to mention that this was what was best for you and Matteo."

"No, Mami," I say, her words settling in. All the lies didn't even have anything to do with me. This was about them and their life choices, their missed opportunities. Mami's explanation wraps around my throat and squeezes. Their meddling and lies were meant to protect everyone else's dreams. They assumed if I knew the truth, I would have walked away from my plans and run back home. Is that how little they thought of me? I worked hard to get into the Army. I chose to join the war after 9/11. This was my decision. My calling.

My family's intervention allowed me to move forward without all the facts. Did their intervention twist fate? Was it because they altered destiny and lied that my course changed? My family doesn't understand.

Mami awaits my response.

I am angry, but even more so I'm drowning in regret. My family's intervention meant I was able to join the Army, but because I joined the Army, a young man died.

I imagine a balanced set of bronze scales. My life was spared, another was taken away. Mami is right—their lies stopped me from returning home.

*If only things went as they were supposed to go.*

As Teó steps off the bus, I see grass and mud stains caked across the knees of his khaki pants, spreading upward on the right side toward his waist. His shirt is untucked, and his collar stands straight up. My trained eyes look him over from a distance. There's a tear in his left sleeve, a slightly swollen lip, and a small, fist-size red circle near his right eye.

Ave Maria, Teó was in a fight. *Not again . . .*

I swing open the car door and jump out, prepared to run, but he sees me first.

He looks back at the other kids dismounting the bus. His eyes beg me not to move. I can almost hear the pleading: *Please don't, Mamá.*

My fists clench at my sides, but I hold still. The passenger-side door shuts behind me.

Mami walks around to where I'm standing. She raises her hand to tent her eyes, gasping when she sees Teó. "Ay, bendito, la escuela se acabó como el rosario de la aurora," she says, using an expression that refers to an event ending in a fight.

I want to rush to Teó's side to examine his every scrape and scratch, but the last thing he wants is for me to fawn over him like he's a helpless baby in front of the other kids.

The bus attendant waves him on through and points in my direction.

When he reaches the car, I hold open the rear door. Neither of us speaks until we are all safe in the quiet confines of the vehicle.

*Sniff.* "Hola, Abuelita." *Sniff.*

"Hola, mi amor," Mami replies. "What happen, Teó? Who fight you?"

My fingers squeeze the steering wheel. I want to hurt whoever hurt my boy. This isn't supposed to be happening here.

I turn the key.

"Can we go to the beach?" *Sniff.* "I wanna go smell the ocean."

He isn't purposely avoiding Mami's question. I know my son; he is waiting to see how I react.

I remain silent.

"Sí, let's go," she agrees. "Lina, there is a park for Teó at the beach. That is good, Teó. Yes?"

I know precisely which park she is referring to. She used to take me all the time when I was a little girl. I always loved it because the swings face out to the Atlantic, and when you get high enough, it feels as though you're flying over the great blue sea.

"That's a great idea." My voice strains with false calm. "Let's go to the park."

# CHAPTER TWENTY-FIVE

"Matteo Salvador LaSalle-Rivera, I have only one question." I am holding him at arm's length, looking him over while he squirms against my grip. "Did you start the fight at school?"

He raises his right hand in the air.

"Don't you dare try and plead the Fifth," I say sternly. "Tell me what happened."

"But, Mamá, you didn't read me my rights."

"Teó, I'm not going to ask you—"

"Okay, okay. I didn't start it. I promise."

"But you were in a fight?"

Now he is staring down at his shoes. "Well . . . yeah . . . sort of . . ."

"What do you mean, sort of? Either you were, or you weren't. Did someone hit you?"

When he doesn't answer me, I try a different tactic. "Did you hit someone trying to defend yourself?"

"No, Mamá. I didn't hit anyone," Teó says solemnly.

"Teó, please tell me what happened."

He kicks at the dirt and shrugs his shoulders. "I got hit because I was protecting Sophia. I used my body as a shield. Then Tomás punched me in the face, twice. He tried to pull me off so he could punch Sophia in the face, too, but I held on to her very tight—even when Sophia and

I both fell into the mud. I wouldn't let go. Then the teacher came and took Tomás to the directora's office." He points back to the car. "There's a note in my backpack for you to sign."

"A note? They didn't think this merited a phone call? Look at your face!"

Teó's hand inadvertently moves to the swollen red bump near his eye. "My maestra was going to call you, but I told her I was fine. After the iguana bite, I didn't want them to call Abuelita to pick me up again. Everything happened when we were lining up for the buses. So I asked her to please let me ride the bus home. She said only if I promised to give you her note and make sure you sign it."

Teó sniffs uncontrollably. I hold him until his tiny chest calms against mine. When I pull away, I'm surprised by the tears welling up in his eyes.

"What's wrong, son? You know you're not in trouble, right? Defending someone else was very brave."

"I know, but I'm so mad that Tomás was trying to hurt Sophia. He said she was betraying her people because she was being my friend. He called her a 'gringo lover' and said he would make her pay. She looked so scared, Mamá. I had to protect her."

"I understand. I'm very proud of you. Sometimes when I get really angry, it might seem like I'm crying because I'm sad, but I'm actually crying because I'm mad. It's okay to be mad about what happened today. Tomás decided something about you because of where you come from, which is wrong."

Teó wipes the tears from his eyes and looks over toward the swings. "Tomás isn't even from here, Mamá. He's from Texas but said he isn't gringo because his parents were born and raised here."

"I'm confused, Teó. So was I. Didn't you tell him that?"

He shrugs. "Nah. Besides, I don't care if Tomás calls me gringo. I think it means I'm American, and I am proud to be an American. Like you, Mamá. You're an American soldier. Titi Kika told me that you protected the soldiers when you went to the war. She said the Army gave you a medal for being so brave. I knew you wouldn't be mad if I protected someone else."

I pull him close, desperately wanting to transfer that childish innocence back into my psyche. My brave boy.

*You protected the soldiers when you went to war,* I repeated silently. How much does he know? That has to be the extent of it. It's all I told my tía Kika when she saw the article on the base's social media site about my award ceremony. I had no idea my tía had mentioned anything to Teó about my time in service. The pride behind his expression pierces through my shame. My actions inspired him to protect someone . . . it's strange how easy it is for my head to understand what my heart can't seem to reconcile.

"I'm not mad, Teó, not one little bit. I'm proud of you for doing what was necessary to protect your friend. Now go, grab a swing before someone else does. If you swing high enough, you'll feel like you're flying over the ocean."

I sit beside Mami on a blue wooden park bench as Teó runs over to the swings.

"Is Teó okay?" she asks me under her breath.

"Yes, he was defending a girl in his class." I swallow, determined to continue. "The boy called her a gringo lover and tried to attack her. Teó used his body to protect the little girl but refused to stand up and defend himself, because he doesn't know enough about his own heritage . . . about his father . . . to confidently proclaim who he is."

"Lina—"

"No, Mami, it's true. I haven't told Teó anything at all about Leonardo. Not one single thing, because I was embarrassed and ashamed I got pregnant by someone who could walk away from me and the baby so easily. I was terrified my son would somehow feel responsible for the abandonment. I chose to suffer that loss in silence—to pretend I wasn't suffering. Instead, all I did was cause more pain now. Teó feels lost without any knowledge of his family history. He won't admit it, but I can feel it."

I turn to her, unable to hold back the anger spilling from my words.

"And all of it could have been prevented if you would have just told me the truth."

Mami shakes her head slowly, wanting to deny the validity behind my words. She stares straight ahead. "How did you find out, Lina? Papi told you?"

I can hear the hurt in her question, the suspicion that Papi betrayed them. She still doesn't get that they have all betrayed me.

"No," I say, standing up. "I saw him. I saw Leonardo at Chiquitas. You can imagine how that went. He was shocked when I chastised him for abandoning his son, a son he didn't even know existed. And then extremely guilty when I told him about Teó's condition. Now he wants to see Teó."

Her fingers spread out in a fan against her chest. "Ave Maria. Guilty? Why he's guilty?"

"Yeah, *Ave Maria* is right. He is guilty because he had the same illness as a boy. So all this time, while I was busy hating myself, wondering if I'd done something wrong—" I stop, unwilling to make this about me. "It appears Teó's condition is nothing more than some random genetic mutation from his father." My voice rises, approaching a shout. "Maybe now you can understand how your lies and meddling have put my son and me in a horrible mess. Y no solo eso—now I have to figure out a way to clean it all up."

There are two other sets of parents at the park. They glance over at us. If I don't calm down, they are likely to come over. This isn't the US, where people tend to mind their business. Mami is thinking the same as she looks over at them and offers a half-hearted smile, assuring them everything is all right.

"Por favor, Lina, tranquilízate." *Calm down.*

I laugh, but the sound carries the sharpening of a blade. "I need to get out of here. I can't deal with all of this right now."

What I really mean is that I need a drink. But I can't tell Mami that.

"Okay," she relents, "let's get Teó home, and we can discuss what to do about Leonardo."

My eyes widen, and I'm nearly forced to a seat at the impact of her words. "We are not going to discuss a damn thing," I shout.

"Catalina Noelia!"

"Lo siento, Mami, ¡pero ya! You are not understanding. This is *my* son. It is *my* decision to make. This idea that you and Papi and Abuela have the right, the authority, to make any decisions about Teó's life—about my life—is what started this mess in the first place. No more! Stay out of it. I don't need your help."

She looks as though she is about to say something more but doesn't. She rises slowly, grabs her purse, and walks to my parked car.

I turn to get Teó from the swings, but he is already running after her. He must have heard me yelling at his grandmother and isn't happy about it.

"Teó. Come here, papito."

Glancing back at me angrily as he reaches Mami, he places his hand in hers. Lines have been drawn, and Teó has chosen his side.

# CHAPTER TWENTY-SIX

I contemplate Chiquitas, but I don't want to see any familiar faces. I'm definitely not in the mood to strike up a conversation or pretend I'm interested in what anyone has to say. *Qué revolú,* I tell myself—this is all one big mess. Alone. I want to be alone. This trip back to Puerto Rico may have been about escaping solitude and gaining family support, but in my darkest moments, alone is my default for comfort. Especially when I'm by myself with a bottle of whiskey or rum or vodka—right now I'm not one to play favorites.

Mami had agreed to watch Teó. Truthfully, they both seemed to prefer the arrangement. The impact of that had me so disoriented, only the warm buzz of a stiff drink felt like it could soften the blow. When we arrived, Dolores was sitting on the patio, talking on her cell phone. She could tell something was off when I didn't join them up the path to the house. Dolores raised her phone in my direction. I understood. I could call if I needed to.

I nodded before driving off.

Despite not having a specific destination in mind, I knew the right area to find what I was looking for was La Placita. La Placita in Santurce, a neighborhood within the capital, is a daytime commercial marketplace of bodegas and professional offices. Once the sun goes down, however, the area's bars, restaurants, and food trucks come to life, and people of all ages roam the streets and take in the tropical energy of music under the stars. This early in the week, I anticipate it'll be a bit calmer than the loud music and crowd-filled streets during the weekend. La Placita is designed as a place to party and listen to shirtless drummers play the rhythmic sounds of batucada. It's the right kind of place to escape and celebrate.

This isn't that kind of night for me. The escape, yes, but I don't have anything to celebrate. I'm lost, without purpose, without a clear path to a future. I can't even get myself to show up and start working, despite my dwindling funds screaming at me that time is running out. Not tonight. Tonight, I want to wallow. Tonight, I want to scream. Tonight, I want to rebel. I want to lose myself on the island and pray it finds me on the other side. The truth of my family's betrayal, the rejection from my own son, watching him find his footing so easily and his place within the island while I still feel so lost, cuts to my core. It has me grappling on the inside like I'm drowning out at sea, the riptide pulling me farther from shore without any trace of a lifesaver.

Fortunately, after parking the car in a random lot, I quickly find the perfect place, a quiet little bar in the corner called Charlie's. There's outdoor seating, and the tables are all still empty. I can hear the music playing inside, so I know they're already open, even if the skies aren't yet dark enough to transition La Placita to its alter ego. I can be alone here. It's exactly what I'm looking for.

I walk in the front door and look around at an empty lounge.

"Una?" a presumed waitress calls out as she wipes down the tables at the far back of the restaurant. I almost didn't see her.

"Yes, one—just me."

She grabs a menu and glares at me suspiciously, keenly aware I speak Spanish, even if I'm pretending I don't.

"I won't need that," I say, pointing at the menu. "Outside, please?"

"Adelante." She points to a table out on the patio.

When we reach it, I take my seat and offer my smuggest of smiles. I don't know why, maybe it's my bad mood, but I just feel like being a pain in the ass. She stands there with one impatient hand on her hip as the crowds in the street grow larger. My early arrival must be disrupting her plans to prepare for this evening. I don't think she anticipates me spending much money, particularly since I said I'm not ordering any food. She is a fool. Alcohol can be pricey here, but at least for tonight, I have enough in my bank account to drink until my heart's content.

"Cuba libre—doble, por favor."

"Coming right up," she says in perfect English. I like her feisty spirit.

I relax as dusk steps in, and the sky darkens. The neon lights of the nearby establishments blink on, and the music in the street grows louder. Sitting alone at the table, I feel hidden. Finally.

The waitress returns with my drink and sets it down.

"I'll go ahead and order another one now."

Her expression makes it clear what she thinks about that, but she takes my order anyway and walks away.

I think about the past few days, letting the straw dance on my lips. I'm angry at my parents' deception, but that's only one part of it. So much more has unraveled in my first month on the island. I feel like a pinball bouncing against the flippers at every new revelation.

My mind replays my encounters with Dolores and our trip to Maria's house, then Eli's kiss on the beach. I let myself linger on that one. Eventually I press the handle on my own red toy binoculars. Teó's in the first image, chasing the chickens in the backyard. I pause for a moment and allow myself to linger in my parents' fondness for Teó's presence. Why couldn't I ever make them feel that way? Press. Dr. Robles and her intuitive eye sit across her desk, unveiling all my secrets in her blank expression. Press. A snapshot of the scene I re-create from imagination between Leonardo and my family when he surprised them seven years ago. Press. Tía Lisandra's judgmental observations as she assesses my new life from across the dining table. Press. The screen goes blank, and there's nothing left but a voice in my head, asking how I'm going to manage the paradigm shift behind my supposed truth of living as a single mother. Leonardo never even knew about his son. Teó knows nothing about him. I've entered an upside-down world with an entirely new set of characters. And since arriving, I haven't had a minute to come up for air or figure out my place in the chaos.

Let's be real.

A few months ago I knew who I was. I was a single mother and a soldier. Then my driver was killed just a few feet from me on my final mission in Iraq, and I aimed my rifle at a young man who was still more kid than adult and took his life. Those are the facts, the boundary lines for my existence. Now everything has changed. I have changed. I'm not a soldier anymore. I'm not a healer. I don't have a mission. I don't even know if I have a country. Wearing a uniform kept me in this space of patriotism. I walked away from that and returned here to the island, a place I was told would hold me back, a place that didn't have anything for me. I am no one. It's like my identity and my hope died that day alongside that boy.

I am sipping the last of my drink when the waitress returns with a perfectly timed refreshed glass.

My driver was killed . . .

As the rum settles in, it reminds me how little time I've spent grieving the other major loss that day—Sergeant Fuentes, my driver. Fuentes . . .

"Gracias," I tell the waitress offhandedly, as she takes the empty glass. She didn't ask me whether I wanted anything else. I'm sure she knows I do, but it's wise if we pace this out . . . for both of us.

This time when she appears again, it's to escort a young couple to a nearby table. The woman in the pair has long, jet-black hair that hangs low down her back and thick gold hoops dangling from her ears. She is exposing as much skin as possible without technically being in her underwear. Her oversize escort is covered in thick gold chains, a pair of hoops in his ears, and a heavy diamond bezel watch. His flashy jewelry contrasts harshly with his slightly faded black T-shirt, blue jeans, and sneakers. Their accents are heavy. New Yorkers.

The waitress places them at a metal table in the center of the patio. Given the size of her breasts and his belly, they'd likely have struggled to sit comfortably in one of the available, small wooden booths.

Their table is slightly off-center from mine, still giving me a direct view to the street. I take another sip of the rum and Coke. The warmth of the alcohol spreads along the tops of my shoulders and tips of my ears. I like this part—the early stage—when my mind relaxes, and my truths open up.

The woman's left arm crosses self-consciously across her exposed stomach. I'm a trained observer. She's self-conscious about her weight. She shouldn't be. I think her curves are the envy of most women. Betty Boop. The neon-pink acrylic nail on her index finger taps rapidly on the tabletop. Why is she nervous? Her long, thick legs cross at the ankle. She leans in close to whisper something to Big Guy. I bet she's telling him a lie. Papi is right—girls are mentirosas. Tía Lisandra lied to Leo, Mami lied to me, I've lied to Teó about who I am and what I'm capable of.

My gaze shifts over to Big Guy. He is fidgety . . . and overheating. He pulls a handkerchief from his back pocket and wipes the sweat from his brow. His entire body is in motion, feet tapping the floor, his body shifting in his seat. He leans back, then forward, and glares down the street. Big Guy could be high or hyperactive. His demeanor isn't quite as obvious as hers. There is a bit more mystery about him.

He keeps licking his lips. Big Guy's gotta be high on something. Betty Boop leans forward, whispering something near his cheek, but he isn't paying attention. Instead, he peers down the road. I think he is expecting someone. The idea heightens my own sense of alertness. *Damn, Big Guy, don't you understand I don't want to be on alert? Come on, I'm running from a really crappy day? I want to be free.*

Enough.

I force myself to look away from the couple and turn around in search of my waitress. I don't immediately spot her, so I raise my hand in the air, desperate to get someone's attention. *I need another drink.*

At least now I know the alcohol is eroding my inhibitions and sense of manners. I hold the empty cup in one hand, keeping the other hand raised high in the air.

The familiar clipped voice calls from behind me, "¿Sí, señora?"

I should have the decency to be embarrassed. I'm way past that.

"Una más, por favor."

"Are you sure I can't get you something to eat? An appetizer?"

"Nope." I shake my head. "Only another one of these." I raise my empty glass to her nose, probably a little too close to her face.

"Another double, señora?" she says, looking back toward the bar.

I nod, enjoying that feeling of outright giddiness. All the day's earlier frustrations are already floating away to a place I can't reach, not that I want to. I like this state of mind much better, but I know not to push my luck and continue the chitchat. Saying something more means I'm likely to erupt with something I shouldn't and get cut off. This level of warmth is where I can get a little brazen . . . okay, let's be real—obnoxious.

"I'll be right back with your drink," she says, but Big Guy waves her over. Damn him for being an unnecessary delay between me and my escape to a warm oblivion.

"Don't worry, I'll be right back," she says before walking over to their table.

As I wait, a nagging thought returns . . . something about my deployment. What was it? I search my mind, tempted to drop it, but something deeper won't let me. Not just yet.

Oh, right . . . the sergeant . . . the new arrival . . . the one who died . . .

What is it that's bugging me?

Moody waitress gives Mafia couple a megawatt smile as she takes their order.

I roll my eyes. What the hell did they say to get her to smile like that? Whatever. It doesn't matter. *I want my drink.* I cough loudly to voice my objections.

Yup, definitely cruising into obnoxious.

Moody waitress looks over at me. Her smile evaporates, offering me blank disinterest as she closes a small notepad with their order and passes me on her way back to the bar without so much as a polite nod.

The crowds grow heavier as more people make their way to the streets. One of the phenomena of this city's slice of nightlife is that it attracts everyone.

Proving my point, a white-haired woman with a cane and an equally old man saunter along the sidewalk in front of me, crossing a group of loud, boisterous young tourists dressed in their best American-yuppie attire. I bet that group came directly from Dorado's golf courses to drink at the local spot they heard about on Yelp.

The waitress returns with my third drink as Big Guy stands up and leans over the railing, shouting something to a group of young hoodlums standing in a gaggle across the street.

"¡Siéntate!" his girl hisses, insisting he sit, but he ignores her. I can't quite make out what he's hollering, in part because of the thick New York accent, but more because of the gibberish street slang he's using. It doesn't make any sense.

"The bartender says you should take your time with this one or eat something," the waitress says, placing a fresh napkin on my table. "Otherwise, this one's it."

I don't bother to look at her. My focus is where my instincts pick up danger. Aware I'm not paying attention, the waitress follows my gaze to the couple.

Big Guy turns back around as his woman stands.

He coaxes her with a loud, deep voice. "Okay, relax, mami. I'll sit down. Chill out. They're on their way." He points over at the group of guys across the street.

I don't feel good about these two or what they may be involved in.

I turn to address the waitress's original point.

"Don't worry, you can cash me out after this one," I say with more than a trace of attitude.

She nods, relieved, and together we look back at the couple. They are again seated, heads joined together in hushed whispers.

"You may want to keep an eye on them." My words are slurring.

She raises one eyebrow. I know what she's thinking. It's me she needs to keep an eye on.

"I'm serious. I know what I'm talking about. I think the man is high."

When she purses her lips sarcastically, I can't help myself. "Trust me. I'm a medic."

She pats me on the shoulder. "I'll go get your check."

*I bet that makes you a damn good medic . . . Stay down, Sergeant.*

My mind slams two images together like a car accident. Sergeant Fuentes—my driver—the new arrival from the support battalion. Oh my God. It's him. How did I miss the connection?

Sergeant Fuentes's face flashes before my eyes—a replica, albeit older, of the young man in the photo at Maria's house in Ciales. Maria's son, Christian. Christian was my driver. Sergeant Christian Fuentes, the new arrival, Dolores's love, and the young soldier Eli was grieving, told me he was from Puerto Rico.

The realization settles on my chest with the weight of a wrecking ball. Christian did not die on the mission with Eli. He died on the mission with me.

I'm dumbfounded. Could I have this wrong? Maybe my memories are playing tricks on me, especially after two double Cuba libres. Could they just be two different men who looked a lot alike?

I close my eyes and think back to the photo in Maria's living room as my pulse increases.

No, it's definitely him. He was much younger in the picture, but remembering our conversation, I recall how he told me he was from Puerto Rico. He told me he had someone waiting for him. The smile when he mentioned his girl . . . Dolores . . . it's the same smile he had in the picture on the wall. My driver was Maria's son—Christian. He was killed in action, but he was killed in my convoy—not collecting soil samples with Eli.

But how?

I think back to Eli's story, although it isn't easy with the amount of rum and Coke in my system. The room is beginning to spin. I force myself to take a few deep breaths and focus my memory on what Eli said about the night he was on his last mission.

*It was my own selfishness, handpicking him to join me, a decision that cost him his life . . . I, at least, managed to radio for the medevac even though I was leanin' into shock . . . When the chopper arrived, he lost consciousness . . . I never saw him again.*

What if Christian survived the blast and was released back to duty?

I'm halfway through drink number three when I put the pieces together.

Eli was transported back to Germany for treatment. He was cut off from the world. It's possible once he found out Christian was killed in action, he assumed it was because of the tragedy with him—on his mission. It made sense. There would be no reason to consider otherwise.

Our mission was supposed to be low risk. It's not too much of a stretch to believe he recovered and volunteered to go back. Then I remember the rumor . . . *Rumor is he had contact with the enemy but survived and insisted on staying in country to finish his tour.* It fits. The Army wouldn't have hesitated to deploy a volunteer who insisted on staying—particularly a hero.

And it's his face. Again I picture the image of the boy on the wall and the man on the battlefield. The driver. The man on the wall. It was the same man. It was Christian.

I tell myself once more, knowing it to be true: Christian didn't die collecting samples with Eli. Christian died on the convoy with me.

My lips widen into open-mouth shock when my waitress returns again with the check.

"Are you okay?" she asks.

I shut my mouth, but everything else is moving slowly. Sipping through my straw, I finish the last of my drink. No reason to let a single drop go to waste.

"Yes, sorry. I . . . uh . . . remembered something."

She looks at me, waiting for further explanation, but I don't offer anything more.

I may need to walk around La Placita, at least a little, before I attempt to drive back home.

I place my credit card in the black binder, but it falls to the floor at the sound of an ear-piercing scream from Betty Boop at the table ahead of me.

Big Guy has fallen from his seat and is now on the floor, convulsing. My instincts immediately spring me into action.

Hispanic male, likely mid to late twenties, approximately six feet tall, two hundred and fifty pounds, presents with a generalized, tonic-clonic seizure. I look down at my watch—6:45 p.m.

After jumping up from my chair, I rush to the ground next to him. The adrenaline helps to sharpen my senses, but the six shots of rum I've consumed in less than an hour are slowing my response time. Dammit. Not now.

I don't ask permission. I use all my strength to turn him onto his side and check for breathing. Relieved, I confirm warm air on my fingertips. "Sir, can you hear me?"

"What are you doing?" Betty Boop yells. "Somebody help!"

"Señora," the waitress calls out sharply from behind me.

"Listen," I shout, doing my best to control the slur, "I'm an EMT. He is having a seizure. Give me your apron."

The waitress hesitates but complies, pulling it off and handing it to me.

"Call nine-one-one," I tell her.

I want to reassure Betty Boop and keep her from distracting me. "Everything is going to be okay," I tell her, doing my best to sound as sober as possible.

I ball up the apron and place it under his head, attempting to keep him on his side without constricting his body's convulsions. I stick my fingers in his mouth, ensuring he doesn't have food, a garnish from their drinks, or a retainer—anything that could cause choking.

A crowd of people gather on the other side of the patio fence, watching and shouting different instructions. I ignore them. Even with the rum coursing through my system, I know exactly what to do. I focus solely on the man on the floor.

"Are you his wife? Is he diabetic?" I ask. "Does he have a history of epilepsy?"

She shakes her head, her body trembling. "No, we are dating. I don't know. It's only been a couple of months . . . I don't know . . ."

"Has this ever happened before?" My watch ticks—he's been seizing for one minute.

"N-n-o-o." Her lips and chest tremble. With that tiny top, I'm convinced I'm about to get a direct view of her nipple if she isn't careful. I'm sure this is not what she planned for their vacation from the Big Apple, and there isn't much time before she shuts down completely.

The man's body finally relaxes against my arms. The muscles in his back and extremities release. He looks as though he is sleeping peacefully on the concrete floor. I know better. He is unconscious. Keeping him on his side, I scan his wrist for a medical ID bracelet, but aside from the gaudy watch, there's nothing there, no sign of any preexisting medical condition.

"Sir, can you hear me?"

He is still unconscious.

The sound of the sirens approach. I breathe a sigh of relief.

Turning back to Betty, I say, "Listen, this isn't the time to hold back."

The waitress is no longer behind me. I lower my voice. "Has he taken any drugs? We need to know so we can help him."

While checking his pulse, I wait for her response. His heart is racing. He needs to get to a hospital.

"You need to tell me."

She is rising to her feet and backing away. "We were on vacation . . . you know how it is . . . Is he going to be okay? Oh my God, is he dead?"

"No," I shout, "but every detail counts." As the terror increases on her face, I lower my voice. "What has he taken?"

She shakes her head. "Nothing," she mutters.

We are getting nowhere. Betty has probably taken the same stuff Big Guy did, and now she's afraid to be caught. I peer out to see if the men he was talking to earlier are still there, but they're gone.

The ambulance pulls up to the sidewalk on the other side of us. Three young men dismount. The waitress and an older man in fancy clothes, most likely the manager, escort them directly to us.

Big Guy is regaining consciousness as they approach.

"What's . . . what's . . . happening . . . where?"

"It's all right, sir," I say, trying to soothe him. "You're here at Charlie's at La Placita. How are you feeling?"

Before he can answer me, one of the EMTs is lifting me to my feet. "It's okay, ma'am. We got it from here."

The abrupt rise to a standing position throws me off balance. I sway, unsteady, and grab the table beside me to keep myself from toppling over. I turn away, hoping the EMT doesn't notice.

"You want to tell me what happened here?" he asks, looking me over carefully. He noticed.

"You may want to start with her," I say, pointing at Big Guy's girlfriend. "It looks like a possible drug overdose."

"And you are?"

"A friendly bystander." I shrug. "I'm also a licensed EMT and an Army combat medic." He looks impressed, but I think he can tell I've been drinking.

"Listen," I deflect. "It looks like Big Guy had a generalized tonic-clonic seizure. It lasted approximately ninety seconds. No restrictions on the airway. Pulse is elevated. When I questioned his girlfriend about drugs, she got really cagey."

He looks confused.

"Suspicious," I clarify.

He nods. "Got it." He glances at his two counterparts as they load Big Guy on a stretcher. "I think I'd better go assist. Thanks for your help. They were lucky you were close by. Do you have a ride? Someone who can drive you home?"

"Yes, of course. A friend of mine is on his way," I lie.

"Okay, great. Be careful out there." He moves to join his team but stops and turns back to face me. "Hey, if you live here now, the Puerto Rico National Guard is looking for people. Rumor has it the governor is getting ready to mobilize units in the area." He pulls a card from his back pocket. "Let me know if you're interested in joining the unit. I can put you in contact with the local Mafia." He smiles when he says it, but I understand exactly what he means. In Puerto Rico, it's all about who you know.

"You're in the guard?"

"Sixty-eight whiskey—like you." He extends his hand. "Sergeant Cabrera."

"Nice to meet you, Sergeant. I'm Lina. I was Sergeant LaSalle-Rivera a few months ago," I say, and shake his hand.

"It's nice to meet you, Sergeant . . . er . . . Lina. Un placer." *A pleasure.*

"Gracias, igual." *Same.*

"I've gotta go," he says, glancing at the crew. "Good luck to you. I hope to see you at the unit."

I smile and thank him, then watch as they heave Big Guy into the ambulance. I'm not at all surprised to see Betty Boop slip away into the crowd.

When the ambulance drives off, I look down at my hands. They aren't trembling; they're still. In fact, for a beat everything inside me is still and certain. Springing into action, helping someone in distress, felt eerily like a big yellow lifesaver tossed out into the middle of the raging sea just before my head dipped below the waves.

# CHAPTER TWENTY-SEVEN

Walking should help me gather my bearings, and La Placita is the perfect place to do it. The night sky is spotted with neon signs brightly advertising each of the bars and restaurants turned into nightclubs. Sidewalk bands play live music at the more traditional places. Trendier spots post DJ booths near the entrance to seductively solicit hundreds of young and eager pedestrians. I'm not paying attention to any of it. I have this swirling storm of thoughts colliding in my head between the realization of Christian's identity and the rush of being pulled back into action.

Even with everything I've had to drink, the satisfaction, the instinct of helping someone, filled me with power and purpose in a way nothing else has since I walked away from the military—a reality I've been trying to drink away and forget about. I thought my ability to help people died that morning in Iraq. I keep telling myself that watching that boy fall to the ground is the only thing I'm ever going to see again when trying to heal . . . but maybe I was wrong. It came so easily to me tonight.

Everywhere I turn, there are people. Some walk aimlessly, taking in the sights and sounds from one staple to the next; some sit at tables on the outer edges of the street. And still others are fixtures standing on the sidewalks with drinks in hand, watching as the intensity of the night increases with every passing minute.

It's still early, but it won't be long before the older crowds head home for the night and La Placita is filled with the lustful energy of people my age and younger. Some are looking for a vacation experience, wanting to trash their inhibitions, and others, like me, are looking for an escape.

The exhilaration from earlier is fading, replaced by the echo of a message that continues to play on and on in my head: *You're not a healer, you're a murderer. Don't kid yourself. You took someone's son from them, and now you want to forget all about it and move on as though it never happened. What if it had been your son?* The shame of the kid's death starts to blend into the memory of Sergeant Fuentes getting shot. Wasn't that my fault, too? He was responding to my call for help. That day taught me the deadly implications of getting caught in my path.

My heart begins to pound, and I can feel the panic rising. I keep walking, trying my best to shove it all inside, lock it deep down where my own thoughts can't torture me on an endless repeating reel.

It's easy to hide behind the loud music, the growing crowds, and the readily available alcohol. I feel invisible among the crowd. I like that. Tonight, I'm a ghost.

"¡Toma, mami!" A young girl in tiny vinyl shorts and go-go boots approaches me on the sidewalk with a round tray of bright-pink Jell-O shots. She picks up one of the small white paper cups and brings it directly to my lips.

Jell-O does not look appetizing amid my heightened nerves. I shake my head. "I can't." I hope my English puts her off.

It doesn't.

"Yes, you can!" She smiles, tilting the cup to my lips and leaving me no choice but to swallow the gelatinous concoction.

Oh God, what the hell was in that?

"Join us." She points to the entrance of the bar behind her.

I know I shouldn't. I'm alone. This isn't safe. But . . .

A police car—its lights flashing—passes alongside us. Flashing lights here are the norm, used to warn of police presence. They remind me of the ambulance, of the battlefield, of the convulsing body I just triaged. This girl in the tiny shorts doesn't get it: I don't want to party; I want to forget. I look away, searching for another table in a dark corner where I can drink by myself and in peace.

"No, thank you. Gracias," I say and keep walking.

Whatever was in the Jell-O shot leaves me even more unsteady. I struggle to walk a straight line as one foot steps off the sidewalk and onto the street while the other remains fixed in place. The difference from beneath me causes me to nearly tumble to the ground, but I'm able to catch myself just in time. A woman looks over worriedly while I'm bent at the waist, hands on my knees, focusing on the star printed on my tennis shoes. I know zeroing in on a fixed point will help avoid puking.

"I'm okay," I say to her in my friendliest voice, raising my hand.

She forces a small smile, unconvinced, but walks away anyway.

The moment allows me to reorient myself and take a deep inhale in an attempt to sober my senses with fresh air. This walk was supposed to help me clear my head so I can drive myself home. It isn't working. The post-adrenaline lull and my continued consumption have only worsened things.

It's better if I sit for a few minutes.

I cross the street, spotting an empty table. Reaching for my phone in my back pocket, I text Dolores:

Hola. What R U doing?

Her response immediately swipes in:

Chacha . . . jangeando con el corrillo . . .

Great. Dolores is already out with friends.

I am contemplating my options when another text from her comes in:

Mami "L" come 2 casa 2nite. She no easy. U want 2 go dancing?

My heart sinks. Tía Lisandra came by the house. Not good. Given the situation with Mami earlier, this feels ominous. I'm sure they told her that I found out about her lies and her intervention in my private affairs. I wanted my confrontation with my aunt to be on my own terms, but now she can prepare her excuses in advance. I need to get home.

No, I have 2 get back 2 Teó. Have fun. B safe.

OK. U 2. C U Soon.

Well, that's a bust. Dolores will not be picking me up and bailing me out of this one now that I've found myself too drunk to drive.

Reluctantly, I am considering the one other person I can call to pick me up, when the pinprick of goose bumps breaks out along my neck and arms. My head swings to look around, making me dizzy.

Someone is too close.

Maybe I'm getting overly paranoid, but I continue to search for the trigger that caused me to sense danger. The Army taught me situational awareness. An assessment of your area of operation (AO) can prevent you from getting killed.

The lights from the club trail across my field of view like comets, but still I spot him.

Older man, late forties, possibly early fifties, only a few feet from where I'm sitting. He's hiding behind a group of tourists much younger, likely drunk, and not paying him any mind. I know he isn't with them. They are all speaking English, and there isn't even a glimmer of comprehension on his face. His exposed forearm bears a Puerto Rican flag tattoo. He's got to be a local. There's a drink in his hand. But he's standing at the entrance of the bar, all alone—out of place.

I knew it. I'm not crazy. The man tries to remain inconspicuous, but I'm trained to spot a threat. And I can read a body. Rage in his eyes tents the sneer on his lips.

I may be a bit underwater, but something primal tells me to beware.

He catches me staring at him and raises a red plastic Dixie cup to his mouth. He likes that I see him.

It's not safe for me to remain here alone, but I'm in no condition to drive my car. I need to get a ride home, and it won't be Dolores. A taxi in this area at this time of night is hit or miss. In most cases they can't locate you and end up picking up another fare. I'm not up for it.

I swipe open my phone, returning to my earlier conclusion—Eli. This is so humiliating, but the only other option is Papi. That would be worse. I scroll down to search for the South Carolina area code.

Eli answers on the first ring. "Well, howdy, Lina. I wasn't expecting to hear from you so soon."

"I need your help," I slur into the phone when a waitress approaches my table.

"What can I get you?" she asks.

I raise my index finger. "Um, one second," I say, but Eli assumes I'm speaking to him.

"Lina? Is everything all right? You're worrying me. What's goin' on?"

"Yes, yes," I start to tell Eli, but now the waitress is looking at me, confused.

"Hold on, Eli. One sec." I place the phone on mute and face the waitress. "I think I'm okay, for now. Thank you."

"No, sorry," she says, shaking her head. "You want to sit here, you have to order something."

"Lina?" Eli's voice rings through the speaker, sounding freaked out.

"I can bring you a Medalla?" she offers.

Flustered, I say, "Okay, sure, that's fine." A beer shouldn't be too bad. I don't want to get up from the safety of my table, even if that means another drink.

I turn back to look over at Creepy Guy. He is still standing at the entrance, but now he's looking away in the opposite direction.

I take the phone off mute. "Eli, I'm sorry. I was hoping, umm, maybe you wouldn't mind giving me a ride home?"

"You don't sound so good there, Lina. You all right?" He sighs, and I bristle at what he says next. "Had a lot to drink, I assume?"

My pride hurts, and I don't appreciate his tone. "Never mind. I shouldn't have—"

"No, wait," Eli says. "Now don't go gettin' all twisted up. I'm just concerned. Of course I'll pick you up, but will you be okay to sit tight until I get there? It could be a minute."

The crowds are swelling before my very eyes. It should be all right to sit here in plain view and wait. "Yes. Just hurry, please. I gotta get home."

"Text me an address," Eli says. "Better yet, drop me a pin. Addresses here can get . . . uh . . . tricky."

"You're sure you don't mind?" I'm wondering why I bothered to ask. I don't care if he minds. I need to get home.

"No, Lina. I'm glad you called." I can hear the concern in his voice. "I'm heading out the door now."

"Thank you. I'll send you the name of the bar. I'm at La Placita. Do you know where that is?"

"Yes, I know it," he answers. "I've been told it's best to go with a crowd, especially if you're not a local. You there all by yourself?"

His question makes me feel like an idiot. My response sounds angry. "Yes. I'm alone."

He is quiet for a moment before saying, "Sit tight. I'll be there soon." The line clicks. He's gone.

The waitress returns to the table with an ice-cold beer. "Here you go. This one was already paid for."

"Paid for?" I look at her, confused. "Who paid for it?"

"Another group that ordered Medallas. When I go to pick it up, they order an extra one. Told me to keep it." She winks at me, then pushes the beer closer and saunters back into the crowd.

I rise from my chair and look around. Searching my surroundings, my eyes move from one building to the next. Lights streak across my field of vision like lasers. Music plays, couples dance, and bystanders continue crowding the streets.

I return to my table and drop Eli a pin, then take a big swig.

I drink the rest of the beer slowly while waiting for Eli. Even I know my limits, and tonight I'm damned near plunging headfirst into mine.

Placing the empty bottle back on the table, I immediately spot when Eli's curls come into view. He is taller than most of the people around him, and he's easy to spot because he walks like an athlete. There's this confidence he carries. I wonder if the Army taught him that. Even walking through the streets of La Placita, the man seems to know exactly where he is and where he is going. It makes him easy to spot. Thank goodness he is finally here.

He looks a little blurry. I don't wear glasses, so I can only assume it's the alcohol. As he approaches my table, his eyes meet mine. I smile, but he looks worried and uncomfortable.

"Good thing you're all right," he says. "I think I know what all this is about, but I think you may need to get a grip."

I stare at him but don't really process what he's saying, I just take it all in: golden hair, green eyes, tan skin, white teeth. He really is a mix of beautiful colors. I want to sink my finger into the dimple in his cheek. I lift my hand to do just that, but his sudden frown stops me midway.

"What's wrong?"

"You had me really worried about you tonight. You all right?" He is staring behind me.

I shrug. "That's kind of a loaded question." My words slur against one another. I hear how sloppy I sound. "Oh, and hello . . . by the way."

I should have warned him—I can be an obnoxious ass when I've had this much to drink.

He looks back at me, assessing the extent of my condition, then puts his arm around me to help me off the high-top.

"Yeah . . . hi, yourself," he says. "An odd fella over there is looking this way. He was about to approach when I started walkin' over. I reckon he was surprised I beat him here." He turns back to me and gives me a once-over. "It's not safe for you to be out here all alone, ya know. Especially if you're going to be drinking this much."

His tone feels condescending. I don't appreciate being judged, especially from some fancy gringo—even if he did drive all the way over here to pick me up.

I cross my arms in front of my chest, prepared to tell him exactly that, but his eyes darken, not finding anything about this funny, and I find myself unusually quiet.

"I had a mess of things going on tonight, but I dropped everything on a dime to help you. Don't get me wrong, I'm glad I did. You never leave a fallen comrade, remember that? The Soldier's Creed." I grimace, but he isn't done. "Lina, what if I wouldn'a made it in time?" He glares behind me again. "It ain't safe . . . or wise, for you to be taking silly risks like this. You're a mama. That's all I'm sayin'."

I drop my arms, angry and frustrated, but even I can't convince myself it's him I'm angry with. Eli's right. Damn him.

"Okay . . . you win." I sway on my feet with each word. "I'll be more careful." I lift my finger in the air and point directly at him. "But not because you said so, Mr. Smarty-Pants, but . . . because I know with Teó . . . things are different." I almost whisper the last part.

His stiff demeanor relaxes a little. He keeps his arm wrapped around my shoulder as he leads me toward his car. His steadiness helps keep me on my feet. I like being close to him.

People stare down at his prosthetic as we pass them on the streets. They can't seem to help themselves. Their eyes move down his tall frame, starting at his handsome face, then trickle down to where he's missing half of his arm. Their expressions shift as their eyes reach his handicap. They go from admiring him to pitying him. It pisses me off.

How does he live like this? How can he stomach people looking at him and feeling sorry for him all the time? As we continue to walk, I wonder how frustrating it must be to feel whole, the same way you've always been, but then be forced to see yourself through others' eyes as broken or damaged.

Who am I kidding? I'm no different. Except for me, it's the opposite—everyone sees me as whole and strong, but I'm missing a part of myself, too.

When we reach the car, Eli buckles me into the passenger seat and takes his place behind the wheel.

"Eli, there's . . . something . . . I need . . . to tell you." My words are choppy, but I push past it, wanting to tell him about Christian.

"Oh boy." Eli lets out a little whistle. "Are you sure it's something you need to tell me right now?"

I ponder his question. "I think so . . ."

"Lina," he cautions. "I would not be a gentleman if I don't at least try and talk you out of saying something in this . . . uh . . . condition. You might wish you waited until morning."

Is he right? Am I being selfish trying to get the truth about Christian off my chest for my own benefit?

"Maybe you're right. But . . . I don't know . . ." I stare up at the roof of the car. "I think it's important."

He lets out a puff of air. "Your call. But try and remember in the mornin' I did my part to warn ya. It's been my experience drunk confessions are never the kind you look kindly to once the sun's up."

"Drunk confessions?" I chuckle. He thinks I'm going to profess my feelings. "No way, lover boy. It's nothing like that."

Eli clears his throat nervously. "Well, pardon me. That's embarrassing."

"No, I mean . . ." I'm determined to clear up this whole mess, but my laughter leads to nausea. A combination of gelatin, rum, and beer sloshes in my stomach and up my throat.

Oh God, I'm going to puke in his car. "I think I might be sick."

"Should I pull over?"

I shake my head and close my eyes. My confession is going to have to wait. I breathe and try to steady the spinning images behind closed lids. "Talk to me. Distract me until we get there."

"Lina, are you sure you're okay? Do you need to go to the hospital?"

At the mention of a hospital, I panic. "No! I'm fine. I had . . . a little . . . too much to drink to drive myself home." I just said *home*. I bite my lip. "There was the Jell-O shot . . . down my throat . . . damn waitress . . . and then the beer." And the three Cuba libres. I know I'm not making sense. I roll down the window and let the night's warm, salty air hit me squarely in the face. "Don't make a big thing."

"I can't help it. I guess I shoulda warned ya. My mama always said I was an excessive worrier. It came with being responsible for them at such a young age."

"Them? I thought you only had one sister?"

"I do. I meant my sister and my mama. My daddy died when I was thirteen. I think I always felt responsible for them after that."

"You lost your father? So young?" I want to have misheard him, but I'm drunk, not deaf.

"Yes. Sepsis."

"What? How?"

"Flesh-eating bacteria. He made contact at a lake with an open sore in his leg. As a diabetic, it only compromised his condition. Once the sepsis crept in, there was no savin' him."

Eli's father died from an environmental cause . . . even in my jumbled mind, I can piece this one together. "Is your father's death why you chose to study environmental science?"

He looks surprised, probably given my current condition. "Boy, nothin' really gets past you. Even . . ." He pauses and clears his throat. "Even when you're like this."

I give him my best sarcastic expression. "No, it really doesn't, and I don't appreciate the judgment."

His voice lowers. "I'm the last person in the world to judge you, Lina. I think you're a special lady who's dealing with a whole hell of a lot of hurtin' from the war. I get that."

I don't want to talk about the war. "I'm not a lady, Eli. I'm a Taíno warrior."

He shakes his head, but I can see the worry in his eyes. "How 'bout you take the rest of the night off there, warrior. It's time you give yourself a break."

I *want* to give myself a break. I want to curl up in a ball and give up altogether. But if I even start to think I have a right to feel sorry for myself, all I have to do is look over to the driver's seat and know better. Eli knows tragedy, real tragedy, and somehow he is still pressing on, finding ways to honor the losses in his life by moving forward and staying positive through it all. I honestly can't fathom how he finds the strength to do it.

"I'm sorry, by the way," I say awkwardly. "I had no idea you lost your father so young."

"Shucks, there was no way for you to know. I hadn't told ya."

"It must have been tough for your mother and sister when you left for the Army."

"Yes and no," he replied reflectively. "Mama met her current husband during my first year at the Citadel. He is a good fit for her." He leans over and offers a conspiratorial smile. "Now, there was the matter of my leaving for college. Once I knew I had a choice between West Point or the Citadel, as far as Mama was concerned, the choice was between stayin' true to my roots or crossing over to no-man's-land. Thankfully, I saved her a heart attack and chose wisely."

He winks, but it's a facade. I can see him keeping a close eye on me. I'm a medic. I know what it looks and feels like to have someone assessing you. Still, my heart warms for him. I also understand his family's identity as Southerners. Puerto Ricans are proud to be Americans. Still, we, too, hold fast to our individual identity and independence as Boricuas.

I realize I've gotten it wrong. Eli isn't an outsider. Despite our differences, we have many similarities. Over the past couple of weeks, we've shared a love for deep-fried food, lazy sunny days, and love of country. We also share the heaviness of guilt from service to our country, even if that guilt has manifested itself differently.

Eli is honorable. He sacrificed his life, dreams, and culture to honor a young man whose life he believes he is responsible for. Eli hasn't prioritized his own loss, even if it is a life-altering disability that would bring most people to their knees. He sure hasn't allowed the injustices to lead him to the bottom of the bottle, where my pain has taken me. No, Eli uses *his* tragedies to move forward, help people, and build a business. He gave Christian's mother and Dolores a sanctuary—a tribute to remember the man they loved. Eli suffered a tremendous loss and immeasurable guilt, consumed with the belief that because of his decision, a boy died. And what did he do about it? He ran to Puerto Rico to build.

On the other hand, facing the same reality at a similar crossroad, guilt over ending someone's life, I, too, booked a flight to Puerto Rico, but not to build—I came to hide.

I am a coward. And now I've become a drunk.

The revelation brings a new layer of self-disgust as Eli rounds the corner onto my street.

The porch light is on, but my parents' car is not parked in the driveway. It's the same fancy car as the other day. Tía Lisandra.

I'm surprised she would still be visiting at such a late hour. I'm not thrilled about getting past her in my current condition. I was hoping I could tiptoe through the living room and into a house where everyone had retired to their rooms for bed. But if Tía's car is here, people are still visiting.

"I'd be happy to walk you in. If you don't mind, that is," Eli says. We both turn toward the front window as a light from the living room turns on. "Someone knows we've arrived. Probably waiting up for ya."

"Teó," I whisper. It sounds more like a breath than a word.

I can't face him in this condition. What the hell was I thinking? I was sure he'd be asleep when I made it home.

Eli exits his side of the car and comes around, opening my door and extending his hand. I place one leg out onto the gravel below, trying to stand up, but both legs are shaking as my surroundings spin. My muscles are heavy, making it difficult to put one leg directly in front of the other. My body keeps moving sideways instead of straight ahead. Eli's arm wraps around my lower back, holding me up as he guides me ahead.

"Lina, I don't like this. You weren't quite this bad off when we left the bar. Something doesn't seem right. Maybe we do need to get you to the hospital."

"No," I snap. "I already told you—no hospitals. I will not scare my son. I need to lie down and sleep. I'll be fine in the morning. Help me to the door."

He shakes his head in frustration. "Woman, you sure are stubborn."

Eli's arm is wrapped around me as we reach the door, propping me up, but my chin drops to my chest. I take a couple of deep breaths.

Any sudden movement will undo my best intentions to maintain control. It doesn't matter. As the door swings open, a forceful heave beginning in my gut pushes its way through my chest and up my throat. Yellow bile and bits of orange Jell-O spray from my mouth, splaying across my shoes and onto the concrete pad at our feet.

The smell of vomit combines with a potent waft of Chanel No. 5.

Angling my neck up, I'm surprised to see the furrowed brow and curled lip of Tía Lisandra's disdained expression. But it isn't her disapproval that pushes me to the edge, nor is it the rush of the familiar cool, sweet air from inside my parents' home. No, my stomach's violent rejection is my intestines twisting from Tía Lisandra's deliberate decision to answer the door with my son at her side.

Teó's tiny hand is interlocked with hers. His big blue eyes stare at me in widened terror as he looks over at the stranger beside me. Eli can barely hold me up with his one good arm. I'm doubled over, in shock, by the mess I've made at our feet. My head hangs with the heaviness of shame, a weight my neck can no longer bear.

I look up at him again, wiping my mouth with the back of my hand, pleading for forgiveness. "Teó, please."

"Mamá?" His voice is small. He looks up at Tía Lisandra, terrified as he says it.

Unable to stop myself, I lean over again and heave forcefully—only this time, nothing comes out.

# CHAPTER TWENTY-EIGHT

When I wake up in the morning, my son is gone.

I shoot up from the bed—the one I've graciously ceded to my boy since moving here—and look over to the sofa bed, confused and disoriented by the change in our arrangements. It is empty, never even pulled out. The throbbing in my temples and the pressure behind my eyes punish me for last night's bender, but they don't deter me from whipping my head in every direction, searching for any trace of my son.

Maybe he slept somewhere else. Maybe Dolores's room? I bet he's at the breakfast table eating oatmeal and pan de agua, waiting for me to join him.

As I rub the sleep from my eyes, last night's images invade my new day. I remember the scene at the front door. I threw up when Tía Lisandra answered it. Teó was with her. I almost blacked out, but Eli held me upright.

Oh my God . . . my son witnessed everything.

Once released, the images pour into my mind like a raging river. First, there's Eli leaning down and slinging me over his shoulder with his one good hand, then carrying me into the room. Then there's the sadness on Teó's face as he wordlessly pointed him in the right direction.

Eli laid me down. He and Teó stood at the edge of the bed, each removing one shoe and one sock.

How did this happen? Why were Teó and Tía Lisandra in my parents' home alone? Where was everyone else?

I suck in air, shocked by the next blurry memory—Eli propping me on my side and my son watching, worried.

Oh my God—his face.

Teó's eyes were dark pools of disappointment—and fear—watching as Eli bunched the blankets and the pillows on the bed to prevent me from falling backward and aspirating on my own vomit. How could I let this happen?

Throwing my feet over the edge of the bed, I stare ahead into nothingness. I replay the softness in Eli's explanation, telling Teó it was important I remain on my side all night.

What an impression I must have made on them both.

The last thing I remember when Eli led Teó out of the room is the spinning ceiling, as though I were lying on my back in the middle of a merry-go-round.

I finally fell asleep, positioned on my side, mumbling incoherently about the tragedies of children in war. It all goes black from there.

This is not good. This is a new low, even for me.

Convinced Teó is at the breakfast table, waiting for me, I shuffle to the bathroom. It's important that I shower and brush my teeth. I don't want Teó to see or smell any remaining instances of last night. My boy needs to see the mother he recognizes, a woman he can trust.

Undoubtedly I've broken his sense of safety. How do I ever forgive myself for that?

I'm not sure I can, but I have to try to make amends.

I'm dressed in less than fifteen minutes, and from the archway, I see that all traces of last night's escapade are washed away. The traditional morning activities are underway in the kitchen, as though last night's travesty never occurred. There's no sign of Teó. The screen door is open.

I peer out to see if maybe he's outside. Abuelo is swaying gently in his rocking chair on the front porch. My eyes automatically search the ground just outside the door, but someone made sure the vomit on the front stoop was washed away.

Papi starts the car and is pulling away from the driveway when he suddenly stops, seeing me standing at the front door. I look to see if Teó is in the passenger seat, but it's empty. He rolls the window down and pops his head out. "She lives?" he shouts.

"Very funny. Where is my son?"

This time, it's Papi who shakes his head. "Catalina, I already warned you to get yourself under control. You want to be out there on the streets like a man in heat. We will discuss this tonight when I return."

Before I can shoot back a rebuttal, he reverses out into the street and drives away. The bubbling of my own scorn simmers in my stomach when I turn back inside.

Abuela is in the kitchen, rinsing the last of the breakfast dishes clean. From the scent of burned grease, I can tell she fried bacon.

I'm surprised Dolores is already up, wearing a tiny pink camisole covered with red hearts and matching shorts. She is sprawled like a cat on the corner seat, sipping coffee and staring down at the table. Her troubled expression deepens when I approach. Mami sits beside her, peeling and grating the yautia by hand. She must be preparing the masa for alcapurrias. The deep-fried fritter stuffed with ground beef is usually one of my favorites, but today the smell of the bacon combined with the very thought of food makes me nauseous.

"Lina, qué bueno, you're awake," Mami says, as though my altercation with Papi at the door didn't just happen. Her tone carries a bite. She doesn't bother to look up.

"Where is Teó?" I ask, looking around, well aware he isn't nearby. My heart quickens.

"Your tía Lisandra took him to school this morning."

"What do you mean?" My voice rises. "Did she stay here last night? Why did she take him to school? Why didn't anyone wake me?"

Mami finally looks up. "Lina, calm down. She took him to her house last night. Apparently *you* were in no condition . . ."

She doesn't finish her statement. We all know what she means. Mami's expression dares me to deny it.

Dolores stares down at her coffee, her expression further darkening. I know she wants to come to my defense, but I haven't given her anything to grab on to so she can help defend me.

They aren't wrong. I wasn't in any condition to care for my son last night, but that was last night. This is the morning—a new day. I am fine, and Teó is *my* son. They had no right to take him anywhere without my consent.

I made a mistake bringing him here. I'd forgotten how intrusive family can be on the island. The idea of boundaries is foreign when it comes to the household. There aren't roles to respect; the village raises the child, especially when the village shares a roof.

The LaSalle and Rivera blood flows through Teó's veins, which means I'm not the only authority in his life, not as long as I am living with my parents and grandparents. My aunt's actions are stretching it, but it's obvious, as far as they are concerned, she isn't totally out of line. Not that I care. To me she sure as hell is. Teó is *my* son.

Tía Lisandra's innate desire for her own son is deep at the root of this thing. She has utterly rejected and abandoned her daughter. By Dolores's own admission, her mother has spent the entirety of her life chastising her for not being the boy she wished for. I can relate. Papi has done the same to me, damn near blaming me for being born a girl.

I won't risk Teó serving as some type of retribution for my tía. If my actions in Iraq made one thing abundantly clear, it's what I'm capable of doing to stay close to Teó. God help anyone who tries to separate him from me.

I look directly at Mami. "My condition last night is no one's business. Teó was supposed to be safe here—with you. Where did you go?"

Abuela turns from the sink to face me. "I think your condition when you come into this house falling-down drunk is everyone's business. Especially when you bring a strange man with you."

Mami cuts in. "Papi was playing in the band last night. I went to support him. I didn't realize you were planning to be out so late, Catalina. I agree with your abuela. Isn't it a bit soon to be bringing someone to the house to meet your family? And then to bring him here when you're in such a state . . ."

My cheeks flush with embarrassment. "Mami, it's not like that. He's just a friend. I needed a ride."

"Irresponsable," Abuela murmurs before returning to the dishes.

"Al contrario," I counter. "Calling him was the most responsible thing I could do, because I knew I was in no condition to drive. Eli is someone I trusted to get me home safely."

I cross my fingers, hoping they don't refute my logic, stating that *not drinking* was the most responsible thing I could have done. I know that, but I need an edge right now, a reason they shouldn't have taken Teó. Thankfully Dolores comes to the rescue.

"It's true, Abuela," she says. "Eli is very honorable and responsible."

I want to reach out and hug her.

Mami doesn't say another word. She continues grating the taro root as though the conversation is over. They believe Tía Lisandra's actions are justified. I was out of control, and my tía stepped in and saved my son from my debauchery. Case closed.

Teó and I have to find our own place. We cannot continue to stay here. We've been on our own too long. If I don't regain my independence, my relationship with the people who mean the most to me will be destroyed.

I know what I have to do. I think back to last night, before things got out of control. I remember the feeling of purpose, the sense of unity with my own soul while triaging the big guy amid his seizure. I need to stop the voices in my head, the ones saying I can't—my son's future depends on it. I need to choose loyalty to myself and to my calling over the life of the young man on the battlefield. Which means I have to find a way to release my guilt at the child I took from someone else. I can't get myself to sign up for factory work, and I know why. As much as I've been willing to sacrifice, something deep inside me is urging me not to give up. I need to fight for my own identity the same way I fought to get back to my boy, which means shoving down what I did in Iraq even deeper. I need to bury those memories so deep they can't keep coming back up to destroy me.

*I have to forget.* The words carry the sound of my voice but are coated with the mourning of a grieving mother. What choice is there? I know what I can do; the option literally landed at my feet. That can't be a coincidence.

"Dolores, can you take me to pick up my car?" Before she can answer, I turn back to Mami. "Last night I found out the National Guard is looking to mobilize soldiers. I am going to stop by the office in Toa Baja and see how quickly I can sign back up to serve with a unit here on the island. It'll give me an opportunity for full-time employment and allow me to get my own place."

"Good idea, Lina," Mami says. "It will be good for you to get back to work. And I strongly recommend you stop drinking so much, because we all agree it's not good for Teó to see his mami in the condition you were in last night."

Abuela reenters the conversation from the kitchen. "And nearly every night since you arrived! I know all about your little routine on the back patio when you think everyone is sleeping and no one is paying attention."

"Sí, Mami. Gracias," my mother says, cutting Abuela off before turning to me. "If you have a drinking problem, there are places that can help you. In the meantime, Tía Lisandra would happily look after Teó while you get the help you need."

"Tía!" Dolores gasps.

My head shoots up. I was staring at the floor as they chastised me. But now my hands and feet are pumping with adrenaline—this is fight or flight in its most primordial sense. My fingers grip the edge of the dining table, poised for attack. She is calling for war.

My glare meets my mother's, and when her eyes meet mine, I see terror.

The drumbeat of my heart pounds in my ears as my breath comes in short bursts. She crossed the line by threatening to take my son away and give him to my aunt.

Mami's dark, soulful eyes search my face. Her lips tighten grimly. Her fear shifts into something else. Despair. She sees something she wasn't expecting from me. Vengeance.

"Don't you dare," I growl. I turn to Dolores. "I think it's time for us to go. Right now."

Abuela turns in time to see Mami and me facing off. A dish towel falls to the ground as her hand rises to her mouth. "Bendito sea Dios. Ya, muchachas. Stop. No more."

Dolores rises from her seat and swipes the purse hanging on the chair over her shoulder. She rushes to where I'm standing, grabs my arm, and leads me to the front door. "Okay, everything is okay. Let's go, prima."

Dolores doesn't let go of my arm until we reach the car.

It isn't until we turn the corner and pull away from the street that I realize I didn't even give her an opportunity to change out of her pajamas.

# CHAPTER TWENTY-NINE

"I will not let her take him," I shout, slamming my palm on the dashboard. The burn from the impact of flesh against plastic travels to my wrist. I ignore it. "I will not let anyone take him. Do you hear me?"

I may be shouting, but Dolores understands my tirade isn't aimed at her. She is more a victim of Tía Lisandra than anyone. My face remains straight ahead, yelling at a ghost and at my own reflection in the glass.

"No one is going to take him from you," she says, attempting to soothe my frayed nerves. "No one will—ever. That boy's heart belongs to you."

I wipe my nose, unsure what is making me cry more—my anger over my family's betrayal or my shame over what Teó witnessed last night. Maybe it's the fear they have grounds to take him from me, especially knowing that my aunt is a power player on the island, and with her long list of political connections, it wouldn't be a stretch for her to get support from the local child and family administration office. I don't want to believe she's capable of that, but my tía has always maintained an iron will. If she believes something to be "for the best," there's no stopping her. The lies she told Leonardo, life-altering lies, prove exactly that. I know better than to underestimate her.

"I'm sorry, Dolores," I say, yielding.

"For what?" Dolores reaches over and gently pats my thigh.

I plan on saying "for this morning," but I realize I'm holding a big truth about Christian that I haven't yet revealed. "For all of it. I didn't even let you get dressed."

She rolls her eyes and smiles. "Qué importa. It doesn't matter. I'm taking you to pick up your car. I'll call Mami to make sure she took Teó to school and help calm things down."

"Actually, I think I'm going to go over there myself. I think it's time I face her one-on-one." Seeing the trepidation in her eyes, I ask, "You don't think that's a good idea?"

"I guess I don't have a better one." She turns onto the area marked as La Placita.

"I mean, I could go pull my son out of school, book two tickets to Florida with Tía Kika, and never look back."

"Lina, I hope you're not serious," Dolores says solemnly.

*I'm entirely serious.*

Dolores reads my face. "You made a big decision to leave Tía Kika's house seven years ago and join the Army. You grew into a powerful woman. Why would you go backward?"

I look away from her. "Isn't that exactly what I've done? Gone back to where I started?"

"Yes and no," Dolores relents. "Returning to Florida to be alone doesn't make sense. Yes, Tía Kika is there, but she has her friends from the retirement community. Her own life. She's independent, Lina, and she loves it. I know she's dropped everything to help you in North Carolina, while you were deployed, but isn't all her sacrifice worth it if she sees you thriving and moving forward with all our family here?"

Dolores is right. "Teó said the last time they spoke on the phone, she was so happy to hear about us starting a new life back here with the family," I admit softly.

The young, wise Dolores always has a way of making a point.

"I know if Tía Kika were here right now, she would agree with me. Don't run away, prima. Remember Teó's doctor appointment is coming up. He can get the care he needs here, on the island. I know you're afraid, but there's a reason you're here with us. It may not seem like it right now, but family is important. It's everything. Tía will be visiting us for Christmas, like always, and I'm sure she will tell you herself. It's good for you and for Teó to have us surrounding you; you both need it." She looks over knowingly, but the corners of her lips rise tightly in cadence with a shrug of her shoulder. "But sometimes that means family is around to point out things you don't want to hear or see."

She returns her gaze to the road.

"Trust en tu familia," she says softly. "We will always be here to help you. And Lina?"

"Yes, go ahead," I say with a sigh.

"Teó is happy here. He needs you. He needs his mami to be strong and healthy. I know you can be both of those things and still be happy here with us."

We pass the first empty parking lot, and I point to the street up ahead, remembering now where I parked.

"I won't lose my son, Dolores."

"Then don't, prima. Don't."

The wisdom of her words cools my anger. I understand what she's saying. The decision is mine to make. It's up to me how I choose to handle my grief. I can continue to drink it away until morning, where it sits patiently at the side of my bed, waiting. Or I can take a page from Eli's book and allow my grief to push me forward into doing something good with the life I have left. At the end of the day, it's my choice.

I point to my car at the same time Dolores sees the hatchback all alone and pulls up alongside it.

"You will be stronger with your family here to support you," she says, knowingly. "We will never stop looking out for each other, even if we don't always get along."

I reach across the seat to hug her and kiss her cheek, much calmer than I was when we first got in the car. I'm thankful she's talked me off a ledge. Now it's my turn to do right by her. Eli too. There's something I need to make sure I tell them both.

I step out but peek my head through the open passenger window. "Dolores, there's actually something I'd like to talk to you about. You and Eli. Can you meet me at Chiquitas in a couple of hours?"

Dolores knows the primary connection between her and Eli is Christian, but any glimpse of concern disappears swiftly.

"Of course I will." Dolores flashes the wicked grin I've come to love. "Everything is going to be good. Don't worry so much. I know Mami took Teó to school. She wouldn't have it any other way. After you two talk, everything is going to work out. You've always been her favorite, Lina."

She shrugs, and I'm surprised at the guilt that pricks like the tip of a syringe. I've never thought about how my relationship with Tía Lisandra might look from my cousin's eyes.

I wave goodbye. "I'll see you at Chiquitas. I'll text you when I'm heading there."

She nods and drives away.

Dolores is right. I can't keep running. I came home for a reason. In the little time I've known him, Eli has shown me the power of using tragedy as a mechanism to move forward and build something. I have to change. It's time to stop running and hiding in a mind-numbing state of drunkenness.

Truthfully, the thought of not drinking anymore makes me desperately want to drink. Which is exactly why I know I need help.

I unlock my car and slide into the driver's seat, forcing myself to replay the image of my son removing my shoe the night before. Teó probably thought I was dying. I would have.

One thing that's been made absolutely clear this morning: if I don't get it together, I will lose my son. Hell, if I'm not strong enough to do this for him, I don't deserve to be his mother.

And now Leonardo knows about Teó. That changes everything. I am in no position to risk Leo's concern over my ability to care for our son. If anyone had seen me last night and told him . . . the thought shakes me to my core, especially because he'd probably get my tía

Lisandra's connections and support. Maybe that's a stretch, given her opinion of Leonardo, but at this point I can't be sure of anything, except that things have gotten out of control and I refuse to fail either of us. This can't continue. I must make a change—for Teó's sake.

The quiet countenance of La Placita fades away in my rearview mirror. I contemplate the memories of the night before. I was so drunk and put myself smack in the middle of a potentially dangerous situation. My family was right to have taken Teó away, given the state I was in when I finally made it back. Who knows what else Teó might have seen or heard had we shared the room.

This time, my tía did the right thing, and my parents were right to support her. That realization hits me hardest of all.

Before the day's up I need to go see Dr. Robles.

# CHAPTER THIRTY

As I approach the entrance of my aunt's gated community, my phone rings.

"¿Hola?"

It doesn't matter that it's been a decade since we spoke regularly. I instantly recognize Leonardo's familiar baritone and thick accent.

"Lina? Qué bueno. I found you."

"Yes, you found me. What is it?" My words escape a little short, but I'm not sure how to react to him or to this great big bow we have tying us together.

"It's good to hear your voice," he says huskily.

I know that tone. I remember that tone with surprising familiarity. It's the one he uses when he's trying to get what he wants. It was the same one he used when we agreed to going all the way, knowing it would be my first time.

When I don't respond, his words come out clipped. "I think I've been patient. Have you decided when I can meet my son? I don't want to wait any longer."

Leonardo is getting anxious. I know it's not fair to him, but my newest reason for delaying this meeting has nothing to do with the stress of an introduction. Teó has been through a very traumatic night. Thanks to me.

I run my fingers through my hair, gripping the phone against my ear. "This isn't about what you do or don't want. Things have been a little intense for us lately, Leo. Moving here and starting school, it's a lot for a young boy. He is going through so many changes in his life. I think we need to take things slow. You can understand that, can't you?"

The tone in his voice softens. "I'm his father, Lina. Meeting me isn't a burden for him; it's a blessing. Finding out about me isn't going to bring him pain; it will bring him happiness. Why would you think otherwise?"

I wish we could be having this conversation face-to-face. Still, however it's happening, Leonardo has a point. Perhaps I'm allowing my relationship with *my* father to cloud my judgment. Leo wants to establish a connection to his son. How can I stand in the way of that?

I imagine the two of them meeting for the first time. My heart warms at the thought of Teó looking up to see a face and a demeanor so similar to his own. Leo's right. Bringing them together will be good for him. I remember the conversation yesterday about the boy bullying him at school, his parentage, and his tics. Meeting his father and knowing Leo went through similar circumstances means they can relate to one another in a way that Teó and I can't.

"Okay. You're right, it's time. But just you, okay? I know you want Teó to meet your family. But please, we need to move slowly. Will you respect that?"

"Yes! Claro que sí. Of course I will." He sounds happy. "Whatever you want. I only want to meet my son. So when can we make this happen, Lina?"

I think about all the uncertainties in my and Teó's life and the resolution I must make with him first.

*One hurdle at a time,* I say silently, affirming that my top priority is to protect my son. "This weekend." I push away the fear of how fast it's all moving. This is it. I've already said yes. There's no turning back now.

"How about the science museum—in Bayamón?" I propose. "Teó loves science. We can meet near the entrance in front of the rocket at ten in the morning on Sunday."

"Yes, that's a great idea, linda . . . I mean, Lina."

He said *beautiful.* Is he flirting? I picture the wife who sat at his table at Chiquitas. The woman he returned to after our summer and married—the mother of his other child. I need to be careful. I don't want him getting the wrong idea.

I grip the steering wheel a little tighter and push away the thought.

"Don't be late. The thirty-minutes-after Puerto Rican grace period will not fly," I warn. "Teó is all about punctuality. It won't make a good impression if you're late."

"Gracias," he says ardently. "I won't be late, I promise. I will see you both there on Sunday. Ten a.m., en punto."

"Okay, see you then."

"Cuídense, Lina."

"You take care, too, Leo."

I nod even though I know he can't see me. I nod again because it's all I can do to convince myself I'm doing the right thing. Reaching the gates of my aunt's housing community, I steel my resolve and prepare to slay a different dragon.

The security guard at the entrance walks over and taps on my window. "Su licencia, por favor."

I hand him my driver's license, then wait as he disappears into the guard shack.

Tía Lisandra's haughty tone bellows through the speaker on his desk. "Sí, está bien."

"Adelante," he says, directing me forward as he updates the visitors' log. "Last building on the right, facing the ocean."

I nod. I remember.

The car travels down the curved asphalt, framed on each side with lush, manicured grass and swaying palms. I drive around the last bend toward the ocean. My eyes graze the rolling green hills and bright floral landscaping. It's been years, but the familiarity of the neighborhood fills me with a distant sense of home. I learned to dream here, studying at my tía's desk after a full day of class. She pushed me to believe in myself in ways I probably wouldn't have otherwise. No one else in my family seemed to have any expectations that I'd do anything big with my life. I always assumed it was because they never had big dreams of their own. I didn't even know about Abuela's desire to join the Army and travel the world until yesterday. When I was growing up, Tía Lisandra was the only one who talked about my future as a professional. She saw something in me that no one else either saw or admitted to. Her vision pushed my parents to send me to Florida for a bigger life. I didn't understand it at the time, but now I realize the gift that it was. If I hadn't gone to Florida, I wouldn't have had Teó, and I don't think I'd have joined the Army. Our relationship is complicated, but I can't deny that my tía Lisandra's influence and my tía Kika's welcoming arms and solid support have manifested some of my best experiences. Looking over at the manicured homes, it hits me: Would Teó be better off here, living the country club lifestyle? The sudden thought scares me.

Each paved walkway leads to a freshly painted angular house. They look like little yellow brick roads leading to their own private Emerald Cities. This is how some of the island's most elite live.

*Don't forget, Lina, Dolores could be living here.* Instead, she's chosen the pueblo that surrounds my parents' humble neighborhood. She ran away from all this.

It reminds me of the other side of the coin: the sterility of my tía's nature, her hard-edged discipline with little room for mercy, and especially the mortal sin of simplemindedness if you don't agree with exactly what *she* wants for *your* life.

The thought offers some comfort when I arrive at unit 101.

*No, Teó belongs at home with me.* I can give him both the inspiration I've gotten from my tía Lisandra and the affection he deserves that I've experienced from Mami and my tía Kika.

Crests of waves crash against the sand, filling the air with the quiet rustle of low tide. A private exit to the beach opens directly to my right. Another security guard is parked there in his golf cart, watching my every move.

Before I can knock on the frosted glass panel, my aunt pulls the door open, looking freshly prepared. Her makeup, painstakingly applied, is framed by jet-black hair, once again blown out into an iron-straight pageboy, just past her shoulders. She wears a sleeveless silk shirt patterned with hibiscus flowers and a starched folded collar. The tropical top is paired with creased tangerine-orange chinos, the colors coordinated to an exact match.

Chanel No. 5 fills the air as she draws closer to greet me, and I'm reminded of the pride I always felt when she would pick me up at school in her shiny new car, perfectly pressed and looking like someone in charge.

"Buenos días, sobrina," she says politely, offering an air-kiss.

"Buenos días, Tía." I make sure to sound equally polite. Seeing her, nostalgia transitions to anger and indignation when I remember why I'm here. I wish I could tackle her to the ground after discovering how she lied to Leonardo and to me, but given last night's events, she could very well take my son away. My tía has a slew of suitors and connections in San Juan and a way of exerting her influence. She did it when she convinced Papi I'd be best off going to high school in the US. When she insists on something, it tends to happen. I won't risk her perseverance when Teó's custody is on the line.

She waves me into the ultramodern townhome with a perfectly manicured hand. "Entra."

"Gracias." I follow with a begrudged "Bendición," wishing I didn't feel compelled to ask for her blessing.

"Que Dios te bendiga, Catalina."

"Is Teó . . . ," I say, looking around, but I don't finish my sentence.

"No, of course not," she says. "He's at school, exactly where he should be."

She's remodeled the living room since the last time I was here twelve years ago. The newly hung modern-style paintings are lined in a perfect row above the white leather couch. They remind me of soldiers standing at attention. The decor is classy but cold.

My eyes graze around the room to confirm, and it still holds true—she doesn't hang or display any family pictures. My aunt's living room could be used as a showroom, modeling the units for prospective tenants. There is no trace of her individual life—at least not in the living room. It's so sterile, although it's always been this way. When I was little, I thought that was how smart, rich people decorated their homes. Now I see it for what it is—an impenetrable defense, a way to ensure people can't see who she is just by standing in her living room. They have to be invited in, in more ways than one.

"Why don't you have a seat." She points to the pristine white couch.

It doesn't look like anyone ever sits on it, but aside from an oddly shaped bright-red chair in the corner, there is no other choice. And I'm not sure I can figure out how to sit inside the chair's weird design. The couch is crisp, flat, and low to the ground.

I choose the couch.

My aunt chooses the red chair.

Its raised height compared to the couch makes her appear on a throne and me below her. Well played.

Attempting some semblance of my own power, I scoot forward to the sofa's edge and place my elbows on my knees. The faint sound of classic salsa plays in the distance from another room. It's the same station Abuela listens to in the kitchen while making breakfast. The traditional rhythms soften the tense air between us. Even in this residential museum of modern architecture, the sounds of our heritage break through.

"¿Cómo te sientes?" she asks, a loaded question I must carefully answer.

"I'm feeling much better, thank you."

She looks me over.

"That's good," she says tersely. "We were all very *worried* about you last night."

My instinct is to defend myself and fight back. A sarcastic rebuttal dances on the tip of my tongue. But again I force myself to stop. It isn't the way. I need to try humility. At least start there and see where we land.

"Tía, I want to apologize for last night. I went out because I was very angry after hearing what you and Papi told Leonardo when he showed up inquiring about his child. I needed to calm down and I think someone may have spiked my drink. I realize it doesn't matter and it's not an excuse for the condition I was in, but . . . I'm just trying to say I understand why you brought Teó here. I was not in a good place."

I lean back, satisfied by the humility and thoroughness of my explanation while still holding her accountable for her part in this disaster.

"*Not in a good place.* Hmm. That's one way to describe it." Her eyes look to one side as her lips point to the other.

I hate when she makes this face. Sarcasm definitely runs in our family. She isn't going to make this easy for me. I didn't expect she would. When has this woman ever made anything easy? Her technique has always been refinement by pressure and fire. Her motto has always been that to improve, you must be stretched to your limit.

I think back to our shopping trips when I was a little girl—just the two of us. She would tell me all the stories of the greats. José Barbosa; Pedro Albizu Campos, the first Puerto Rican to graduate from Harvard; Dr. María Cadilla, who fought for a woman's right to vote. My aunt was always pushing me to stretch the possibilities of my dreams. There was a time when we were close, when I felt like she had my best interest at heart, even if her approach always carried a diabolical twist. I still remember the drives we would take once every summer when I was in middle school, navigating through some of Puerto Rico's poorest areas. We would slow to a crawl in places where children ran through the dirt roads barefoot, and where families used outhouses behind dilapidated buildings due to the lack of indoor plumbing. She would pull the car over and roll down the window and say, *Lina, take it in. Take it all in. If you don't study and commit to your full potential, you will end up living like this, with nine children of your own. A simple woman with a simple mindset.* Then she'd drive me through the gates of her beachfront community to spend the afternoon studying, ensuring I understood the stark difference between the two possibilities before me.

*Lina,* she would say, repeating Barbosa's quote over and over, *superiority is not proved by color, but by the brain, by education, by willpower, by moral courage.*

Reflecting on it, I see how she thought lying to Leonardo meant she was protecting me. It doesn't make it right, but I get that, from her jaded point of view, she believed she was doing what was best to ensure my success.

"It isn't going to happen again, Tía," I insist. "That's why I'm here. I wanted to assure you—face-to-face—I'm serious about getting back on track. What you witnessed last night was a wake-up call."

Her eyebrows arch. "For you, Lina? Or for Matteo?"

It's the first time in my life the sound of my son's name makes me cringe, and I damn near hate her for it.

"I don't know what that's supposed to mean, but Teó is my life. He doesn't need a wake-up call. I would never do anything to hurt him."

Only one eyebrow lowers. The doubt in her expression is loud and clear. Or maybe she is silently saying what we both know—I have already hurt him.

It's time for a Hail Mary. "I'm going to see my therapist today. I'm serious about getting better. I'm working some things out. I know I need to change, slow down the drinking."

She's unable to hide the surprise that registers across her powdery white face.

"Is that so?" she muses. "Bueno, I'm glad you said something, because I was about to offer you a drink." She leans forward in the red throne chair. "Are you sure I can't offer you something, Lina? You can always begin sobriety tomorrow."

I roll my eyes, well acquainted with her games.

"I understand why you might have doubts, Tía. Why you feel the need to test me. I was out of control last night. I'm not going to let that happen again."

"Is that why you couldn't answer your phone when Ma—when Teó," she corrects, "was hurt at school? You were drinking?"

My eyes shoot up from my lap, surprised.

"What do you mean? You saw me as soon as I arrived at the house. The cell signal wasn't strong where I was. You know I wasn't drunk. Why are you doing this?"

My aunt answers with the iciness of her familiar mind games. "What is it that you think I'm doing?"

There's no reason to beat around the bush; she has pushed my patience too far.

"Threatening to take my son from me. You've already kept him from his father his entire life. Haven't you taken away enough?"

She sits rigidly still and stares at the coffee table between us as though my accusation sits at its center.

"Catalina Noelia, all I've ever tried to do is help make sure you had every opportunity for greatness. Do you know how many women on this island believe the only thing they're good for is cleaning houses and having children? I wanted more for you and for your son. Once you got pregnant, you could have lost your chance. I made sure that did not happen. That's what family does. We protect our own."

This is what aggravates me most. She isn't wrong; family is supposed to protect one another. However, not through lies and deception and not by eliminating the opportunity to make the decision for myself. Essentially she'd admitted she believes that left to my own devices, I'd have given up my future for Leonardo. I would have fallen into this endless trap of "simplemindedness." That truth generates a deep-rooted sense of indignation in me.

Worse yet, she believed she had to save me from failing even further, since I'd already gotten pregnant and begun down a path she deemed irreparable and destined for failure.

"You know, Tía, for some women, being a wife and a mother is a gift, not a failure. Even if the road that leads to motherhood is cracked and bumpy, it doesn't change the fact that raising a child can be life's greatest reward, even more rewarding than a thriving career."

I stand by what I'm saying, but hearing myself speak, I can't help but grip the reality that I want both. I want it all.

"Do you really want what is best for Teó, Catalina?"

I recognize her games, her ploys to try to keep my son. "How could you ask me that? Of course I want what is best for him. I am his mother. Don't you have any idea what that means?"

Her lips part in rebuttal, but I refuse to stop. I'm fighting for Teó, and I have to gain the upper hand to win this battle of wits with her before she will crown me victorious and release her hold on my boy.

"No, you don't. You can't possibly. Dolores left you. Apparently you weren't cut out for the role."

I brace for her to stand up and ask me to leave, but she doesn't move a muscle. The whites of her eyes glisten. This time my words have cut deep.

"Catalina, you have been gone for a long time," she says coolly. "It's dangerous to assume you understand the details of a circumstance you had no part in."

I picture Sergeant Fuentes's blood pooling on the ground beneath his neck, followed by the shouts from the commander, and the target's crumpled body.

My voice drops. "I could say the very same thing to you."

Her shoulders slump as she tilts her head and looks at me. Match point for me.

"He is an extraordinary boy, sobrina. God has given you a gift. Don't take such a gift for granted. There's no reason for him to suffer because you can't get yourself under control. He is exceptional, brilliant—he could be the next Dr. Barbosa."

I release my fingers, balled tight with fear. My words must be chosen carefully to sever the responsibility I see her formulating over Teó's future.

"That is something we can wholeheartedly agree on. Teó *is* an extraordinary boy, and I won't take him for granted. Never again." I say it and I mean it.

She considers me, her hands clasped on her lap as she leans in closer.

"When I was pregnant with Dolores, I prayed for a son."

I nod. "I know." I pause before finishing the thought. "So does she."

This time her eyes don't glisten. A cascade of tears wells up and spills down her cheeks.

I catch my breath. I've never seen my aunt cry before. Come to think of it, I've barely even seen her smile. She has long since mastered the mystery of the blank expression, just like the other day at Mami's dining table or at the door, when she opened it wide enough to allow Eli to carry me through. It's always a blank expression. But this ends the battle. Through her vulnerability she has directed me right into a checkmate. I'm done fighting. I want to hug her and tell her that we need to put the past behind us and find our way back to the relationship we once had.

She doesn't wipe the tears from her cheeks. I look down to the tightly clasped hands on her lap and damn near surrender. I don't doubt the authenticity of the moment, but still . . . *Well played, Tía.*

She looks me directly in the eyes. "God knew what I needed, Lina, even if I couldn't see beyond my own ideas." She straightens in her chair. "He gave me a beautiful daughter, so beautiful I was sure she would throw her life away on a few romantic words or some childish fantasy. I thought having a father figure, even a jíbaro like your father, would keep the scoundrels away from her. I wanted to protect her, but in the process I destroyed my chance to be her mother."

I think about the generosity in my cousin's heart and the emptiness she carries from the fractured relationship with my tía Lisandra. I need to tell her it's not too late.

"Tía, *my* son is no one's replacement. He is my gift from God, and from now on I will do better to act like it. I will do better." This time I lean forward to meet her halfway. "You have not lost your chance with your own daughter. Dolores is extraordinary. You should feel very proud of the confident and selfless woman she has grown into. But she still needs her mother. You need to tell her what you told me today."

She looks down at her lap, then glances back up and considers me carefully. I see the stoic strength return to her face as the tears in her eyes begin to dry.

"You don't have to worry about anyone trying to take your son, Catalina."

I exhale the breath I've been holding.

"As long as," she warns, her tone again ice cold, "you make good on your word. Teó is the priority. He should never again see you in the condition you were in last night. I will be watching, and none of us will allow that boy to be hurt that way again. Can we agree that in order to avoid your family stepping in, you must behave more responsibly?"

"Agreed," I say. "And Dolores?"

She glances toward her front door. "One matter at a time."

I know my aunt. That's the best I'm going to get, and I need to take the win. I offer an apologetic smile as we both rise to our feet.

"Thank you, Tía, for hearing me out and for understanding. Things are going to be different."

She doesn't answer right away. Not until we reach the door.

"I hope so, Lina," she says holding the door open. "For both your sakes."

Something tells me the matter isn't fully settled. My aunt has a history of testing my resolve. I summon the courage inside for what I know is still coming, but I can feel the shift, the softening between us. Today I got a glimpse of a relationship I once held very dear. I do hope we can find a way back to a similar place one day.

"Bendición, Tía."

"Que Dios te bendiga," she offers, closing the door behind me.

# CHAPTER THIRTY-ONE

Stabilizing the situation with Tía Lisandra and knowing Teó will come home today allows me to ease my most pressing fears, breathe, and prepare for another moment of truth. I'm not going to lie to myself—I'm scared. The voices in my head want me to believe that once Eli learns the truth about how Sergeant Fuentes really died, he'll assume I did something wrong. I failed a fellow soldier on the battlefield out there, just as Eli has seen me fail my own son. A part of me wants to allow him to believe that. That today not only absolves him of the guilt he's carried for Christian's death, but that I can offer myself as an alternative target at which to aim his loss, his anger, and his shame. I think that way it'll make it easier when he tells me he doesn't need to stay in Puerto Rico anymore. This revelation will change everything. Eli is free now.

*Except you didn't shoot him, Lina. Sergeant Fuentes was a tragedy of war, an unexpected casualty.*

Had the marksman's rifle been aimed one degree over, it could have easily been me shot that day. Besides, I don't think I can handle the deaths of two innocents on my conscience, even if some would argue that a young man wearing a device filled with explosives around his waist is anything but innocent.

In either case, the facts remain the same. Sergeant Fuentes didn't die collecting soil samples with Eli that day; he died on the battlefield with me. Which means Eli doesn't have to sacrifice all his own hopes and dreams to honor the young soldier's legacy. He can return to South Carolina, if that's what he wants, and begin life on his own terms. The thought of him leaving hurts. Eli's presence in my life and watching how he's handled his postwar recovery are starting to help me to see my own circumstances through a different lens. I don't want him to go, but if freeing him from the heavy chains of guilt and shame results in him leaving, I understand. It's the least I can do, especially after everything he's done for me.

As for Dolores, Christian was her first love. She deserves to know the truth, and it felt nearly divine that the young sergeant's final moments were alongside a blood relative of the woman he loved in return. That had to mean something. I can't help but think I'm being called to complete some mission and deliver the truth to them both.

The first pangs of trepidation kick in when I reach the foot of the dreaded stairs leading to Chiquitas's rooftop bar. I can do this.

I lift my foot onto the first step. My mind is made up—I will not be afraid this time.

Eli must have been monitoring the security camera over the parking lot, because he is waiting for me at the top of the stairwell. He extends his right hand as I reach the landing.

"It's okay. I'm good."

"Shucks, good for you. Well, come on in then." He holds the door open and waves me in.

There's enough tension in his gait to reveal the truth. He is worried about what I've come to say. Or perhaps the tension is coming from what he plans to say to me. I surely haven't behaved like someone he should be spending time with.

He offers a sympathetic smile. "How are you feeling this mornin'?"

"Honestly? Like there's a desperate policeman swinging a battering ram inside my head."

"That's usually what happens after all that drinkin'. I will admit, you may have been seeing double and feeling single last night," he teases, "but you look pretty good this mornin'."

I've already learned to recognize how Eli uses humor to mask his discomfort.

"Aren't you the charmer," I say. "But I promise I understand if you'd rather I didn't come back here for a while after I say what I came to tell you."

He shrugs, obviously undecided. "I'm glad to see that you're all right. You gave us all a pretty good scare."

My shoulders drop in resignation and embarrassment. This is turning out harder than I expected. Seeing Eli forces me to really see myself from his perspective. I don't like who I've become. "Yeah, about that . . . I want to thank you, for, you know . . . putting me to bed last night."

He nods, but it's awkward to see him accept thanks for a gesture that should never have happened.

"That isn't why I'm here, though," I say, grateful for a reason to change the subject.

A slow smile dominates his face, but I'm not fooled. I can see the nervousness in his eyes. "Right. I got your text. The confession. I had Anita prepare us a table out on the balcony. The skies are beautiful today, but Dolores isn't here yet."

"Fresh air sounds great. Outside is perfect."

As we walk alongside the bar, I notice an ice-cold pink mojito in front of a young woman in a flowery sarong, sitting alone. The crushed mint leaves press against the edges of the glass, and the lemon wedge on the rim makes my mouth water. I can nearly taste the parcha. Truthfully, I can nearly taste the rum.

*Stop. I won't do it.*

Eli asks, "Would you like a drink?"

I glance over my shoulder at him. When our eyes meet, it's obvious he sees my struggle.

"We brewed iced tea this mornin'," he says quickly. "It has a hint of parcha. It's local."

"That sounds delicious."

It's charming to hear him say *parcha* instead of *passion fruit.*

Anita walks out the swinging kitchen door just as we reach the end of the bar.

"Hola, Lina," Anita says, not at all surprised to see me. Her smile throws me off. Eli must have said something.

I lean over politely and kiss her cheek in greeting. "Hola, Anita, it's nice to see you."

She puckers her lips and uses them to point to the back door. "The table is ready outside. This way."

Eli winks at her before turning to me. "I'll be right back."

"I think he is going to go get me a tea," I tell Anita, following her out onto the balcony. I can hear the regret in my voice.

"¿Un té?" There's no effort to hide her surprise.

"Sí. I need to stop drinking. Tea seems like a good place to start. At least it still has parcha."

She laughs nervously, waving her hand toward the table Eli has chosen for us.

A pink-and-gold dahlia, fire bright, rests in the center of the table. I'm impressed by the selection. I've always thought this ferocious round flower is so much more vibrant than the common carnation. It sits alone in a crystal vase, giving off an aura of power. The dahlia has stolen the show.

"Please take a seat, and I'll be out shortly with the appetizer," Anita says, pulling out my chair.

I grab the flower, break the stem, and tuck it behind my right ear, then sit down. The fiery beauty caresses my cheek.

"It looks beautiful," Eli says, surprising me from behind.

"Gracias."

"I thought the dahlia would make a lovely centerpiece, but it's clear that ornament was made for you."

"I think so, too, prima. You look like you are doing better." Dolores waves at us from the balcony's entrance as she meanders over to our table. "Things must have gone well with Mami?"

I nod. "Better than I expected."

Dolores is uncharacteristically muted this morning, with minimal makeup, her hair piled high on her head in a messy bun, and a pair of loose overalls with a tight baby tee beneath them. Round, extra-large sunglasses hide her stunning gray eyes.

"I'm glad you made it." The shrillness in my voice gives away my emotional state.

She gives Eli and me each a hug and light kiss in greeting before taking a seat beside me. Eli sets down my tea and a glass of ice water before he takes his seat.

I eye my glass, trying desperately not to feel disappointed by the lack of alcohol. The seeds float to the top, pushing past the larger unraveled tea leaves. "Thank you."

"De nada," Eli replies with a wink.

Summoning my strength, I take a moment to observe the beauty around me. In my last session with Dr. Robles, we talked about taking in what I see, what I hear, and what I smell in the moments when my anxiety begins to spike. It's an exercise in mindfulness and centering oneself in the moment. This is as good a time as any to practice. I look over at the chango perched on the balcony. A small insect flails with desperation in the bird's small, dark beak. It cranes its sleek black neck sharply, acknowledging me, before flying into the nearby trees. I look up and *see* the bright-blue-sky canopy above us, then focus in so I can *hear* nature's most beautiful soundtrack, with the waves crashing below in a rhythmic lullaby at our feet. My heart rate begins to slow as I focus on the *smell* of the sweet, floral scent of the dahlia tucked behind my ear.

"Thank you both for meeting me here on such short notice," I begin. "Last night was pretty wild, for a couple of reasons. What I'm about to tell you is probably going to sound ridiculous, but I've thought about this from every angle, and there's no doubt left—it's the truth."

Eli straightens in his chair but doesn't utter a word.

"It's about Christian. I . . . I recognized him."

This time it's Dolores who shifts, and I feel the depth of her stare. Neither one moves a muscle, waiting for me to continue, but I can see that Eli is holding his breath, waiting for what will come next.

"Last night I remembered where I recognized him from." I glance over at Dolores. "It was the night I went to Maria's house for her cancer treatment." My lips feel dry against the ocean breeze, my tongue like sandpaper, a combination of all the talking I've already done today and the dehydration from last night's alcohol extravaganza. I pause to sip the fruit-flavored tea, savoring the refreshment, before I continue.

"No entiendo," Dolores says.

"I know you don't understand," I answer. "Let me explain. When I first saw Christian's picture on the wall at Maria's, I didn't recognize him right away. I mean, he looked familiar but much younger in the photograph, so the realization didn't settle in at first . . . but then yesterday, at La Placita, it hit me. That's when I remembered."

Eli's brow furrows as he leans forward on his elbow, his hand splaying across his lips. He glances over at the tea, and I wonder if he thinks I've actually shown up here drunk.

"I haven't had a single drop of alcohol since you brought me home last night. Please listen to what I'm saying. Christian didn't die from the blast you suffered while collecting soil samples. He must have recovered from his injuries and returned to duty, to my unit."

His blank expression starts to crack with uncertainty. His head shakes ever so slightly as he bites his lower lip. I look over at Dolores, and her head tilts, still processing but confused.

Anita steps back out with a platter of seared ahi tuna. The food looks delicious, but the timing is horrible.

"Buen provecho," she says, placing the large plate at the center of the table. One of Alvin's young cousins from the other night stands behind her and sets down three small plates, one for each of us.

"Thank you," Eli says offhandedly, but both he and Dolores remain focused on me.

Anita senses the intensity at the table and hurries the kid back through the door, inside.

Alone again, I lean slightly closer, hoping to clear this up once and for all. With Dolores wearing sunglasses, I'm unable to see how she is responding to everything I've said so far.

"Eli, the other night you told me you were medevaced out of the area and never saw Christian again. You only found out later, after you returned from Germany, that he passed away. Right?"

He nods slowly. "Yes, that's right." Hints of anger brew in his stare.

"And Dolores, the only thing you were told was that Christian died on a mission in Iraq."

Her shoulders rise with frustration, as though that should be sufficient to know what happened. I've never seen her agitated before, even when she faced down her mother in the living room after bringing Teó home early from school. It's unnerving. I take a breath and try to slow my delivery to ensure they both understand everything I'm trying to say.

"Dolores, that still holds true. Christian did lose his life while on a mission in Iraq. Except that mission was with me, not Eli."

Dolores pulls her sunglasses up, resting them within her nest of dark hair, and wipes at her eyes. She is shaking her head but keeps silent, processing.

I reach for her hand. "Let me explain." I look across the table at Eli.

"Eli, you assumed Sergeant Fuentes passed away on the mission with you, but he didn't—he survived. In fact, his injuries weren't as bad as you thought, because he returned to duty. When he arrived at my unit, there was a rumor about him. One of the cooks mentioned that the new arrival had survived contact with the enemy and insisted on staying to finish his tour—"

"Lina," he says, interrupting me before I can continue. He runs his hand through his hair. "What are you talking about? You're not making any sense. You're saying Christian didn't die but returned to duty and was transferred to your unit? Why didn't he tell me that? He could've contacted me while I was in the hospital."

"Did you scrub all of your emails from the time you were in Germany?" I ask softly.

He shakes his head. "No, there were hundreds. A lot of generic Army stuff."

"What about your phone? Are you sure he didn't call?"

Possibility spreads across his face. "I lost it in the blast. We used his to call a medevac. I had to set up a new account after leaving the hospital. But listen, I asked around, looked him up myself when I was back online, and found out he was killed in action. I guess I just assumed I knew exactly how he was killed."

Before I can answer, my earlier words settle.

"Wait. You said he was on a mission with you? How is that possible?"

"I think I understand," Dolores finally breaks in quietly. "Christian called me, but the connection was no good. I couldn't understand everything. Only that he was going to a new unit in Iraq. I assumed with you, Eli. That was our last call."

Eli glances down at the prosthetic, then looks up at her. "I guess we never really talked about the details, did we, kid?"

I glance down at the tuna, keenly aware that none of us is inclined to eat, and focus on the execution of the whole truth.

I bite my lip momentarily to keep my voice from cracking. "I recognized Christian's picture because he was stationed at my FOB in Iraq. Only a few days before our"—I swallow the imagery thickening in my throat—"before our final convoy. We didn't speak before we rolled out that morning, but he told me he was from Puerto Rico."

I look down at my lap when I feel Dolores's hand on my arm. "He was my driver."

Eli stands up from the table abruptly and walks to the edge of the railing. I don't move, giving him the space to process what I've said, and prepare for everything I have yet to say.

When he turns back to face us, I look over at Dolores, and she offers a gentle nod. "Go ahead."

I take another breath, channeling Stone Cold. I need to tap into her essence if I'm going to finish my story.

"Three days after Christian arrived at the unit, he was assigned to join us on the convoy. My truck was the designated ambulance. There were three of us. Christian and I were in the front, the chaplain was in the back. We got stopped. There was a suspected IED ahead on the road."

My eyes close, and I'm right back there. The hot, dusty desert air surrounds me. The faint scent of trash and oil from my memories fills the air.

"We were attacked. They stopped the convoy by placing an IED in the middle of the road. Then, while stopped, we were attacked by sniper fire."

I let out a deep whoosh of air. "Everyone dismounted the vehicles. We heard shots."

I leave out the rest. The boy isn't relevant to the purpose of this discussion, and I can't bring myself to go there anyway. I've said enough to free Eli from the burdens of guilt he carries every single day and to give Dolores closure on the truth of how Christian's life truly ended.

"Christian was taking position in front of our vehicle. I was on the other side. He stood up to help me and was shot in the neck by enemy fire. His body fell beside where I was crouched. I was about to render aid. But it was too late."

I hear the whimper as Dolores takes in a breath. I squeeze her hand. Eli's eyes scan the ground as though the answers lie at our feet. Finally, he breaks the silence.

"He was killed by sniper fire?"

"Yes, instantly," I say. "He didn't suffer."

I can't explain why, but it feels unjust to them both that I would be the one to see Christian last. "It was chaos," I say to Dolores, then hold

Eli's gaze. "The kind of chaos you know all too well. We were faced with multiple threats. The IED. The snipers."

"All this time . . ." He trails off, his eyes closed.

It's settling in. Christian's death was not his fault.

"When I realized it was the same person, that Christian died in Iraq with me, not in the explosion, I had to tell you both."

I look over at Dolores, but her face looks strangely peaceful. She offers me a soft smile, her expression growing concerned as she looks over at Eli. I'm not sure he hears me. He stares down at his hands. From the loss and confusion in his eyes, I can see the flurry of images racing across his mind.

He looks over at Dolores. "I was certain this was all my fault. I believed I killed him."

Dolores shakes her head in response. "No, Eli. I have told you this already. None of this was your fault."

Eli faces me again. "Are you absolutely certain?"

I nod. "There are ways to prove it. Military records. But yes, I'm certain. Christian died on the convoy with me. And yet, somehow, we both—you and me—ended up here on the island. I believe it's because I was supposed to free you, both of you," I say, leaning closer to my cousin, "with the truth."

Minutes pass before anyone says a word. We sit quietly, our breaths in sync as we stare out into the water. Finally, Eli lets out a sigh.

"This is going to sound nuts, but doesn't it seem like death was just out to get him? I mean, could it really be that we all just have a set time?" His question isn't directed at either of us, but perhaps at God.

I get what he means. It isn't very different from a young man who entered the world healthy and able-bodied, only to end up a pawn in a monster's game of war. Maybe it's not up to us to determine how things are going to end?

Dolores shifts her gaze from Eli to me. "Maybe we do have a set time," she agrees. "But God is merciful because he spared Christian the first time so that he could be beside you and, by default, through our bloodline, beside me, before he finally died. I'll always take comfort that through my connection to you, I was there with him when he needed me."

Dolores pulls her sunglasses back over her eyes, and my mouth drops open at the realization that she's voiced exactly what I thought myself earlier. I realize this is one more coincidence, or more likely an answer from heaven that it's true—a part of her was there, through me. Neither of us knew it then, but I have a feeling he's watching us from los cielos and taking part in this moment now that we all know the truth: nothing about that convoy was chance.

I just don't understand what that means for me and what happened next on the battlefield that day.

We managed to pick at the tuna—just a few bites, before agreeing no one had much of an appetite. Eli is doing his best to remain upbeat, but he is quieter than usual as he walks us back to the parking lot. I know the weight of today's revelation is heavy on his shoulders. I can also tell he needs time and space to process everything I've said. We stand side by side in the parking lot, watching the taillights fade as Dolores drives off.

"So I guess this means you'll probably be leaving Puerto Rico, right?" I say in a lowered voice.

He shrugs. "Hell, I don't know about any o' that right now. What I do know is that everything is going to be all right, Lina. This is a lot, but I'm glad I know the truth."

I know there is much more to it than he wants to admit.

"Eli, can we talk later?" I need to get away from the bar. I can't help but picture that passion fruit mojito, wanting so badly for the numbness to carry away the weight of this moment.

He pauses and looks down at me. "Yeah, I'd like that." He pats me on the back with what I interpret to be a boundary line. "I know you got a lot going on today, but call me later if you're not too tuckered out."

Given the almost unforgivable and unstoppable craving I'm having for a drink, I know I've got one more stop to make before I go to pick up Teó.

"I'll try, but first I've got to beg my son to join me on a long, bumpy road to forgiveness. If I'm lucky, I may even make it all the way to redemption."

"Lina," Eli says, "something tells me that boy is going to show up on horseback for ya. I know we didn't really talk much about what happened last night, but ordering tea is a great first step. Keep at it, and when it comes to little Teó, I don't think you have a thing to worry about." Eli points his finger up. "Just be sure to keep any promises you make to him. Promises are important to us guys."

"I will," I say, making him a promise, too.

# CHAPTER THIRTY-TWO

"Buenas," the bartender says amicably. He recognizes me from my 11:00 a.m. visit a few weeks back. I guess that's what happens when you tip well.

I don't know how I ended up here. At least that's what I tell myself.

"What can I get for you, pretty lady?" he asks me in Spanish.

Talk about the question of the hour. I picture the bright-pink mojito I saw earlier at Chiquitas, but I don't answer right away.

"A mojito?" he asks, reading my mind and pushing me to the very edge. I look up at him.

Who am I kidding? I can't do it.

I try to picture Teó peeling off my shoes the night before. It had worked all day, but the need for the numbness is growing stronger by the minute. I nod, giving in. "Sí."

He confirms my order with a tilt of his head and turns to prepare my escape.

I can feel the tears of failure threaten an appearance. I swallow them back when my phone springs to life with a voicemail from Papi. I never even noticed him trying to call.

I bring the phone to my ear and press play, surprised at the comfort I find in the sound of his voice. "Lina, you are not alone. Things got bad yesterday, but you are with your family now. We are here, and we are going to help you. The women were speaking nonsense about Teó going to Lisandra's to stay. I believe in you, Lina, and I know you will never let something like last night happen again. I won't let anyone separate you from Matteo. I wanted to tell you face-to-face, hija, when you got home, but something told me not to wait. I love you. See you soon."

The bartender puts the drink down as I tuck the phone back in my pocket. I reach into my purse and pull out a crisp ten-dollar bill, then lay it down beside the sweating glass.

"Gracias," I say, silently thanking Papi for his intuition.

I stand and walk away, leaving the drink untouched. I wish I could say it feels good to be strong. It doesn't.

Dr. Robles looks back at me curiously as we reach the door to her office.

"Welcome back, Lina. I'm glad you're here, although I wasn't expecting you until next week."

Her hair is flat-iron straight, her makeup light and flawless. The diamond-studded hoops in her ears and the Cartier on her wrist remind me of her flair for the expensive. The dark-blue jeans and Chanel T-shirt under a navy-blue blazer dominate a more casual but still classy look.

I follow her into the modern seating area, passing the white leather couch and electric-blue coffee table, entering through the set of glass-paned double doors into her office.

"While waiting in the lobby, I was thinking about that photo in your office. You know, the one with the other women, your battle buddies. I ran a Google search on you, and a local article featuring your career said they used to call you 'Rambina.'" It's a clumsy attempt to make conversation as I take my seat in front of her desk.

Dr. Robles looks genuinely surprised I knew this. "I'm familiar with the article. They used to—yes, a long time ago." She leans back and examines me. I think she wants me to get to the point of why I'm here. I don't know how to.

"My team said you called the front desk on your way here."

"Yes." I nod. "I did." Unsure where to start, I revert to my babbling. "*Rambina* doesn't sound like something a communications soldier would be called. It sounds more like . . . uh . . . combat."

"Lina, you told the team it was an emergency. What's happened?"

She's not in the mood to chitchat.

"You read my file, Dr. Robles, didn't you? I mean, come on, let's be straight with each other. You know about the situation with the boy during my deployment, don't you? Last time I was here we kept it pretty light, focusing on my childhood and dreams of becoming a doctor. I don't think either of us felt like stepping on the real land mine, but you do know, right?"

She opens the same drawer as before and pulls out the trusty Montblanc and black leather binder, then shuffles it open to a fresh page. But she doesn't write; she eyes me carefully instead, poised at the ready.

Her next words come out slow and cautious. "I've reviewed the psych evaluation after your return from deployment. It's part of your medical file. When you say 'the boy,' do you mean your son, Teó?"

I scoff. This isn't going to work if she isn't going to be honest. "No, not Teó. I mean, I guess he wasn't a boy anymore. If you don't know about him, then how did you know about the Silver Star? You mentioned it the first time I came to see you."

At least she has the decency to blush. She *is* lying about what she knows.

"My assistant told me about your award right before we first met. She must have googled you." The usually militant, unwavering doctor clears her throat. "I've made it clear she isn't to do that again. In her defense, she didn't tell me in a manner of gossip. She was proud that of only three women to earn such an honor since 9/11, one of them was Puerto Rican. I'm unsure how or why she tracks these things, but she does. Your bravery was—is—a source of honor and great pride for all of us.

"It was wrong all the same," she says quickly. "I should never have brought it up. It was unprofessional. I apologize."

So she doesn't know what really happened on that convoy. Well, she shouldn't. The information is classified. I made sure to google myself before moving here, and it never came up. But something still doesn't make sense. Her face changed when I mentioned Teó during my last session. I know I didn't imagine that.

"It's fine," I tell her, waving a trembling hand dismissively. My head pounds from last night's bad decisions. "I'm curious about something else. When I mentioned my son before, you seemed surprised."

She sat up straighter. "You're very perceptive."

"So I've been told."

"I will admit," she began, "I was surprised when you mentioned having a son. I knew you were from Puerto Rico, and as you know, it's not common for . . ." Her cheeks color. "For a Puerto Rican woman to leave her children for what is normally considered man's work. It's bold because it's not traditionally applauded in our culture."

I bite my lip. Old paradigms in our culture are stupid. At least we agree on that.

She straightens in her chair for the third time. I can't imagine this woman sitting any straighter. This conversation must feel very awkward from her side of the desk.

"The truth is," she says, "I have great respect for you and all the barriers you've broken."

"You do?"

"Yes."

"But you served, too."

"Yes, I served, too, but not as a single mother. I wasn't willing to even consider motherhood during my service . . . or thereafter, to be honest. I know firsthand what the Army asks of its soldiers. Choices have to be made. Yet somehow *you* found a way."

I'm taken aback by her praise. "It was the best option *because* I was a young mother. The Army gave me an opportunity to study in the future, hold a full-time job, and provide things like medical care for my son I wouldn't have been able to afford otherwise."

"It's admiration, Lina. That's what you saw on my face. You didn't just put on the uniform; you rose above the ranks to shine—a hero. And you did it representing all the things these white male generals often believe are impossible: young, Latina, and maternal. I find it glorious."

*Glorious* . . . I never really thought about the stigmas I was breaking. Joining the military seemed like a desperate act for a young woman with no options at the time.

After a momentary pause, Dr. Robles breaks the silence: "Now please tell me. What's the emergency that brings you in today?"

I think of Teó and what he witnessed last night.

I raise my hand, physically stopping the direction of this conversation, blocking her praise from reaching me. "Your words are very kind, but you don't know everything that happened during my service or what has become of me ever since."

She doesn't respond. Her silence allows me the freedom to begin.

"I am not a hero, Doctora Robles. I am a murderer—of the lowest kind. I murdered someone. I told myself he was dead the minute he stepped out with that belt on. But that isn't true. He was very much alive. The truth is—I killed him. I did it. Me." *I could have waited a few more seconds. I didn't. I failed us all: him, his mother, Teó . . . me.*

With one admission, the entire canvas of her face transforms from admiration to travesty.

"Lina, let me stop you for a moment because you're going so fast. Close your eyes and take a deep breath."

As I close my eyes, she uncaps her pen.

Her voice lowers just above a whisper. "Start at the beginning. Slowly."

I keep my eyes closed and let out my breath in a long, slow stream. I replay the moment at the bar less than an hour ago. I know where I need to start if I ever plan on regaining control of my life.

I begin.

"During our last mission, we encountered the enemy. They used a kid, no more than eighteen or nineteen if I had to guess. His life was taken in exchange for my recognition as a hero."

She allows that statement to hang between us before she speaks again.

"Is that why you took his life? So that you can be called a hero?"

My eyes snap open, but no words come out. I swallow the irony of her question. *No.* Finally, I answer, "No, obviously not."

"Then why did you do it?"

I don't hesitate. "He was wearing a belt filled with explosives—a human bomb. The man behind the wall was going to detonate the device and kill us all."

"How do you know that for sure?"

"I saw it. He was taped around the middle with explosives. They used him. They pushed him toward our convoy and used him to try and kill us." My head hangs close to my chest. I repeat, "He was heading in our direction."

My heart is pounding. I raise a clammy palm to my chest, trying to calm the rapid beats. My memories are amplifying everything that happened. It's as though he is here, running toward us. Then he stops and stands in front of me as clearly as he did that morning. I think I might be sick.

"No one else saw him approaching your convoy, did they?"

I feel my eyes widen. "No. But how could you possibly know that?"

"Because your records indicate you served as a medic, a noncombatant, and yet somehow it was *you* who had to use force to protect the rest. And because I've already seen how observant you are."

I slowly shake my head. "No. No one else. There were six other vehicles, but no one else saw him." I correct myself. "Except the unit chaplain. And he couldn't do it. As you know, they are not allowed to carry a weapon. There was no way he could help. He wasn't trained to shoot. I was."

"Te entiendo," she says. *I understand.*

She leans forward, closer. “Why are you here today? What was the emergency this morning?”

I drop my head into my hands, giving me a direct view of my feet nervously tapping the floor.

“I can’t seem to forget this boy and what I did to him. And now I need to return to work, and I can’t get past it.”

“Tell me what that means. Are you having trouble sleeping? Eating? Conducting regular daily activities?”

“Yes, yes, and yes. And then there is . . . uh . . . the drinking.”

Again, the room grows quiet. I am thinking about the desperation I had to drink while sitting at the bar in Chiquitas, the empty bottles of rum I threw away in a public dumpster a few days back, my first visit to the chinchorro . . . last night’s sloppy mess.

“Do you have a history of binge drinking or using alcohol to cope with difficulties? Even before the trauma in Iraq?”

“No, I rarely ever drank. Maybe a little coquito at Christmas.”

“Okay, then tell me how the drinking began.”

This is easy. I knew exactly when it began. “One of my soldiers asked me to meet him—to talk—shortly after we returned from deployment. He was having a hard time. We met at the bowling alley on post. We drank—a lot. It was innocent. We talked about our families and our childhoods. We joked. We drank beer, then tequila shots, until we could barely see straight. Finally the bartender cut us off. We each called a cab and went home. It was the only time since returning that I was able to forget. I got a reprieve from constantly reliving the convoy. For those couple of hours, I finally stopped seeing the young man and his lost future in my head.” I wipe a tear from the tip of my nose. “Then I kept drinking. I kept wanting to forget.”

“Was his death your first encounter with death?”

I think back to Lieutenant Colonel Rafferty and the massive coronary he had our second day in country. He died instantly. I was first on the scene. Then I think of Sergeant Fuentes, and the tangible scent of his blood pooling beneath him fills my nose.

"No. Not even the first encounter while on this deployment."

"So it wasn't seeing him dying that affected you?"

"No." Dr. Robles doesn't understand. But then again, how can she?

"Then what is it? What is it about the young man's death that is haunting you?"

"Isn't it obvious?" I ask. "I'm the one who killed him. I killed someone who wasn't even old enough to be making life-altering decisions but somehow ended up with a waist covered in explosives. It wasn't supposed to be me. I wasn't there to take lives; I was there to save them."

She doesn't answer right away. I think she wants me to process what I just said. After a few seconds, she continues.

"Why do you think that is, Lina? Why do you think that happened?"

The answer to this one isn't as obvious. I consider the doctor's question. I reach over to the box of tissues on her desk and extract one. After wiping my nose, the answer comes to me.

"I don't know, maybe to humble me. I was getting too comfortable, cocky even, in my abilities. They called me Stone Cold Healer. I was proud of how I could just turn off my emotions and save lives. But I had no right to be so arrogant."

"Why not? Why have you lost your right to be proud of your ability?"

"Because I'm never going to measure up in anything. Not as a healer, not as a soldier, not even as a fellow mother. My birth was a big cosmic joke on my father, who desperately wanted a replacement son. Instead, he got a daughter—a sad reminder of a child who would never measure up to what he wanted. This experience in Iraq was another reminder that, once again, I was not enough to save that boy's life. Even worse, I had to kill him and take him from his own mother. He was already dead, but I still had to be the one to pull the trigger. Even when the Army called me a hero, I couldn't find a way to justify it to myself as a soldier. I am a failure in every sense of the word."

My hands are covering my sobbing face. I bring my head down close to my lap. With each forceful heave, I can feel the pain of the young man's death coursing through my chest. It's the first time I am crying like this. My hands are wet with a combination of sweat and tears.

I reach for another Kleenex as Dr. Robles stands up and moves to the vacant chair beside me, taking a seat and turning in my direction.

"Lina," she says softly, "I want to recap everything you've told me this morning, and I want you to be honest if there's something I'm repeating that is incorrect, okay?"

I lift my head from my hands and nod, unable to speak, trying to transition my sobs to stuttered hiccups.

She begins. "The experience of stopping the suicide bomber . . . the young boy . . . is a source of shame, despite the military recognizing you as a war hero. You feel responsible for taking someone's life—even though he posed an imminent threat to you and the other innocent soldiers with you. You were the only one who saw him, so you believe the universe punished you by forcing you to take his life, reminding you that you are not good enough. You believe you were not good enough to please your father, and you were not good enough to save that young man and instead took him from his mother. Is that right?"

Hearing her speak my words back to me . . . I'm speechless. I stare at her silently. I don't know what else to say.

"I need to know if I've understood you correctly, Lina."

"Yes," I whisper.

"Okay, good. Since you returned from deployment, you've begun to drink alcohol excessively, culminating in an event you've deemed an emergency. Is that correct?"

"Yes."

"Are you or is anyone around you in immediate danger of harm?"

I know what she is asking. She wants to know if I'm a suicide threat . . . or worse . . . if I am capable or planning to hurt anyone else.

"No, of course not." I shake my head. "But I don't want to lose my son. My family is wondering if I can take care . . ." I trail off, unable to say the rest.

She nods. "I see."

"Do you?" I ask doubtfully. She admitted earlier she doesn't have children.

"Lina, it is not unusual to suffer from post-traumatic stress disorder, especially given the events you were exposed to. I didn't find anything indicating a diagnosis of PTSD anywhere in your file. Although, so far, you've confirmed many of the symptoms."

"I've never been diagnosed with that." There's no emotion in my voice; it's a simple fact.

"Weren't you given a mental health evaluation upon return from deployment, or even a thirty-day follow-up?"

I wave my hand dismissively. "A quick one when we got back. That was it. The big focus on our return was ensuring all our supplies were accounted for. What does that have to do with anything? You think I have PTSD?"

"Lina, you were a medic. Think like one and consider the symptoms. Don't you?"

Allowing myself to process her question, my eyes again flood with tears. So much for Stone Cold Healer. We both know the answer is yes.

"Dr. Robles, what do I do? How do I fix this? I'm going to sign back up to serve with the National Guard here in Puerto Rico. I have to get better."

She takes my hand and smiles at me. "You are tougher than you realize. Look, I want to try something unorthodox. It's a type of treatment we take a few weeks to build up to, so it's not something I would recommend for nearly anyone, but I think it might be exactly what you need today. And it will kick off a protocol we can work on over the next couple of weeks. Are you willing to try it?"

"Claro que sí. I'm willing to try anything."

She stands up and walks over to the cabinet in the corner of the office. Reaching into the pocket of her blazer, she pulls out a key and unlocks it. Inside, she removes a small tripod and a long, thin tube about an inch in diameter. She opens the legs of the tripod, no taller than a ruler, and places it on top of her desk. The fluorescent tube is secured to the tripod horizontally. After she powers it on, five consecutive blue squares light up, glowing in the center of the tube.

"This is a light tube. It is part of a treatment protocol called eye movement desensitization and reprocessing therapy. You may have heard of it before, by the acronym EMDR. What we are about to do is called bilateral stimulation. I want you to allow your brain to roam freely as your eyes follow the lights from one end of the tube to the other. We will treat your memories and experiences as open wounds in the brain. These wounds are unable to heal because of debris inside that needs to be cleared out. By allowing both hemispheres of the brain to be stimulated, we can replace negative beliefs—debris—with positive ones."

I'm not sure how a light tube is supposed to help me, but what other option do I have? "It seems easy enough."

"This treatment has proven to be very successful in reprocessing memories and emotions associated with trauma."

The doctor presses a button from a wireless remote, and the light travels from one end of the tube to the other, creating a hypnotic rhythm.

"As your eyes follow the light, your mind processes memories. We will mimic what happens when you reach REM, the state of dream sleep. This will help us move your memories from the amygdala-hippocampal complex—the emotional part of your brain—where the debris is stuck, to the rest of your brain for processing. Does that make sense?"

"I think so," I say. "You really believe it can help me?"

"I do," she replies. "This will be one of a few things we will work on to assist you in the healing process. Are you ready to get started?"

I swallow the fear. The face I've memorized sits at the edge of my memories, preparing the haunt, but what choice do I have? Something has to change. "Yes. I'm ready."

"Okay, let's begin. First, I want you to tell me about the image. Walk me through the moment you saw the young man and knew he was a threat."

I close my eyes and force myself back to the convoy. I start to relay the details. My hands and feet tremble as I speak.

When I stop, I open my eyes. Dr. Robles is watching me.

"Is there a belief you hold in your heart that goes along with that image?"

My heart aches with my truth. I use every ounce of energy I have in my dehydrated and exhausted system to stutter out a response. "Yes. I believe I am a murderer and a failure. I killed someone; I was there to heal. I was not good enough to find a way to save him, leaving a mother somewhere grieving in the most unimaginable way."

She turns on the machine. "I want you to follow the light with your eyes. Think about the image and this overarching thought until I tell you otherwise."

After a few seconds she stops the machine and looks at me.

"Where do you feel the trauma?"

"My eyes. It hurts behind my eyes, like an immense pressure in the back of my lids that will turn into a migraine."

"Lina, is there a belief you would prefer to go along with that image?"

Goose bumps explode along my arms and legs. I've never thought about countering beliefs.

"Go ahead," she coaxes. "I want you to voice the belief you would prefer out loud."

What does she mean? Does she want me to lie to myself? Is that what therapy is supposed to be? Lying to myself?

"I don't understand," I tell her. "What do you want me to say?"

"Lina, you said you believe you're a murderer and a failure because you couldn't save the young man wearing the belt. What do you want to believe about the experience?"

I swallow, thinking through the gravity of her request. With trembling lips, I begin. "I want to believe there was nothing I could have done to save that young man on the battlefield."

"Think back to that moment. Is there anything you could have done?"

I close my eyes again.

"He was going to kill us. He was running in our direction, and the man behind the wall was going to detonate him. The man held the trigger in his hand, but I saved us before he got close enough. I don't know what else I could have done. I screamed for help, but no one understood." I thought about Sergeant Fuentes. He died trying to help me.

"Dr. Robles, I want to believe the boy was going to die no matter what I did, and I saved as many lives as I could."

"Very good," she says. "Now I want you to follow the light and picture the young man. Imagine the moment when you realized he was a threat. I want you to mentally tell yourself what you just told me. I want you to tell yourself that he had no chance that day. You did what you had to in order to save as many lives as you could."

I do as she says, allowing my mind to wander freely. Once again I begin to cry.

Dr. Robles turns off the light. "What images came up?"

"His body is on the ground at my feet."

"What is he doing there, Lina?"

I shake my head. "I don't know."

Dr. Robles stares at me. "Don't you? Why did you bring his body to where you are standing?"

My voice is thick with emotion. The first word pushes past the pressure in my throat with a loud croak.

"Because I want to hold him. I want to tell him that I'm sorry." I look down at my arms, unaware I've moved them into a cradling position. "I had no choice."

"You look like you're holding something, Lina."

I nod. "I want to hold him and say goodbye."

"Close your eyes," she says. "Pick him up and hold him."

My head whips back and forth as my body rocks. "I can't," I yell. "I can't do it. I don't deserve to. This is my fault! This is all my fault. I wasn't good enough to save him."

"But, Lina, you did save them. So many of the mothers and fathers and daughters and sons on that convoy. You saved them. The man behind the wall would have used the young man to take all of you with him. But you saved them. His death is on his handler's hands. Not yours."

My howls fill the room as I allow my body to process and release the sorrow and guilt of taking an innocent life. Dr. Robles is right: the monster behind the wall pushed that boy out into the open.

"I want you to close your eyes and hold him close to you."

My arms tremble at her words. "I cccaaannn'ttt." I raise my head, eyes closed, but my head shakes, refuting her idea.

"Yes, Lina, you can," she urges. "Hold him close and say what you need to say."

Wrapping my arms around my chest, I bow my head, eyes closed, and imagine the little face with the dark curls that looked so much like my own son's. I pull his body close to mine and smooth back his hair. "I'm so sorry, sweet angel. I'm so desperately sorry."

I rock him as though he were only sleeping. I allow myself to feel the tenderness of a mother to her son, holding him close as he falls asleep. This boy will sleep forever. *Rockaby, baby . . .*

I open my eyes and tell Dr. Robles about what I've imagined and how I want my last interaction with this boy to be.

"That's good," she says. "I want you to hold this image and follow the light with your eyes."

Again, I picture him in my arms. At times I picture Teó, and it brings an even deeper sense of comfort. I reiterate the positive message of doing what I could to save the other soldiers.

My message is getting stronger.

There are more details each time we discuss what I saw. Each time I speak with more conviction, focused on saving the others. Soon it isn't the young man I picture, but the man who pushed him toward us. I am imagining myself taking down the real enemy.

We repeat this process four more times.

After each round, my eyes following the light, I believe the message more and more.

When my positive belief has risen from a one to a four, on a scale of one to seven, we stop. Dr. Robles moves to the watercooler tucked in the back corner and pours me a cup of ice-cold water. I take it gratefully, allowing the cold to soothe my dry throat.

"You've done great work today, Lina," Dr. Robles says, shutting off the light tube. "This journey is long, but you've taken a big first step. I want to see you back here in one week."

I empty the paper cup and close my eyes, allowing the peace to slip over me despite the trepidations of my hurting soul. There's a sense of calm and possibility that I want desperately to hold on to. It's the large yellow lifesaver, only this time I don't slip beneath the water. I hold on to it tightly.

Dr. Robles returns to her side of the desk and jots something on a Post-it Note before handing it to me. "This is the contact information for a local Alcoholics Anonymous group. I recommend contacting them immediately to connect with a sponsor."

I don't ask how or why she has the information committed to memory. Rambina may be more familiar with my circumstances than she can let on.

"Thank you, Dr. Robles. I mean it."

She gives me a warm smile. "You are very welcome, guerrera." *Warrior.*

As we walk to the door, I turn and throw my arms around her. I allow myself to embrace her with pure gratitude, hoping the depth of my thanks moves forcibly from my heart to hers.

She laughs nervously as she steps back from my embrace and smooths her blazer. I don't take it personally. I get it. All that matters is the catalyst coursing through me and the amends I've begun to make, which start inside.

"You did great today, Lina. I look forward to seeing you next week."

"Thank you, Dr. Robles," I say gratefully. "I think you may have just saved my soul."

"I didn't do anything. You did all the work. I'm only here to help facilitate the effort."

I offer a small smile, a sense of relief budding inside. It's the first in a series of wrongs that need to be made right.

# CHAPTER THIRTY-THREE

As the folded doors collapse open, Teó jumps from the top step of the bus onto the sidewalk. His knees bend low, dropping him into a full squat and a simultaneous thump on both feet. He smiles, satisfied by the perfect landing. I'm satisfied by the victory on his face. It's a temporary celebration—terminated once he sees me standing at the outer edge of the parent circle. His smile immediately disappears as his eyes drop. My stomach turns, witnessing the joy evaporate as he shoves his hands into his pockets, visibly sighs, and walks over to me.

"Hi, papito." My voice is congealed with apology, trying my best to ignore the heartbreak at seeing him reject me for the very first time.

"Where's Abuela?"

I swallow the lump in my throat. What have I done? I'm losing him.

"I'm pretty sure she is back at the house waiting for us. Teó?" I try to catch his eye, needing to feel our connection after the ordeal at Dr. Robles's office. My boy has always been my respite, and I, his refuge. "I thought we could spend a little time together, you and me, before we go home."

I stand there, nervous as he looks me over, feeling vulnerable and exposed. I think he's trying to assess whether I'm sober. I need to make this right. I need to find a way to pave the road to reconciliation. I crouch down and grip his waist, seeing the baby who slept beside me his first year of life, the toddler whose hands always reached up for me, needing my warmth the same way I'm needing his today. This is me reaching for him.

"Teó, I think I owe you an apology. No, forgive me, I know I do. I'm so, so very sorry, papito."

My little boy doesn't say anything right away, but he reaches out his hand—a bold move in front of the other kids exiting the bus. I look over at them, but he shrugs and takes my hand anyway. I stand to follow alongside him as he leads me to the car.

Once we are both buckled in, I brace as he turns toward me. His dark eyelashes flutter against the pockets of his eyes. The blinking is more aggressive today.

Guilt slices through me with the razor-sharp edge of a stainless-steel blade. It's me. I'm the one creating this pain. The memories of my condition last night are causing him excess stress, forcing me to witness the sour fruits of my selfishness. I've managed to fight off the desperate and physical desire to get a drink throughout the day, but seeing Teó like this strengthens my resolve into iron. I can't hurt him like this again.

Before I can start the car, Teó says, "You scared me last night, Mamá. I thought you might be dead."

His chin twitches up toward me—the rarest of his tics. I think about the reality of seeing someone die. I remember the pain that seared itself into my heart watching Sergeant Fuentes transition into a forever sleep. That's what I did. That's how I made Teó feel. I try to swallow down the anger I have at myself. How could I be so callous?

I start the car, anxious to turn on the air-conditioning before the heat inside suffocates us both.

"Tía Lisandra told me you had too much to drink," he says knowingly. "She told me I had to leave you and go sleep at her house so you could rest. I told her I wouldn't bother you. I told her I would let you rest." He sniffs twice. "But she said I had to go anyway. I thought she was lying—that you were dead, and she didn't want to tell me the truth. I even asked her. That's when your friend, the man with the Captain

Hook arm, made me a promise. He promised me that you were just sleeping and that he would check on you and make sure you were okay."

*Oh, Eli.* I close my eyes and whisper a silent thank-you.

"Teó, none of that should ever have happened. I can't apologize enough for scaring you that way. Let's go back to the park. I have some very important things I need to tell you about. Especially how sorry I am about last night and what I'm going to do to prevent it from ever happening again."

*Sniff.*

I hope for a reluctant yes, at best, but Teó doesn't answer right away. He stares straight ahead and considers my request. All is not forgiven so easily. I take pride in knowing my son is no pushover.

"Teó? Please? Can we go talk?"

"Okay, I guess," he mumbles.

I release a sigh of relief and hold on tight to the inkling of possibility that I may find a way to earn his forgiveness. The car begins down the street toward the park and the coastline.

Trying to reset the tension between us, I ask, "So how was school?"

Teó sighs. "Sophia was right. The kids keep making fun of me."

My stomach clenches in anger, but I don't let my reaction show. It'll make things only worse. I don't understand why kids can be so damn cruel. I channel my inner Stone Cold and maneuver the next question as calmly as possible.

"Why is that?"

"Because of my tics," he says under his breath. "I tried to tell them I can't help it. I can't stop myself. It feels weird for me, too, you know." *Sniff.* "I can control everything else, like when I use the bathroom." *Sniff.* "Why can't I stop myself from doing it?"

My heart breaks a little more, knowing the question is rhetorical. He knows I can't answer that.

"The kids tell me: 'Cut it out, sniffer,' or they keep staring at me, making it worse." *Sniff.* "Or they ask me: 'Why are you doing that? Can't you stop?'" *Sniff.*

"Are you trying to hold your breath, the way Dolores showed you?"

"Yeah, I tried that."

The resignation in his voice pushes the fisted grip of pain from my stomach to my heart.

"It helps most of the time"—*sniff*—"but sometimes it's like there is another person inside me, Mamá, and I can't stop him. I'm just a kid."

Why do things have to be so hard for us both? I picture the kids surrounding Teó on the playground, and the breakdown I just had in Dr. Robles's office. I'm so tired. But I can't give up. I have to push forward, for both of us. *Focus on Teó, Lina. He needs you to be strong.*

"Teó, next week is your appointment with the neurologist. I really think they can help you. Do you remember when Dr. Stevens in North Carolina told you about CBIT?"

He bites his lip in concentration. "I think so . . . kinda . . ." His eyes are focusing on the swing set now in view. I'm losing him.

"Dr. Stevens said it was a way to teach you how to identify the feelings in your body before you start to sniff. Like when you said you start to feel a tickle in your nose. If you identify those things, then you can try to stop them."

"Oh yeah, I remember now," he says. "Dr. Stevens said I should try . . . uh . . . cog-tat-ive behaving inter . . . uh . . . somethin' for tics." *Sniff.*

"Yes, that's right," I say proudly. "Cognitive behavioral intervention for tics—CBIT."

Teó's eyes widen. "Oh yeah, CBIT." He smiles. Learning always makes him smile.

I park in the spot closest to the slides and turn off the engine.

"You can start trying some of the things she talked about whenever you want. And I promise things are going to be better once we finally see the new doctor here in Puerto Rico next week."

"Okay, Mamá. Can we go swing now?"

He is already jumping out of his seat.

"Um, wait. Teó, there's something else I need to tell you."

His shoulders slump. "Before I can go to the park?"

I don't understand how I can be both thankful for his innocence and frustrated that he doesn't grasp the gravity of what I need to say, but I feel both.

"It's important. Can we go for a little walk on the beach first? Then you can swing."

Teó looks up at me. "Is this about last night?"

I nod, heavy with guilt. "Yes, some of it. But there's some other stuff, too. Important stuff I need to tell you about."

"Okay, Mamá." *Sniff.* "We can take a walk. And then—swings."

When we meet behind the car, he extends his hand again. I'm touched by his insistence at hand-holding today, even if I know it means I really scared him last night.

I think back to sitting at the bar less than a few hours ago. How do I get off this never-ending Ferris wheel of self-destruction? I know I can be a better person. I'm not sure I even recognize who I am anymore. Where did this woman come from?

I take Teó's hand and lead him toward the powdery-soft sand, trying to decide where to begin.

*How about when he thought you were dead?*

"Teó, I haven't been feeling very well lately."

"You haven't?" he asks. "Could it be a bacterial infection? Because a bacteria can be treated with antibiotics."

I ruffle the top of his head. My future scientist. I picture him (as I often do) a grown man in a white lab coat—a great man, like Dr. José Celso Barbosa. It's easy for me to imagine him grown, with signature horn-rimmed glasses and an inquisitive gaze in his sapphire eyes. He will look so much like Leonardo.

"No, Dr. LaSalle. It's more like I've been heartsick."

"Heartsick?" he repeats.

"I've been sad, Teó—very sad. The things I saw when I went overseas with the Army this last time . . ." I swallow. "The things I had to do there made me very sad."

I brace for what I know is coming next.

"What did you have to do, Mamá?" *Sniff.*

How do I tell him that I had to take the life of someone who in many ways was still a kid? Someone who didn't have any choice but to do what others were forcing him to do. Will I ever be able to admit to my son that I was the one to pull back on the trigger of an M4 rifle, ending someone else's life forever?

Readying my answer, I stare straight ahead, knowing if I look down at Teó's face, I will see the young man on the battlefield, and I will fall apart.

"Even though I was scared, I had to protect my team from getting hurt by the bad guys."

We are both quiet as we step to the edges of the wet sand. I reach down and slip off my shoes. Teó smiles and does the same, handing me his balled-up socks. I place them in my pocket. Finally, he breaks the silence.

"If you were protecting your team, you were a hero. Especially if you were scared. That makes you very brave. So I'm confused. Why does being brave and protecting others make you sad?"

It's the same question I've been asking myself for months. Today Dr. Robles helped me understand it all a little bit better.

"Because I never, ever, want to have to hurt *anyone*, son. I am at my best when I can help people and make them feel better if they're sick or in pain. That's why I wanted"—I clear my throat—"why I *want* to become a doctor one day. So that I can help people feel better."

"What about you?" he asks. "Who is going to make you feel better?"

I shake my head. It's supposed to be him. My son is supposed to be enough of a reason for me to keep it together. "I don't know. I guess when you're a grown-up, it's all up to you to do that for yourself."

"Isn't that why you drink alcohol, then? 'Cause it makes you feel better?"

His question leaves me breathless. However I respond will be stored in his treasure trove of lessons for life. I need to be honest with him;

anything less would make me the kind of mother I can't bear to look at in the mirror. A fake.

"I used to think so. But, actually, it does the opposite. When I drink alcohol, it makes me feel worse."

Teó stops walking. His hand tents his eyes to block the sun as he looks up at me. "I don't understand." *Sniff.*

I take a step closer to cast a shadow over him. I want him to see me, really see me, as I answer.

"I know, papi. Sometimes grown-ups don't make much sense. That's why I'm seeing a doctor, too—just like you, but my doctor will help me manage the symptoms that come from my sadness. She and I agreed today—no more alcohol. Zero. That's it. I will fight very hard to do my best and never scare you again like I did last night."

Teó's eyes search my soul, and I can see the depth of his need. He needs to know I'm telling the truth. If only he could see how much I'm needing that, too. Teó is fighting the doubt as much as I'm trying to force it away. I don't want to fail him anymore.

I kneel down, placing myself as his equal. "I'm going to try my very best."

It's the longest we've been eye to eye today, and Teó hasn't had a blinking episode. His lips spread slowly into a smile. He's found the assurance. "That's all you can ask. Right? Isn't that what you always say? Try your very best."

I reach my hand out to shake his, making the deal official, but he wraps his arms around my neck and lays his chin atop my shoulder instead. Holding his little body tightly to mine, I whisper, "Thank you," and give him an extra squeeze.

"There's something else," I say, releasing him. He drops my hand and resumes walking.

"More, Mamá?" *Sniff.* "Okay, what is it?" He looks back over his shoulder at the swings.

"I'm thinking about going back to work for the Army." I rush to the next part before his worst fears spread between us. "But this time it would be with the National Guard. That means my missions are going to be here, on the island, with you. I wouldn't be leaving you anytime soon. Especially since it hasn't even been a year since I got back from my last tour."

He exhales, relieved. "Can you promise that, too?"

We both know the answer to that one.

"No, Teó, I'm sorry. I can't. But I really don't think I will have to leave you. There's a lot of work to do here. And if the worst-case scenario does happen and I do have to leave for a little while, you have so many people here who love you and will ensure you never get lonely."

I pause, knowing how to sweeten the deal. "Including Dolores."

His eyes brighten at the sound of her name, but his lips slip into a frown. "Will you start right away?"

"Soon enough," I say. "Once I find us our own home."

"But if we have our own home, who will take care of me if you have to work late or on weekends? Tía Lisandra or Abuela?"

"Abuela," I say firmly, still recovering from my encounter with my aunt.

"But I like living with Abuela and Dolores. Who will feed the chickens?"

I'm surprised at how the island's magic has cast her spell and filled an unknown loneliness I didn't realize existed in Teó. I've always believed having me was enough. I told myself having him was all I needed, too. Maybe that's the thing about this whole experience: both of us are coming to understand the possibility of how things *could* be, leaving us wanting even more.

"Don't worry. We will choose a home close by so you can continue to spend time with the family." I close my eyes and brace for what I'm about to say next.

"And with someone else who very much wants to spend time with you." It's time. I have to tell him.

"Someone else?" *Sniff.*

"Let's sit down for a minute." I pull him gently onto the wet sand.

He looks confused by our sudden stop but sits down beside me without a word.

"I bumped into someone I hadn't seen in a long time," I say. Except even I don't believe that. "Well, maybe fate intervened," I mumble.

"Whad'ya mean, Mamá? Who did you bump into?"

I sigh. This is it. No turning back. "I bumped into your father."

Teó pulls off his glasses and rubs his eyes. He puts his glasses back on and turns to face me. *Sniff.* He whispers the words in awe. "My father?"

This time the pressure in my throat is so strong it leaves me unable to respond. I nod.

"My father," he repeats on the cusp of a breath.

He brings his knees up to his chest and wraps his arms around them. His body language is shouting self-protection. I wonder if it's from his mysterious father or from me.

"I didn't think I had one. You've never talked about him. I just assumed he was . . . maybe dead . . . or gone."

"I'm so sorry, papito," I say, realizing how cruel my silence on the matter has been. It was selfish and cowardly for me to avoid such an important part of Teó's life under the guise of protection. "His name is Leonardo, and he lives close by."

His eyes widen, the shock filling them behind his lenses. "He does?"

"Yes," I say carefully, "and he would very much like to meet you."

*Sniff.* "He would?"

*Yes. Oh, yes, he would.*

Teó's hands wring together, a gesture I know means he's contemplating something deeply. "Why now?" *Sniff.*

I considered earlier how I would answer this. I don't want Teó to blame the family he is bonding with for keeping him away from his father. This is another one of those unique cases where the specifics don't make the situation any better—only worse.

"There was a mix-up," I say, wanting to remain as honest as possible. "He didn't know you were born. And I thought he chose to stay away. I recently found out I was wrong."

Teó's lips purse with consideration. "Well, that's unfortunate," he answers logically. "All this time . . ." It's exactly what his father said.

After seeing how immediately Sergeant Fuentes was gone—forever, the kid on the convoy, stumbling one minute, dead the next—it hits me. Time is a gift. Neither Teó nor Leonardo deserves for me to waste another minute.

"Now that he knows about you, he can't wait to meet you. But first I wanted to know how you feel about it. Would you like to meet him?"

"If I say yes, will it make you sad?"

I grab him and pull him against me, resting my chin on top of his head and closing my eyes. How did I get so lucky to raise this exceptional boy?

"Not at all, son. I think getting a chance to meet your dad and getting to know him is good—for all of us."

Teó pulls back and smiles at me. "I think so, too, Mamá." *Sniff.*

"Do you think he will like me?" he asks behind a series of blinks. "Does he know about . . . uh . . . you know . . . the tics?" *Sniff.*

Forcing out the question puts his tics on overload. He shakes his head, the sniffing frustrating him. He brings his hand to his nose, but three more sniffs push through.

"Teó." I rub his back slowly. "Take a deep breath. Your father does know. He told me he had the same thing."

Teó releases his breath in one smooth motion and closes his eyes. His words come out slowly. "He had tics, too?"

If only I had thought about this possibility before, if I'd even considered Leonardo, I could have reached out to him to inquire. All my family's lies would have been brought out into the open sooner. Teó would have had answers . . . sooner.

"Yes. Your father had tics, too. So, you see, you didn't do anything to cause this."

"Dr. Stevens said my condition could come from a mom or dad, but you said you never have tics, Mamá, so I thought it was just a case of bad luck."

I don't respond, already overwrought with guilt at how much better I could have handled all this.

"When can I meet him?"

If it were up to Leo, I'd be taking Teó over there right now. But I can't take on much more today. I need at least one good night's rest to be prepared for this massive shift in our life. "How about this weekend?"

This surprises him. "This weekend?" *Sniff.*

"Yes, I suggested we all meet at the local science museum."

Teó's eyes brighten with excitement. "My father likes science?"

I shrug, entirely unsure.

Sensing the heaviness between us, Teó pats my hand and offers a much-needed reprieve. "Okay. That's it, right? Can we go to the park now?" *Sniff.*

"Yes," I answer, feeling the weight of the entire day lifted from my shoulders. "I'll race you." I force myself to ignore the ache in my limbs from one hell of a hangover as we both stand up and get into the starting position. I look over at my little boy. "Okay, ready? One, two, three . . . go!"

Teó shoots forward, and I chase after him, fast enough to give him competition but slow enough to let him win.

When we get to the park, he turns around and smiles triumphantly, raising both arms above his head and pumping them into the air. "Victory!" he shouts.

"Yes! You win!" I cheer. "Now go and have some fun on the swings. And then maybe we can get a piragua on the way to Abuela's."

His smile widens at the mention of a sweet, icy snow cone. "Do you have chavo?"

I chuckle, but I can hear the exhaustion in my tone. "Yes, Teó, I have money."

He pumps his fist into the air, then stops at the edge of the swing set and turns to face me. "Mamá?"

"Yeah?"

"Don't forget to tell your friend I said thanks for taking care of you last night."

By *friend*, I know he means Eli.

"I won't forget. I'll be sure to thank him."

And as Teó jumps up onto the swing and kicks his feet out for momentum, it hits me how much I mean it—Eli really deserves all the thanks for making sure my son was comforted amid the disaster of my arrival home.

# CHAPTER THIRTY-FOUR

I spend my time doing my best to exercise myself into exhaustion and distract my mind from the new sense of sobriety. In some ways the world is clearer, and I'm noticing details in the things around me, seeing colors and hearing sounds in ways I haven't in months. On the flip side, the sharpness of the world is flooding my senses and leaving me with the unsettled inner tremor of anxiety. I'm exhausted after waking up sporadically throughout the night, bolting up each time in a cold sweat from adrenaline-fueled dreams with worries that I'm about to die before Teó even grows into a man. I know where this newfound fear is coming from. During the last snippet of my most recent nightmare, Leonardo was at my door with two police officers, declaring he would be taking my son away from me—forever.

The heaviness of my angst and the depth of unending despair while I screamed at him to leave our house and stay away from Teó still linger well into the afternoon, even though I know it was all just a bad dream. We have less than forty-eight hours until Sunday, the day Teó and I are going to meet Leo at the science museum. Between my brain's attempts to reorient itself within a sober nervous system and the impending fears I keep trying to push away of my son loving his father more than he loves me, I'm a nervous wreck, and I keep thinking about how easy it would be to just pour a little rum over ice and indulge in a brief reprieve.

The long runs up the island's rolling hills are made only harder by the nonstop headaches I've had since the morning after La Placita. Still, I keep showing up to the starting line of my own homemade running track, pushing away the nausea and the ache in my muscles. As long as I can focus on the future and getting back into the kind of shape expected of a soldier, I have something to strive for, something beyond who I am to everyone else, but who I want to be just for me.

If only the runs, followed by push-ups and sit-ups until my muscles reach failure, could also quiet the terror of how my life will change when Leo becomes a more permanent part of the dynamic with Teó. I've never had to share my baby before. From the moment he was placed in my arms, he's been all mine. I'm not sure how to parent him any other way, and yet something deep within my heart knows this is what's best for our son.

The ride home is unusually silent. Teó has always been a sensitive child, attuned to my emotions and state of mind. He stares out the window quietly during the short drive home. That's when it hits me. Of course. I'm not the only one nervous about meeting Leonardo.

The cars are gone when we arrive at my parents' house.

"Where is everyone, Mamá?"

"I don't know, love."

"Oh wait! I remember," he says, lightly slapping his forehead. "Abuela told me this morning that everyone was going to el culto; that means church. She said you would have to cook dinner tonight because no one would be home when I got out of school."

It would've been nice if she'd let me know.

He looks up at me, visibly disappointed. Has Teó lost faith in my ability to do something as simple as make us dinner?

"How about if I whip you up your favorite—scrambled eggs and french fries?"

"Mamá, I don't think Nana or Abuela keep a bag of Ore-Ida french fries in the freezer."

"Well, that means I'll have to peel the potatoes from scratch. They taste better that way, anyhow."

His rosy lips purse into a circle. "Oh yeah! That's how Titi Kika made them when she stayed with me in North Carolina. You can do that, Mamá? Nana keeps the potatoes in the basket in the kitchen."

"I sure can," I say, using my key to let us in through the front door. The mention of my aunt makes me long for the sound of her voice. I make a mental note to call her on the weekend, once I have the strength to tell her about everything: the good and the bad . . . and now the path to the better.

"While I get started, how about you refill the water dispenser for the chickens out back and check the nesting box for today's eggs?"

When we walk in, Abuelo is sitting on the couch. A telenovela plays on the TV across from him. Looking up, he says, "Bienvenida, Catalina," welcoming me. His gaze, however, moves directly back to the TV before I can respond in kind. He's drawn to the screen by an intense argument between a mother and daughter as they battle over the affections of the family's butler.

"Gracias, Abuelito. Bendición."

He doesn't respond. I didn't expect he would. Instead, he whistles a tune to a song I recognize from my youth, one of his favorites back then.

"Hola, Abuelito," Teó says from the entrance. He runs over to him and kisses his cheek, but my grandfather continues whistling, lost in another world.

"Go on, Teó." I usher him past the living room and drop his backpack on the dining table. "Let's see if the eggs are ready for dinner."

"Okay, Mamá, I will check. By the way, did you know chickens have a unihemispheric slow-wave sleep cycle?" *Sniff.*

I look over at him. "Huh?"

"It's where half of their brain is sleeping, and the other half is awake. Chickens can literally sleep with one eye open."

Despite my pounding headache, I chuckle. "I did not know that, Teó, but I'm not surprised you did. It sounds super creepy. Now stop delaying and get. I have to start dinner.

"And make sure you wash your hands when you come back in!"

He sticks his tongue out, the more prominent of his tics, and sighs. "Okay," he grumbles, then sprints to the back door.

Abuelo remains as still as a statue with a tune on his lips, staring at the ongoing argument on the screen. The mother and daughter have escalated into slaps and hair pulling.

"Are you okay?" I ask, but Abuelo doesn't respond.

I put my phone in my back pocket and walk into the kitchen to peel potatoes.

My breath catches in my throat as I round the corner, coming face-to-face with a brand-new bottle of amber-colored spiced rum, a big red bow tied around its neck. A white tag hangs from the bottle. It's addressed to me and signed by my tía Lisandra. Sometime since we last spoke, she decided to drop off this "present" at our house. Here it is. Her test.

I swallow hard, nearly tasting the spicy liquid on my tongue. My mouth waters. So do my eyes. I should have known she would do something like this. I knew the meeting at her house earlier felt a little too easy. That isn't my aunt's style. Pushing me to the very edge, testing my resolve, daring me at the brink of collapse to remain strong—that's much more in line with how she does things. Tía Lisandra isn't going to walk away from Teó without absolute certainty that I will do right by him.

I walk over and grip the neck of the bottle, wanting to hide it somewhere I don't have to see it or discuss why the mere appearance of alcohol is more than I can handle right now. I realize as soon as the bottle is in my hand that it's better if I don't touch it. The amber liquid swirls inside the thick glass. The temptation is so strong, and I don't want to break. I glance down at the label and blink back the overwhelming desire to crack open the cap. I won't do it. I have put the bottle back down on the counter, knowing it's better to just walk away, when I hear a shuffling at the front door. Papi grunts as he fumbles with the lock before the door swings open and he gets a full view of me standing in front of the unopened rum.

He stares at me, and I try to find the words, to tell him that it's not how it looks, but the fogginess of my sober mind, combined with the weight of so many recent life-altering revelations, renders me mute and exhausted. Holding my gaze, Papi shakes his head. "You can't be serious, Lina. After everything that's happened? What is wrong with you?"

"It's not what you think," I manage to say, keeping an eye out for Teó. "Papi, it's not."

"Lina, please." He reaches out his hand. "I keep trying to fight for you, to help you, but you insist on destroying yourself. Don't disappoint me. You're better than this. You're my legacy, Lina, the only child . . ."

The impact of his words makes contact. *Don't disappoint me. The only child* . . . I hear what he doesn't say . . . *the child that I actually wanted is gone.*

"There's not much left to destroy, Papi. I guess we both just have to accept that I'll never be enough for you." I march directly to my room, ignoring the power of the silence that fills the hall behind me.

# CHAPTER THIRTY-FIVE

Late at night once everyone's gone to bed, I return to the kitchen for a glass of water. I pull off a piece of paper towel and wipe the sweat from my forehead. I toss it in the trash and see that someone has thrown the full bottle of unopened rum into the trash can.

I think about all the late nights out on the patio with a glass of rum on ice, and my entire body trembles with a craving so strong I can feel myself breaking out into a fresh sweat. I look down at the brand-new bottle resting atop a pile of trash and I reach in and grab it.

I focus on a new countering belief. *This poison is preventing you from becoming who you were meant to be. It is only delaying the pain and the weight of everything that has happened until morning. This is not a solution; this is the problem.*

I crack open the cap and rush to the sink. I can't. I can't keep living like this. Still, I find myself raising the bottle to my lips and taking one small sip. *No,* I scream silently, spitting out the oaky liquid before tilting the bottle in one smooth motion and pouring its contents down the sink until it's empty.

When I turn around, Abuelo is standing there in the kitchen with me, alone in the dark. He is hunched over slightly, his knees trembling, too, looking me over. I understand why he is standing there. He is serving as my witness if the question arises about the now-empty bottle of rum in the trash can. He doesn't have to say it—I know. I recognize the gesture for precisely what it is. This is him offering his full support.

I nod back at him in appreciation. We are in this together, and he is standing there, silently encouraging me to be proud of what I've done—pouring it out. He grins at me before losing himself again and returning to pass under the archway, down the hall toward his room.

In the morning I will call the number of the local AA group Dr. Robles gave me. It saddens me to think I've allowed things to get this out of control, but it's where I am. Rebuilding my inner strength and the new picture of who I am starts with admitting the truth. I can't crawl out of this hole alone. I need help. If there is something the Army taught me, it's the power of the team. It's time I stop trying to survive alone.

I realize after tonight's experience with Abuelo, returning home has given me a new Army to fight alongside.

The next morning I wake early to see if I can catch Papi before he leaves for the fields, but I'm not early enough. I want to clear the air, although it seems like he had the same idea and woke up even earlier than usual to avoid seeing me. Perhaps it's better this way. I think the conversation he and I must have will go better if I can explain that I've already begun attending AA meetings. I'm unsure how he is going to take that news. I don't know if it means he will be hopeful that I've taken another step toward healing or if it will only solidify his disappointment that by attending meetings, I'm demonstrating how seriously I've lost control.

Either way, I am going. Last night's near slip, after all the promises I've made and intended to keep, proves I can't do this on my own anymore. After doing a little research on Alcoholics Anonymous and learning about the program—the principles and the steps—I dial the local group and make an appointment to meet during the 9:30 a.m. session.

It gives me plenty of time to drop Teó off at the park with Dolores and drive to the local library, where the meetings are hosted.

When Teó and I reach Dolores, waiting at the park's entrance, he waves goodbye, and I take a mental snapshot, knowing it's that little expression of the hope and faith he has in me that will get me through all twelve steps of this journey.

*Honesty. Being truthful with oneself.*

Similar to the VA building, the library has both the US and Puerto Rican flagpoles posted side by side, waving big and boldly against the tropical breeze of a bright-blue-sky morning. The waves of both fabrics point together toward possibility in a kaleidoscope of red, white, and blue. I stop and stare at them and suddenly realize that maybe I don't have to be lost anymore. Maybe I don't have to choose one place over the other. Today can be the beginning of something new. I can move forward as a woman with the identity of two places inside her. The idea strengthens my resolve.

I'm ten minutes early when I enter the private conference room in the back of the library, a military tradition I can't help but continue. Fortunately it gives me first access to the freshly steamed cafecitos a woman with her back to me is partitioning out on a long pop-up table. My eyes move across the table to multiple trays of freshly baked pastries. Pastelitos filled with a combination of guava and cream cheese and dusted with powdered sugar on a buttery, flaky crust, and quesitos, a golden cigar-shaped pastry, also filled with cream cheese and glazed with honey and caramelized sugar, make my stomach growl, but given the underlying tremble of trepidation, I think better before picking one up and taking a bite.

Needing to put my nervous energy to good use, I clear my throat, hoping to catch the woman's attention before blurting, "Is there anything I can do to help you set up?"

At my request, the lady turns to face me, and I'm shocked with recognition.

"Oh, excuse me. Milly? Right?"

Maria's nurse looks equally surprised to see me, but quickly her eyes soften, and she offers me a gentle smile, a stark contrast to the silent, no-nonsense woman I met that night during Maria's treatment.

"Sí," she says, nodding. "I remember you. You were with Dolores. Please forgive me, I don't remember your name."

"That's okay. It's Lina. Don't worry, I don't think either of us was feeling very friendly that night." I nearly slap a hand over my mouth at the brazenness of my response.

Milly's expression agrees, but for some reason she doesn't turn away and resume setting up the coffee station. Instead, she offers grace. "You're probably right, Lina. I tend to be very focused when I am working. I don't recall seeing you here before."

I look around, remembering exactly why I'm standing there, and I can sense the warmth in my cheeks. "No. It's my first time."

"First time here?" she asks.

"Ever."

She nods again, and I can see a glimpse of her stoicism from that first night in Maria's living room, but as she assesses me, I pick up on her effort to remain warm and open. "I've been coming here for five years now. Five good years."

"Really? That sounds like a long time." My cheeks grow even hotter when I realize the callousness of my response. I didn't intend to sound harsh or judgmental. It's more that I'm curious whether it takes that long to get through all twelve steps, but I don't know how to explain that without making a bigger fool of myself. "I'm sorry, I didn't mean . . ."

Milly reaches out and squeezes my arm. "It's okay. I understand. I've completed the program, but I like continuing to help the group. It's part of the twelfth step. This is a lifelong journey. It's important to have people that you trust around you. This group has been essential in giving me five good years. That's why I've decided to serve as a sponsor now."

"A sponsor?" I ask, unsure exactly what that entails.

"Yes, someone you can work with one-on-one to help you. But don't worry about that right now. Why don't you help me get these cafecitos set up and we can sit together? It can help to have a friendly face nearby, especially your first time."

"Yes, of course." I try to smile, but the flood of all the emotions coursing through me makes it feel like more of a grimace. "I'm sorry."

I can't seem to make my feet or my hands move. As people enter the room, the reality of where I am and what is happening threatens to take me under, and I contemplate sprinting out the door to freedom. Milly reaches out her hand and grabs mine. "One second at a time. That's all you have to focus on. The right here and right now."

"I'm . . . scared," I mutter, nearly unable to choke out the words.

Milly reaches for a tiny cup of café con leche in the corner. "Here, this one is decaf. Take this. You and I can go have a seat over there." She waves over at an older man in a pressed white guayabera and creased khakis. "José, would you mind taking over for me?"

José winks at her. "Claro. With pleasure."

Milly mercifully leads me to a seat beside her, and over the next twenty minutes, the room fills with approximately twelve to fifteen more people. Only one other—a man—looks about my age. The rest range from midthirties to possibly seventies, if I had to guess. No one pays much attention to me; they all take their coffee, a pastry, and their seats. Some faces mirror the despair I feel; others look bright and shiny. Even so, they are here, and what Milly said earlier begins to settle in. These meetings are not only helping those who are burdened by a rock bottom, but helping those who are sober stay that way.

A tall woman with elegant clothes and perfectly styled hair stands at a small podium in the front of the room. "Buenos días, everyone."

"Buenos días," we all reply.

"I'm glad you are here this morning. Is this anyone's first time here or at a meeting in general?"

I want to lie and keep my hand at my side. I look around the room, almost begging someone else to have the kind of courage failing me now. Milly looks over at me and places her hand on top of mine. "It's okay," she whispers.

Two hands go up around the circle, and reluctantly, I raise mine and quickly bring it back down. The host looks at Milly, and they exchange a nod.

"I'd like to offer a special welcome to those of you who raised your hands. We are grateful you are here today. Don't feel any pressure to say anything you are uncomfortable saying, but know that this is a safe place, and we are here to listen if you feel compelled to share. The first of our twelve steps can be one of the hardest, but the fact that you are here shows your bravery and ability to do hard things. We only require one thing of our participants. Only one: the desire to quit drinking. If you are here because you want to stop drinking, you are in the right place, and we will do everything we can to help you. My recommendation to all new members is the 'ninety-in-ninety principle.' We will talk more about that at the end of our meeting. For now, let me introduce myself. My name is Rosa, and I'm an alcoholic. It's been two thousand seven hundred and forty-eight days since my last drink."

The room applauds, and I'm overcome with a feeling of inadequacy. How shameful will it feel to admit that, for me, it's been less than one week?

Rosa scans the room. "Who would like to begin?"

The young man whose hand went up earlier, indicating that this was his first meeting, shoots up a hand again. I'm a bit taken aback by his bravery, deepening my dread that maybe I'm not ready for this, because all I feel is weak and insufficient.

"Yes, go ahead," Rosa says to him.

"Buenos días, my name is Christian, and I'm an alcoholic. Today is my first time at this group, because I just recently moved here from

Vieques, but I've been attending meetings for two years since I got out of the Navy. I was doing well until yesterday. Nothing specific triggered me. I'm sure you all can probably tell that I'm pretty hungover. It was just a bad day. And now it's been"—he looks down at his watch—"thirteen hours since my last drink. Or more like thirteen hours since I made myself stop and decide to try again, back at the beginning."

My eyes fill with tears at his pain and at the uncanny coincidence of a service member named Christian paving the way with his bravery for me to set aside my pride and reveal the truth of my misgiving and missteps.

"Gracias, Christian," the room replies in unison.

"Bienvenido, Christian. We are here for you. Would anyone else like to introduce themselves?" Rosa asks.

I feel the very light squeeze of Milly's hand over mine. I nod and raise my other hand before wiping my eyes.

"Please, go ahead," Rosa says to me. Her voice is soft and encouraging.

I stand on shaky knees and take a deep, cleansing breath before releasing it slowly. I place my right hand over my heart while Milly, seated beside me, keeps a hold on my left.

"Buenos días. I'm Catalina, and I'm an alcoholic. I've been sober for almost five days. And I want nothing more than for this to be the first day of the rest of my life."

I allow myself a moment of hope in the solidarity of the room's gentle applause.

# CHAPTER THIRTY-SIX

*Hope. Believing in the possibility of recovery and a better future.*

I stand at the base of the rocket in Bayamón's Science Park with Teó's hand in mine. Leonardo has been incredibly patient, and I personally can't wait to see the two of them come face-to-face for the first time. Especially when they get to see for themselves the similarities in both their features.

I glance down at my watch. Ten minutes until our scheduled time. *Please don't be late,* I think, knowing how much Teó is counting on this to go well . . . and on time. But my concerns are unnecessary—not only is Leonardo punctual, he's early.

Our eyes lock as he approaches slowly. Leonardo is wearing dark jeans, shiny black loafers, and a pressed royal-blue polo shirt that matches the nearby ocean. I can see the level of care he put into his appearance. His hair is freshly cut, and the lines are cleanly drawn from a recent style of his trim beard. I can still see the high school boy I knew ten years ago, but my pride swells at the man he's grown up to be, even though my feelings for Leo are more nostalgic than romantic. I think it's normal for me to feel something, given the insurmountable love I have for the child we share, but if the past week has taught me anything, it's that I've got a lot of work to do on myself before I can get involved with anyone.

"Is that . . ." Teó doesn't finish the sentence. His index finger pushes his glasses farther up his nose, taking in the grandeur of the father he's never known.

"It sure is," I say softly, refusing to take any offense when he releases my hand.

"He looks just like me," Teó says.

"He does."

Leonardo stops a few feet from us, and I'm overcome with compassion at the hesitancy and worry in his eyes, blending with pure awe at the sight of his son.

Teó looks up at me, and his eyes gleam a deep, bright blue, bluer than I've ever seen before, and I realize he is overwhelmed with emotion, too. It looks like it's going to be up to me to bring these two together.

"Hola, Leo. I'm glad you could make it. I'd like you to meet your son, Matteo Salvador."

Leo angles his chin down like a true gentleman, but he can't stop the wide spread of the smile across his face. "Es un placer, Matteo." He clears his throat and steps in closer. "I mean, it's very nice to meet you."

"You can call me Teó," he says. "Everyone does." Teó extends his hand for a proper shake, and Leo's eyes fill with tears.

He looks up at me. "He is so beautiful, Lina."

I nod, and we both notice Teó blush as Leo takes his hand and shakes it. "It's very nice to meet you, Teó. I have been praying every day about our meeting since I found out about you, especially knowing that you and your mami were living here in Puerto Rico. Your mami and I got mixed up, we had a misunderstanding, and I didn't know about you. If I had . . ." Leo releases Teó's hand but crouches down to meet him eye to eye, graciously changing the subject. "Your mami tells me you love science, and . . . um . . . Bolly Huddy."

Teó breaks into a fit of giggles. "You mean Buddy Holly." *Sniff.*

Leo smiles, but his eyes look sad for a moment, recognizing Teó's tic. *Sniff.*

At Teó's growing embarrassment, I can sense the tics coming on stronger. I reach out and put my hand on his arm. "It's okay," I say softly.

Leonardo swallows. "I'm really sorry, Teó. I know how difficult it is to live with these . . . um . . . tics. I had them, too."

"You did?" Teó asks. "Like me?"

Leonardo nods. "Yes, it's my fault that you have them. I'm sorry." He stands and lowers his head, ashamed.

"Don't be sorry," Teó says. "I kinda like them." He shrugs.

I swallow back the lump in my throat from the pure and honest graciousness and forgiveness my son has just offered his father. He is truly a remarkable kid.

Leo swallows hard, and I can tell he is equally moved.

"Thank you . . . son." He says the last word with great hesitancy, but Teó smiles at him.

"You called me *son*. I like it. What should I call you?"

In unison, Leo and I both say, "Papi," without ever having discussed it. Because that's who he is, and it's the only name that makes sense.

"I'm glad to meet you, Papi," Teó says and takes his hand again.

"May I?" Leo asks, and I wave them on ahead of me, hand in hand. Father and son.

# CHAPTER THIRTY-SEVEN

*Surrender. Letting go of control and surrendering to a higher power.*

Dr. Robles once again sits across her desk from me. I sip a tiny cup of foam-topped espresso while she finalizes her notes from our most recent EMDR session.

"Your responses show that you are making great progress, Lina. How do you feel about it?"

"Stronger," I answer.

I could almost predict what she will ask next, and when the question comes, I hold back a smile, knowing I was right.

"What does stronger feel like?"

"I knew you were going to ask that."

The pretty doctor smiles. "Of course you did—you're very astute—but don't deflect."

I shake my head at the undeniable truth that the good doctor has already gotten a strong sense of who I am. "I feel lighter inside—most days, anyway. It's been nine days since I've had a drink, so I'm significantly more alert. I'd forgotten how sharp the world looks when you're not buzzed all the time. I feel more present, like I'm seeing and hearing things I would have normally missed under a drunken fog. Most times it's good and I feel strong and capable. But sometimes it can be a little overwhelming. I feel like the world is moving around me so bright and fast, and there's a silent pressure urging me to keep up. And I think I'm afraid to fail."

I pause and take another sip of the nutty local roast. It's extra sweet, my new preference since I quit drinking.

Dr. Robles places down her pen. "That's a lot to unpack, but that's good. I can see a significant difference in your demeanor and your self-reflections from that first visit."

We both smile at the memory.

"Let's begin at the top," she continues. "Nine days is a wonderful milestone. Congratulations. I'm glad the local group is helping you. Are you connecting well with your sponsor?"

I nod. "Yes, I think it was serendipity that we found ourselves at the meeting. My sponsor is very diligent and focused on the guidelines. I appreciate her rigidity. It reminds me of the way things are done in the military. I also like the idea of moving through twelve defined steps. It gives you a goal and makes the process of recovery transparent and clearly outlined. By the time I got to the meeting, it wasn't as difficult as I'd expected to face myself honestly and achieve step one: an admission of powerlessness. I couldn't deny that the alcohol was in control when it threatened my ability to keep my word to Teó that I'd stop drinking. Step two wasn't a big stretch for me, either, because I've always had hope and believed in God. I can easily admit that I need help from heaven and from Mama Lina watching over me to get me through this. So that brings me to step three, an act of surrender, which means putting my beliefs into actions, knowing that I need to engage in a more spiritual existence through attending church and daily prayer and meditation to help guide my thoughts and my choices."

"And how do you feel about turning your beliefs into a daily practice?"

I pause to consider the question. "I feel like that makes this whole thing more real. It moves getting sober from an idea in my head, a concept, to something that's now a physical part of my life. It's like incorporating exercise. This is muscle memory for my brain. I can understand why it's required, and I'm looking for ways to incorporate prayer or time with God in a way that feels authentic for me. I don't want it to become a chore or a box to tick off. I want it to count."

Dr. Robles glances down at her journal. "Can journaling be part of your prayer sessions? Do you find the process of journaling effective?"

"I do," I say sincerely. "Funny you should mention that, because it was during a recent journal session that I realized the time had come for me to move out and begin building my own home for Teó and me. I wasn't really sure when it would be the right time, but sitting there and journaling my thoughts, I just knew. So, today, my friend Eli and I are going to look at a few available apartments near the beach."

Her eyebrows arch at the mention of Eli. "It would be remiss of me not to highlight the importance of avoiding any new romantic relationships during your first year of sobriety, Lina. This is a crucial time for you to put all your energy and focus into your recovery, your stability, and your son."

My heart twists at the truth of what she's saying. "I know. I agree and I don't plan on letting our friendship get romantic in my first year." I let out a small sigh. "I just hope he is willing to wait. We haven't really discussed it."

"Well, you know what they say, at least what my abuelita always said to me: if he isn't willing to wait for you, he doesn't deserve you."

My voice lowers to near a whisper. "I know. I just hope he does."

Dr. Robles opens her journal and flips to a fresh page. "One more thing I'd like to discuss before we end our session for today. I know you may be a little mentally spent after the light therapy, but it's important. You said that the world is moving so fast you feel the pressure to keep up, creating a fear of failure. Did I understand that correctly?"

I stare down at my hands. "Yes, that's correct."

"Lina, who are you afraid of failing?"

I move to offer an immediate response, but I hold back the words, realizing I need to let my mind process the question. My response matters. I look Dr. Robles directly in the eyes.

"I'm afraid to fail my family and my son. But mostly I'm afraid to fail myself."

The normally proper and pristine therapist props her elbows on the desk and brings her hands together beneath her chin, making her seem uncharacteristically warm from her more clinical demeanor.

"Listen, I want you to remember that feelings and thoughts are not facts. It's important to recognize limiting beliefs such as 'I am failing' or 'I feel like a failure' and acknowledge that thinking them doesn't make them true. Just as they can be given power over your sense of self, so can the opposite be true. So try engaging in self-compassion and reword the limiting belief to include acknowledgment and a shift into a more positive direction."

I take in what she's saying but answer honestly. "I'm not sure I'm following."

Dr. Robles nods encouragingly. "That's okay. Let me give you an example. The next time you find yourself thinking or feeling like you are failing, I want you to tell yourself: 'I'm struggling with this feeling of failure because of my inherent desire to do well, and that's okay. I'm human and things have been very hard, but I am a good mother who loves her child, and I'm doing my best. I won't fail if I keep working at the things that bring me joy and fulfillment.' Can you do that?"

I welcome the assurance that blankets me from the inside. Honesty. Hope. Surrender. These are the principles for the first three steps, and I can already feel them working at removing the darkness I've been harboring inside since returning from Iraq.

"Yes, Dr. Robles. Yes, I can definitely try that." And I mean it.

Eli is waiting for me outside the VA building. We coordinated my appointment with Dr. Robles to align with his physical therapy session, making the commute to the first of three apartments I've scheduled to see even easier.

He looks amazing in a pair of designer jeans, an emerald-green polo shirt, and a pair of aviator sunglasses. His golden hair shines beneath a brilliant sky. And I find myself struggling with the idea that we can be only friends for the next year, but I know that if I want to offer him my best self, then I need to be strong. Eli still hasn't told me whether he is planning to stay in Puerto Rico, and honestly, I'm too scared to ask. If he is planning to leave, I don't want to know yet.

"Howdy, Lina," he says, giving me a customary kiss on the cheek. I smile at how seamlessly he has adapted to local customs. "How'd it go today?"

"Really good, actually. I didn't start these sessions expecting them to work. Honestly, I just wanted to make sure I did what I needed to do to maximize my military benefits, but now I really think it's helping. I'm feeling stronger and have a clearer sense of who I am. I mean, don't get me wrong, there's still a way to go, but I feel like I'm moving in the right direction."

Eli puts his arm around my shoulder as he leads me toward his car. "That's really great, Lina. I know talking to someone really helped me when I first got back from my tour across the pond. I damn sure thought there were days I wasn't gonna make it. Some pretty dark days when the reality of, well, you know." He glances over at the prosthetic. "No one ever really tells you about phantom limb pain, or the challenges of learning to live your life in a whole new way. Some days you feel like a little baby learning to walk for the first time. I spent my whole life leading in sports, academics, even leading things around the house for my mama and my sister. My career as an Army officer felt like a natural extension to continue leading. Then, one snapshot of a moment and everything changes. And you gotta find a way to pick up the pieces and learn to live a whole new life." We reach his car, and he walks over to open the passenger-side door for me.

"How did you do it?" I say in awe of the man I've come to know. Listening to him really talk about his injury for the first time, I see the severity of what he's been through with a clear perspective and sober eyes. "What pushed you through the darkness?"

He smiles that beautiful wide smile as he leans into the car and pulls my seat belt out for me. "Purpose, Lina. At first, I knew I had a purpose to come to Puerto Rico and honor Sergeant Fuentes. Now it's about trusting that I came down here for a reason and that maybe all that preparation to lead was for the life I'd be given right here, where I'm happier than I've ever been—in paradise . . . with you."

He closes my car door, and I can feel my heart racing at the impact of his words as he makes his way around to the driver's side. Eli is planning to stay in Puerto Rico. For me. I have to tell him about the one-year waiting period. He may change his mind after he knows.

I look over at him as he slides into the driver's seat. "I'm attending AA meetings," I blurt. "I was trying to figure out a way to tell you, but I'm still trying to say it out loud without feeling ashamed."

Eli starts the car, graciously filling the inside with cold air before buckling in and turning to face me. "You don't have a damn thing to be ashamed about. Most people ain't got a clue of what it's like over there or what it takes to get over the things we had to see . . . and do. You're a strong and capable woman. And you're getting some help so you can be your very best for yourself and your son. That's commendable and I'm proud of you. I will do whatever it takes to help support you through this journey, ya hear. Whatever it takes."

My heart fills with tenderness at the endless compassion that exudes from this man. "It means a year of remaining single and focused on my recovery."

He chuckles, understanding that his supporting me means we can't indulge our mutual attraction. "And how do you feel about that?"

I laugh. "You sound like Dr. Robles. But, seriously, as much as I'd like to explore what's happening between us right away, I think it's important that I follow the rules and take my recovery seriously, for Teó's sake and my own."

Eli grins. "I understand. Lucky for you, I'm a patient man, even if this relationship is taking off like a herd of turtles." We are exiting the parking lot when he turns to me and says, "Now that we got that outa the way, you ready to go pick out a new home?"

# CHAPTER THIRTY-EIGHT

*Courage. Facing fears and taking action despite uncertainty.*

After a busy first week unpacking in our new apartment, I wake up with a wish to return to sleep for a couple more hours, but no such luck. Today is a big day—the day I sign back up with the National Guard. I reach for my phone to make sure there haven't been any last-minute changes emailed to me since I went to bed the night before, but after rubbing the sleep from my eyes, I don't see any new updates.

Teó spent the night at Mami's so I could focus on reporting for my appointment on time. As tired as my body feels this morning, I'm grateful.

I scroll through my phone, but I don't see any new texts from Eli. He's been unusually quiet since the afternoon he took me to pick out my apartment. I know the reality of everything I've revealed has taken its toll, and he's still working to process it all. Dolores also mentioned that a large tourist convention in the area has kept Chiquitas full of patrons. She's even stepped in to waitress and help him cover the growing crowds. I'm proud to see her working and finding her footing again.

Neither of them has said anything about selling Chiquitas, which means Eli is still planning on sticking around for a while. Whatever he decides, I have to stay focused on myself, my recovery, and moving back into life in a uniform. Today is the first step in reclaiming my dreams to heal and one day become a doctor.

"Con permiso." I walk up to the glass window in front of a series of cubicles. Only one young female—a private first class—is working quietly at her desk.

"I'm here to see Sergeant Melendez. I spoke with him on my way here. He said to go ahead and come on in."

"Have a seat. Sergeant Melendez will be right out." She points toward two dilapidated chairs behind me against the wall. Government buildings on the island don't get much of a budget for furniture and facility upgrades.

"Thank you," I tell her and cautiously take my seat.

To Sergeant Melendez's credit, he leaves me waiting only twenty-five minutes, a small favor where the norm is long hours in a waiting room, particularly in buildings like these.

"Sergeant LaSalle, un placer," he says in a loud voice that rings with song, opening the door to the inner sanctum of cubicles.

"Gracias, same," I respond politely. "I appreciate you seeing me last minute."

"Claro," he says, "especially now that I know I'm in the presence of a certified war hero. Qué orgullo."

Pride. He's referring to a Puerto Rican actually earning a Silver Star. Dr. Robles shared the same sentiment. I get it. He sees this as a victory, and one Puerto Rican's victory is a celebration for all of us. I wish I could share in their pride, but even if I'm clearer on culpability, the word *hero* still feels foreign.

Sergeant Melendez's eyebrows are waxed into flawless shape. His bright-white, perfectly rectangular teeth fill his smile from corner to corner. I bet someone recommended him for recruiting duty. He has charm oozing from his cologne-scented pores. I bet he's got the women in the unit swooning. I'm confident there are many. Not me, though. Today he serves a clear and defined purpose.

Despite the glimmer of invitation in his eyes as he leads me to his office, I am not even ruffled with interest.

"Do you think you can help me out, Sergeant?" I ask as he holds the door open for me. "I really need to get back to work."

"Oh wow, all business." He waves me in. "I was about to offer you a coffee, but it's all good. Have a seat. I think I can help."

I sigh, relieved, taking the seat across his desk.

We are talking rank to rank now—the glimmer is gone.

"Just so you know, we aren't offering any bonuses for medics to get back in. I just want to put that out there in case your rush to get back in is tied to some extra cash."

I shake my head. "No, that's not it. I don't need a bonus. I need to put my uniform on and get to work."

He leans back in his chair and smiles, looking me over.

"I like your fire, Sergeant LaSalle. I could tell over the phone you meant business."

"I keep my MOS and rank, right?" I say, wanting to stay on task. "Even though it's the National Guard and not active duty?"

"That's right, you remain a medic and a sergeant," he says. "Plus, I already looked you up in the personnel database and confirmed an honorable discharge. I also saw that you're a Silver Star recipient. That's pretty impressive, Sergeant. You must have done something that went above and beyond. Giving a Puerto Rican female a Silver Star, that's no joke."

"Yeah, well, I didn't apply for it. I didn't even know my unit commander submitted it until they were ready to present the award."

He waits, likely wanting me to expound on what I did to earn such an honor. I'm sure the more feral side of him wonders whether I managed to *earn* the medal. It's no secret men still think most women earn an award like that on their backs or on their knees. I don't hold it against him. But given the level of prominence an award like the Silver

Star represents, even a blond bombshell with an agenda couldn't jockey that level of recognition without genuine merit. I know that. He knows it, too. Still, he is curious.

"I know you want to ask me about it," I say firmly. "It's all over your face, but I'd rather not get into the details. I'm still working on accepting that sometimes we have to do impossible things on the battlefield, and not everyone will make that choice and protect the mission. You understand?"

"A war wound," he says knowingly. "Understood."

He claps his hands together and rubs his palms as though trying to generate a spark. "Can I ask a different question? Maybe related, maybe not."

"Go ahead."

"Why did you get off active duty? Your records say your last duty station was in North Carolina. It looks like you had it pretty good out there."

I prepared for this question ahead of time. Our lack of boundaries on the island doesn't pertain only to family. They extend to fellow Puerto Ricans. It's unlikely Sergeant Melendez would "go there" if I weren't from here, but he's seen my records. He knows I am local.

"I have a son." I prepare to rattle off the simple, clear-cut response I rehearsed, but then words I wasn't expecting begin tumbling out. "His father lives here. It's important to me they are close to each other."

Where the hell did that come from?

My subconscious arrived at this conclusion. I swallow deeply. "And besides," I say, ready to go back on script, "my parents and grandparents are here. It's all about family, right?"

Sergeant Melendez smiles. Bull's-eye.

"Yes," he agrees, "family is everything. I get it. Now let's talk about the unit."

I visibly relax, leaning back into my seat, relieved we are finally done playing twenty questions.

"LaSalle, I don't know how much you know about the Puerto Rico National Guard—it's a little different from the National Guard in the States. Most people don't know this, but we provide direct support to the local police department throughout the island. In fact . . . ," he says, accentuating the words with his large hands.

I smile, inadvertently tuning him out. I'm endeared by how we speak so animatedly. The Italians don't have a thing on us. He is still speaking, but I've gotten distracted by all the hand movements.

"I'm sorry, the largest what?"

"The largest sustained support to a law enforcement mission in modern US history. And the rumor is the governor is about to cash in his chips and mobilize us to provide law enforcement support in the streets."

"Really?" He's right; this is different from the States. In the US, everyone knows the military is a foreign defense element; our mission is abroad. I find it bizarre to picture US military and their M16 rifles in the streets of San Juan.

"That's right," he reiterates. "In fact, before you got here, we were all trying to get information on the strike happening at Plaza. So far it sounds like it's been peaceful, but hundreds, if not thousands, of people are protesting the layoffs right now."

"Layoffs?" I haven't done a very good job keeping up with the local news.

"Yeah, tensions are pretty high, which means for you—right place, right time."

He's right—right place, right time—but the civil unrest makes me nervous. "So you think we will be mobilized soon?"

"Yes, very soon." He strokes his freshly shaved cheeks.

I bet he used to have a beard. I have to admit, Sergeant Melendez is really good-looking.

"Okay, so where do I sign? I'm ready to get the process started."

He pushes a manila folder with a small stack of documents toward me from across the desk. "Everything's right here. You can start in about a week; just report here to the unit." He snaps his fingers as something comes to memory. "Medic, right? ¡Mano! I almost forgot. You will be perfect for an upcoming volunteer effort we've got going in two weeks, on Saturday at the VA in San Juan."

"What's the mission?"

"Medical exams and flu shots for kids living in an orphanage in Hatillo. We welcome them at the VA twice a year and do routine medical exams. You know, test eyes and ears, provide vaccines, and any other basic medical care they may need. It's a special initiative we do here. Honestly, everyone on the medical team looks forward to it. Kids are cute and well, imagínate, they live in an orphanage. This is one way they get to leave that place, come all the way to the capital, and make a day of it. You understand what I'm saying, right?"

"I think it sounds wonderful. Cuenta conmigo. Count on me. I'd be honored to help."

"¡Excelente! Then let's get these forms filled out and processed immediately. You can stay here and turn them in to Private Sanchez on your way out. I'll call you tomorrow and confirm everything's complete. I'll get you the details for reporting at the unit. And then that following Saturday, we'll meet in the VA parking lot at zero eight hundred sharp."

It is warm and familiar to hear the Army lingo. I confidently reach my hand into his outstretched one and shake it, thanking him again.

Back in my car, I feel lighter, a whisper of my darker self. Without thinking, I consider stopping at a chinchorro. I imagine a celebratory mojito and nearly taste the sweetness of the rum on the tip of my tongue, craving the warmth on my insides.

*Stop it, Lina.* I repeat the first tradition in my head. Honesty. *I am powerless over alcohol; my life has become unmanageable.* I won't go back. I think about the children attending the clinic. I can help them. They will be counting on me.

# CHAPTER THIRTY-NINE

*Integrity. Living in alignment with one's values and principles.*

The knock on the door surprises me because Teó and Leonardo are out having lunch, and they wouldn't knock on the door even if they returned. Teó loves using his new key to our apartment, which he gets to keep with him when he is spending time with his father or our extended family.

"Who is it?" I call out.

"It's me, Lina. Your papi."

*Papi?* The sound of his voice catches me off guard. We haven't talked about him coming by. We haven't spoken about much of anything since that night he thought I was going to drink the rum, made worse, I'm sure, by finding an empty bottle in the trash can the next morning. I planned on telling him the truth: that I'd poured it all out into the sink, Abuelo as my witness (for all the good that might do), except his indignation and assumptions only served to push me further away, until weeks had passed and we'd transitioned to operating in each other's shadows, avoiding any direct contact. When I told him and Mami that I was moving out, I couldn't tell whether that was relief on his face or concern. With a grunt, he stood and left out the front door, and I haven't seen him since. Mami must have given him my address; otherwise he wouldn't even know where I moved.

I turn the lock and swing the door open.

"Buenos días, Papi. Bendición," I say, extending my cheek as he leans down and gives me a polite kiss.

"Que Dios te bendiga, mi hija," he says. "Can I come in?"

"Please." I open the door even more and step out of his way. "We are still unpacking things, so please forgive the mess. But the movers brought the furniture a few days ago and then just dumped all the boxes yesterday."

As my father passes the kitchen, I see his eyes scan across the countertops, and it's obvious what he's looking for—alcohol. That's probably why he showed up unannounced, wanting to see whether he could catch me drunk. I shake my head, frustrated. "Would you like something to drink?" I ask.

His eyebrows shoot up. "What do you have?"

My voice bites. "Only water, apple juice, and club soda."

"Water, please," he answers tightly. "I'm playing in the band tonight. It's important that I'm well hydrated."

"Sure," I say.

I pull out a frosty water bottle from the refrigerator and hand it to him. "So what brings you by?"

He looks around the cluttered living room before looking back to assess, obviously pleased by my sobriety. "I wanted to see if you needed any help. You know moving isn't easy, especially for a woman living by herself." At the mention of my solitude, he realizes I actually am alone. "Where is Matteo?"

I roll my eyes. "Teó is having lunch with his father. They should be back any minute."

"You are allowing that man to spend time alone with Teó?"

I fold my arms across my chest. "Of course. Why wouldn't I?"

Papi shrugs. "I mean, he is a stranger. Teó doesn't even know him."

"Thanks to you," I snap. "Besides, up until a few months ago, Teó didn't know you, either, but I let you into his life, too."

His head twitches as though I've physically slapped him. "It isn't the same thing, Lina. But you're right. I'm sorry. I trust your judgment."

This time it's me who jumps back like I've been hit. "What? Since when? You were pretty quick to challenge my judgment when you mistakenly thought I was going to drink that rum Tía Lisandra sent over."

This time he rolls his eyes. "Come on, Lina. You're going to tell me I'm wrong? I throw out the trash in the house, remember. I saw the empty bottle the next morning. What else was I supposed to think?"

"How about that maybe I waited until everyone was in bed and I went to the trash can to find a full bottle and I poured it out into the sink to avoid any unnecessary temptation?" I decide to skip the gulp I almost took before spitting it out.

"You expect me to believe that?" Papi asks, incredulity dripping from each word. "Come on. I'm no fool."

"Abuelo saw me. Ask him," I answer, equally indignant.

The possibility of a witness throws him off. That and that I may have proved to be a drunk, but not a liar. Papi knows I've never been a liar, despite his thoughts on women in general.

"Do you blame me for having my doubts? You've been out of control since you got here, Lina, meeting strange Americanos out on the street and letting them bring you home so drunk you can't even walk. Don't you know how dangerous that kind of behavior is? What's happened to you?"

I walk over to the fridge and pull out a bottle of water for myself, needing a moment to gain my composure before I start yelling. I twist the cap and take a big drink. "Wrong again," I say tightly. "I went to La Placita that night by myself. I did drink too much, Papi, and yes, my decisions were dangerous, but I called Eli to come pick me up and get me home safely. And that's exactly what he did. I called him because I trust him and I know he is the kind of man who does the right thing. He was as disturbed by my condition as you were; trust me, he made his opinions very clear. In fact, he's a big reason why I'm finally getting help, Papi. That's right, help."

I allow the silence to linger in the air, needing, wanting, everything I've said to sink in.

Papi takes a long sip of water, and when he speaks again, his voice is softer. "Lina, you're seeing a doctor? What kind of help are you getting?"

"I'm going to therapy, Papi, at the VA hospital." I look down at my shoes, still working through having to admit the next part, as it falls under step four of the program, taking a self-inventory. "And I'm going to daily AA meetings. I have a sponsor, Milly, who is helping me."

"Daily?" Papi looks at me with sympathy in his eyes. "Is it that bad?"

"Yes," I admit, not wanting to soften the reality of my situation. "And no. I go every day because I promised to attend ninety meetings in ninety days. Which is supposed to help solidify the habits to change for life. But there are days I don't think about drinking. Others when I can't get to a meeting fast enough."

Papi sits on the couch, almost as though the reality of my situation weighs so heavy on his own shoulders, he is unable to remain standing.

"I had no idea," he mutters, staring down at his hands. "I knew you were drinking, Lina. I assumed with the stress of motherhood, being out there all alone. I'm so sorry."

I move to sit beside him on the couch, but I can't bring myself to offer any affection; there is still so much unsaid between the two of us. Things I've done he still doesn't know about.

"It's all right, Papi. I know this is a lot to take in."

"I just wasn't sure you were being honest with me or with yourself about the path you were on. I believed you thought everything was about having a good time and ignoring your responsibilities."

"You know, Papi . . . not all us girls are mentirosas. Some of us really believe the lies we tell ourselves. Especially when we try to convince ourselves that we are enough for those who are supposed to love us."

Staring down at our hands, side by side, neither of us hears the key in the door or notices when Teó and Leonardo walk in, until Teó interrupts the silence. "Abuelo, did you call my mom a mentirosa?"

Papi's head shoots up. "No, Matteo. Of course not. I want your mami to know that I love her." He looks over at Leonardo and does a double take, probably surprised by how much Teó looks like his father. The two of them standing together, side by side . . . it's uncanny.

"Leonardo," Papi says formally, standing to leave.

"Señor," Leo replies, but keeps a possessive hand on Teó's shoulder. I can hear what he isn't saying: *I will not relinquish hold of my son.*

Papi crouches down to look at Teó face-to-face. "I would never call your mami a mentirosa. She is my princess."

I look over at him sharply, his affection making my heart pound.

Teó pushes his glasses up higher on his nose. "But you said all girls were mentirosas."

Papi smiles, embarrassed, when I break in. "Teó, your abuelo's values can be a little old-fashioned, but he is very good to admit when he is wrong. Right, Papi?"

Papi stands upright, towering over everyone in the room, but he bows his head in humility.

"That's right, Lina. I can always admit when I am wrong." He looks directly at Leonardo before glancing down at Teó and then back up at the father he helped keep from his son. "And sometimes I can be wrong, very wrong, even if my heart was in the right place."

Leo nods at Papi, making peace.

No one says another word until Papi leaves and the click of the door fills the silent room.

# CHAPTER FORTY

*Humility. Recognizing one's limitations and seeking support.*

My first day at the unit has finally arrived. Today is a turning point. A new chapter. Abuela insisted on pressing my uniform, so I decided to get ready at my parents' house, and they agreed to drop Teó off at school to give me some extra time to navigate my first morning at Fort Buchanan. Standing in front of the bedroom mirror of my old room, I stare at the reflection of the woman who dares stare back at me.

Appreciation at returning to service, at the stethoscope that will hang on my neck, at reuniting with the mission to help and heal others swirls together with a sense of despair. I'm afraid I will fail, that I will freeze when I need to move, that I will draw a blank when I need to act. But my instincts, my natural reaction to Big Guy at La Placita, allow me a little drop of hope and faith in who I was born to be. I remember the little girl who checked her tía Lisandra's pulse and listened for her heartbeat after hearing stories about the power of doctors in the world, and I take another step forward.

The mirror reflects a woman I knew not too long ago—Sergeant LaSalle-Rivera. She's back in uniform.

I never thought I would look like this again: a tan T-shirt, gray-and-white digitized pants, an Army rigger belt wrapped around my waist, and a brand-new pair of tan combat boots on my feet. I complete a full turn in front of the mirror and face forward again. The brown bun at the top of my neck shines, wrapped tightly in place over the doughnut shape of a rolled-up sock. My uniform is pressed to starched perfection. The brand-new boots feel heavy, but familiar, on my feet. A dash of mascara extends the curtains of my chocolate-brown eyes, enhanced with a dollop of pink gloss on my full lips. I stand tall, legs slightly apart, arms behind my back, elbows pointed out, chin and chest raised high with pride. My eyes move from top to bottom, carrying a strong sense of nostalgia as I assess the reality that I'm back. I don't crouch underneath its force. I hold still—strong. Stronger.

*I am a soldier and a healer. I am battle ready.* I repeat this in my mind one, two, three times. *Own it, Lina.*

Still standing in front of the mirror, I bring my feet together and salute myself with deliberate precision. Then, before I can process what is happening, I'm down on my knees as the image of the young man crumpling to the ground splays before my eyes. It's no longer my reflection but his terrified face staring back at me from the mirror.

My palms lay flat on the ground, allowing the heaves in my stomach to settle. I really don't want to start my day vomiting. Desperately working to regain control, I suck in air, forcing myself to inhale through my nose and exhale from my mouth.

Rocking on all fours, I ask myself: *What is your countering belief?*

I repeat the statements I've come to memorize from my therapy session. There was nothing I could have done to save that young man on the battlefield. He was going to die no matter what I did, and I saved as many lives as I could.

I wait patiently as my mind channels me back from Iraq and to my bedroom, where I'm crouched on the floor. It's over.

My gaze returns to the mirror. The boy from the battlefield is gone, and his return is spreading across a wider and wider span of time. Seeing him still hurts, but I'm finding myself stronger each time I take control of the visions and my countering beliefs.

Slowly I rise to my feet and smooth out the wrinkles in my pants. The mirror waits for me to return. *Look at yourself. See who you are. It's me. I can do this. I know I can.* The small space fills with serenity.

"Catalina! Diantre, nena. You look so beautiful."

Papi leans on the doorway of my bedroom. I turn around shyly.

"Gracias, Papi," I say, my fingers trembling. I'm not sure why I'm so nervous for him to see me this way.

"Lina, I've seen you in pictures with your uniform, but, wow, this is different. You look so . . . powerful." He smiles at me with the same type of admiration he gave Teó when he first saw him in the yard. "Mi hija poderosa." *My powerful daughter.*

I'm not sure what to say; the approval in his gaze throws me off balance. I don't remember him ever looking at me this way before. He's proud.

"Papi, I didn't think you would be happy about me signing back up for the service. I assumed you were hoping I would find work in one of the local factories."

He shakes his head in disbelief. "Catalina, all I've ever wanted is for you to follow your heart and find happiness. I know it hasn't been very smooth between us since you got here. I'm not so good with words, but I believe in you. It has been frustrating for me to see you falling apart when I know what you are capable of. You are a soldier, Lina. A good one."

"But, Papi," I counter, "you were so against the idea of me joining the Army in the first place. You remember our conversation, right? About this career being the better choice for my brother, if he had lived . . ." I don't continue.

I wait for his justification, for his eloquent and poetic discourse about how I couldn't possibly understand, because for men it's different, but he enters through the doorway and crosses the room, stopping behind me. He stands an entire foot taller than the top of my head. His height alone commands reverence, but I won't back down. I won't be intimidated.

We are both facing the mirror as he begins.

"Lina, I have done you a great injustice. As a father, it is natural for me to want to protect my only daughter. Don't fault me for that.

You're a parent now. It's natural to want your children to be safe, and I am a traditional man."

I open my mouth to placate him. Years of habit are deeply ingrained in our interactions, but he squeezes my shoulder.

"Let me finish," he says. "When your brother, Levi, didn't make it past one day on this earth, I didn't think I would survive another night living in a world where my son ceased to exist. Your mother is a saint, and somehow she held strong for both of us, despite the intensity of her own loss. It was her strength that pulled us through those next couple of months."

To my shock and amazement, Papi's eyes shine with the fullness of fresh tears wavering on the cusp of overflow. My lips move to speak again, but he blinks the tears back into place and continues.

"My pain was still very fresh when we discovered your mother was pregnant again. I was terrified. I worried I might be cursed, and you would die, too. For nearly nine months I prepared myself for the loss I knew was coming." He swallows the memories but replaces the pain with the faint edges of a smile. "But you didn't die, Catalina; you came into this world screaming with life. A beautiful baby girl who looked so much like the woman who already owned my heart. I had no idea God could be so generous, giving me another child so quickly—a daughter to protect."

I can't believe what I'm hearing. It's not making any sense. My heart pumps with thirst for such words, but my conscience refuses to accept a sentiment that contradicts what I've spent my life experiencing.

"Papi, I'm sorry. I'm confused. I can't recall a single moment where I ever felt cherished. It was the exact opposite. I felt like a failed consolation prize, a daughter instead of the son you so desperately wanted. I told myself time and time again that if I could try a little harder, work a little more, be a little better, you would love me the way you loved my brother—the ghost."

My words hit with the power of a right cross. I hear the sharp inhale before I feel his hands turn me around to face him directly.

"You are no consolation prize. You are a gift."

He takes a step back but keeps his large, calloused hands on my shoulders.

"Look at you, Catalina. You are beautiful, and you're wearing an American soldier's uniform—my daughter, the sergeant. How can I not be proud of you? I always knew you were meant for greatness. It broke our hearts to send you to Florida, but we knew you needed to have bigger experiences and more opportunities than we could offer. And look at you now, Lina. You've given us a beautiful grandson. You are a soldier protecting Puerto Rico. And you are so young, nena, and still there is so much more ahead of you."

"I'm scared," I admit. "I want to do a good job, but I'm still working through some things . . ." I swallow. "Some things from my time overseas."

Papi leans down, ensuring I capture every word.

"War is cruel. My father left the island to fight for the US in the Korean War when I was just an infant. He never came home, hija. I'm no fool. I know you didn't leave the Army so quickly after returning from Iraq because things went flawlessly over there. Don't you understand what I meant when I told you that it's justified to do whatever you must do to get home to your son?"

"But, Papi, I thought you were referring to returning home from a night out."

"I think you knew what I meant."

I stare at him until the truth stands firmly between us. "I guess I did."

"Lina, my father never made it home to me, and I have suffered that loss ever since. Whatever you had to do out there, be peaceful. I know you. There was no other choice. You did what you needed to do to return home to Matteo. That's all that matters. Your son will always be proud of you for returning home. We all are."

The vise loosens and falls at my feet, allowing me to take in everything he's said. "Thank you, Papi."

His strong arms wrap around me and squeeze tight. "You are a warrior, Lina. Una guerrera. I couldn't be any prouder of you. Tragedy may have brought you into our lives, but I am deeply grateful I was blessed with such a strong and capable daughter."

I kiss everyone farewell and head out, pushing into the first day of my new life in uniform. Teó's eyes light up as I walk out into the living room. "You look awesome in your uniform. I'm so proud of you, Mamá," he says, squeezing me tight.

"Thanks, honey. You look great in yours, too."

Teó waves goodbye, standing between Mami and Papi on the front porch. I pull away from the street and wave back.

It's time to get to work.

I'm six weeks sober. Today begins the next phase of our lives, and I'm determined to do it in my element as a healer.

# CHAPTER FORTY-ONE

*Willingness. Being open-minded and willing to change.*

After clearing security, I park beside a government van with a generic white license plate and pull down the visor to ensure my beret is positioned correctly. The bottom edge must be lined parallel to the eyebrows. My finger traces it, stopping just below the stainless-steel sergeant rank centered on the light-blue rounded patch directly above my left eye.

"I'm ready," I murmur before a forceful knock on the driver's-side window startles me. A bronze-skinned man, with dark-brown eyes and unnatural bleach-blond hair poking out from his beret, stands outside my window in a matching Army uniform. He leans down to get a good look at me and taps his index finger on the face of his watch.

I glance down at my own watch.

There are still fifteen minutes left until I'm scheduled to report to duty.

I turn off the ignition and step out, grabbing my backpack from the rear seat before locking the car doors.

"Sergeant LaSalle," the man confirms, towering in front of me as he takes in my name tag. "We've been trying to reach you."

The rank on the center of his chest and the last name beside it give me quick and necessary information: First Sergeant Miller. I heard about him in my welcome letter. He's the unit's highest-ranking non-commissioned officer (NCO) in charge of the unit's mission.

He doesn't have an accent; must be from the States. I'm surprised. In a National Guard unit, it's usually someone local.

"Good morning, First Sergeant. My cell phone is in my backpack." I lift the strap over my shoulder. "Is something wrong?"

He gives me another once-over, making me increasingly self-conscious that something on my uniform is out of place.

"We were going to have you report directly to the base clinic for duty instead of the unit headquarters. They have your onboarding packet ready to go. I told your section sergeant, but it looks like they forgot to make contact. Communication is a soup sandwich around here, Sergeant. As a new leader on the team, I expect you will help me improve that."

"Roger that, First Sergeant."

He nods in approval after appraising my boots, my uniform, my hair. I've passed his informal inspection.

"You see that vehicle over there at your six o'clock," he says, pointing directly behind me to a Humvee parked under a group of flamboyán trees.

I turn to see where he is pointing. "Yes, I see it."

"Sergeant Melendez is driving. You can leave your POV here," he says, pointing at my car, "and ride over there with him."

"Roger that," I reply.

"Dismissed, Sergeant. Double time."

*I'm still early,* I think but jog as instructed over to where Sergeant Melendez is waiting anyway.

"What's up, LaSalle?" Melendez greets me. "It's so good to have a Silver Star war hero in our ranks. Looks like you just met First Sergeant Miller. He's new."

I grimace as I slide into the passenger seat and buckle my seat belt. "What's his deal, anyway? He seems kind of intense."

"That's the consensus at the unit," Sergeant Melendez says, tossing the clipboard into the front seat of the Humvee. "But he just got here from the States. He recently returned from a tour in Afghanistan. Miralis, my mother's best friend, is our office manager. She says he keeps trying to get an appointment with the chaplain or the psych team, but they haven't been able to get him in. The psych team is backed up. Doña Lupe in the cafeteria is cousins with Miralis, and she told her that he walks around the unit late in the day when everyone is heading home and talks to himself. Shouts like he's pissed about something. Miralis thinks it's PTSD. That's all the story we know." Melendez lets out a light whistle. "Whatever it is, the guy's definitely wound up tight. So we'd better go."

Newly returned from deployment. PTSD. Wound up tight. It all makes sense now. I get it. PTSD is a monster that can morph into many shapes. Given the formalities of the rank structure, it can be tricky for me to discuss this with a higher-ranking NCO, especially one in my direct chain of command, but that doesn't mean I don't feel for him. I may be able to slide some resource information for Dr. Robles under his office door during off hours. He'll never know who sent it. I don't know if First Sergeant Miller is drinking to cope with his pain, too, but it's possible. I'll have to pay close attention.

I lean back into my chair and count my blessings on my first day back on duty. I take in the moment, the uniform, the camaraderie with Sergeant Melendez, the mission and focus on the dreams that might come true in my life after all.

My first week at the unit is incredible. Serving in an Army environment melded within the Puerto Rican culture is different; the coffee is way better than any unit stateside, and the language between the team is a blend of English and Spanish, but I like it, and everything about my experience feels like I'm exactly where I'm meant to be. As I start my second week, First Sergeant Miller calls me into his office. I walk in, only to find him staring off into the distance. He doesn't acknowledge me until I close the door, the sound seeming to stir him from a trance. I remember what Sergeant Melendez said about the rumors and possible PTSD, so I tread carefully, wondering if maybe he found out that the list of resources and pamphlets slipped under his door came from me. I step forward and stand in front of his desk at position of parade rest, with my feet hip width apart, my hands together positioned against my lower back, my elbows pointed out in a sharp angle.

"Good morning, First Sergeant."

"At ease, Sergeant LaSalle. Good morning."

At his command to release my posture, I bring down my hands and stand at rest.

"Why don't you take a seat?"

"Roger," I answer, my medical training kicking in as I observe him.

"Looks like you've made a great impression this week. I've already spoken with the commander down at the clinic and she says it's been a while since she's seen someone with such a detailed eye and excellent manner around the other soldiers."

I smile on the inside, his praise confirming the sense of belonging and completeness I'm beginning to feel within myself.

"Thank you, First Sergeant. I'm happy to be back in uniform. I, um, took some time off, leaving active duty to return to the island with my family. It isn't easy to feel like you've lost your mission."

He looks at me strangely. "You got out and came back in? To find a mission?"

"Something like that," I say. "There was a little more to it, but I realized I was meant to continue my mission and serve. I'm interested in the Army's medical school program. I'd like to submit my packet."

First Sergeant Miller bites his lip and stares at the desk. His silence worries me that perhaps he isn't on board with my career goals. I need his help to recommend my packet for signature. The Army can be very bureaucratic . . . and competitive. If he doesn't recommend me, it's unlikely my submission will get any traction. I've had only a week on the job for him to make an assessment, and he just said I've made a good impression. It doesn't make sense. I push aside my own worries and continue to observe him. His pupils are dilated, his breathing slightly belabored, and I can see a slight tremor in his hands. These are all possible symptoms of a reaction to medication, but I'm unable to know definitively—

"Did you say something, Sergeant LaSalle?"

I rewind to put us back on track. "I said I'd like to submit my packet for consideration in the Army's medical school program."

"Right, right." He nods. "I heard you were interested in going to medical school. That's great, yeah, really great. Keep up the good work and we can get you a letter of recommendation from the colonel in charge of the clinic and one from the post commander. I mean, if that's what you really want. I guess if you were already out and came back into the military . . ."

He trails off again, and I'm conflicted between taking his yes for an answer and recognizing the symptoms and pain behind his odd behavior. The familiarity hits close to home, and I fight to maintain my military bearing, knowing it's the most effective way to get through to him. Baby steps.

"That's right, First Sergeant. It's always been a dream of mine to go to medical school. I'd be very grateful to get the unit's support on my packet."

He bites his lip again and nods. "Yeah, sure. Keep up the good work. I don't think you will have any trouble. I see you're a Silver Star recipient. Should be easy to push through."

I'm the first to ignore the power of my medal because of what it took to earn it, but I'm genuinely surprised at how offhandedly he brings it up. This is the kind of thing leaders are usually pushing us to capitalize on. His lack of interest doesn't sit right, furthering my concern. "Thank you, First Sergeant. I mean it."

"You can call me 'Top' if you want, Sergeant LaSalle. I don't mind."

Again, he surprises me. "Top" is a token nickname for the role of a unit's first sergeant, but usually soldiers who use it are already within their leader's confidence. There's a camaraderie there, which I don't believe I've earned yet.

"Okay . . . Top," I say, feeling a bit foolish. I make a decision. If I don't address my concerns, what kind of medic am I?

"Umm . . . Top? Respectfully . . . is everything all right? I mean, are you feeling okay? I . . . uh . . . just got back from deployment, too. It hasn't even been six months and, umm . . . well, it got pretty intense over there. My transition back . . . has been difficult . . . at least until recently, when I started to get help . . ." My eyes move down to his shaky hand.

The dynamic between us changes instantly. I can feel the piercing of his dark eyes grow hard as they land directly on my face.

"What are you talking about, Sergeant LaSalle? Did I ask you to triage me? I don't think so. I'm doing just fine there, Sergeant. Mighty fine."

I see the puff of his chest as he straightens in his chair, challenging me to continue. I think about my packet and my future and swallow any developing retort.

"Understood, First Sergeant. Thank you."

"You're quite welcome, soldier. Dismissed."

I complete an about-face, spinning on the ball of my foot until I'm facing the opposite direction, and exit his office. *He is not doing well.* I shake my head, wondering what in the world I can possibly do about it.

# CHAPTER FORTY-TWO

By the time I reach drill weekend and prepare for the mission at the VA, I'm settling into my groove. I am now past the eight-week mark of my sobriety. My cravings aren't entirely gone, but I've learned to distract myself with walks on the beach, studying for the MCAT, and drinking freshly squeezed juices from the local bodega to help transition my palate.

I brush back my hair and zip up my uniform jacket before grabbing my keys and heading out. Teó gave me a high five for good luck before heading out to the grocery store with Mami and Dolores, so I slip out from an unusually quiet household, hearing only the crow of the rooster in the backyard.

When I arrive at the VA hospital, our local unit administrator (UA) is positioned at the designated area in the parking lot where we were instructed to meet.

"Good morning, Sergeant LaSalle," she says. "Sergeant Melendez is in there waiting for you." She points at a white unmarked van. "He drew your weapon from the arms room."

I stare at her blankly. My weapon.

"Is it something I said, Sergeant?" she asks.

I blink back at her in surprise. "My . . . uh . . . weapon? Aren't we going into a hospital?"

A voice rings out from behind me. "Do you think she's confused, Sergeant LaSalle? Our UA is following instructions. Is there a problem?"

I turn around to face him, although I already know who it is. "No, First Sergeant. No problem," I say, trying to get my bearings.

"Good. Then go get your holster and your weapon and get to formation. Don't be late."

"Roger that," I say, my voice on autopilot while my mind races to stabilize my emotions. My weapon. I knew this day would come. I thought I was ready. Am I ready?

Before I can answer that question, I jog over to where Sergeant Melendez waits.

Upon reaching the shaded vehicle, I shake my head, attempting to force away the sounds of screaming and explosions pounding in my mind. The sky is filling with a bundle of thick gray storm clouds. The sun is gone. My surroundings have changed from a screen saver to the preludes of a horror film complete with guns and monsters.

In the distance I can see First Sergeant Miller staring up at the clouds, too. The tension in his shoulders and the grimace on his face mirrors the apprehension I'm feeling in my chest.

Sergeant Melendez steps out from the passenger side of the Humvee with a black binder in his hand. The bulge at his waist reveals his own pistol, holstered for concealment, but it screams at me.

"Sergeant LaSalle, good to see you."

"What's with the weapons?" I glance up at the darkening skies. "We are going to be around kids."

"Unit protocol," he replies offhandedly, handing me the open binder. "Here, verify the serial number and sign there." He points to the last line on the page, then pulls a 9-millimeter from its case, handing me the weapon and the magazine, fully loaded with thirteen rounds.

My chest pounds. "You mind loading it?"

Sergeant Melendez considers me briefly before sliding the loaded magazine into the pistol grip. He gives it a once-over, checks that the switch is on safe, then hands it to me, aiming the weapon toward the ground opposite our direction.

I compare the serial number on the page with the one on the pistol. A perfect match. With trembling fingers, I sign my name, catching the pen afterward when it nearly slips from my hand.

"You okay?" Sergeant Melendez asks cautiously, his eyes on the pistol.

I want to say, "No, I'm not okay," but I think of Teó and how well he's progressing with the extra medical benefits and physical therapy sessions he qualifies for now that I'm back in uniform, and I summon the courage to proceed.

"Yeah, of course. I'm okay."

"Bueno," he says, smiling. "Then let's get to work before the first sergeant makes an example out of us."

"How many of us are here for this detail?"

"Five. It's you, me, the first sergeant, and two civilians—the unit administrators."

"Pretty small crew . . ."

"This mission is an in-and-out, Sergeant. It's a small group of kids. Local media will stop in and take some pictures. Shouldn't be a big deal."

The cinder block building sits proudly ahead of us. Large palms sway closer to it as the winds kick up.

"Looks like we are on the edges of a nice afternoon storm," Melendez says.

I could get back in the car right now and drive home and pretend none of this ever happened. I can leave now and never look back. But what would I be giving up? My dreams, the extra medical benefits for my son, the chance at a fresh start.

*Buck up, Lina.*

The voice in my head carries Tía Lisandra's sharp tone. It's what I need. Her presence, even in my memories, gives me strength and resolve. The kids are waiting to get our help. The pistol is protocol, nothing more than a part of the uniform, and the storm hasn't even registered strong enough to make the news.

This is not a big deal, not a big deal at all.

"Let's do this," I tell Sergeant Melendez, but he's already two steps ahead, waiting for me to catch up.

When we arrive at the waiting room sectioned off for this event, I count fourteen little faces seated together, one next to another, along the back wall.

I'm surprised how well they are all following the rules. None of these little angels look older than eight years old. The youngest one looks to be about four. They squirm anxiously but remain seated.

Each unit administrator wheels to the center of the room a gray cart filled with balloons, stuffed animals, crayons, and candy.

"Okay, niños. It's time. Surprise!"

Together the adults in the room regard their tiny faces as they transform from wide-eyed hope to open-mouthed circles of wonderment. The snaps of a camera echo behind me from the local reporter covering the event.

My eyes water at the reality of their lives and how this small gesture lights up their expressions like it's Christmas morning.

"Wow," one of the little girls calls out breathlessly. She stares at the glossy coloring books under a pile of yellow-and-green crayon boxes.

A little boy in the corner reaches out his hand to the jars on the carts' bottom shelves, filled to the brim with chocolates, lollipops, jelly beans, and hard candies wrapped in a strawberry-patterned gold foil.

"Dulces," he whispers in amazement.

The boy is underweight, I note, looking over his coffee-colored, gangly limbs. Based on their length, he is one of the older boys, maybe seven or eight years old. His lips pucker into a large circle as though he is whispering "wow," but beyond the word *dulces*, silent amazement seems all he can muster. I study him even closer. The familiar yellow tinge in his eyes—jaundice—is accompanied by shallow breathing. His head tilts to one side weakly, like it feels too heavy for the protruding tendons in his bony neck.

My body tightens when I lean forward, preparing to hand him a chocolate from one of the jars, when a little voice interrupts my intention.

"Is that for us, maestra?"

A chubby little blond with pigtails like Slinkys grins sheepishly.

This one's a hustler. She knows the carts are for them.

Her eyes open so wide the entire diameter of the aqua-blue irises contrasts starkly against her pale porcelain skin. I guess her to be about five or six years old.

"Sí, Clara," the teacher in charge of the group says. "Pero, primero, tenemos que hacer unos exámenes médicos."

Fourteen little faces fall at the mention of doing medical exams first. I don't think they expected a catch before tearing into the treasures only a few feet away.

"How about if we at least pass out the balloons?" I ask loudly enough for the children to hear, making it impossible for the teacher to say no.

"Yay!" The children cheer, jumping and bobbing their little heads in concert with one another.

Sergeant Melendez shoots me a grin. "Good call, LaSalle."

The window of the waiting room provides a direct view of the darkening skies as a second teacher, an older, sterner-looking woman, loudly clears her throat. Instantly, the children stop in their tracks and turn toward her. One little girl in the back with a long dark braid has the saddest eyes I've ever seen. She doesn't seem to be moved by any of the surprises happening around her. If I didn't know better, I would think she wasn't at all interested in any of the treats, only in returning to the orphanage. My heart breaks at the trauma that must have caused her to build such thick walls so early in her life.

"Excuse me," the teacher commands in a thunderous voice. The children freeze as though their feet are in quicksand. They wait for her to speak again.

"Hagan una fila," she instructs, walking over to one of the carts and pointing to a spot on the floor.

The children do as they are told and obediently form a line behind her.

"That's our cue," Sergeant Melendez says under his breath. "Let's go take our positions."

I follow him, but as we reach the door, I glance back and admire our two UAs passing out balloons to the smiling children. These babies have lost so much. Teó and I are blessed to have both a home and a family to love.

I follow Sergeant Melendez through the door and down the hall to the medical stations the staff has graciously set up for us in an adjoining room. A nurse is already inside, finalizing all the placements of supplies in anticipation of our arrival.

"Buenos días," she says, admiring our uniforms. "You guys must be here from the National Guard unit. We are almost ready for you and the children."

"Nice to meet you," I say, extending my hand. "I'm Sergeant LaSalle-Rivera, and this is Sergeant Melendez."

"Ah, yes," the nurse says, smiling at my battle buddy. "I remember you from last time."

Sergeant Melendez gives her his signature smile, and she blushes. I clear my throat, ready to get to work. Despite my nerves at the darkening skies, I can feel my adrenaline pumping—in a good way. My entire sense of self has clicked into place.

I give the room a quick scan. Five stations are set up in a circle, filling the entirety of the space.

"Where's First Sergeant?" I ask openly. "I haven't seen him since formation."

Melendez looks over at me. "I'm sure he's wandering around here somewhere. You know leadership. Somehow they always find an excuse to stay out of the action. Trust me, LaSalle, better for us."

Both Sergeant Melendez and I chuckle, but "finding an excuse to stay out of the action" doesn't ring true. Everything I've seen so far shows me that First Sergeant Miller is the exact opposite, the kind of leader who wants to be right smack in the middle of the action.

I turn back to the nurse. "How can I help?"

She points to the eye station. "You think you can handle eyes and I'll take ears?"

"Sure, but what about Sergeant Melendez?"

Melendez answers. "Not me. I'm a forty-two alpha, a human resource specialist. I'll be checking everyone in and ensuring all the little darlings are accounted for and processed through."

"Okay. No problem, I can do it—eyes and ears," I offer, pulling my lucky stethoscope from my pocket and wrapping it around my neck. I don't plan to use it, but the sight of it will help me keep the kids in line.

The lights in the room flicker as the wind outside howls.

"I didn't hear any news about a hurricane coming through this weekend," I joke, but I don't think I'm fooling anyone. It's evident by the tremble in my voice the weather is making me nervous. I picture First Sergeant's worried glance at the gathering clouds earlier, too. Where is he?

I glance away, trying to hide my embarrassment, then pull the clipboard with a roster of the kids' names from Melendez's hand and scan the list. *Yup, fourteen,* I count in my head. I wonder which name belongs to the serious little girl with the long black braid.

The sound of the children murmuring outside the door is superseded by thunder crashing overhead. A familiar trembling of my insides takes flight. Thick sheets of jungle rain grow louder against the building as the force of water from the sky pelts down on us. *Breathe, Lina.* Deep inhale. I breathe deeply through my nose. *One, two, three.* I hold my breath, then quietly release it through my lips. *Slow exhale, one, two, three . . .*

Lightning beacons above us, and three sets of eyes turn to see the crackling of light outside the window. This time, as the thunder booms, there's a rumble in the walls and the floor beneath my feet.

I close my eyes and fight the instinct to seek shelter and hide. I failed my son when I couldn't be strong enough to handle a storm—I won't fail these kids. I hear Dr. Robles's voice in my head. *Come on, Lina. Come up with a countering belief.* But my heart is pounding so strongly I can't get there. I hold my breath, channeling Tía Lisandra once more. *Superiority is built on my willpower and moral courage.* I let out a breath, sensing the shift and my fortitude strengthen. *You are not in Iraq; you are in Puerto Rico. It's just rain. This is normal. Everything is going to be okay. You're safe.*

"Sergeant?" a voice calls in the distance. "LaSalle?"

The voice is getting closer.

"Earth to LaSalle. Hey, you all right?"

I didn't realize my eyes were closed until I opened them. Melendez's hand is on my shoulder, but I don't look at him right away. His worried gaze remains fixed on my face as my eyes scan the room.

"Welcome back. What is it? Is it the weather outside? The rain? Are you okay?"

"Yes," I say, returning to the here and now. My fingers move up to my temples. "I'm just trying to ignore a growing headache. I'm okay; seriously, it's not a big deal."

"You sure?"

Before I can respond, the double doors swing open, and the younger teacher from earlier walks in, followed by a single-file line of children, each holding their own balloon.

Sergeant Melendez turns to greet them.

"Bienvenidos," he welcomes the little guests as they file in. "Today we are going to check you guys out and make sure all your important body parts, like eyes and ears and noses, are in good working order."

He lifts up the tip of his nose with a pencil to simulate a pig snout, and the kids erupt with laughter.

"Let's get started, niños." He points to my station on his left. "This is Sergeant LaSalle. She is going to check your vision at the white table. Half of you will start with her, and half of you will start with our nurse at the hearing booth."

I hold up my hand and wave as Melendez continues.

"Once you're finished checking eyes and ears, you will form a line at the table over there."

The nurse raises her hand politely from the back of the room and waves at the children. Melendez was smart enough *not* to highlight the vaccines.

He reaches into each of his side pant pockets, pulling out two handfuls of lollipops, and spreads them across the table.

"Everyone who follows the rules and completes every station gets a lollipop. Any questions?"

They shake their heads and reply "No, señor" in one singsong voice.

Thunder cracks overhead again, but this time I barely hear it. My focus is on the first child in line. It's the boy who's ill. He approaches Sergeant Melendez with a heavy limp. He is moving through short, stilted breaths. The little girl with the long dark braid and the eyes full of betrayal follows directly behind him. I fight the urge to wrap my arms around her and promise everything will be okay.

"Bueno, let's get started," Sergeant Melendez calls out cheerfully. He marks the first child on the list, writes his name on a name tag, and places it on his chest, then directs him my way.

The little boy limps over to me. We focus on each other, ignoring the flicker of lightning that fills the room with light.

"Hello," I say in greeting.

"Bonjou," he says.

The boy is Haitian. The word sounds fatigued. Something tells me his journey here to Puerto Rico, to the orphanage, has been an arduous one.

"Bonjou bèl ti gason," I answer, offering the extent of my Haitian vocabulary. However, calling him a "handsome" boy makes him smile. I'm gifted with a display of tiny, bone-white teeth behind full violet lips.

"How do you pronounce your name?" I glance at his name tag.

"You can call me Rudy," he says, simplifying the richness of the name written down.

"Okay, Rudy. Follow me."

He stands dutifully on top of the taped X.

"I'm going to ask you to raise your left hand and cover your left eye. Then I want you to read line number four." I point a red penlight at the lighted chart on the wall in front of him. "Are you ready?"

"Sí, señora," he replies. I'm impressed. Spanish is not a native language in Haiti, and he understands me when I speak to him in English, so the child speaks at least three languages.

He covers his eye and reads. As he recites the letters perfectly, the sad little girl approaches my station. I nod at her so that she knows she is next. She turns back, unsure if my eyes have actually fallen on her. Her thick, jet-black braid hangs over her shoulder, nearly reaching her waist. As she turns around to face me, she points to her chest, next to the name tag that reads "Analise." I nod again. *Sí, tú,* I mouth.

"Good job," I tell Rudy. He's called each letter out perfectly.

Rudy's chest puffs with pride. He likes the challenge. As he reads the letters in the opposite order, I'm drawn back to little Analise. The remaining children are now forming a line behind her. She ignores the animated conversation they are engaged in, instead standing there stoically as she waits her turn.

Her obsidian eyes stare out into nothingness. I recognize the trauma bundled and tucked away behind them. Her lips are pressed together tightly with her hands clasped in front of her khaki waistband. There's not only disappointment in those eyes; there's wisdom, too. She's thinking about something, seemingly far from here. I can't figure out if she's solving calculus equations or trying to rationalize how those who were supposed to love her best abandoned her.

She's a mirror of my own disappointment when I first returned home from Iraq. That expression on her serious face, the pain in her eyes . . . I recognize it plainly. This child has suffered disillusionment. I wonder whether she often questions why her family couldn't keep her, or how she ended up in an orphanage all alone.

I pull back and return my attention to Rudy.

"That was an excellent job," I tell him.

Analise continues to wait patiently for her turn. I am entranced by the similarities I sense between us. Her angst feels so familiar.

I force myself to focus on the last row of letters Rudy calls out. He repeats the line again, backward. "Great job," I tell him. "Your vision is perfect. Twenty-twenty."

Rudy's proud smile reaches his eyes when the light behind the screen switches off. Analise's solemn glance tears at my heart, as though she's expecting things to go wrong at her turn.

"It's okay," I tell her softly. "Probably just needs a bulb replacement. An easy fix."

The nurse witnesses the malfunction and immediately steps into action and begins ushering the children in her direction. "Sergeant Melendez can take my key for the supply closet. It's the first door on the left at the top of the stairwell."

Sergeant Melendez looks up, but for reasons I can't explain, I'm compelled to be Analise's hero. I want to show her that sometimes unexpected things may happen, but a solution may be just right around the corner.

I bend down, eye to eye with the children. "Rudy, go ahead and follow everyone else to the hearing station. Analise, would you like to come with me to the supply closet to get a new bulb?"

She nods slowly, her expression blank. The girl's experiences have likely taught her not to trust anyone, but it looks like her instincts calm her trepidations. I look up and ask the teacher, "Is that okay?"

The teacher is now trying to wrangle anxious children as balloons stream up to the ceiling. "Sí, sure, go ahead."

Analise slowly reaches out her hand, and I take it and lead her out into the hall.

*Familiar*—that's the first word that goes through my mind. Then *peligro. Danger.* I know this place. The threat has once again arrived at my doorstep, except this time the threat isn't running toward me and my unit. This time the soldier sits crouched at the top of the landing one flight of stairs above us with his eyes closed and the barrel of an Army-issued 9-millimeter tucked beneath his chin.

*Oh God, not again.* I blink as the image of the boy on the battlefield, the dirt-smudged face, the dark, heavy curls, looks down at me. *No. This isn't happening.* I blink again; this time the boy is gone, but the nightmare is still present. My mind fights an out-of-body experience as though this moment is happening to someone else. *Not me. Not again.*

A beret no longer covers the bright-blond spikes on First Sergeant's head. His long, thick legs are tucked beneath him in a prayer stance. Because his eyes are closed, he doesn't see us enter. Analise stands silently beside me, looking up, slowly raising her hand to cover the silent scream of her open mouth.

Instinctually I squeeze the tiny hand that still rests in mine, but my feet remain frozen with shock as the heavy door closes behind us. The sound of the door clicking shut forces his eyes open to stare directly at us.

What am I supposed to do when I can't bring myself to move? My mind is racing. This isn't an enemy with a suicide belt; this is a fellow soldier, a friendly. What is he doing?

First Sergeant Miller has a gun. I have to do something.

With a pause that lasts a lifetime, I finally manage to whisper a stuttered "Please" as my eyes move back down to the innocent child beside me.

Analise has miraculously managed to stay completely still, without uttering so much as a sound.

He stares directly at me, and I'm devastated by the mirror of pain I see in his eyes, the pain that can come only from the battlefield.

Almost like hearing a ghost, I imagine Christian Fuentes beside me. I can still recall the distinct tone of his voice. *Lina, you have to do something,* he urges. My hand is trembling, but with a soldier's instinct to defend and protect, I force it up . . . slowly . . . I have a gun, but this is a stairwell, ricochets will kill us all.

Miller lowers his gun but shakes his head, seeing my hand twitch. "Don't move," he says.

I know enough about trauma and facing the enemy to remain completely still.

"What are you doing here?" he asks. "Did you see them, too? You did, right? All the wounded out there. Why won't anyone do anything about it?"

His voice relays thoughts far off into the distance, indicating some type of mental displacement from the here and now. I can relate because I keep seeing the man behind the wall, screaming at the kid. Miller's face keeps flipping to the one who's haunted my nightmare for months. I force myself to key into him.

"I did, Top. I did see them. That's why I'm here. That's why I'm trying to be a doctor, so I can help them. All those wounded soldiers. I want to do something about it."

Beads of sweat glisten across his forehead as his chest pulsates with adrenaline.

"No. It's too late. You're not supposed to be here," he says, his gaze moving down to Analise. "None of us should be here. We're supposed to be okay. We're all supposed to be okay."

My ears fill with the pounding of my beating heart. My words stick to the roof of my mouth as my mind works to assess the immediate priorities. I need to protect the child. I need to stop my first sergeant from hurting himself. I need to leave this moment alive for my son's sake. My own breathing grows shallow at the realization of my circumstances and the combating memories of a similar moment not too long ago, when I faced life and death directly on.

*Mama Lina,* I pray silently, *ayúdame.*

"I think I *am* meant to be here," I say quietly, surprised by the courage in my words I do not feel.

"What the hell are you talking about? Don't you see? No. They're broken. We are all getting sent off and destroyed. Then we come back, and no one cares. They just send us on our way like we don't matter. Like none of it matters."

His words hit hard because he's right. No one came to check on my mental health the day after I killed a young man in Iraq. The congratulations kept coming in, the applause, the pats on the back, calling me a war hero. A hero. I can still taste the bitterness of that word, especially then. I remember the inspections when we returned from overseas. It was all about weapons accountability and the diseases we might have contracted. I get it. I know what he's talking about, but there is another way. Images of Dr. Robles, Eli, Milly, Dolores, and all the tiny victories I've had that have helped me get to this point flash before my eyes. He can find another way.

"It matters, Top. You matter. I can help you."

He is looking directly at me, but it's like I don't exist. I can see the lack of recognition in his eyes. "I need to end it," he shouts, although it sounds like he's talking to himself. "I can't take it anymore. The visions. The sounds. No one will help me."

Tears pool in his eyes. He is grieving. I look down at the gun he waves around in his hand, bracing against the summoned sound of rifle fire going off in my ears. I look down at Analise, and she meets my gaze. If the threat rises and I have to pull the trigger in this tiny concrete space, she could get hurt in the cross fire. The thought nearly brings me to my knees. Analise's expression goes blank, and I see the visible effort to hide away inside herself in a place that feels safe.

I squeeze her hand again, praying she understands. I will die protecting her today if it comes down to it. This means leaving my son, but I know that he has his father now and my family, and the island, to protect him. I have fought, given up parts of myself, to return to my boy, but in this moment, these two souls have only me. I don't know if waiting a few more seconds on that battlefield would have saved that young man's life, but I do know I won't leave this moment without being certain I did absolutely everything I could to save both her and First Sergeant Miller's lives.

I swallow and delve deep into my instincts. "Top, it's me. It's Sergeant LaSalle. Lina. put down the gun. It's not an accident I walked in when I did." My voice is quiet but holds the military authority I know he will understand. "I know you feel helpless, but you are not alone. You can step out of the darkness. I'm here. Look at me. Take my hand."

I push Analise back behind me, closer to the door, while I take a step forward, but his eyes spring wide with terror.

"Stop," he shouts, aiming the gun in our direction before realizing the horror of his actions and bringing it back up to his temple. "I swear to God, you take another step . . ."

I consider pulling open the door. Even if he shoots himself, she can run out while I administer aid, and I'll have saved her. But that would be history repeating itself. I survive but someone else has to die. If I'd just waited a few more seconds . . . No. I can't take the easy out. I have to save him, too.

A tear streams down his cheek.

My eyes close briefly, and I see the boy, running in our direction. I remember how badly I wanted a different outcome.

"I need to let the little girl out of here, Top. She's a child. I'm going to open the door and let her out, and I promise I will stay. We can agree this isn't about her. She doesn't need to be here."

Miller slumps from a high kneel onto the backs of his calves, resigned, and nods. "Okay. Just her. Please. Stay."

If I leave with her, I will be safe and returning to my son. And Miller will kill himself. I will have given him permission by abandoning him. I can't do that.

I take a step back and swing the door open, nearly pulling Analise through it. "Go. Run. Now," I tell her before shutting the door behind her. The musty stairwell fills with the sour scent of my fear and my unit leader's angst.

My voice quivers with the truth that I'm barely holding on. "Okay. I'm here. Just us."

His eyes open, and he wipes away the tears with the back of his free hand, keeping the pistol pressed firmly against his temple.

A splay of images: the boy, my flight's descent into Puerto Rico, my arrival at my parents' house, the storm at Chiquitas, La Placita, facing my tía Lisandra, the blue light tube during my therapy session, my AA meeting at the library, putting my uniform back on. All the images stack one atop another, proving to me that I need to find a way to show Miller that he can crawl up this hill and make it onto the other side. It's up to me. I can help guide him back into the light because I know the strangling hold of the darkness.

"Top, I'm coming up. I'm going to help you."

He looks at me as though utterly at a loss at my words.

"Help me? Sergeant, don't you get it? You can't help me. No one can. I just want to stop the screaming in my head."

I take his resignation as a cue to move ahead on trembling legs.

"I know it feels that way right now, Top, but that isn't true. It's a lie we all tell ourselves."

I reach halfway up when his face reddens at my approach. "Stop right there. I swear to God. I will pull this trigger."

I stop and reach out. I swallow the fear building in my chest as the images in my head flicker between Teó's smile and the crumpling body of the boy I couldn't save. I look back up at a man tortured by a demon I know all too intimately. His leg trembles beneath him as his free hand rises to his chest. I understand. I know the vise of trauma on the battlefield.

"I won't move," I coax. "I promise. But please, let me help you."

He looks at my extended hand, staring at my reaching fingers before his eyes move to my face. He blinks back one, two, three times. I can see the disassociation as his mind fights to make sense of everything that is happening.

"Put the gun down," I say firmly. "You don't need to find freedom like this. There's another way."

"What are you talking about?" he says, his words wavering. "There's no escape. The screaming, the bodies. I can't do it anymore. There's no way out."

I take another step. Four more and I will reach the landing.

"I'm saying I know what it's like to want to escape the memories, First Sergeant."

I take another step. "Put the gun down." Each word carries a pause. "Let me help you."

"You can't," he urges, but I can hear the relentment in his voice.

"I can," I say, nodding, holding his eyes as the gun in his hand trembles with fatigue. I take a final step.

We are now eye to eye. I reach my hand out, holding my breath, and place it over the one on his chest.

"I killed someone. In Iraq," I say, barely above a whisper. Footsteps pound in the hallway, heading toward us. "All I've ever dreamed of was healing and helping people. Believe me, no mother can ever fathom taking the life of an innocent, just barely a man, until his waist is wrapped in explosives. Until the choice is his life or yours and all the innocent people you have out there with you. I had to do it. I had no choice."

At my revelation, the fog in his expression clears. "You . . ." He doesn't say another word. It isn't necessary. We stare at one another, joined in tragedy.

"Somehow I made it through that. You can, too."

We hold our gazes, memories passing between us of dry desert air, the metallic scent of bullets fired, the feel of a pounding heart when an IED has been identified on the roadway, the sounds of women crying and men shouting their pleas in Arabic. I don't know if his memories are exactly like mine, but the air between us is heavy with shared experiences.

His eyes lower and his mouth sags in resignation.

"I'm sorry, Sergeant LaSalle," he says quietly.

"Me too," I answer, blinking back my tears.

"How are you able . . ." He can't finish past the croak of the last word. His eyes close for a moment before he opens them and looks directly at me.

"By choosing to endure for at least one more day," I answer honestly.

He brings the gun down to his side and releases a heavy sigh. "Okay. One more day, Sergeant. But tomorrow is never guaranteed."

I shake my head, refusing to give in to his grief. "I know it feels that way, Top, but you get to choose to live as though it is."

With shaking hands, I extend a firm grip and remove the gun from his hand. The stairwell door bursts open, and we both brace for what will happen next.

# CHAPTER FORTY-THREE

The detective looks at me with more than a trace of suspicion as he points his final question my way. "So there's nothing else that you can tell us, specifically, I mean, that Nathan Miller might have said to you about his intentions with that gun."

I roll my eyes, tired from my fourth response to the same question, only worded differently. "No, Detective. Nothing beyond what I've already told you. He didn't mince words. He went to the stairwell alone. That's how I found him. Alone. He planned to end his life because of the trauma from his war experiences. At least that's what he talked about. I got there before he could carry out his plan, and I managed to stop him in time."

"And free the girl from getting hurt, no less. At least that's how it looks on camera from the hallway just outside the stairwell. Unfortunately, we are having trouble accessing any audio."

I remain silent because, for some reason, it feels like any additional details could easily get twisted into something I don't mean. My personal opinion: First Sergeant doesn't belong in jail; he belongs in a hospital, where he can get the mental health support he needs. But that's far from up to me.

The detective leans back in his seat, folding his arms across his chest. With great sarcasm he says, "From everything we've seen so far, you're quite the hero, young lady."

*Hero.* What a complicated relationship I have with that word. The detective doesn't want to believe I've done anything heroic today. That's all right; neither do I.

"Whatever you say, Detective."

"Well, I think that's all for now," he says. "Since, again, you are stating you have no information about anyone else Nathan Miller intended to harm."

"That's exactly what I'm saying," I answer with a huff, reaching the end of my patience. "If he'd planned to hurt anyone else, why would I keep that from you?"

"I know how tight the brotherhood"—his lips curl into a sneer—"and sisterhood, in this case, can be in the military. Especially when you're not from around here. I just want to make sure you know this isn't about protecting one of your own. This is about stopping a potential criminal from ever hurting anyone else."

I give the detective a pointed stare. "I am from here," I said. "Just two towns over, and I don't believe First Sergeant Miller is a criminal. I believe he's a man distraught with post-traumatic stress from his experiences overseas while fighting for our country and the rights of all Americans—including you."

He puckers his lips, unconvinced, and shrugs. "Okay, no need to get sanctimonious. I'm surprised. You don't sound like you're from here. My mistake." He pushes a legal pad across the table. "And for the record, we aren't in the habit of putting innocent people in prison. If what you're saying is true, I'm sure justice will be served, and he will get the help he needs. Please put your contact information here in case we have any additional questions."

I jot down my name, cell phone, and email and push the notepad back in his direction. "Will that be all?"

He nods and uses his mouth to point toward the door. If I weren't so anxious and fired up, I might laugh. But I am far from lighthearted; in fact, I haven't wanted a drink this bad since the night over the sink with my tía's little present.

I close my eyes, trying to block the vision of the little bar I know is within walking distance of where I'm standing. *Don't, Lina, don't do it.* This time I imagine Milly's voice and pull out my cell phone to call her, but the six missed calls from Mami prioritize me in a different direction first.

Given the news vans in the parking lot, it's obvious we've already made the local news. I know my abuela, and through her the rest of the household will have heard about the VA from the satellite radio's news updates.

Mami answers on the first ring. "Lina, ¡Dios mío! Abuela just told me there was some kind of active shooter at the veterans' hospital. Oh my God, are you okay?" *Too late.* "Why weren't you answering your phone? My heart almost stopped. If anything should ever happen to you, mi hija . . ."

"Mami, I'm okay." I sigh, touched by the genuine concern in her voice. Now that I'm a mother, I understand her in ways I never could before. "Does Teó know? Did he hear about any of this?"

A kiss rings through the phone, and I can tell Mami is crossing herself and thanking the heavens that I'm okay. "No, no. He and Papi are in the backyard with the chickens and planting a new tree your father brought home. Abuela and I just heard the news a minute ago." Her voice is muffled through the receiver as she tells Abuela I'm okay and not to scare Teó or Papi. I wait for my abuela to respond before breaking back into the conversation. "Mami, I'm on my way home now. I'll explain everything when I get there."

"You're coming directly home?" she asks, her words marked with worry. I know what she isn't asking: *Are you going to stop at a bar?*

It won't help to admit that I want to. What matters are my actions. "I'm heading directly home, Mami. Maybe Abuela can start a café for me? I could really use one."

I hear the relief in her voice. "Yes, un café. Of course. We will be here waiting."

My eyes close for a moment, and I let the setting sun soak one last shot of energy into me before I head to my car and home to my son. When I open them and look up, the two teachers from the orphanage are exiting the children in a single-file line to two awaiting vans.

Analise is last, her tiny hand gripping the end of the bright-red rope each child is holding on to to keep them in line and together. She must feel my stare, because she looks over at me, and I can see the relief on her face.

Did anyone tell her I was all right? Or that the soldier with the gun was so sad he didn't realize what he was doing? Suddenly the urgency of making sure she knows this propels my feet forward, and I jog over to the children as they prepare to cross the parking lot.

A small smile spreads across her naturally downturned mouth, eliminating any sense of logic I have as I drop into a crouch beside her and take her into my arms.

"You're okay," she whispers into my neck. "I didn't know if I should believe the maestra when she told me that you weren't hurt."

I give her a gentle squeeze. "I'm okay," I say and swallow. "And so is the other soldier from the stairs.

"You helped save him, you know," I say to her. "He saw you, and I think it helped him see that he couldn't hurt himself. You bought us some precious time."

"No." Analise shakes her head. "*You* saved him," she says. "Good job." She shrugs as though there's nothing left to say. Looking over at her teachers and the fidgeting children, she says, "I gotta go now."

"Okay, of course. Thank you, Analise."

"You're welcome," she says and faces straight ahead, no trace of the earlier smile, and that's when I realize, for her, today was a peak in an already heartbreaking existence. I offer a half-hearted wave at the teachers and stay standing still until I see both vans are loaded and driving off.

When I reach my car, my nervous system is pounding with a flood of emotions so deeply integrated I can't tell one from another.

I scroll through my contacts and dial Milly. She answers on the first ring.

"Hello, Lina. Is everything okay?"

"I guess that kind of greeting is pretty standard when you're a sponsor, isn't it?"

"Comes with the territory," Milly says in her most practical voice. "What's going on, Lina?"

"I take it you haven't seen the news."

"No. I have not."

I wait for more, an excuse to prolong my admittance, but Milly is not that kind of sponsor. She is the best kind, refusing to play games.

I look down at my shaking hands and smile at the memory of Sergeant Fuentes's compliment about having great hands. It's progress that I can smile about anything from that day. I take that momentum and begin. "There was an incident at the VA today, and I'm desperately wanting a drink. You think you can meet me at my mother's house for coffee and conversation?"

Milly doesn't hesitate. "Of course. I didn't have anything planned. I'm happy to meet you there."

I take in the respite she offers, knowing things are different now. *I* am different now, and for today, that's more than enough.

# EPILOGUE

I never look back and feel an inkling of honor or pride in the travesty of that day at the VA hospital or the one before it in Iraq. What I do feel is a sense of gratitude that I was there in that stairwell when I needed to be and that the tragedies in my life put me on the road to being present and mentally prepared to save a life.

I still think about the heavy rains and how the island warned me of a man's inner pain. Terror arrived at my feet that fateful morning in the form of someone no one suspected capable of reaching such a point. The following morning I listened silently to the conversations at the bodega after the news first broke. For many locals with no military experience, a tangible reason for what drove a career soldier to lose all hope remains a mystery. Not to me. The investigation concluded with PTSD—a demon I know all too well. I'm sure there were many factors, but I'll never forget how he explained to me that he came home from a brutally intimate war and felt lost and alone. I saw the look in his eyes of trauma, of witnessing the kinds of atrocities most people will never see in their lifetime. For First Sergeant Nathan Miller, I wouldn't be surprised if he'd broken after bearing multiple instances like the one I experienced during that morning convoy. God knows it took only one to nearly break me. And I can only bet it likely that he had his equipment inventoried before being sent on his merry way. Just like me. My struggle led me to hurt myself slowly, under the guise of false confidence. For the first sergeant, his anger turned violently inward.

I can't help but count my blessings again. I had Dr. Robles, and she never dismissed my symptoms or my concerns. The mental health support she provided saved my life. Teó's too. I can't help but wonder whether getting the first sergeant the help he needs, in time, might change things for him as well.

I'm also thankful for Milly, who's been a no-nonsense, solid presence in my journey to recovery. She listens more than she speaks, and when she does offer her thoughts, she's as by the book on the process as she is about her medical patients. I relate to Milly's bedside manner, and I can only pray that one day, when I do become a doctor, I will have nurses like her alongside me.

After reflecting on my journey, I've come to a deeply planted understanding.

I may have taken a life, but I've also saved many lives. It's time to accept all the parts that have made me who I am and trust that they make me better, stronger, and wiser. At a minimum, all my combined experiences have helped me understand the shades of gray we live in and tear down the petty boundaries of black and white. Mami's famous line rings in my ears: *If only things went as they were supposed to go.* She's right. If they did, soldiers would come home safely, and youths would never enter the battlefield.

Yet they do. My journey included the death of another. I did it. I killed him. Nothing is ever going to change that. The Army trained me to accept these things as a casualty of war, a travesty on the battlefield, but a reality nevertheless. When there's war—people die. *War* implies the indiscriminate killing of civilians; age is not a factor. My healing means recognizing that truths of war aren't the final stop for my own distillation of events. I can see the young man as an innocent and my actions as a necessary evil on the battlefield. These two things don't have to be mutually exclusive.

Acts are never random. And for every tragedy we can find a greater purpose. I was meant to be in that convoy in the middle of an isolated desert, just as I was meant to be at the medical clinic in the VA hospital on a regular Saturday morning in Puerto Rico. Sometimes things aren't meant to go the way *we think* they are.

Who decides that, anyway? I think they go exactly the way they were supposed to. It's up to us to accept a bigger commission in all our experiences, the moments, and the tragedies. Nothing has been wasted in my life, because these moments have led me to discover who I was meant to be.

The sentiment reminds me of a lesson I heard in church when I was a little girl. The teacher said that the narrow gate and the difficult road lead to life. That's been true for me. My journey is exactly how things were meant to be. I'm a mother. A Boricua. A soldier. A woman. This is my truth and my journey. Lina's journey.

Dolores spins Teó in the center of the dance floor at Chiquitas. She sashays her hips, kicking her feet one after the other in synchronization with the music as Teó tries to mimic her, hopping from one foot to the other. I hold back a chuckle as he sticks out his backside, leans forward, and shakes his hips the way Dolores has taught him. I give him a thumbs-up from the sidelines.

The song ends, and he throws his arms around his cousin's waist, pressing his sweaty cheek against her bare belly. She leans down to kiss the top of his head, then leads him back to where Eli and I stand.

I sip a piña colada—virgin, with extra coconut milk and a dollop of fresh honey. Honestly, it tastes much better without the bitter bite of rum. I would not have thought so a year ago, but after twelve months without alcohol, my taste buds have changed. I'm grateful for that. My cravings are nearly gone. I successfully completed my ninety meetings in ninety days, which served to restructure my daily habits. Working through my twelve steps in addition to EMDR therapy has radically changed my thought patterns, my view of the world, and how I react to life's normal stressors. My daily phone calls with Milly transitioned to weekly ones until last month, when we spoke only once for a standard check-in. Yoga sessions on the beach early in the mornings, work, and starting medical school have fulfilled me in ways alcohol never did. Weeks can go by when I don't think about alcohol at all, and if I do and I feel tempted, I can always attend a meeting or call Milly.

After careful consideration and twelve months of consistent progress, Teó and I discussed the little girl who made such an imprint on my heart. I told him about meeting her while I was on duty at the VA and how sad she looked because she lived in an orphanage and didn't have a family. Teó's response made our next steps crystal clear. He said "Maybe we can be her family" with the matter-of-fact manner of choosing where to have breakfast. "I mean, you're a great mom, and I think I could be a cool big brother. I can teach her all about science. And we have my nana and abuelito and abuelo and abuela and Dolores."

*From the mouth of babes,* I thought back then, realizing Teó's openness made all the difference in the world.

Three more days and I will pick her up for good, and both Teó and I are counting down every minute as we prepare her bedroom and pick out her school supplies.

Fortunately, after I received my acceptance letter from the University of Puerto Rico's medical school, my Army-sponsored school packet was approved, allowing me to transition to full-time military pay and benefits while studying full-time. It's more than I could ever have hoped for.

"Hey, buddy, you look good out there," I tell Teó, wiping the sweat from his brow as I kiss the top of his head.

"You sure do, champ. I didn't realize you were such a natural on the dance floor," Eli says.

Teó looks up at him. "Eli, did you know dancing boosts the connectivity between both cerebral hemispheres, improving the brain's gooeyness and reducing the risk of disease?"

"Yeah, Eli. Didn't you know that?" I tease, enamored by my boy's brilliance.

"As a matter of fact, kiddo," he says to Teó, "I did not know that. But you just proved why I've got to talk your mamá into dancing with me more often and stop saying she's embarrassed."

I shoot a look at him. "No fair, Elijah Montgomery. You don't get to use my kid's genius against me."

"Well, I'm gonna have to remind you that you can't deny science, Lina, and insist we dance." He glances at his watch. "Which, lookin' at the time, I only have a couple of hours before you turn back into a pumpkin."

"You mean, a full-time mother with an overtired kid," I tease.

"I actually think that's one of my favorite things about you."

"You want to know one of *my* favorite things about you?" I ask.

"I'm all ears," Eli says, leaning his head closer to mine.

"Well, I want to say that sweet southern accent . . . but . . . I think I'm going to have to go with how easy it is to be around you and how when we're together, everything feels complete."

Before he responds, his eyebrows shoot up. I get it; what I'm saying offers an invitation to cross out of the friend zone he's been existing in for the last year.

I offer a slight nod and look into his eyes for affirmation, wondering if it is too late, if maybe our time has passed and getting back there is more than I could hope for.

"Everything feels complete?" He smiles. "I wasn't quite expecting that."

My heart races at the thought that maybe my fears were justified. It is too late. Too much time has passed, and now those possibilities are gone.

Eli nods back at me. The giddy smile playing on his lips makes me want to kiss him.

"My, my, Lina, you sure know how to give a man something to hope for."

"Here's to a whole lot more than hope," I say, raising my glass in his direction.

My beautiful boy gives me a thumbs-up from his barstool, sipping an ice-cold lemonade. I think he agrees.

Papi and his band are finishing setting up on the small stage in the corner. My tía Kika is visiting this week, and this is the first time I've seen Teó give her a little breathing room. He hasn't left her side since she first arrived. Her support about everything I've been through has made all the difference. She and my tía Lisandra are relaxed and laughing over a pitcher of sangria. Mami and my abuelos are seated beside them, sharing a large pilón of mofongo stuffed with shrimp in salsa criolla, waiting for Papi's band to begin.

Mami looks from Eli over to me, then winks. I think she can see the silly schoolgirl energy all over my face, and she approves. It's time.

Eli glances at his watch once more. "I better go back and check on the kitchen. It's lookin' to be a busy night. Your papi is drawing in a pretty good crowd." He waves over at Teó. "See you in a bit, cowboy."

"Later, gator," Teó replies. His cheeks are dotted with ketchup from the basket of fries Anita sneaked in front of him.

Eli gives me a quick kiss on the cheek before going to check on his crew.

I smile. He really is a good guy. I warm at the idea of finally feeling strong enough to give in to the possibilities growing between us.

Papi's band begins to play, and I get swept up in the rhythms of classic salsa and merengue.

"Abuelo sings good," Teó says, his eyes round with awe. "Maybe one day I can sing like that."

I give him side-eye. "I didn't know you liked to sing. You're full of surprises."

"Me neither, Mamá, but maybe I could try." *Sniff.* He reaches down and pops another french fry into his mouth.

"Of course you could try. You can be anything you put your mind to, Teó."

We both turn, pleasantly surprised by the sound of the familiar voice.

"Papi!" Teó says, smiling, raising his arms to his father for an embrace.

Leonardo graciously steps into those gangly arms, lifting Teó high into the air before swinging him back down to his feet.

"Hola, Lina." He leans over and kisses my cheek. "Thanks for inviting me."

"Sure. You know how much Teó loves when you two spend time together."

Teó reaches for Leonardo's hand, and my eyes moisten at the tenderness in my son's gesture.

"Is your . . . um . . . family coming?" I ask.

"No." He shakes his head. "It's only me, Lina. Ziomara and I have decided it's best this way."

"I'm confused."

"Me too," Teó chimes in. "What're you guys talkin' about?"

Leo lowers his voice. "I tried, but the more I've gotten to know . . ." He points at Teó from behind his head, keeping the revelation between us. "I never could get past everything she took from me by sending that email to you. I've recently found out that it was only the first of a series of mistruths for my 'own protection.'" He raises his fingers in air quotes at the last part of the sentence. "This was a long time coming, but don't worry, it won't affect the relationship with his sister. I will arrange visits together as much as possible."

"I understand," I say, and offer a sympathetic smile. Our visitation arrangement has been very open. Leo sees Teó almost every other afternoon, bringing him home in time for dinner, and every other weekend. It worked especially well on the weekends when I had to drill at Fort Buchanan. I was immediately surprised at how easy it turned out to be to allow Leo into Teó's life and share the responsibilities of parenthood.

At his inquisitive stare, Leo looks down to Teó and says, "Don't worry. We are just talking about grown-up stuff, papito."

Teó rolls his eyes and sticks out his tongue. "Boorrringg. How about we go dance, Papi? My prima Dolores is dancing over there, see her? And, Papi, my abuelo is up there singing."

"That sounds like a great idea," he replies. Then Leo stretches his hand out to me. "What do you say, Lina. Can we have this dance?"

"Say sí, Mamá! Say sí!" Teó shouts, jumping up and down.

"Okay, okay, you two. How can I resist?"

My family watches us as we make our way to the dance floor. I return their stare, and together they smile at me and nod approvingly. I smile back, knowing that our relationship has only been strengthened since I was able to genuinely forgive them for doing what they thought was best.

I accept Leo's outstretched hand and clasp Teó's with the other and let them lead me to the very center of the dance floor. My heart warms when Papi begins to sing Sergio Vargas's "La Quiero a Morir," the acoustic version of the song I danced to with Eli on the night I saw Leo again for the first time in ten years. It feels like a lifetime ago, but I'm thankful because that night began the prelude of my and Eli's possibilities. It has been a year of firm friendship and his full support while I worked the program, but it's built a solid foundation for something incredibly real.

I look over at the bar and see Eli organizing the glassware. Our eyes meet and he smiles, recognizing the song, too.

Leonardo lifts Teó up on his hip as we clasp hands. We move into a circle, and I smile as he sings the lyrics to my son.

I settle into the familiarity of the moment, embracing all the new things materializing in my new life on the island. I consider the southern gentleman who's stolen my heart, and the fullness in Teó's life with his father and two new sisters. My deepening relationship with my own father also has a new feel to it. My family and my sense of belonging are a combination of new and familiar. I can finally settle into a sense of wholeness and joy.

And for the rest of the evening, surrounded by music and realizing I've finally been taken by the island's magic, I do exactly that.

# AUTHOR'S NOTE

I remember the morning when I woke up with one prominent thought: What would it be like if, during my time in the Army, I'd been forced to take the life of someone I deemed an innocent casualty of an evil practice but who still posed an imminent threat on the battlefield? I knew through my military training that some extremist groups fixate on the idea of indoctrinating the young to sacrifice themselves in order to get to heaven. As a mother, my heart wept. As a soldier, my soul cried for my brothers- and sisters-in-arms forced to confront such a horrific situation. That day, the thought plagued me, evolving into a deeper internal discussion. What if a mother were forced to confront such a situation? How do you reconcile the concept of duty with the tragedy of someone's stolen innocence?

As a Latina, I felt this deeply because of the cultural roles and responsibilities that we assign mothers and caretakers. That's when I knew I had a story that needed to be explored and a concept—women returning from military service with PTSD—that needed to be addressed. I began my research by reading stories about women in the military navigating the road to recovery from PTSD. It surprised me how few there were. So I began to reflect on the incredible women I've served with since joining the Army in June 2005, and I made a promise to myself to honor their legacy and their sacrifice through this story. Don't get me wrong—this book isn't just about women in the military. I know and have served with some amazing, honorable, selfless, strong, and empathetic men. This story is equally attributed to their impact on my life and the deep respect I have for their service. Especially my husband, a retired Army officer, who deployed four different times and experienced the war on the front lines in Iraq and Afghanistan. But, as a writer, my voice is from a woman's perspective, and I hope I empowered Lina through those shared experiences.

As I contemplated Lina's journey to healing, a magical place that brought me such personal joy continued to come to mind. That's when I knew that my experiences in Puerto Rico, and the facets of both my culture and my time on the island, had to play a significant role in Lina's recovery. I first visited Puerto Rico in January 2008. I walked the streets of Old San Juan and kept repeating, "I could live here." The island's magic was intoxicating. I felt free, alive, and full of possibilities, roaming the cobblestone streets framed with brightly colored buildings and breathing in the rich aromas of the local cuisine.

In October of that same year, my whispered wish was granted. I moved to Dorado, Puerto Rico, for my first job following three years on active duty in the Army. The move also led to my transition to Fort Buchanan as an Army reservist, giving me a unique chance to see two very different worlds come together and create a symbiosis of military duty and island flair.

My move in 2008 was the first of three times (so far) I've lived or worked in Puerto Rico. Each experience has held special meaning and even more special memories.

It's not lost on me that the island continues to pull me back to her. And when she does, I always say yes. After all the gifts she's given me, *At the Island's Edge* is a small token of my thanks in return.

# ACKNOWLEDGMENTS

It is no surprise to me that after multiple attempted manuscripts, the one that finally helped me break into mainstream publishing is the one about Puerto Rico. I began an entirely new career in manufacturing in Puerto Rico in 2008, a journey that spanned multiple states, lasted thirteen years, and taught me to believe in myself in ways I'd never dared before. When I finally finished my doctoral program at Liberty University in 2020, after nearly giving up, it was my dissertation (and the associated research) about strategic thinkers in manufacturing facilities in Puerto Rico that finally helped me cross the finish line. The island's magic has permeated my life when it mattered most and taken my dreams to another level. I have to thank the people of Puerto Rico and this precious little piece of land in the Atlantic for helping inspire me so profoundly that I finally put the right words in the right order on the page to fulfill my life's greatest dream—becoming a published author. I don't think it was a complete coincidence that I named Lina LaSalle after my Puerto Rican great-grandmother, whose full name I didn't know when I began this book, or Rivera, the last name of my great-great-grandmother, something I also didn't discover until after I'd written the book. I can only conclude that it's all part of the "isla magic."

I want to thank my incredibly selfless and inspiring agent (and soul sister), Katie Reed, and the agency's founder, Andrea Hurst. All this began because you both said yes and took a chance on an unknown.

I will be forever thankful for your guidance and your friendship. May this be the first of many to come.

To Lee Ann Ward and the Writing Away Refuge: I am thrilled to spend the rest of my career telling writers about you and your organization. May your efforts be returned to you a thousand times over. I believe we were meant to enter each other's lives; I just didn't realize how profound an impact you'd have on mine.

To my beta readers and friends: your insights and feedback made all the difference. A special thanks to Linda Massarella, David Manno, Amjed McDonnell, Vanessa Rutledge, and Susan Stucker. To Aura Bruno and her husband, Luis Rivera: thank you for sharing the unique authenticity of a family's love on the island.

To the team at Lake Union, especially Tiffany Yates Martin, Carissa Bluestone, and Melissa Valentine—my powerhouse editorial team—and James Gallagher, Kellie Osborne, and Heather Rodino, whose detailed eyes refined this beyond measure. Thank you all for pushing me hard and helping me craft the story it was always meant to be.

To my parents, Alberto and Jeanne; my siblings, Briana and Tico; and my grandparents, Irene, Jim, and Laurie: your encouraging voices have always dared me to dream . . . and write.

To all my children, Alexus, Izabella, Emily, Michael, and David: I hope this shows you all that you can achieve in your own lives if you're willing to go for it. My grandchildren, Melanie, King, and Ahkeem: this legacy is for you, my babies.

To Mike, the great love of my life, for making "I support you" really mean something. I love you—now, then, and forever.

# DISCUSSION QUESTIONS

1. At the beginning of the book, Lina allows her nickname—"Stone Cold Healer"—to define her in many ways. She believes tucking away her feelings makes her a better medic and a better soldier. She justifies her approach as a way to be viewed as "equal" to the men in her unit. Is she right to adopt this persona to survive? How does this affect her later, when she's forced to face her actions on the battlefield?
2. Lina arrives in Puerto Rico filled with despair and a sense of failure. She believes that, by returning home, she is letting down everyone who believed that sending her to Florida would put her on a path to greatness. How does this view change over time? How does her family change Lina's view on her return?
3. Once Lina meets Eli, she is faced with a very different approach following a tragedy on the battlefield. How does this affect her? How does her relationship with Eli affect her own choices about managing the pain from her memories in Iraq?
4. The theme of fate is often discussed in Mami's famous quote: "If only things went the way they were supposed to go." What does this mean to you? How does its meaning evolve for Lina throughout the story?

5. Dolores's presence comes as a big surprise to Lina. Not only was she initially unaware that her cousin was living at her parents' home, but she knew very little about her. Why do you think the family chose not to tell Lina about Dolores's circumstances early on? How does Dolores's presence in Lina's life alter the course of her future and how she sees the world?
6. Lina struggles with the stark contrast of identifying as a healer and the realities of being a soldier in wartime. After reflecting upon everything that happened that day on the battlefield, do you think her guilt is misplaced? Why or why not?
7. At one point, when Lina really begins to spiral, she convinces herself that she needs to tuck the memories further in and forget about what happened in Iraq in order to heal. Do you think this is a common response for trauma and processing difficult choices? What about Dr. Robles's approach helped shift her thinking? Do you have a supportive group or professional resources you can turn to in times of crisis?
8. Despite the inner turmoil Lina is dealing with, she keeps her focus on trying to be a good mother at the forefront of her mind and her actions. Do you think she's successful in her approach to raising a child with special needs? How do you think being raised as a military kid has affected Teó? Do you agree that returning to Puerto Rico was the best decision she could make for him? Why or why not?
9. Lina discovers that everything she believed about Leonardo and his rejection of both her and her child was a misunderstanding. Do you think there was room to forgive her family's actions? Even after the impact on Teó and both his parents? Why or why not?

10. The relationship between Lina and her tía Lisandra is complicated. What are some ways that her aunt showed her best intentions for Lina and her well-being? Why do you think her approach was so unconventional? Do you think these complexities helped Lina in the long run or made her worse off? Why or why not?
11. In the novel Lina goes from an idealist in uniform to a bitter veteran to a woman at peace, realizing her journey, both professionally and in motherhood, led her to her greatest happiness. What were the most profound moments that helped her get there? Was it Eli? Her family? Getting into AA? Returning to service? How do you feel about Lina at the end of the novel? Do you wish she'd found a way back to Leonardo, or are you happy about the possibilities with Eli? What do you think her future looks like?
12. At the end of the book, Lina finds herself back in uniform and feels as though she is where she was always meant to be. Did this feel right to you? Discuss a time in your life when you may have veered off course from your heart's truest desires. Did you ever find your way back? If not, are there ways back onto a path of fulfillment, even on an unexpected road?

# ABOUT THE AUTHOR

*Photo © 2024 Tina Combs*

C. I. Jerez, who has a blend of Irish, Puerto Rican, and Cuban parentage, grew up near El Paso's Mexican border experiencing a true cultural amalgamation. After graduating from the University of Texas at El Paso, she commissioned as a signal officer in the US Army and rose to the rank of major before transitioning out of the military. Cherisa holds an MBA from Webster University and a doctorate in international business from Liberty University. When not writing, she serves as cofounder and vice president for Ashire Technologies & Services Inc., a cybersecurity firm specializing in securing federal information systems. She lives in central Florida. For more information, visit www.cijerezbooks.com.